THE LAST
SECRETS

McKenzie Dempsey Dawe

ALSO BY MCKENZIE DEMPSEY DAWE

Spirit Hearts

The Last Acer
The Last Crystal
The Last Stand

GLAC

TRAZON'S CASTLE

BLAGASIAN
MOUNTAINS

LUC

MIRA

AREEM

OUTLOOKER'S BAY

TANTILLUS LAKE

AFON

SENDOA RIVER

SENDOA MOUNTA

ZELOPHEHAD

PORTAL TREE

WOLF PACK CAMP

ANIMA FOREST

DRAGON-WING RIVER

SPEED SPRUCE

ACER CAMP

CAPRICIOUS OCEAN

PELAGIUS

LACERPENNA ANIMI
(DRAGON HEART)

FEROC

LAK

VALOR RIVER

FIRMARA

DS

DERYA

ALTASEN

PROFUNDUM OCEAN

MYRDDIN

CAVE OF MORALITY

UNVENTURED LANDS

The Last Secrets
Second Edition
ISBN: 979-8-9913307-2-5 (paperback edition)
ISBN: 979-8-9913307-3-2 (ebook edition)
Library of Congress Control Number: 2024916770

Printed in the United States of America

THE LAST
SECRETS

SPIRIT HEARTS · BOOK TWO

M^cKENZIE DEMPSEY DAWE

ACKNOWLEDGMENTS

This book is dedicated to many people, of whom without, this series would never have begun to flourish.

To my teachers at St. Peter Lutheran School and Valley Lutheran High School, for without their teaching skills and patience in class, I would have never learned how to write and enjoy it.

To all my friends who continue to read my works and enjoy them. Especially my best friend, Kaylee. We spent countless hours discussing my characters and editing my stories together.

To my family, who were patient and considering enough to listen to my explanations and plans for this book. Without their insight and enthusiasm, I would have never thought to finish this tale.

And most of all, I thank my lord Jesus Christ for giving me my Christian education, my home, my family, my teachers, my friends, my talents, and over all for giving me his love and kindness that inspired my book

CONTENTS

PROLOGUE

Darkness shrouded the spacious throne room. The only light came from a candle with a sinister-looking flame. The air smelled of snow and frozen air amidst misery and danger—the only feelings that were aroused when he was around.

The doors and the windows were barred, but not sealed. Because of the castle's northern location and the open windows, the summer night carried in a cutting chill. Outside, the tall grasses of Glacias Valley were covered in frost. The stars shone brightly on the cold night but the sliver of the moon was hardly noticeable.

There were three figures in the dungeon-like room. The first and second knelt before the third, who could bring tragedies merely by his presence.

The first silhouette was quite tall, but not lanky. He was built with a strength that could be seen in the way he walked and spoke. But though he was strong, he now cowered in fear as he bowed to the third form, which sat on a large throne.

"Master," the man began his plea. "Please forgive me. I was unaware of what the boy was capable of. I had no idea he could—"

"Silence!" The figure on the throne cut him off with his icy voice. "The more you plead in cowardice, the less I am convinced to let you live." The muscular man dropped his gaze and stared at the floor.

The man on the throne turned to the other figure, which had remained silent. "Sievan, I don't suppose you know the location of our little friends?"

Sievan struggled to bow even lower. "I'm afraid not, your majesssty. We ssscouted the whole arrrea around the portal but could not find them."

The leader sighed but asked him with a straight face. "What was the radius?"

"Sssir?" Sievan asked, puzzled.

"What was the radius of the area you searched!" He demanded.

"Oh, uh," Sievan stammered, daring to glance up at his lord. "We sssearched ssseventy-leagues or better, my lord."

"Who searched with you?"

"Ssseveral mcn, but I named Shassstor and Trayka group leaders."

The leader glanced at the doorway. "Guard?"

"Yes?" came a nervous reply from the entrance.

"Find Shastor and Trayka—execute one and make the other watch."

"Yes, my lord," the timid voice replied and the guard's footsteps echoed down the hall as he ran as fast as he could.

Then the sinister lord turned to the strong man. "General Donigan, grab your cloak. You'll be visiting every city and town near the portal in Firmara. Remember, the gryphon won't show up unless chaos comes to her friends. And most likely the other two will be entirely disguised. You'll need to take the bane to draw them to you. You know the one."

"My lord?"

Trazon shot Sievan a dark glare. "What is it?"

"What shall I do?" Sievan asked timidly.

Irritated, the dark lord reclined back into his throne. "Fly above Donigan and follow where he leads."

"Sssir, there is jussst one problem with that."

Lord Trazon lifted an eyebrow.

"During the battle of the porrrtal, the grrryphon removed mossst of my tail. And then, durrring my flight back here, I crrrashed because I could not ussse my tail to fly" Sievan said, shuffling his front bird-like feet nervously.

Lord Trazon let out an exasperated sigh but then leisurely twirled his fingers as he pointed to Sievan's backend. "There, are you well enough to go now?"

Sievan looked to his rear to find a new tail in the place of his old one. Instead of a slippery dark green tail of a snake, it appeared to be made of an ice-like crystal. It was the same length of his old tail, only now he could extend it to the length of his body by flicking it in any direction. He then turned back to Trazon with an enthusiastic sinister smile. "Thank you, Massster."

Lord Trazon ignored Sievan's thanks and continued, "You will fly over top of Donigan and follow wherever he leads. And when he has drawn at least one of the three near, help him to take our little friends to your castle in the mountains.

"If you two succeed, this war may be over for good."

THE MEDIATOR

Stepping to the left, Zack easily avoided a blow from Travis's staff. He heard Travis grunt as the staff hit the ground, missing its mark.

While Travis tried to regain his posture, Zack easily used his own staff to rap Travis twice on his legs—once on his knees and once on his ankles. Like a small tree in a tornado, Travis lost his balance and fell to the ground. No sooner had the younger boy hit the ground than Zack was upon him. With ease, he held the pointed end of the staff at Travis's chest in a pose ready to kill.

"You're dead," Zack broke the small lapse of silence. Their grapple hadn't lasted five minutes but Travis was still drenched in sweat. August in Firmara could get very hot, but today the weather was fair even though the sun shone brightly. *Travis still wears out too quickly,* Zack thought to himself. *If he can't catch up to Sarora and I, then what good is he in battle?*

Travis tried to force on a grin. "But I wouldn't die if you had a change of heart, would I?"

Zack frowned at Travis. "No one on the dark side, who is paid by their own lives aside from the mountains of gold and treasure, will give you any last words. Compassion doesn't exist in their hearts." Zack backed away from Travis to let him up.

Travis shakily stood to his feet. "How do you know what is written in someone's heart?" Travis challenged Zack.

"I know because anyone who seeks help from the darkness becomes it," Zack explained, trying to control his emotions. Why was he so argumentative? Why wouldn't Travis just listen to him and agree? Anger welled in his stomach as the two of them clenched their fists. The fire in Travis's eyes met Zack's as he felt the hair on his arms stand on end from the growing electricity.

"Would you two stop it already?" Sarora finally broke up their dispute as she stepped between them. Her glossy feathers reflected the sunlight, adding more texture to her exotic beauty. Zack looked to Travis, who had already dropped his gaze.

"Sarora, would you please tell him what is in the hearts of those who side with darkness?" Zack demanded as he continued to glare at Travis.

Travis brought his gaze back to Zack's. "Sarora, why don't you tell him, as you once told me, that we don't know what is written in anyone's heart?"

"Both of you shut UP!" Sarora finally screeched at the both of them. "When will the two of you grow up?"

"Sarora, in my defense—" Zack began, but Sarora cut him off.

"You," she glared at Zack, "don't need to be a perfect 'know-it-all'. Travis is trying his best. Also I'm not your servant, so stop the demands!" Then she turned to Travis, her golden eyes glowering. "And you should show more respect to Zack. He may only be a year older than you, but it was Master Racht's wish that he would continue your training, remember?"

Zack finally looked away from Travis and Sarora and to his feet. Out of the corner of his eyes he saw Travis hang his head in shame. *Why does he question me? What am I doing wrong?*

"Sorry, Sarora." Travis awoke Zack from his thoughts with his apology.

Zack quickly apologized, so as not to be outdone by Travis. "Yes, me too. Sorry, Sarora."

"And so you should be," Sarora replied with a huff. "What's

the matter with you two? Ever since we read Master Racht's will, you two have behaved like cats and dogs. Why can't you two just get over whatever problem you have with each other and be friends again?"

"We are friends," Travis began. "It's just, well, I don't know." He regarded Zack. "What is the matter with us?"

Zack shook his head. *Maybe it's because you're boneheaded beyond belief? Or that you have no patience? Or maybe you don't respect my leadership?* But as frustrated as he was, he couldn't let the storm grow. So instead he took a deep breath, clearing the thunder clouds from his mind. "Sarora's right, what are we doing? Friends?" he asked, holding out his hand for Travis to shake.

"Friends," Travis smiled and agreed. Even though outwardly it appeared that they were getting along, Zack still wondered what Travis was thinking. He was, after all, the grandson of Racht, the last true Acer. How could Travis and Racht, two entirely different people, possibly be related to each other? He supposed he could see some similarities—small facial features and such, but Travis's outlook on the world seemed alien to Master Racht's.

"Good." Sarora woke Zack from his thoughts once more. "Now that that is settled, let me teach you how both of your fighting skills are faulty."

"Both?" the boys asked.

Sarora nodded. "Yes, both." She turned to Travis, "Travis, you're focusing too much on hitting Zack. Instead, try wearing him out first so that he will be more likely to leave himself open to an attack." Travis nodded in reply.

Then Sarora turned her golden gaze to Zack. "Your moves are faulty because you don't strike enough. Evasion of attacks is the main goal, but you still need to defend and attack directly so that you won't be caught off guard if your opponent uses magic."

"Hey, I thought I was the teacher!" Zack teased Sarora.

Sarora smirked and looked at him. "You may be the official teacher, but admit it, I'm much better at it." She lifted her head and tail up high and spread out her wings as she sat, declaring her pride.

"Yeah, and you're really modest about the whole thing," Travis snickered and Zack laughed as well.

Sarora smiled at Travis. "The eldest may be most experienced, the youngest filled with the best ideas, but those who sit in the middle are granted both virtues."

"Ooo..." Travis acted as if he were amazed. "Where did you read this line, in the Book of Proverbs?"

Sarora flicked one of her feathery ears. "No, a friend taught it to me."

Zack remembered the saying quite well, but he didn't quite remember where he had heard it before. He wasn't all that surprised, though, when Travis asked him, "Zack? Have you been teaching Sarora more sayings?"

Zack shook his head. "It wasn't me who taught her that, I know that someone else did but I can't exactly remember who." He looked to Sarora.

Sarora shot a little glance at Travis and then looked back at Zack. "You know, it was someone from a long time ago, but I can't exactly place who."

Maybe one of the wolves during our visits with Master Racht?" Zack suggested. He knew Sarora was trying to cover her tracks regarding her past. Zack wouldn't be the one to let anything slip before she was ready to be open with Travis.

"Oh," Travis said, obviously showing that he believed them. Travis was hardly ever a hard sell.

Zack, trying to change the subject, looked to the sky to find that the sun was gradually getting lower. "What do you say, guys? It's getting late—you two want to head back?"

Sarora nodded. "You two go ahead, I'm going to stretch my wings for a little bit."

Zack grudgingly gave her the okay. "But not for too long. If you're not at home ten minutes after we are, you'll be in big trouble."

Sarora chuckled. "No offense, Zack, but you don't frighten me any more than a worm frightens a bird." She turned and took to the skies before Zack could counter her jest.

Zack heard Travis laugh under his breath. "Come on, let's go." As they began to walk, Travis sped up from behind Zack and tapped his shoulder as he ran by. "Bet I'll beat you home!"

"Hey!" Zack, slightly irritated at the surprise but ever competitive, made chase. "No fair!" And they raced each other across the golden fields toward their home.

Zack watched the candle flicker in the darkness. It was late at night, and his other friends were fast asleep in their own quarters. Outside, a few clouds painted the sky, circling the moon. Zack stiffened as he heard a noise but was able to relax again quickly when he recognized the sound of Travis rolling over on the mat in Zack's old room.

Even though they had found the truth of Travis's heritage, the younger boy wouldn't take their master's old room. "He was more of a grandfather to you than he ever was to me," Travis had told Zack when Zack had offered to trade rooms. However, no matter how Travis put his hidden feeling into words, Zack was aware that Travis felt more now for Master Racht than he had ever felt.

But Travis's inheritance wasn't the only reason why Zack wanted to give him the room. The real reason was because every time Zack surveyed his master's old room, he felt a pang of guilt inside himself. Any corner of the room he looked at might hold one little thing that would remind him of the fate-filled day. He recalled Sievan's killer blow, and how the blood poured out of the three deadly wounds on Master Racht's chest. His heart beat faster as he remembered Travis disobeying their master and tossing the sword to Zack. How easy it was to promise to do his Master's bidding, and how unfathomable it was to follow through and kill the man who had always been there for him. Lastly he recalled the sweat from his hands that slickened the handle of the sword, but the feeling hadn't stopped him from crying out one last time before his hand brought down the weapon. Only for a split second had the sword pierced Master Racht and then reached through his body to the other side. Tears filled his eyes as Zack pondered what he could've done differently that day that would have made life continue on the way it always had.

———

HYDROPHOBIA

Travis slunk out of the tent, tired and hungry. His stomach growled at him as he continued to walk away from their makeshift home as if it rationalized home meant food. Paw steps padded almost silently behind Travis as he made his way across the field and over to the woods.

"Pran?" Travis asked suspiciously as he turned to look at the young dog. "Why must you follow me every time I go to the stream?" The dog cocked his head as he continued to trot slowly alongside Travis.

Travis gave in with a sigh. "Fine, you can come, but when I get in, no peeking." Pran wagged his tail in agreement.

It was a fair morning—the sun shone warmly and few clouds blotted the sky. But even though the morning had begun fairly cool, Travis could already feel the heat beginning to rise.

As Travis reached the woods, the shade of the trees cooled his body. Not far from where he entered, he could hear the horses grazing. Travis stood on his tiptoes to see over a bush in front of him. He spotted Shadra, his dark bay mare, grazing next to Abendega, a mouse-gray stallion. Travis smiled at the two of them, sharing the same patch of grass the way a couple would share a drink. Strangely, at this sight, a question crossed his mind, *Will I ever have a connection like that with someone?*

He shook his head, trying to rid himself of the worry. "Here," Travis mumbled to himself as he continued his walk to the stream. "I will list reasons why I won't ever find a link like that with someone— one, I'm busy all the time, two, to some degree, I still think that girls are weird, three—I'm undercover, and four—even I know that I'm not the sharpest knife in the drawer, even without Sarora telling me so a hundred times a day." Travis couldn't help but smile at himself.

After a while, the woods broke out to a small riverbank by a chest-high stream. As soon as Pran saw the cold, rushing waters, he gave Travis a 'yeah right' look and then took off back toward where they had seen the horses. Pran was used to Zack and Travis bringing him down to the river to try to clean some of the filth off of him. Unfortunately, Pran was not so enthusiastic about the whole idea and he hid every time they took him near it.

Taking a moment, Travis gazed at his reflection in the moving waters. His brown hair was shaggy from weeks without a proper trim, though it wasn't much longer than a couple inches. Since his time in Firmara, Travis's boyish face had begun to disappear and his jawline had become squarer. His eyes were bright and a warm russet-brown color.

Quickly, Travis glanced around and listened for any sign of another person in the area. Once he was sure that no one was looking, he took off his tunic and leggings and jumped into the freezing waters.

Underwater, Travis opened his eyes and took in his surroundings. He was completely submerged in the cool water and he felt the bottoms of his feet wipe against slippery rocks that covered the entire bottom of the river.

Just as his lungs felt like they were going to burst, Travis forced himself upward to the surface. As he broke the surface of the water, his lungs revived themselves as he gasped for air. Carefully, he placed his feet on top of the slippery, rocky riverbed and began to wash himself.

The cool water refreshed Travis's skin and it seemed to both calm him and keep him alert. Nearby, he could hear birds singing in the treetops. In a small clearing near the river, Travis could see a few wild chickens scuffling among the dead leaves searching for bugs to eat.

Travis felt something slippery wipe against his leg. Startled, he looked down into the water and spotted a tiny minnow swimming around his legs and pecking at his toes. He smiled as he watched the little fish flicker in the rays of sunlight.

Distracted by the fish, Travis did not hear the figure approaching from the sky. Suddenly, he heard a twig snap and he turned around to see...

"Sarora!" Travis exclaimed, trying to hide himself by diving in the water. "What are you doing here?"

Sarora had not seen Travis beforehand and as soon as she swiveled her head to look at him, she quickly turned around so that even her peripherals could not spot him. "Sorry!" she called. "I didn't mean to surprise you."

Travis spotted a clump of reeds. "Just watch where you're going next time!" Travis replied as he ducked into the tall reeds.

"Sorry," Sarora repeated. "I was just out looking around for food when I thought I heard a big fish flopping in the water." Travis could picture Sarora with a huge 'gryphon smile'. "Anyways," Sarora continued, her head still turned away from him, "when you're finished scrubbing the stench off yourself, not to mention when you are fully clothed, I'll be over by the horses. I thought that we could go scout together today."

Travis felt a wave of excitement pass through him. "Okay, sounds great!" he called to her and began to work his way back out of the reeds. Almost everyday, Zack would send Sarora out to fly the area around them to make sure that they were still hidden well. Travis had never been on a scouting trip with Sarora. He found himself both glad to be doing something other than training and excited to be alone with Sarora. It had been months since they had time alone—before they met Zack and Master Racht.

"Good, I'll meet you there then and I'll bring your staff," Sarora replied and Travis heard her walking away.

Travis let out a sigh of relief when he thought that Sarora had left. Wanting to be done with his river-bath, he didn't spend much time looking for a good footing on the slippery rocks. Travis was just out of the reeds, when he unexpectedly placed his foot on a large, algae covered boulder. Unable to hold his balance in the swiftly moving current, Travis fell into the water. Travis had never been known for being an excellent swimmer, but he could still easily hold himself above water—until now. The current drug Travis down away from where he had hidden in the reeds. He struggled to get his footing back but he just couldn't place his feet anywhere before the water would drag him farther along.

Travis managed to hold his mouth above water for a moment, and a frightened yelp escaped his lips. "Help!" he cried, hoping that someone would hear him. Travis's heart pounded heavily in his chest, begging for air from the lungs. But when his lungs could not supply his heart with oxygen, his whole body began to strain. With great effort, Travis struggled to hold his mouth shut and refrain from taking a breath. His senses began to dull. In his vision, there were red flashes of light as blackness began to envelope everything else. Travis was blacking out.

Suddenly, Travis felt his body being lifted out of the water and he was laid out onto dry land. A firm hand struck him on the back and he coughed up a large amount of water.

As Travis coughed up water and gasped for air, his gaze drifted up and he spotted Zack, who was draping a thick cloth around Travis. Travis's face grew hot with embarrassment as he realized that he was still in his underwear.

"Don't worry about it," Zack voiced Travis's thoughts. His friend then looked around and asked, "Which way are your clothes?" Unable to speak, Travis shook his head and shrugged his shoulders. Zack waved him off as he replied, "I'll go and look for them. You stay here and rest a bit." And he ran upstream before Travis could reply.

After Zack had left, Travis worked his way back over to the edge of the river. He shivered as he peered at the water. Never before had he been so afraid of something that wasn't even alive. As he began to wake from his state of shock, Travis took in his surroundings—he was still in the woods, but instead of grass underneath his chilled body, the riverbank was made of sand.

Travis forced his gaze away from the rushing waters and kept an eye out for Zack. Five minutes later, Zack returned with Travis's clothes and since he was nearly dry, he was quick to put them back on.

When Travis was dressed, Zack smiled and rested his arm on Travis's shoulder and asked, "Do I really want to know why you were in your underwear, drowning?"

Travis couldn't help but smile as well. "It's not a long story, but you really don't need to know."

Zack chuckled and patted Travis on the back. "At least you're alive." His expression became a little more serious, "You have to be careful, what would have happened if I hadn't spotted you drowning? We'd all be in trouble if you died."

"I know," Travis sighed, "I'm sorry. I'll be more careful next time."

"I was also going to wash myself, but let me walk you back to the tent. After all that excitement, I'll postpone the training until tomorrow, okay?"

Travis nodded his head. "Fine." And as they walked away together, Travis glanced once more at the riverbank and suppressed a shudder. *I'm never going in there again*, he vowed to himself as they walked on.

TRICKY TEACHERS

Travis and Zack sat outside of the tent, relaxing as they waited for Sarora to return. With all that had happened, Travis had completely forgotten that he was to go scouting with her. The sun shone in his eyes when Travis spotted Sarora walking over to them from the woods. Travis wondered why he thought that he saw mild annoyance glowing in her eyes as she approached them. *What's her problem?*

When Zack spotted Sarora, he called out to her, "Good afternoon, Sarora! How did the scouting go?"

Sarora did not reply until she had reached them. Her gaze was like a knife cutting through Travis. "So, did you forget something?" she asked him.

Travis looked at her confusedly. "Forget something?" he pondered.

"Here," Sarora spat, "let me try to jog your memory. This morning, you were bathing in the swift river. I came walking by, scared you out of your wits, and as you hid in the reeds, I asked you..."

"Oh shoot!" Travis exclaimed, remembering the scouting trip that he had promised to go on with her. "Sarora, I'm so sorry I forgot—"

"Obviously," Sarora cut in, looking away from him and back to Zack. "Scouting was fine. The whole area is clear and there is no sign of anyone that may cause us trouble. I'm sorry I'm a little late, though. I could have been here earlier if I hadn't wasted so much time waiting for a friend of mine to not show up."

"I'm sorry!" Travis did his best to apologize. "I didn't mean to forget! I just got, well, um, distracted." He didn't feel like sharing the tale of being swept down the river and nearly drowning while in his underwear.

Sarora's glare was harsh. "If you'd wanted to sit here in the sun all day with Zack, you could have just told me instead of leaving me there waiting."

"Sarora," finally, Zack came to Travis's rescue, "Travis hasn't had the best morning, and I ordered him back here to give him some rest."

Sarora looked at Zack. "What do you mean?" she asked him.

"Travis got swept down river and nearly got himself killed," Zack explained.

"Oh, I see." Sarora seemed to brighten up before crossly glaring at Travis again with her strangely cold-warm sarcastic reply. "Rather than spend time alone with me, death was your first choice?" She shook her head, obviously trying to settle herself down. "Just, next time, could one of you at least find a way to send a message to me to let me know that you are unable to attend? I could have been hunting that whole time instead of just sitting there."

Zack nodded. "Will do. Sorry about that."

Sarora shook her head and sighed once more before turning back to the tent. "I'm going to take a nap, don't wake me." Neither Travis nor Zack opposed her decision.

"She's really ticked off with you," Zack commented as he leaned back and stretched his arms.

Travis heaved a sigh. "I know, but when isn't she? It's like she wants me to walk the straight and narrow and not put a hair out of place. I'm not perfect—she knows that, you know it, and even I know it."

Zack chuckled. "You are the only one who seems to put her off-edge. Just take it easy on her and let her throw her tantrums; don't be fazed by them. Eventually she'll get tired of yelling at you and just learn to relax."

Travis glanced down at his feet, and then out to the expanse of golden plains. "If it were only that easy. She just seems to have her own perspective on things."

"As we all should," Zack put in.

Travis sighed. "I know, but it's as if she thinks that she knows everything."

"Well, I guess you could say she's like Master Racht when it comes to knowledge, but more like you when it comes to expressing feelings."

Travis gave Zack a funny look. "What's that supposed to mean?" he asked him.

Zack chuckled again. "You'll understand someday. But as for tomorrow, since you are all good and clean, why don't we head into the city?"

Travis felt his spirits lift. "Really? That'd be great!" He had not been to the large city that was set about ten miles from where they were staying.

"As long as it doesn't rain, I think we'll leave a little after dawn," Zack told Travis.

"Rain?" Travis wondered aloud. "I don't believe that I've ever seen it rain on these plains before. Are you sure?"

Zack shrugged his shoulders. "The weather here can be very unpredictable so just don't always expect a clear day. And even if it rains tomorrow, we'll go once it dries up again, sound good?"

Travis nodded.

"Good," then he smiled, "now let's talk about this whole thing about Sarora coming by while you were in the river?"

"Well, um, I don't think we should go into details." Travis's face grew warm.

"Well, I believe that this is a story that I must hear for myself..." Zack smirked as his eyes twinkled with mischief.

Travis sat in the candlelight the next day, reading from one of Master Racht's old books. *Not master,* Travis thought to himself, *Grandfather Racht.* The thought made Travis feel ridiculous. He didn't know how Master Racht could have ever been his grandfather, but still he accepted it. It at least felt good to have had some living relative for a while, even though he hadn't known at the time.

Outside, thunder clapped. The summer storm had prevented Zack and him from going to the city. Travis had been a little disappointed at first, but now he was too busy trying to focus on reading a book with info about magical animals. Sarora had told him to study hard and in a while she was going to test him.

Travis read the first page to himself:

Water Dragons have long, slender bodies, unlike the bodies of most other dragons. Instead of sleek, shimmering scales, the water dragon has fur on its head and the back of its body. The fur can be many colors, but the most common are teal, light blue, black, and white. The water dragon's underbelly is made of a material similar to scales, but they aren't very strong and are more like skin.

From their heads, two sleek horns protrude backwards, usually colored in black, white, or the common tan. They also have a set of whiskers at the muzzle of their dog-like heads. These are used to sense prey in the large bodies of water that they live in.

Once, there was thought to have been a countless number of water dragons living in the oceans and lakes, but today, their numbers have greatly dwindled.

Travis studied the picture that the description had told about—
the sketch of the water dragon had white fur, a tan underbelly,
two white horns, two long whiskers, and a line of greenish-blue
spikes on the dragon's back that seemed more like fins used for
swimming than for protection in battle.

Travis read through the pages of the old, tattered book, trying
to soak up all of the information.

*The phoenix comes in nearly all hot colors—red, orange,
yellow, and even pink... There are many varieties of talking
animals including wolverines, wolves, snakes, and foxes.
Most talking animals are not magical, but many magical
species still speak... Firmarian lions have two long fangs
that are exposed even when the mouth is closed...*

"Are you ready?" Sarora's voice woke him from his deep
studying.

Travis looked up from the book with sore eyes. "You won't
give me a choice, so I guess I am." Carefully, he shut the large
book and placed it on the floor.

Sarora's eyes glittered. "You know me so well. Remember,
Zack may be here to strengthen your muscles, but I'm here to give
your brain a workout, something that it never had."

"Haha, very funny," Travis smiled. "So are you going to test
me or tease me?"

Sarora cleared her throat and began, "Okay, name the three
types of dragons."

Travis thought for a second. "Well, I know water is one, ice is
the second, and the third is..."

"Do you give up?" Sarora asked him.

Travis shook his head. "No, I know. Or at least, I thought that
I knew."

"Want me to give you a hint?" Sarora inquired.

"Yes, please."

"Your Crystal."

20

Confused, Travis answered, "The Courage Dragon?"

Sarora hung her head and sighed. "Oh, Travis, it's a wonder how you've made it this far in life."

Finally, it clicked. "Oh! It's the fire dragon! I'm right, aren't I?"

"Yes," Sarora side, shaking her head though she smiled. "Next question, what is the sccond most dangerous creature in Firmara?"

"Oh, that's easy—dargryphs," Travis replied almost as soon as the question was finished.

"I only went easy on you because I didn't want to lower your self-esteem," Sarora joshed.

"Right," Travis replied sarcastically. He thought for a second before asking Sarora, "If dargryphs are the second most dangerous animal, what is the first?"

Sarora clucked her tongue and shook her head. "Know what I teach you now, learn what is taught later."

Travis sighed. "Fine, next question?"

"If an electric gryphon and a tiger-wolf were to fight, who would win?"

Travis had to think the question through for a moment before guessing, "An electric gryphon?"

"Neither," Sarora smirked naughtily.

"What?!" Travis exclaimed.

"Well, you see, electric gryphons don't exist and tiger-wolves are extinct." Sarora's eyes gleamed with amusement.

"That's not fair! You tricked me!" Travis complained.

Sarora wagged her head a couple times as she spoke. "Master Racht taught knowledge–I'm handing down wisdom. Life is full of tests and tricks and you need to be able to solve for answers you don't already know."

"But you said this was a test," Travis argued.

"It still was."

Both Travis and Sarora turned their heads to look at Zack. He was standing by the entrance to his room, arms crossed and a twinkle in his eyes. "Isn't it funny how when I'm teaching him, you have to break up our fights, and when you're teaching him, I have to break up your fights?"

"It wasn't a fight," Sarora began to explain.

"Oh, really?" Zack faked a shocked expression. "Then what was it?"

"It was a fiery debate." Travis spotted a twinkle now in Sarora's eyes, understanding that she was only goofing around with Zack and not trying to prove a point.

"Ah, I see," Zack nodded his head in understanding. "Now, if you two don't mind, I'm going to catch up on my studies, so I'd greatly appreciate it if the two of you kept your 'fiery debates' down to a minimum."

Sarora smirked and nodded, "We'll try." Then she turned back to Travis. "One more question. Why do some animals speak while others do not?"

Travis thought for a second and then replied, "Wait, I don't remember anything about that in my readings other than that most magical creatures can speak."

Sarora smirked. "That is your next assignment." She turned her head and used her beak to point at the huge bookcase. "See the middle shelf?"

Travis nodded, "Yes?"

Sarora turned her head to look back at him. "One of those books contains your answer. Happy reading!" She turned to walk into her room.

"Wait!" Travis exclaimed. "You mean that I have to read all of those?"

Sarora turned her head back to look at him. "Not if you pick the one with the right answer in it first." She smirked and then turned to walk into her room.

STOWAWAY

The dew glittered on the tall grasses in the morning sun. A few clouds floated high in the sky, all round and fluffy. The day was far more beautiful than yesterday.

Travis walked beside Sarora as the two of them left the tent. The wet grass drenched Travis's boots but it didn't faze him at all. He glanced over to Sarora, who was walking with her eyes closed, soaking up the sun's rays.

They were going out to scout this morning. Even though Travis had wanted badly to go into the city, he wanted even more to spend time alone with Sarora. The day was beginning beautifully and Travis could see it ending that way. A bow strap held his staff against his back since he did not want to carry his backpack around all day. He put an extra skip into his step as he walked next to Sarora, waiting for her to speak.

Finally, Travis grew tired of waiting for Sarora to speak up, so he began the conversation. "So, when are we going to fly?"

"Patience is a virtue." Sarora exhaled a deep breath as she opened up her eyes. She then looked at Travis. He forced himself not to flinch as he spotted the scar that Sievan had left over her right eye. A few months ago, during the great battle at the portal, Travis, Zack, and Sarora had joined with Master Racht to defeat Sievan and

Lord Trazon's army. She and Sievan fought the fiercest out of all of them, and with the battle drawing to a close, they each took massive blows from each other—Sarora chopped off Sievan's tail and in return, he swiped hard at her with his talons. Luckily, her eye hadn't been damaged at all, but the pink scar that stood out like a blemish on a smooth stone would be a constant reminder of the battle.

Sarora's voice spoke him out of his memories, "Soon. But the more you begin to bounce off of the walls, the more that I am tempted to leave you here. Now remember, when we begin the scout, you must remain silent on land, but you can talk in a regular volume in the air. We don't want to attract any unnecessary attention to ourselves."

Travis nodded. "Right." They were silent for a few more seconds before Travis asked, "What are we exactly looking for?"

"Anything unusual." Sarora's reply was short.

"Like...?" Travis tried to pull a more specific answer out of her.

"Like if you see a rabbit with wings."

Travis was puzzled. "Rabbit with wings?"

Sarora used an expression more familiar to Travis. "Or as some say, something that sticks out like a sore thumb."

"Oh, well, you see a lot more sore thumbs than you do rabbits with wings."

"I'm glad you noticed," Sarora laughed softly. "If you began to see rabbits with wings, I'd be even more concerned about you than I have been."

Travis stopped walking as Sarora continued on. "Concerned about me how?"

Sarora just flicked her tail.

Travis caught up to her quickly but she stopped by the time he reached her. "Are you ready?" she asked him.

Travis nodded and hoisted himself up onto Sarora's back. For some reason, it felt different from the last time that he had ridden on Sarora's back a few months ago.

"You haven't shrunk, have you?" he asked her curiously.

Sarora laughed. "If I was shrinking, I think that I would be shorter than before. No," she shook her head, "you've grown at least three inches since we first met."

"I have?" Travis looked down at his legs. He didn't feel any different but he could tell that he had definitely grown since he had first met Sarora.

"You have. Haven't you noticed that you are almost Zack's height now? It won't be long before he'll be craning his neck to look up at you."

Travis chuckled. "I doubt that. Come on, let's go. We can't spend the whole day celebrating my growth."

Sarora faced the open plains. Travis's mind was flooded with memories as Sarora counted the ground like a horse before she took off running. The wind that Sarora made as she sprinted whipped against Travis's face and ran through his hair. Sarora snapped her wings open and began to beat them, slower at first, and then more rapidly. Travis let out a laugh of joy as he felt Sarora lift off the ground. His whole body surged with excitement as he saw the plains far below them. *It's just like the first day we flew, only better!*

A grunt from Sarora awoke him from his thoughts. "You're not just taller—I feel like I'm carrying a horse on my back!"

Travis just let her comment roll off of his shoulders as he continued to gaze in marvel at the scenery around him. As Sarora lifted higher above the ground, the lowest clouds began to surround them, covering both of them in water.

After they were a few hundred feet in the air, Sarora leveled them out so that they could see the land below them without being spotted. "Let me know if you even think that you see some-thing. You can never be too careful," Sarora instructed him. Travis scanned the horizon. For half an hour, they did not see anything except for the occasional bird flying beside them.

Suddenly, as they passed over the woods, Travis spotted movement far below them on the ground. "Sarora—?" he began but his friend silenced him.

"Sh… I saw it too," she replied as she began to circle the area, trying to fly in the clouds, out of sight of the forms. Again, Travis saw a flicker of movement below them and he pointed it out to Sarora, who nodded silently and then descended slightly.

"I don't like how suspicious they're acting. I am going to attack and get some answers," Sarora whispered to Travis so quietly that he could barely hear her. "As soon as I dive-bomb them, jump off of my back with your staff in hand. Be prepared to fight."

"Why don't we just hide from them?" Travis asked as Sarora continued to descend, but she did not answer. Once more, Travis saw the flicker of shapes. There were at least four figures, and as they came closer, he could see why they were so easily spotted. These men wore shining brass armor that glittered in the sunlight. The men obviously didn't see them coming—they were scuffling around a wagon that sat in a clearing in the trees. Two horses were tied to the wagon, one a dark bay and the other black.

"Ready?" Sarora whispered so quietly that Travis could barely hear her. He nodded in reply and leaned forward as Sarora dove through the sky.

As they neared the trees, Sarora let up a little on her dive to make sure that they would land in the clearing. As soon as Sarora dove, the men below them cried out in fear. "It's coming!" they called to each other as they reached for their weapons.

"Now!" Sarora told Travis as she came closer to the ground. Immediately, Travis leapt off Sarora's back and somersaulted as he landed on the ground. As he recovered, the man nearest to him pulled out his sword and lifted it high, ready to strike.

Fast as lightning, Travis reached back and grabbed his staff. By the time the man came down with his blow, Travis held the staff up in front of himself to deflect the attack. Even though he had been ready for the attack, the hit still jarred his bones as he struggled to hold the wood against the sharpened blade.

As Travis worked hard to stand, he caught glimpses of Sarora fighting the other men. By the way they all fought, it seemed as though his luck had given him the hardest of the four—their leader.

He wore only a brass breastplate, unlike the others, who were completely covered in armor, and he had shoulder length, almost black hair. Compared to his comrades, he appeared younger than them. While his friends seemed old and battle worn, the young leader looked to be possibly in his early twenties. His eyes were electrifying blue, and as they stared at Travis, they held hatred and... *Is that fear?*

Travis began to feel his arms give away. Praying he wouldn't mess up, Travis leapt to the side so that his foe would stagger forward. Sure enough, the young man took a couple of faltering steps forward and Travis tried to bring down the side of his staff onto the man's head. But the leader was not about to give up. Just before the staff hit his head, the man flashed his sword back up into position and blocked Travis's attack.

Travis struggled against the young man for another minute before he decided to call upon his powers for help. Focusing his energy, Travis quickly held out his hand, aimed, and tried to recount the first time he had ever used his powers. *Now!* Travis told his powers to come, but they didn't. Travis risked a second to glance at his hand. *Why won't you work?* he asked himself.

The leader noticed Travis's distraction and took the moment to attack. Before Travis could defend himself with his staff, the dark haired man was upon him, striking down. Travis was too afraid to move and he couldn't even blink.

At the last possible second, Travis spotted Sarora behind the man. Easily, she grabbed him with her talons and dragged him backwards. "Ah!" the man cried out in shock as Sarora flung him across the clearing and he landed on the ground. With lightning speed, Sarora stood on top of the man and pinned him to the ground. The man could not fight back because he had dropped his sword out of fright when Sarora had grabbed him. With a flick of her tail, Sarora signaled for Travis to come stand beside her.

"So," Sarora eyed the man with her intense eyes as Travis stood beside her, "I'm a reasonable being. You tell me what I want to know and then perhaps I'll let you live."

Even though Travis had seen fear flicker in the young man's eyes before, now that fear was barely visible. The man held his chin up, clearly exposing his throat. "I would rather not share information with you."

"And why is that?" Sarora asked, her tone and facial expression steady.

"Whether I tell you the information or not, you are going to kill me. So why betray the one who I have pledged my allegiance to if I will not benefit from it in any way?" the man replied with a sly grin.

"Hm, clever," Sarora commented in fake admiration. "You know, I haven't killed your friends—yet. I was wondering whom you were to be sneaking around the woods, obviously keeping an eye out for someone like me. Why would that be?"

"I will not utter a word unless I will benefit." The man, though still pinned to the earth, stood his ground.

"You would benefit by having the privilege to keep your life. Now speak!" Sarora barked at him, but the man did not reply.

Travis could tell that Sarora was becoming impatient. "Maybe we could offer him a proposition. Something that clicks better than the gift of life?" he asked her.

Sarora kept a firm hold on the man as she looked at Travis. "And what would you propose that we give him?"

Travis thought for a moment and then replied, "Possibly a treaty in which we promise not to kill him when we see him passing by next time."

"I may be willing to agree upon something like that." Travis was surprised that the dark-haired man would agree so easily.

"Oh, really?" Sarora asked. "Then what is the agreement?"

"Exactly what your friend just said," the man replied. "I will give you information if you promise us safety."

Travis could tell that Sarora was fighting herself inside her mind. He felt the same way as she did; he really wanted to know what was going on, but didn't want to give their possible enemies a chance to inform their leader of their whereabouts.

"Fine," Sarora finally gave in. "I grant you safety while traveling through these woods."

"Him too," the man said, gesturing to Travis.

Sarora had specifically tried to avoid this, Travis thought to himself. *She had obviously been hoping that the leader wouldn't have caught that she was the only one to promise.*

After sighing inwardly, Travis bowed his head for a quick second. "I grant you safety as well. Now, speak."

"First, I wish to stand up if you don't mind. I prefer not to be pinned down to the ground when I share information about his dark majesty."

Sarora gave him a hard look before letting him up. The man stood, wiped the dirt off of his pants, and then moved over to where there was a log. With great ease, he sat down on log, regaining his composure before he spoke.

"Please, sit," the young man invited them.

Sarora glared at him and didn't budge.

The man nodded. "As you wish. There is a stump over there for you to sit on," he said, turning to Travis and suggesting the seat. Though wary, Travis moved over to sit on the stump.

"Now begin with your name and position," Sarora ordered the man.

He bowed his head once before lifting his blue gaze and introducing himself. "My name is Trayka. As for my position, it is more like, how do you say... a fugitive?" the man began.

"So then what are you and your friends doing here?" Sarora questioned him further.

Trayka waved his hand towards his men as he explained. The three men glanced nervously at Travis and Sarora, but since they were generally good-natured men, they attempted a nervous wave. "Like I said, I'm running away. I met these three, and they decided to follow me. Since they were the owners of the horses, I let them come so that I could have an easy method of transportation."

"Why would you run away from Trazon, Trayka? Why betray someone who could kill you with the snap of his fingers?" Sarora asked him.

Trayka sighed. "I will tell you." He looked around to see that his comrades were beginning to stir. "But only after they have all left. They do not even know the full extent of what is going on."

"Then please hurry with it. I do not wish to spend my day conversing with an innocent face that hides a fox's sly attitude."

Trayka smiled. "That was almost a compliment, you know."

"Just get rid of them."

Trayka nodded and turned to his men. "Get up. All is well. Why don't the three of you go take a walk to get yourselves feeling better? And while you are walking about, you could keep an eye out for a possible campsite." The three men looked nervously at Sarora and Travis before nodding to their leader and taking off. Trayka then turned back to them. "Now, let me begin my story so that you may be on your way."

WARNINGS

Trayka began his tale steadily, describing every detail. "After the battle of the portal, at which we where we all fought, I and my comrade, Shastor, were ordered to go and search for you. After three days of endless searching, we finally gave up and came back to Sievan and Donigan with the news that you were nowhere to be found.

"When Sievan reported to Lord Trazon, Sievan told him that the two of us had been responsible for not being able to find you —although, he had spent the whole time cradling his stump of a tail like the cry baby he usually is—so Lord Trazon sentenced one of us to death.

"Though the Dark King knew Shastor was a magician, he was not aware that Shastor could see glimpses of the future. And while the two of us were in our room, he saw that my death was nearing if I stayed there. And so before the men came to take us to the executioner, he helped me escape through the window in our room, and I ran until I was far away from the Lord Trazon's castle and could run no more.

"I woke the next morning alone and hungry. I spent the next few days searching for food and shelter, and finally, I came across the men that I am traveling with. They told me they were veterans of the King of Firmara's army, and—for some strange reason beyond my comprehension—they became interested in my story and decided to follow me. They returned to their homes and donned their old armor, convincing me to travel back to the capitol city with them. And now, I still ride with them back to Olegraro, hoping for the good King's acceptance to let me join his army as payment for my treacherous deeds." Trayka finished with a sigh.

"You are running away from troubles that are difficult to hide from," Sarora commented.

"They are, but it is better to wait in the wings until you are strong enough to play your role," Trayka replied.

"Very true, Trayka. You are crafty for a man with little experience in leadership. I wish you well on your journey." Sarora dipped her head to Trayka. Seeing Sarora's change in demeanor confused Travis.

"Thank you, noble gryphon. I am afraid that I do not know your name, for those that are for the darkness call you names of which I refrain from speaking for fear of you biting my head off and ripping out my entrails." Trayka's smile was friendly as he stood and bowed to her.

Sarora chuckled quietly. "How wise of you... My name is Sarora."

Trayka turned to speak directly to Travis for the first time. "And what is your name?"

"Travis."

Trayka nodded understandingly. "Ah, yes. I believe that I heard your name while I was in the dark army. You are the one who holds the Crystal of Courage. Congratulations on that, and I respect you for all the effort you put forth to protect those who do not know how much they really need to be protected. But I do caution you that Lord Trazon has someone searching for you at this very moment." Then he smiled. "To you, that should both be a concern and a compliment—he only hounds the people that he sees as absolute threats and desperately is trying to kill."

"Uh, thanks." *I think,* Travis silently added, stunned by the kindness coming from the former rogue.

"Now," Sarora stood and looked to Trayka, "we must get going. We grant you safe passage through these woods as long as your heart continues to clean itself and be kind once more, and so long as you do not speak of our whereabouts to anyone."

"I swear on my life I will not tell a soul. I would not dream of turning you over to the likes of that scum, Lord Trazon."

Sarora nodded to him before turning to Travis. "Come on, let's go." And she turned and began to walk away without another glance at Trayka.

Travis began to follow her when a firm hand gripped onto his shoulder. Travis turned to see Trayka holding him in place. His eyes were filled with both interest and worry. "Travis, I must caution you to be careful about those who you choose as friends. Not every book with an appealing cover will have every page of itself filled with the reflection of that cover. Do you understand?"

Warily, he nodded. "I understand, thank you, Trayka. I will be careful. Best of luck to you and your new friends." And he followed Sarora. *What exactly had Trayka meant by what he had said?*

Zack stretched his muscles as he got out of bed—his shoulder still ached terribly from sparring with Travis the other day. The sun was already in the middle of the sky and Zack scolded himself for sleeping in as late as he did. *I'll have to remind Sarora to roll me out of bed next time. I would be a poor excuse for an Acer if I had actually ever become one.*

As he rubbed his eyes in the bright sunlight outside of the tent, Zack was aware of his dog, Pran, walking beside him step-for-step. The little dog just didn't seem to be the independent type—he was always with someone, whether it was Travis, Zack, or occasionally Sarora. Pran was still unsure about the large gryphon, but he was finally beginning to warm up to her.

Zack watched Pran as the young dog sniffed around the tent. His nose twitched back and forth as he continued to bring in the familiar scents. After he had scented what he needed to, Pran returned to Zack and the two of them walked out to where the horses were staying.

It felt weird for Zack to be alone and not working with Travis on his sparring or chatting with Sarora as he usually did everyday. Since Sarora had still insisted that she wanted to take Travis with her on a scouting trip, he had finally been given the chance to check on the health of the horses that day.

As he approached their clearing, Mesha lifted his head and let out an impatient nicker. "Yes, I know I've been gone for a while," Zack told the gelding as he patted his shoulder. "But can you blame me with all that I've been busy with? It's hard to have time to relax and pay attention to two trouble makers who are constantly trying to get themselves killed."

Mesha whinnied in a way that sounded like laughter. His horse seemed to be the one of the four that had the best sense of humor.

"Now," Zack continued as he examined the tan horse, "I didn't just come over here to chat with you all day. How are you feeling? Any part of you sore?"

Mesha shook his massive head.

"Are you sure?" Zack asked the horse again. Mesha bobbed his head up and down.

"Alright then. Where are the others?" When Mesha didn't respond, Zack asked differently, "How about, where is Seraphi?"

Mesha used his head to point behind himself to where Seraphi was standing farther over on the edge of the woods, staring out blankly at the golden summer fields.

"He's still depressed, isn't he?" Zack asked Mesha, who bobbed his head up and down. Ever since Master Racht had passed, Seraphi had seemed to be caught in a spaced-out state. He wouldn't usually respond to anyone or anything unless he thought that it could possibly be Master Racht.

Zack sighed. "Fine, I'll go and talk to him." He approached the old stallion whose fur used to be pure white but was now caked with dirt and mud. His face was filled with sorrow but his eyes were expressionless. Zack sat on a log that stood beside the regal horse.

"Seraphi," Zack began with a sigh. "You can't go on like this. It pains me to see you this way. You are the wisest of all the horses, and yet, you are the one who mourns when you know that mourning will not bring Master Racht back."

For once, Seraphi shot a quick look at Zack and then lowered his head to the ground as if to say, 'I know.'

"If you know, then why do you still blame yourself?" Zack questioned the horse. "I should be the one in this state, not you. I'm the one who finished Master Racht off. It's not your fault for listening to his orders to leave him in the battle—and deep down inside, you know that." This time, Seraphi did not reply.

"Come on." Zack was persistent in trying to get the stallion back to his old ways. "If you aren't going to do this for me or yourself, could you at least do it for your friends? When they see you like this, it disheartens them greatly." When the horse still did not respond, Zack tried to look into his deep, sorrowful eyes. "If not for them, then for Master Racht. What would he say if he saw you like this? He surely wouldn't want his best horse to let his death get in the way of bringing you happiness."

Finally, Seraphi swung his head around to look at Zack. "Please, Seraphi, will you agree to try to move on?" Seraphi seemed to ponder this thought before he finally bobbed his head, brightening a little.

"Good," Zack smiled. "Now, you wouldn't happen to know where the love birds would be, would you?"

Seraphi lifted his head to point past Mesha and over towards the river. Zack followed his gaze and then turned back to the old horse. "Thanks."

Pran walked beside Zack once more as they searched for Shadra and Abendega. After a few minutes, Zack spotted the dapple-gray coat of Abendega standing next to the dark bay coat of Shadra.

"Good afternoon you two," Zack called, smiling as the horses lifted their heads to greet him. "Could I be of service in any way to the two of you?" he asked them.

Strangely, Abendega and Shadra nodded their heads simultaneously. "And what could I help you two with?" Zack asked them curiously.

Abendega swung his head to Shadra and rested his muzzle on her belly. Fear rising inside him, Zack's eyes searched her side for a wound. When he saw none, he was confused.

Abendega stepped back to make room for Zack, but he kept a watchful eye on Shadra. Shadra watched him with her gentle eyes as Zack approached her and laid his hand on her belly. "What..?" His hand froze. Shadra's stomach had widened since he had last looked her over. It took him another moment to realize what the pair was trying to tell him.

Zack smiled at them. "And so the next generation begins. Congratulations, you two. Your foal will be the most beautiful one in the world."

In The Background

Z ack walked back into the tent with a smile on his face. A new horse would be both exciting and hard work for Travis and him to take care of. But at that point, it didn't matter. As happy as he was for Shadra and Abendega, he knew that the couple had long ago, before he was born, had a foal. But because of its lineage, the foal had been stillborn.

Acer horses were very rare. Not just because of their talents and stars on their foreheads, but because their talented blood was also closely related. Most Acer Horse foals were miscarried, aborted, or stillborn because their parent's genetics were too similar.

Zack knew how much it would hurt the pair to lose their second foal, but it was likely that would happen. So they would be stuck with two problems: Shadra would be unrideable because it would be too dangerous for her to do much of anything with that unstable foal, and if the foal survived, Shadra and Abendega would both be busy caring for the foal for a year after it was born.

As Zack walked past Travis's room, he felt a strange urge to take a peek. After a quick look around the room to make sure that nobody was watching, Zack parted the opening to Travis's room and quietly walked in. The room was nothing spectacular

—there were no decorations, only a mat that Travis slept on and a cylinder-shaped pillow at the end of it. Everything else was plain and boring. Zack was just about to walk out of the room when he spotted something shining underneath Travis's pillow. With another look around, Zack knelt down, lifted the pillow, and carefully picked up the book that Master Racht had given to Travis.

On the cover, as always, were the three animals of destiny: the dragon, the gryphon, and the qilin. The animals on the book were known as caretakers of the world, or, at least, the magic-loving people had known them as that long ago. Nowadays, mortal persons despised anything with magical powers.

Zack remembered how Travis had opened the lock to read the book's contents. Part of Zack begged him to open and look inside of the book and learn more about Master Racht. Travis had only read the will to Zack and Sarora, but Zack knew that the book must hold much more because of its thickness. But he held himself back. No matter what the others thought, Zack wasn't always on his best behavior because he believed in doing right, but rather because his guilty conscience would eat him away until he told the truth. It was an awful gift to feel guilty and to know right from wrong because no matter what path Zack chose, it all seemed to have some consequence. Zack bit the bottom of his lip as he struggled to make a decision. *Master Racht was my teacher, and he left the contents of the tent to me. Wouldn't that include the book as well?* Zack swept his hand over the top of the surface of the book.

Just as it had done for Travis, the three animals whirled in a circle, chasing each other around until finally, they spun off of the page and onto the floor. The three life-like animals now all had their own personalities. The dragon snorted in disbelief at him, the gryphon shook its head in disappointment, and the qilin glared at him curiously.

"Sorry," Zack apologized to them. "I just want to take a quick peek, okay?" the three of them just continued to glare at him unhappily. With a feeling of unease, Zack opened the front of the book and began to read:

To Travis,
*   May all your dreams live in your heart, and may you*
live long and happily.
*   —Master Racht*

Zack quietly flipped past the pages of the will and to the next section of the book where Travis had stopped reading to them:

I know that this knowledge may have come as a shock to you. Trust me, I felt the same way when I figured it all out. But now that you know who I am, it doesn't mean that I am about to tell you your entire lineage—that's for you to find out later.

*   Now, as I mentioned before, Seraphi will show you exactly where my gift that was mentioned for you is. You'll just have to be careful when retrieving it, however, because not everything's bark is worse than its bite.*

"What's that supposed to mean?" Zack asked himself as he continued on to read:

The road will be rough for you, Travis, but I believe that you, along with the help of Sarora and Zack will be able to pull through it all. You three make a great team, and I wish that you will never forget that. For when all else has been lost, your true friends will always stick by your side.

*   As for your training, behave and be patient. Sarora can be stubborn and Zack possibly even worse. Can you just picture me sighing right now? Zack is a great kid and he has the potential of a prince. He's not lived the easiest life, the beginning of his story is bleak and dark at best, but from it he has gained much experience. As much as you'd*

like to debate it, Zack probably knows better than you, so just listen to what he tells you. That doesn't mean that you have to agree with him, it just means for you to keep your opinions to yourself.

"Huh!" Zack huffed as he slammed the book shut. "I appreciate Master Racht urging Travis to respect me, but I would have hoped my own master would respect me by keeping my private life mine to share."

Zack quickly swept his hand over the cover of the book as he heard Sarora and Travis approaching. Just in time, the animals placed themselves back on the lock and Zack slid out of the room.

"Hey, Zack!" Travis called to him. "We've got a story to tell you!"

"Just give me a sec!" Zack called back as he tried to put himself back together. *I'll show Master Racht. I'll show them all! I will always remain faithful no matter who is a part of my background!*

Zack sat outside of the tent and listened carefully to the story that Travis and Sarora told him.

"...And so," Sarora continued recounting her tale, "Travis and I interrogated the young man, who turned out to be one of the soldiers in the War of the Portal." And she told him everything that she could remember.

When she had finished speaking, Zack asked her, "Wait, who was this young man?"

"Trayka," Sarora replied shortly.

For a second, Zack's heart skipped a beat. "Trayka?" he repeated.

Sarora nodded. "Yes, didn't you hear me the first time or is your hair growing too far into your ears?" Zack smiled and absentmindedly reached up and grabbed a lock of his hair. It was quite lengthy, each strand a few inches long, but he didn't want to use a blade to cut it.

"Do you know him?" Travis's question woke Zack from his thoughts.

Zack shook his head. "No. I feel that it should, but I can't think where I would have remembered it from."

"Perhaps you heard someone shout it during the battle?" Sarora suggested.

Zack nodded. "That could very well be." There was a length of silence before any of them spoke again.

"So, as the two of you may or may have not noticed, either Trayka didn't believe that there was a third person in this picture, or he chose not to pursue it. Zack, that means if at any chance Trayka may bring us harm, you are the only one who can break that vow," Sarora put in.

Zack watched Travis's face as it once more held that questioning look. "Why couldn't we go back on our promise if he posed a threat to us? For all Trayka knows, we could have both been lying."

"That is one thing that you should never do, Travis," Zack warned him. "If an Acer, or in this matter, an apprentice, goes back on his or her word, not only will they bring shame to the spirits of the other Acers, but they will also have fate turn against them."

"How so?" Travis questioned further.

Zack thought for a moment to put the right words into place. "Well, let's just say that you may have a curse thrust upon you that may or may not be life threatening in one way or another."

Travis still looked confused, but nevertheless, he nodded slowly anyway.

Zack couldn't help but sigh and shake his head. "It is a bigger deal than you know. You'll find out eventually, though. There will come a day when you are forced to make a difficult decision, and the promises that you make will bring you to your knees, whether your intentions were good or bad."

Looking at Travis he saw that the boy's eyebrows narrowed. "I understand," he replied bluntly, but Zack wasn't sure if Travis was really even listening to what he was saying.

Zack inwardly shook his head once more as he turned back to

the tent. "Come on, I'll get us a meal going. Travis," he looked to his friend once more, "get to bed early tonight. We've got a big day planned in the city tomorrow."

Travis's face immediately brightened up. Zack smiled as he turned away from him and walked into the tent. As he clamored around for the food that they had gathered a few days before, Zack couldn't help but think, *How many more times can Travis and I confront each other before we butt heads?*

In New Skin

A faint morning light began to show as Travis let a yawn escape. So far, the sky was clear and the winds over the vast plains barely blew. As he shifted his weight, Travis felt the items in his backpack move. It had been a long time since he had worn his old school backpack, and the age of the item was beginning to show. The old material had many holes covering it, which Travis had feebly attempted to patch up using his old jeans. Now, not only did his backpack look like a first-time quilt, but also maybe it could pass as a commoner's bag in this world.

When the tent rustled, Travis turned his head to see Zack stumble out. If he was as tired as he looked, then Zack was definitely worn out. But if that was so, he didn't say anything about it.

"Mornin'." Travis was the first to speak.

Zack nodded in reply as he took a quick look around at his surroundings. "Well," he finally breathed, "we'd best be off then."

Travis nodded and took what he thought to be the first step of his journey.

"Oh, no, you don't." Sarora appeared from behind them and she snagged the edge of Travis's tunic.

Travis gave her a friendly scowl. "What did I forget now?" he asked her.

Sarora softly chuckled. "It's not what you forgot, but what the sleepy genius over here forgot." Sarora turned her head to give Zack a 'gryphon smile'.

"Oh, right," Zack replied. He walked back into the tent and returned a minute later with a little bottle filled with a silvery liquid.

"Now," Zack explained, "this is a little potion that Master Racht would always whip up for me when I needed to go to the city. It's known as Liquidus Facies. One sip of this, and it'll completely change your appearance. Let me demonstrate how to use this potion properly," and he popped off the cork and held the vial to his lips.

After a small gulp, Zack let out a refreshed sigh, and he put the cork back. Travis watched Zack carefully, waiting to see some change in appearance. But nothing happened.

"I don't see—" Travis began but stopped as he saw Zack begin to transform. His skin seemed to boil all over as it changed color and took new shape. His blonde hair reddened and his blue eyes became a vivid green.

When it was all finished, Travis looked his friend up and down. His skin, that had always seemed to be lightly tanned but still fair, was now a very light color. His once-blonde hair was now flaming red. His muscular frame slimmed, and now his clothes were too large.

"By the way, there are a couple things that won't change," Zack said. It was weird for Travis to hear his friend's voice coming from another figure. "As you may have noticed, my height and age remained the same—no potion can ever change them. Also my voice has not changed. As I'm sure you'll relate to me on this, I can only take it changing once in my life."

Travis smiled at his last comment, but then thought to himself, *Has my voice changed?*

"Now," Zack started again and held out the bottle for Travis to grab, "it's your turn."

"Me? Uh, I'm not so sure..." Travis forgot that Zack wouldn't be the only one taking the potion.

"Come on, don't be nervous." Sarora rolled her eyes at him. "It doesn't hurt, I promise."

"Yeah, that means a lot to me coming from someone who's never taken it before," Travis jested, trying to convince himself that everything would be just fine.

"Don't worry, it only lasts a couple of days," Zack put in, obviously trying to comfort his friend.

"Well, if I have to." Travis reached out to take the bottle from Zack.

"You do. We don't want to risk being recognized and arrested by Trazon's posse." Zack handed him the vial.

With a silent prayer, Travis put the vial up to his lips and closed his eyes. The silver liquid felt warm and sticky as it slid down Travis's throat and into his stomach. And as for the taste, anything else would have been better—the silver potion tasted like iron against his tongue

As Travis forced back the urge to cough up the awful potion, he corked the bottle and handed it back to Zack. Suddenly, Travis felt his skin begin to prickle and his scalp tingled with unease. Travis held his right arm up to his face, and he was shocked to see his skin actually boiling like warm water. Travis felt light-headed, so he closed his eyes so that he would not pass out at the sight of his transformation. Abruptly, the tingling feelings stopped and Travis felt more relaxed as he realized that the process must be over. Nervously, Travis opened his eyes and examined his skin. His dark tan that he had received over the past few months had disappeared and now he was as light-skinned as Zack's had been before the transformation.

Travis looked up to his friends and asked self-consciously, "Well, how do I look?"

"Pretty good for someone with no hair," Zack replied, rubbing his chin with his hand.

Travis yelped and reached for the top of his head... and felt hair. Even though it was still there, he could tell that it was definitely shorter than before.

"Zack!" Sarora scolded the older boy as she raised a front leg and punched him in the shoulder.

"Ow!" Zack smirked at her. "Oh come on, Sarora, like you weren't going to toy with him."

Sarora grinned mischievously. "Yeah I would have liked to, but you beat me to it."

"Guys, please," Travis tried to regain his composure after the awful thought of being bald at only fourteen. "Do I still look human or not?"

Sarora smiled at him. "Well, you do look good for a blonde."

Travis couldn't bear it any longer. In a mad dash, he sprinted into the tent and grabbed the only hand mirror that he could find. With a shaky hand, Travis held the mirror up and revealed to himself his new look.

Sarora had spoken the truth. His hair was a very light dirty-blonde. But that wasn't the only difference—Travis's once-tan skin now had freckles dotting the upper half of his cheeks. As Travis looked for his usual brown eyes, he couldn't recognize them at all, for now they were green, just like Zack's. The rest of his features had sharpened, making him look not unlike a weasel.

"I-I look, I look...so different," Travis stammered, and once again, it was weird for him to hear his familiar voice come out of another's mouth.

Still shaky with shock, Travis set the mirror down and walked back outside to find Zack and Sarora waiting for him. "I feel like myself, but I don't look like anything I've ever even imagined myself as."

"What?" Sarora faked a shocked and hurt expression. "You thought that I would lie to you?"

"Uh, let's just say that you wouldn't always tell the whole truth." Travis shot her a fake grin.

"Touché." Sarora grinned back at him, her eyes sparkling with humor.

"Sorry to break you two comedians up, but we have to get going." The red-haired Zack walked between the two of them.

"I guess you must," Sarora sighed. "I just wish that I could go with you."

"But that can't happen until Trazon is overthrown and every other human on this earth is convinced that humans are gryphon's friends, not food," Travis said, trying to continue the jokes.

"Yeah, no duh." Sarora's flat tone took Travis aback. He hadn't meant to hurt his friend, but at the same time, how would he have known that it would have offended her?

"The potions wouldn't work on anyone but humans though, wouldn't it?" Travis asked.

Zack shrugged his shoulders. "We've never tried because it's already rare enough to find as it is, but it is possible that it could work on animals too."

"It's not like changing my gryphon form would make anyone less afraid of me anyways..." Sarora grumbled.

"Well, we'll be back as soon as we can," Zack cut in.

Sarora seemed to perk back up. "Don't be gone too long, will you?"

Zack nodded. "If we're not home late tonight, expect us early tomorrow morning—we've got lots of shopping to do."

Sarora nodded and bowed her head to the both of them. "Keep your mind focused, your reflexes sharp, and be prepared for the task ahead."

"As well as you, Sarora." Zack nodded to her and then turned to Travis. "Let us be off then!" And together they walked on, two unrecognizable figures. They walked step for step as they strode off into the dawning light.

. . .

Travis felt his muscles cramp and his feet ached. They had been keeping a steady walking pace for the past hour, and Travis was bored—bored out of his mind. The scenery had never changed, not even once, which made Travis wonder how Zack knew the way to the city if the only terrain that they ever saw were wide-open plains. Of course, there was the occasional tree. But to Travis, as much as he saw the woods, he thought that he could live without a few pines for a while.

"Are we getting closer?" Travis asked once more.

Zack sighed. "Sarora was right—you just have no patience, have you?" He reached his hand up and wiped a strand of his currently-red hair out of his whiter, freckled face. "We're farther from home, and closer to there than when you asked ten minutes ago."

"Heh, that helps a bunch," Travis replied sarcastically. He thought for a moment. The only sound that he could hear was the sound of their feet on a dirt road. The road had appeared to them about twenty minutes ago, and it made the whole walking thing a lot easier.

"Zack?"

"Yes, Travis?" His friend had tried to muffle a sigh. "What is it?"

"What is the city like?"

"You'll see when we get there," Zack replied shortly.

"Well, wouldn't it be good for you to tell me? How would I look, a boy that they have never seen before, that has no idea what he is doing and how to pay for his items?"

Zack chuckled. "I guess that would look pretty bad, especially for me, because you won't go out of my sight for more than a minute. Now, let me think. Okay, you'll probably want to know our currency then, huh?"

"Yes," Travis nodded. "That may just help when we're shopping."

"Okay, I'll try to explain it as easily as I can." Zack smiled and reached for a small pouch that was tied to his waist. "See this?" Zack held a small copper coin between his thumb and the finger closest to it.

Travis nodded again. "Yeah, isn't that a penny?"

"No... What's a penny?"

"It's part of the money system that I was used to. You know," he took in his friend's still confused face, "pennies are one cent, nickels are five cents, dimes are ten, quarters are twenty-five..." Zack still seemed puzzled. "You know," Travis continued to try and explain U.S. currency, "one hundred pennies equal a dollar, and one hundred one dollar bills equal a hundred dollars?"

Zack shook his head back and forth very slowly. "No, I don't know. Your form of currency is...odd."

"Well, then, how does yours work?" Travis asked, ready to learn.

"Well," Zack cleared his throat and held up the penny-like coin once more, "this is a zest. Ten zests equal one triller. Ten trillers equal one sham, and ten shams equal one ziess. Simple enough?"

Travis nodded slowly. "How did they get all of those names for the money?"

"They are named after the people who invented them, of course." Zack smiled. "Why? What is your money named after?"

"They, well, I," Travis stammered then looked at Zack, confused. "I'm not really sure."

Twenty minutes later, Zack sparked up another conversation. "So, we probably want to get our stories straight."

"Oh, yeah, right." Travis tried to act as if he knew entirely what Zack meant.

"Here," Zack began, "I'll tell you my story first. I am known as Emeka, which means, "great deeds." You'll want to choose a name with some deep meaning so that they can relate you to the name. I chose my name because the first time I came, I helped a few people out. I am the son of a farmer who lives a great ways to the south of the city. I only come by to gather extra goods that my family cannot supply for themselves. My father's name is Chavdar, and my mother's name is Ada. Are you keeping up so far?"

Travis nodded, "I think so."

"Good. Oh, and I am an only child. Now," Zack rubbed his hands together and gave Travis a mischievous grin, "let's see what story we can come up with for you...To start, let's say you're my cousin."

"Why can't I be your brother?" Travis asked him.

Zack sighed and smiled. "Well, if I've been an only child for my whole life, than they won't buy that you're my long lost brother, especially since we look nothing alike at this point."

"Oh, right." Travis felt his cheeks grow warm with embarrassment.

Zack smiled and then cleared his throat. "So, like I said before, you're my cousin. My mother is your father's sister, and your family just moved close to us. Let's say you're farmers as well, but you work more in the fields and are mainly subsistence farmers."

"Okay," Travis nodded in agreement. There was a pause before he asked, "Then what shall my name be?"

"Hmm..." Zack rubbed his hand against his chin, deep in thought. "You need a name that's somewhat common, and has meaning..." Zack suddenly snapped his fingers. "I've got it!"

"Well," Travis asked. "What is it?"

Zack looked at Travis with a grin. "Devon. Your name will be Devon."

"Devon?" Travis asked with a funny look on his face. "Why?"

"Because that was the name of the great king that ruled here about fifteen years ago," Zack explained to Travis. "He was well-liked, and many people named their children after him. So it only seems fitting that you are to be named Devon." Zack then held his hand out to shake Travis's. "So, what do you say, Devon? You up for it?"

Travis shook Zack's hand happily and smiled, his emerald eyes twinkling. "Sounds wonderful, Emeka, son of Chavdar."

"Hm," Zack mused, "nice touch. You do know our customs more than I thought, Devon. Now let's walk a little faster. I want to reach the city before noon."

OLEGRARO

Finally, Travis spotted a large shape looming over the horizon. As they neared the city, he felt an excited fear begin to well inside of him. What would happen today in the city?

As they walked on, Zack turned to Travis. "Now, do you remember everything that we spoke about?"

Travis nodded, becoming a little annoyed. "Yes, I remember." He'd heard the same question at least three times in the past half-hour.

"What is my name then?" Zack inquired.

"Emeka," Travis replied, more annoyed than before.

"And what is your name?"

"Zack! I think that I would know what I am to be called! What's up with these quizzes?" Travis demanded.

Zack studied his feet. "Sorry," he mumbled. "I'm just a little paranoid about what will happen today."

"Hey," Travis reached out his hand and patted his friend on the back. "It'll be a great day, trust me."

Zack looked back to Travis and nodded. "Yeah, I guess you're right. I mean, as long as we keep our heads on straight and stick to our stories and our plan, we'll be just fine."

Ten minutes after Travis and Zack had spotted the city, they reached its large, wooden gates. The gates stood about twenty feet tall and stretched about fifteen feet wide. As for decoration, detailed carvings were engraved in the large gates, the largest and most detailed of them all sat in the center, between both gates. It was a dragon-like creature, and it had itself wrapped around a cross, with a crown sitting on top of its head.

Alongside of the gates was a long wall that appeared to surround the entire city. The wall was made of some sort of tan sandstone, but it was fairly smooth to the touch.

As Zack and Travis walked up to the gate, a guard on duty stopped them. He wore a cheap looking set of bronze armor. "Where are you boys from and what be your business here?" he asked in a gruff voice.

Zack was the one who spoke. "I am Emeka, and this is my cousin, Devon. We are here to gather extra supplies for our parents who have a farm twenty miles south of here."

"Hm," the guard still eyed them suspiciously. "It's an awfully long journey for boys around the age of thirteen... Ah, well, what trouble could the two of you really cause? Go on ahead. Remember that the gates will not be opened after sunset." Then the guard let out a whistle, and the gates began to part.

His heart beat rapidly as Travis took his first steps into the city. The buildings resembled the city walls. They looked to be made of either cement-like sand, or sandstone. Most of the first buildings stood about three stories high, but as Travis and Zack walked further into the city, the large buildings grew taller; now they averaged six stories.

Travis held a giant grin on his face as he looked all around. There were stores and carts lining the streets, not to mention the occasional entertainer. So far, Travis's favorite entertainer was a man who swallowed fire whole, and then he breathed it out a second later. However, Travis couldn't help but smirk to himself —he was able to use a fire of his own, but he didn't need a life-threatening magic trick to do it.

The people all around Zack and Travis were very talkative and boisterous, but in a merry way. They were so involved with conversing that Travis was convinced that he could have announced his real name to the whole city, and he and Zack would be the only ones who would notice.

"Now," Zack's voice awoke Travis from his thoughts, "we have a list of things that we need to purchase from these stores over here." Zack pointed to his right. "I need you to go over to that little plaza area and look for some more ingredients for the silver elixir. "

"What sort of ingredients?" Travis asked curiously.

"We need what is called an iron mushroom," Zack told Travis carefully. "Don't worry about anybody being suspicious. Iron mushrooms are used also for healing cuts and bruises." Zack then reached into his pocket and pulled out several small, silver coins. "Here, twelve trillers should be enough for a nice batch." Eyes full of worry, Zack looked to Travis. "You will try to be careful now, won't you?" Travis nodded. "Good. Meet me back here, at most, in a half-hour. I don't really want to come looking for you."

Travis nodded again. "Sure thing, Za— I mean Emeka."

"Heh, nice catch. Be careful what you say now." And Zack turned and left Travis standing by himself.

With a little skip in his walk, Travis took his time walking over to the little square where the spice shops were located. The smell of freshly baked cinnamon bread made Travis's stomach rumble, so much so that he had to force himself to keep walking and not to stop and buy some for himself.

A sound of sweet music made Travis stop in his tracks. A little guitar-like instrument was playing the joyful little melody. Travis looked around to see where the noise was coming from and he soon spotted its source. In the middle of the square was a large water fountain. Sitting by the fountain was an older man, playing what looked like a mandolin. But that wasn't what really caught Travis's eye.

His feet held him to the spot, where he stood stock-still,

watching five children dancing. Most of the children looked to be young, probably anywhere from five to ten. They all laughed as they danced to the merry beat of the mandolin, their bare feet smacking the stone pavement.

Travis smiled as he looked at the children dancing, but a different sight made his skin tingle. In the center of the dancing children stood a young girl about Travis's age. She wore plain clothing the color of sand. Her curly, golden hair bounced as she danced with the children. Her eyes were a beautiful gray and her smile flashed a bright white. As Travis stood stock still watching the girl, he felt his heart make a weird thudding noise in his chest. Butterflies flew around his stomach, giving him a warm feeling that both lifted him off of his feet and made him feel sick at the same time.

Travis hardly realized when the music stopped and many passersby applauded the talented young group. A man walked by Travis and he accidentally bumped into him when he took a step forward.

"Hey," the man scowled, "watch where you are going."

"Oh, sorry," Travis apologized as he took one quick glance away from the group to see the man walk away. Quickly, his eyes darted back to the scene where the children were now picking small coins off the ground. A little girl around the age of five was just about to pick up a gold-colored coin off of the ground when a figure broke the circle around the little crowd.

Travis watched with intensity as the man grabbed the little girl by the hand and yanked on it harshly. "What do you think you are doing, you pest?" He pulled her away from the coin and picked the money up in his grubby hands. "This is mine, you hear? Don't you ever steal my business from me again!"

Travis recognized the man. He had spotted him a while back. He was the man that had tried to use sleight of hand magic to perform mysterious tricks. But since most people in the city were superstitious, they chose to give him a wide berth.

"Leave her alone!" Travis looked from the man and the little girl to see the girl that was Travis's age standing close by them. "She hasn't done anything, so just let her go!"

A malicious grin spread across the man's face. "Hasn't done anything? You all have done something! I can't make enough to eat everyday while you lot go from rags to riches!" The man took a step toward the other girl. "But there are always forms of payment that will make me forget about this whole ordeal..." The man tossed the little girl to the side as if she was a rag doll and advanced toward the older girl. Travis couldn't see the man's expression because he had his back turned to him, but he knew that it wasn't warm or friendly.

Travis took a quick glance around to see if anyone would step in to help, but no one moved. They all continued on their way as if this kind of harassing didn't bother them at all.

Before he could catch himself, Travis found himself stepping away from the edge of the circle and into the clearing. "Leave her alone." Only after he had uttered the words had he come to a realization of what he had just done. Suddenly nervous, his palms began to sweat and his heart began to pick up pace.

The man turned his head around to look at Travis. He stood a foot away from the girl, his hand still reaching out to grab her. He smirked when he saw that the voice that had spoken to him was only a boy. "Move along, child. There's nothing to see here." He turned again to face the teenager. The girl's gray eyes flickered with fear as she took a step back.

Travis took another step forward. "I said, leave her alone."

Dumbfounded, the man turned back to Travis. "Look, boy, this is none of your business. I'm just getting what I deserve, so back off!"

Travis took another step forward. He and the man now only stood a few feet away from each other. "I don't want to hurt you, so would you please leave her alone." Even though he didn't know yet how he could fight a man much larger than himself, his tongue seemed to be ready to spring ahead of his mind.

The man's brows furrowed as he glared at Travis. "I don't

know who you are, boy, but you, hurt me? I think you must be mistaken." He turned away from the girl and took a pace over to Travis. The man's thick arms were about double the size of Travis's and he was about a head taller.

As afraid as Travis was, he held his ground and kept his gaze steady. He was not only trying to convince the man that he was stronger than he looked, but he was also trying to convince himself that he had made the right decision sticking up for the girl.

"Ho-oh!" The man chuckled at Travis's glare. "So you do believe that you can beat me! Well, let's just see about that..." The man drew his fist back, aimed at Travis's head, and attacked.

Travis's instincts took over and he quickly dodged the man's blow. Seeing that Travis had ducked, the man took his left hand, formed another fist, and went for an uppercut hit. Just before his fist reached his gut, Travis jumped backward, avoiding yet another harsh punch. The man's face grew red with anger and his eyes grew a fire that literally said, "I'm going to kill you."

Travis held back a smirk of satisfaction as he dodged another blow from the tall man. This time he had jumped to his left. His confidence had grown too large, however, for he had left himself open for another quick attack. The man, seeing a new opportunity, struck with his right arm. Seeing that he wouldn't be able to dodge the next blow, Travis twisted his body so that his right hand caught the fist of the man. As soon as the fist reached his palm, Travis grabbed a hold of it, and using his left hand to help grasp the arm, Travis twisted the man's arm around.

The man groaned in pain as Travis heard a popping sound come from the man's arm. Not wanting to horribly wound the man, Travis pushed the man's arm against him so that the man would be forced backward a few steps.

For a few moments, the man stood still, his body bent over his right arm. Gently, he cradled his sore arm with his left and groaned every few seconds. Travis thought that possibly the man would now give up and leave. But that hope was shattered the same second that the man broke the silence with a loud cry and came at Travis, both arms outstretched.

Seeing the perfect opportunity, Travis fell to the ground just as the man was a few feet away. While the man struggled to stop himself, Travis wrapped his legs around the man's and spun his body while on the ground. With a loud 'thud', the man hit the ground. As Travis stood, he watched the man from the corner of his eyes, expecting him to retaliate, but he didn't—the man was out cold. Side-stepping to avoid the man, Travis backed away. His muscles ached with the strain that he had used to bring the man down. He felt a bead of sweat fall down his nose and into his mouth. Travis licked his lips, trying to rid the taste of the salty water from his mouth.

Travis looked around and spotted the girl his age helping the five-year-old off of the ground. Not expecting any thanks or recognition, Travis walked towards the edge of the clearing.

"Wait! Don't go!" Travis turned around to see the girl his age approach him. Her eyes sparkled with gratitude and a little smile flickered across her lips. "Don't go yet, I haven't had a chance to thank you, brave stranger. Please, come into my family's shop for a drink."

Surprised, Travis wasn't sure how to respond. "I don't want to be a bother..."

"No, not at all. I think we can spare a quick drink for such a hero as yourself." The girl was very persistent.

Hero? Travis thought to himself, mystified. He didn't think of himself exactly as a hero, but he didn't want to turn down the girl's kind offer. "Um, okay then, I'll be thankful for a small drink."

The blond-haired girl smiled and led him into a store that sat only a few paces from the large fountain in the center of the clearing. Her parents' store was small and worn, but it had a cheery feeling radiating from all of its corners. Shelves were stacked high with simple necessities—folds of soft cloth to sew clothing, food, and jugs at the bottom of the shelves held some sort of red drink.

Travis wasn't quite sure what it was but he didn't linger. Travis followed the girl and she led him to a backroom where a table rested with two seats. She sat Travis down in a seat and told him that she would be back in just a second. Travis just nodded and watched her as she walked away, her dress daintily floating around her legs.

The smile that had grown on Travis's face disappeared as a new thought crossed his mind. *Zack is going to kill me.* He was supposed to meet his friend back shortly after they had departed. Before Travis had come to Firmara, his first instinct would have been to look around for a clock. However, it was hard to tell the precise time when clocks didn't exist in Firmara—at least, as far as Travis knew. So instead of checking the position of the sun in the sky as he usually would, Travis estimated his time from what had previously happened. With that, he expected that he had another fifteen minutes or so before Zack would expect to see him back.

The girl woke Travis from his thoughts as she walked back into the room with a tin cup full of clean water. Travis thanked her before taking a quick gulp. The cool liquid soothed his dry throat and he felt it race down to slosh inside his stomach. Travis set the cup down, suppressing a sigh of contentment. He didn't want the girl to think that he was a big-shot, what with all his fighting skills and fairly decent clothing.

Travis looked up at the girl when she cleared her throat, obviously trying to get his attention. When Travis was focused on her, the girl began, "Thank you again, kind stranger, for helping me and my friend. Would you also be so kind as to tell me your name so that I don't have to call you 'stranger'?"

"Oh, yes, my name." Travis racked his brain for his 'fakename'. *What was it again? Oh yeah, now I remember...* "My name is Devon."

The girl obviously believed him. "Oh, a nice name. You are certainly as just as our old king." She nodded her head, but her lips did not break a smile.

59

Not wanting the conversation to die, Travis continued on. "And what is your name?" he asked her.

"Elizabeth. Elizabeth Stealark." The girl smiled once more. "I was named after my grandmother who spent her days as a nurse, healing the wounded during a nasty war that was fought."

"Oh, well, that's nice," Travis smiled, trying to be polite.

"So, where are you from then, Devon?" Elizabeth asked in a sweet voice, her eyes showing great curiosity as she sat down in a chair across from him.

For a second, Travis didn't respond. He was staring at her beautiful blue-gray eyes... He forced himself to stop daydreaming so that he wouldn't slip when he tried to tell his lie. "Oh, I'm from outside of town. I just moved here with my parents from a place about seventy miles outside of the city. Now I live next to my cousin, Emeka. He and his parents have lived outside of the city for a long while."

"Really?" Elizabeth seemed transfixed by Travis's conversation. "I've lived here in the city all my life with my parents. As you noticed, I spend most of my time watching the neighbors' children. They can be quite a handful, but they are wonderful once you learn how to keep them entertained. And Emeka did you say? He wouldn't happen to have red hair and green eyes, would he?"

Travis tried to hide his surprise. He should know by now that many people may have seen Zack around whenever he came into the city. So he nodded. "Yes—do you know him?"

Elizabeth nodded. "A little. He comes into my family's shop every now and then to get supplies. He's very nice, but, and I don't mean this to be offensive to him, but isn't he kind of...rude?"

Travis tried to hold back a nervous look. "What do you mean by that?" He asked Elizabeth.

"Like I said, I don't mean anything negative toward him, but he's very curt when he speaks and he always seems to be checking himself as if he's appraising his appearance. He seems self-centered." When Travis didn't reply right away, she added, "Maybe just a little?"

Travis tried to choose his words carefully. "I'm not so sure about being self-centered, but he is complex."

Elizabeth propped her head on her hands and put her elbows on the table. "Complex?"

"Yeah, complex." Travis tried to convince himself that he had chosen the right word.

"What would make you say that?" Elizabeth asked, her question simple and innocent.

"Uh," Travis drilled his brain for an answer. *Wrong word!* He chastised himself. Complex was a word that was way too close to who Zack really was. "Complex...because he has many different opinions." Travis's statement held a tone of a guessed answer to a question.

"Opinions? What are these opinions?" Before Travis could respond to Elizabeth's question, she spoke again, "Sorry, my parents keep trying to tell me that I always go poking my nose into rough draft books."

Travis thought for a moment on her last statement. *Rough draft books?* Now there was something that he didn't hear everyday. *Maybe she means being too curious about things that haven't fully been told before.* A little voice spoke in Travis's head.

"That's okay," Travis accepted her apology. "I'm told by some of my friends that it's best for me to focus on what's going on now rather than what will happen next."

Elizabeth let out a small, short giggle. "Maybe the two of us are more alike than we know, Devon."

Travis couldn't help but smile. Just talking to Elizabeth made his skin break out in goosebumps. "I don't know about that. I'm sure that you are a lot smarter than I am."

"Oh yeah? Prove it." Elizabeth's eyes twinkled as she dared him.

"Actually, I think that it would take the both of us and the future to prove that." Travis couldn't help but chuckle.

Elizabeth smiled, her lips pressed together as she stood back up. "Then, maybe it would be best that you come by more often, Devon Braveheart."

Travis stood and looked into her eyes. "That would be my pleasure." He gave his best bow, and Elizabeth giggled again and led him out into the main room in her family's store.

"Now," Elizabeth turned to him when they stood at the counter, "am I correct to guess that you came here to buy supplies?"

Travis nodded and smiled. "Yes, Emeka and I came into town for the day. I believe what he told me to get were iron mushrooms?"

"Oh, yes. We just got a new supply in yesterday from some local farmers," Elizabeth told him. "Excuse me for a second and I'll go and get them." She turned and walked behind the wooden counter to a curtain-covered passageway. Travis watched as Elizabeth disappeared and returned in a few seconds. She was now carrying a small basket filled to the top with silver-gray mushrooms. Each one was about the size of Travis's palm and was spotted with little specks of brown.

"Will this be enough?" Elizabeth asked him as she set the basket on the counter.

Travis nodded. "Yes, that should be good. How much do I owe you?"

"Four trillers," Elizabeth smiled and Travis reached into a pocket that he had put in his tunic. He pulled out four small trillers and gave them to Elizabeth. For a split second, Travis felt his hand brush hers. The small touch made his fingers tingle and he smiled.

Elizabeth didn't seem as fazed by the small touch. She simply smiled and put the coins into a storage space below the counter. "Thanks again. Not just for your patronage, but also for saving me. Because of today, I'm sure we'll be great friends for a long time, Devon Braveheart."

"I do believe as well." Travis smiled at her and grabbed the basket off of the counter. "I'll be sure to come back into town as soon as I can, Elizabeth Stealark."

"Farewell!" Elizabeth called after Travis as he walked to the opening of the shop. "May safety always be with you and may you be blessed with good times!"

Travis raised his hand above his head in farewell. "As you, Elizabeth." And he turned around, dreaming of the expression on Elizabeth's face when they first looked eye-to-eye. As Travis walked back to meet Zack, he nearly got himself lost, for he had two things on his mind—Elizabeth and her smile.

Oops

Z ack watched nervously for any sight of Travis. What was taking him so long? Sure, Zack had given him a half-an-hour, but how long did it really take for someone to find a needed item, purchase it, and come back?

Finally, Zack spotted Travis, his usual brown hair now blond. Zack marched over to his friend, one hand holding a basket of newly purchased items. Something in Travis's appearance caused him pause—his walking was lackadaisical, his eyes shone brightly with daydreams, and a goofy grin was plastered on his face.

"Devon!" Zack called to his friend in a greeting, but Travis kept walking, obviously unaware of him.

"Devon!" Zack called again and reached out with his free hand to grab his friend's shoulder.

Under his palm, Zack felt Travis jump and immediately his friend's instincts kicked in. With a duck and a sweeping of the foot, Travis tried to unbalance Zack, but Zack was faster. With cat-like reflexes, Zack jumped over Travis's swinging leg and when he reached the ground again, he paralyzed him with his glare.

"Watch it!" Zack scolded Travis as he recovered from the adrenaline rush.

Now Travis's eyes flashed with recognition. "Oh! Sorry, Zack!" he quickly apologized.

"Uh, Sir Duh Devon!"

Travis's face flushed with embarrassment. "Oh, whoops! I mean, sorry, Emeka, I thought that you were someone else."

"Obviously." Zack rolled his eyes. With a flick of his wrist Zack signaled for Travis to follow him over to a nearby alley.

As soon as they stood inside the semi-private area, Zack glared at Travis. "When I first thought of bringing you here to the city, I thought 'Hm, I'm not sure what to think of this,' but now I'm thinking, 'Hm, was it really a smart decision to bring him after all'!"

"I'm sorry, Emeka." Travis was clearly struggling to remember to call Zack by his fake name. "I didn't mean to attack you or call you the wrong name. But hey, at least I got the iron mushrooms!" Travis's grin just pleaded for forgiveness as he held a small, woven basket up to his eye level.

Zack could only shake his head and sigh. "I know that you don't mean to do things like that, but you really have to be careful. And I wasn't only talking about what you had mentioned previously. No, when you finally returned, you also didn't respond to me when I called you."

"You called me?" Travis asked, his expression filled with bewilderment. Zack simply nodded. "Oh, sorry, I was, um, spaced out." Travis looked down to his feet.

"Spaced out?" Zack questioned him.

There was a small pause before Travis replied, "I-I guess that I was just... distracted by all of the different things around me. I've never been to such a busy city before."

Travis was a bad liar, and Zack knew for sure that his friend wasn't telling him the truth. However, against his better judgment, Zack chose to ignore the subject.

"I suppose Olegraro can be a lot for anyone to take in," Zack said and then reached for the basket. "Since you brought those, I'll take them off of your hands." Zack grabbed the basket from

Travis and inspected the small silver mushrooms. "And, just so that we may avoid any other distractions, why don't you come with me?"

Travis nodded. "Sure, sounds like a plan."

"Because it is the plan." Zack smiled in an attempt to hide a grimace. "Now, let's get going. We still have plenty more to find."

"Oh, one quick question," Travis began.

"What is it?" Zack turned back to him after he had begun to walk out of the alley.

"Why didn't we just ride the horses here?" Travis asked. "My legs and feet are killing me!"

The sun was setting when Zack let out an aggravated sigh. "We won't make it home for sure tonight." They had spent the past seven hours or better searching every nook and cranny of every store for items for the potions that Zack required. Together, Zack and Travis had found nine out of ten of the necessary ingredients for the transformation potion, but the last ingredient that they lacked was the most important—and it was the hardest to find.

After a long day of walking about, Zack and Travis walked up to a small inn for the night. Travis, on many occasions of the day, had asked Zack, "I wonder what Sarora is doing." And every time that Travis asked, Zack would have to shut him up before he exposed them. After Zack would scold him, Travis would cover his mouth with his hand, "Oh right, sorry, Za—I mean Emeka." Zack made a mental note to give Sarora a code name just for the sake of protecting their true selves.

Travis bumped into Zack when the older boy had come to a stop. "Oops, sorry," Travis apologized to him, but not before Zack sent him a small glare. As talented and clever as Travis could be, he was obviously having a difficult time paying attention today. Several times he dropped his many baskets that he was carrying, spilling out their contents. What had gotten into this boy's mind that he would be oblivious to everything around himself? His apologies throughout the day had all been said absent-mindedly. Zack let out a sigh and continued towards the quaint inn.

The inn was made out of the same material as all of the other buildings. The windows were simple holes cut in the stone walls. Only the rooms on the upper floors had glass to cover the windows, but even at that height some were smashed and cracked.

Candles were lit throughout the buildings around them. The faint lights flickered on the tall sticks of white wax as if they were afraid of shining through the darkness.

Zack led Travis through the front door of the inn. The walls were plain, but the ceiling had various carvings dug into them, though they were crumbling. As for the floor, most of it was a solid layer of a sandy-colored rock. In the middle of the floor sat a large green rug. The once-beautiful rug that had obviously had golden threads weaved into it now was covered in dirt and dust.

At the back of the room, across from Zack and Travis, stood an older woman behind a wooden counter. With wary eyes, she watched them approach. Her gray hair was tucked into a bun at the back of her head. Her face held a weary expression and dark gray bags sat underneath her eyes. Although most of her told Zack that she was tired, he could still see the strict look in her eyes.

"Good evening, Emeka," the woman spoke. Her voice held a strange accent that sent a tiny shiver down Zack's back.

"Good evening, Miss Adrais," Zack replied. He then sat down his many baskets and reached toward his bag of coins. "One room for the night, please."

Miss Adrais nodded and she turned around and grabbed a small key from a cupboard that sat behind the counter. As she turned back to Zack, Miss Adrais gave a small smile. "It's been a long time since you last stayed with us, Emeka."

"Aye, it has," Zack replied.

"How many years?"

"Well, I don't know about years—"

"Then months?"

Zack thought for a moment before replying, "I'd have to guess around seven."

Miss Adrais clucked her tongue. "Tsk, tsk. You ought to come by more often. The only people that stay here nowadays are either drunk or on the run. We need more strapping, kind young men like yourself to give this place a better reputation."

"If I could, I would come here every day I come into town. However, it's only on occasions like this that I get a chance to spend the night in the city," Zack explained.

Miss Adrais let out a small sigh. "All is what it must be." Then she handed the keys to Zack. "Here. Room sixteen, top floor. Just like always."

Zack thanked her, picked up his baskets, and led Travis up a set of stairs that sat in the left side of the room. He glanced back and saw that, although Miss Adrais was eyeing Travis cautiously, she still held a smile. Whether that smile was real or just a show, Zack could not tell.

Trying to make himself smaller by pulling his arms and shoulders in, Zack continued up the stairs. There was just barely enough room for Zack and his baskets to get up the small staircase. As he listened to the thud of Travis's footsteps behind him, Zack counted the number of floors in his head as they went up.

One...two...three... he continued. Finally, he counted eight. Moving a little to the side of the door, Zack made room for Travis to stand next to him while he opened it. After he sat the baskets down, Zack grabbed the key to their room and inserted it into the brass-colored doorknob. With a small 'click' the door unlocked. He put the key back into his pocket, pushed the door open a little, picked up the baskets, and walked in.

The room was just as he had remembered it. Miss Adrais made sure that only the most sensible people ever stayed in this room. This was not only because she hated the scoundrels that usually stopped by, but also because she thought highly of Emeka and thought that he deserved better.

With a sigh of relief, Zack breathed in the musty air of the room and set his baskets down next to the bed with the mattress. The room, although small, was warm and welcoming compared to the lobby. In the room were two beds: the one closest to the door had a mattress, while the one next to the window was simply a mat with a straw-stuffed pillow. In between the two beds was a small, wooden stand with an intricately-designed pattern on its four legs.

Zack walked over to where the stand stood. He reached high up on the wall and found what he was looking for. Carefully, he lit the oil lamp and the room was filled with light.

"Wow," Zack heard Travis breathe. "Not a five star but still charming."

Zack turned to Travis and smiled. "I've had this room about five times in the past two or three years. It is in need of repair, but under the rough looking surface lies a deep feeling of protection. Trust me, it is a great place to be."

Travis cautiously walked over to the bed with the mattress and carefully sat down. Using his weight, he bounced up and down a couple times while sitting, as if he was testing the bed's comfort. Looking from Zack, to the bed, and back to Zack again, Travis asked, "Is this, seriously, straw?"

Zack nodded. "Seriously, it's straw, the most comfortable type of mattress in all of Firmara."

Travis cocked an eyebrow. "In all of Firmara?"

"Well, at least what people like us have access to. Only those who can afford feather mattresses get them, but even then, the tips of the feathers poke you."

"At least feathers don't mold," Travis pointed out as he lifted up the corner of the mattress, exposing black specs of mold in the damp corners.

"If you don't want the mattress, I'll gladly take it," Zack said.

"Actually, yeah, I'll take the floor over the mold-covered mattress any day."

Understandingly, Zack nodded. "I guess I'll take the mattress. I'll take every comfort that I can get about now." With that, Zack dropped himself onto the straw mattress. "Ah... Just like the last time that I was here, only with more mold."

Zack heard Travis chuckle as he settled onto the mat by the window. "So, I assume that you come here often?" he asked Zack.

Zack sat up and looked at Travis. "Yeah, I do. Miss Adrais thinks pretty highly of me. I'm supposedly the only person who's ever been kind to her. You know, with her appearance and everything, she can be, oh, how do you say it..."

"Intimidating?" Travis finished Zack's sentence.

"Yes, that's it. Intimidating." Zack nodded at the word. "Now," Zack struggled to hold back a huge yawn, "if you don't mind, I'm going to dim the light in here so that I may..."

"Hit the hay?" Travis put in sarcastically.

Zack smirked at his friend. "Yeah, sure. But first of all, it's straw. There is a difference."

"It makes no difference to me."

"Yeah, but if you were a horse, then there would be a difference." Zack replied as he settled back down onto his bed.

Travis shrugged his shoulders and settled onto his bed. "Horses eat hay, sleep on straw, and produce thirty pounds of manure every day—'tis the life!"

Zack was the one who chuckled this time. Then he recited, "Kings sleep on heaps of gold, knights do their bidding. They work hard to win a maiden's heart, while the slaves do all the fighting."

"And what would thou mean in such a sacred riddle as this?" Travis said, mocking Zack's old lingo.

"By now I thought that you would have figured out that I will rarely tell you what I mean in my recitation."

"But it never hurts to hope that this was one of those rare times." Travis's voice held a chuckling ring to it.

Zack couldn't help but laugh as well. "And may you always find the smallest speck of hope in everything."

"Does that mean that you'll tell me what your riddle meant?"

Zack made up another riddle off the tip of his head. "Those

who hope and those who wish never get their answer until they think."

"I'll take that as a 'no'." Travis's tone was even.

"There, now you're finally starting to understand!" And both chortled at Zack's comment.

As Zack tried to wipe away the tears that had formed in the corners of his eyes, he heard Travis's voice become unusually serious. "Zack?"

"Yes, Travis, boy who never lets me get any sleep?" Zack replied, trying to keep the moment light as he dimmed the lamp in their room.

"I-I seem to have a way of getting on someone's nerves."

Zack sat reclined, intently listening to Travis's every word. "You mean like one day it'll be mine, and the next, Sarora's?"

"Yeah," Travis replied. There was a small lapse of silence before he asked, "Why is that?"

Why is it? Zack asked himself. Surely it had to be Travis's neverending questions or his habit of debating every decision Zack made that got on his nerves. But when he gave himself time to really examine his feelings, he thought he better understood what Travis was up against.

Zack scratched his head. "How can I put this... Sarora and I have been in training for years now. Almost half our lives have been dedicated to our studies under Master Racht and preparing ourselves for our inevitable fight against Trazon. And up until a few months ago, there were only the three of us—a master and his two students. The weight of the world was on our shoulders. And then you came along," Zack turned on his side so he could look directly at Travis, "and we grew hopeful that maybe we would actually stand a chance. And then Master Racht died. Sarora and I went from barely keeping our footing under the crushing weight of our destiny with our Master's help, to having to shoulder that burden on our own."

"But, you're not alone." Travis said. "You have me too."

"I know," Zack admitted. "Though sometimes, I do have to

remind myself of that fact. You are just as naturally gifted as Sarora and I, and you really have learned quickly despite how new you are to all of this. But we..."Zack sighed and corrected himself. "*I* don't feel like you've quite grasped the gravity of the situation, leaving Sarora and I to continue to bear that weight all on our own." Zack searched for Travis's gaze in the dim room. "Travis, if any one of us fails, Firmara will fall to Trazon. And there might never be another soul who is able to stop him."

Travis was silent and his gaze floated away from Zack's to the ceiling. Zack watched as Travis's eyes searched through the darkness.

When he spoke again a minute later, his voice barely escaped his lips. "It's really just the three of us?"

Zack was taken aback by his introspective response. He had expected Travis to start another debate with him. "Well, the wolves will fight with us. And maybe someday we could raise an army to join our cause. But when it comes to fighting Trazon, we are the only three who can stand in his way."

Travis lifted a hand towards the ceiling and examined it front and back, his fingers drumming against his palm contemplatively.

"I'm sorry." He finally said. "You're right. I've been content letting the two of you carry the burden. I'm just not sure..." His fingers froze and he clenched his hand into a fist. "I'm not sure how I can do better. I mean, how can I be of better help to you?"

"Well, for starters you can work on improving your skills and your knowledge," Zack said. "I know you've been doing your lessons, but you need to start living and breathing them. I think the more well versed you are in your abilities will give Sarora and I the headspace to start thinking about next steps."

Travis let his fist rest on his chest. "I've been meaning to ask," he began, turning to Zack, "how do our powers work? How long do they last? Is there like... a recharge period after you use them?"

"I mean, the first answer to all three of those questions is, it depends on the wielder. All wielders should always feel connected to their powers." Zack replied. "However, your ability to use them depends on your stamina—magic stamina, rather than physical, mostly. The longer you have magic and the more you use it, the stronger it will become and the longer you will be able to use it in battle. With continuous use you'll exhaust yourself of magic stamina first, and then the magic will begin to pull from your physical stamina. If you've used both, it may take a while to build your strength back up."

"How long would that take?"

Zack shrugged. "Again, it depends on the user and how great their staminas are. With more experience, your recovery time will only get better. For now, you'll have to train and find out where your limitations lie. Once you've run out of usable magic, your powers will simply cease working until you have gained enough magic energy to call upon them again. I swear Master Racht would've already covered this in your training. Why the sudden curiosity?"

Travis shook his head, "Just finally ready to learn, I suppose." Then he looked from Zack, to the oil lamp, and then to Zack again. "So, you want to turn that out so we can get some rest?"

Zack glared friendlily at Travis. "Sure, but once this is off, you're off too, got it?" Without waiting for a reply, Zack turned and doused the light from the oil lamp.

In With The Old And New

Lazily, Travis sat up and stretched his arms as high as he could. After he felt every inch of his arms wake once more, he opened his tired eyes. Trying to remember where he was, Travis looked around the room, eyelids still drooping. A warm light had just begun to filter through the window in the room of the inn.

Blinking into the sun's light, Travis let out one last yawn before standing. As he stretched his aching back, he gave himself a mental note to take the moldy mattress next time instead of the hard, wood floor. The cold floor had definitely done its job if its plan had been to make Travis's night uncomfortable and unpleasant.

Travis nearly jumped out of his skin when he heard the door to the room swing open. His muscles tensed, preparing to fight, but he began to relax when he saw that it was only Zack. The older boy, though unmistakably his friend, still bore the results of the silver potion—he still had yesterday's red hair and green eyes.

"Good morning, then, Instinct Ivan." Zack smiled at Travis's jump. "Did I wake you up?"

Travis shook his head. "No. I woke up a minute or so ago. I was just thinking about my poor decision on where to sleep."

"Ah, rough night, huh?"

Travis nodded. "What about you?"

"Slept like a rock," Zack said with a smile. "That is, if rocks could sleep."

"Where do all these strange expressions come from?" Travis mused.

Zack merely shrugged his shoulders and then gestured towards the door. "If you're ready, let's get the rest of our shopping done early so that Sarora doesn't have to come storming through the city and give the citizens heart attacks."

Travis smiled at the thought of Sarora, wings spread out wide, beak open in a desperate call for her friends. And as she flew high up and came down, all the people spent their time debating what they were being attacked by—bird, or lion.

"Hey, Sir Daydreams-Too-Much." Zack waved his hand in front of Travis's face. "Your response?"

"What?" Travis asked, still deep in thought. "Oh, yeah, let's get going."

"Hey, Zack?"

"Yes, Devon."

"Oh, um... Hey, Emeka?"

Zack's emerald eyes slid over to look at him. "What is it?"

"Where are our baskets?" Travis asked as the two of them walked out of the inn.

"While you spent the last two hours sleeping, I went outside of the city and hid them so that we wouldn't have to carry them this morning," Zack explained as he chose a path to walk. For such a large city, there were very few people awake and moving about at this time. Of course, Travis couldn't blame them. He still didn't see the need to get up at the crack of dawn every morning.

"Oh, thanks then," Travis finally replied. The older boy just nodded in response as he continued to lead them down the street.

Trying to entertain himself during the walk, Travis looked

around for various shops that may hold the last item that Zack needed. His friend hadn't told Travis much about the ingredient other than it was fully necessary and that it looked like crushed sulfur. Although, the last description didn't help much because Travis didn't really have any clue what sulfur was.

The sun's rays finally began to peek over the rest of the buildings. The warm golden streaks seemed to welcome Travis to the new morning in the large city. Travis squinted to try to keep the bright light out of his eyes. However, the brightness of the light got the best of him when he finally let out a loud sneeze.

Travis saw Zack nearly leap out of his skin. His sneeze must have scared the older boy half to death in the quiet, early morning. Travis couldn't help but smile when Zack turned his head around to look at him, his eyes ice.

"Sorry, did I scare ya?" Travis teased. Zack had never been jumpy before, and it tickled Travis pink that he had spooked Zack without even trying.

"You surprised me," Zack replied. "There is a difference between surprised and scared."

"True, but I believe that you were both." Travis had to stifle a loud laugh when Zack turned away without replying. *Man, I've never gotten his goat like this before!*

After a few more minutes in which Travis felt that they had just been wandering aimlessly, Zack turned into an alley filled with wooden boxes. Reaching into his pouch of coins, Zack pulled out a few trillers. "Here," Zack said as he put them into Travis's hand. "We won't split up for a while, but I thought that I would give the money to you now before someone spots me handing it out. Lots of these people aren't very wealthy, and some would take any chance that they could get to grab a few extra cents, even if it were to mean stealing from another person."

"Stealing? Now, you've never done that before, have you, Goody Two-Shoes?"

Travis's heart skipped a beat. He knew that voice, and it belonged to someone he had hoped to face again. Travis turned and looked up the large wall that sat between the alley and the building. Sitting casually with one knee bent and the other leg dangling off the edge of the wall, was a boy probably a year older than Zack. His clothes were black, and Travis thought that maybe they were made of leather.

"Stephen," Zack said with a nod of acknowledgement.

"Oh, so you do remember me, Zack?" Stephen replied as he leaned on one hand, which was pressed firmly onto the top of the wall underneath him. Stephen's dirty-blonde hair spiked up as it came toward the front-center of his head. Travis had a hard time believing that Stephen was from Firmara and not from some punk-style street in a big city from his world.

"It's Emeka, thank you very much." Zack's voice was angered, but controlled.

"Oh, right..." Stephen smirked at the boys that stood below him. "Emeka," he repeated before looking over to Travis. "Now wait a second, I don't remember you, but your voice is familiar..."

"I'm Devon," Travis replied, completely okay with the idea of Stephen not knowing who he really was.

Stephen chuckled. "No, that's not it—you can't fool me. Wait..." Stephen jumped down from where he sat on the wall and landed right next to Travis. Squinting, Stephen studied Travis carefully. His eyes said friend but his smile said fox. "You wouldn't happen to be Sarora's little friend from back in the woods, now would ya?"

Travis couldn't help but show a surprised expression on his face. How had Stephen found out? Of course, his voice was the same, but Travis looked entirely different from his normal appearance.

"Oh, yes, I'm just that good," Stephen bragged, smiling cunningly at Travis's surprise.

"Yes, just that good," Zack butted in. "What do you want from us, Stephen? We don't have time to gossip or money to be gambling."

Stephen shook his head. "Come now, me, want something

from you? You've got to be joking. I'm what you call a 'self-supplier'. I look out for me and only me. And when the going gets rough, well, let's always say I find a way to get through it all..."

"You mean that you steal. That's not really 'self-supplying,' for your information." Zack glared at Stephen, though he somehow kept his composure.

"Hey, say what you say—'self-supply,' borrow, steal, take... it all means the same to me."

Travis saw that Zack was having a difficult time trying not to roll his eyes. "Stephen, why did you stop us? What is your business with us? Or do you just wish to distract us while someone from your gang pickpockets me?"

Stephen faked a hurt expression on his face. "What? You think that I would do that to you? Is it too much to ask to stay in the info circle? Am I not allowed to know what goes on in the lives of those I know?"

"No." Zack replied shortly.

"Well then," Stephen began, returning to his old, conniving composure. "Just leave me out of the friendship circle. But maybe you'd want to share your info with the newest member of my gang?" Stephen then turned and called into the shadows that sat at the other end of the alley. "Ben, come here!"

Travis watched as slowly, a small shape crept out of the shadows. A young boy, probably eight or nine, walked silently over to Stephen, his eyes not leaving the ground to look at any of the older boys. Ben had light-brown hair and his eyes, though they stared at the ground, were a warm brown. He wore a shirt made of sackcloth, brown trousers, and his feet were covered by worn-out leather sandals.

Stephen looked from Ben back to Travis and Zack. "This is my newest comrade, Ben. Ben, why don't you say hello?" Ben just continued to stare at the ground.

"Stephen," Zack finally broke the silence, "why is Ben in your 'gang'? He should be living with his parents in a nice home, not running around causing mayhem with you and your band of trouble brewers."

Stephen glared at Zack. "Do you think that I am unable to watch out for Ben? I am sixteen you know, not a child like yourself. Ben came to me when he was caught stealing from Olegraro's castle. Luckily, I was in the area and saved him just in time. He had nowhere to go, so I took him in."

Zack glared at Stephen through narrowed eyes, his brows furrowed. He didn't utter a word—there was no need to. As little as Travis knew about Stephen, he was positive that the city boy wasn't about to listen to Zack.

Stephen broke the silence as he looked at the sun in the sky. "Wow, look at the time." Looking back to Travis and Zack, he nodded to each of them and said, "Now, if you two don't mind, I've got some 'shopping' to do." Stephen turned around, jumped, grabbed a hold of the top of the wall, and hauled himself back up. Ben, seeing that he couldn't make the jump, turned back down the alley and scurried back to his hiding spot.

"Ugh..." Zack sighed as he looked at Travis. "I will never understand him. Has he no conscience?"

"Conscience, yes, he has one, but what beliefs guide that conscience?"

Zack gave Travis a you-never-cease-to-amaze-me head shake with a grin. "Why is it that wisdom pours from your mouth but never appears to be contained in your brain?"

Travis shrugged his shoulders. "If I could answer for my reckless ways, nearly all of our problems would be solved."

"My feet are killing me." Travis complained to Zack as they both sat down for a quick lunch. They had been searching all morning, and still, they had not yet found what they needed. Travis's muscles ached from fighting gravity for too long. At least Zack had agreed to sit for lunch, but Travis knew that if he had had the option, his friend would have eaten on the road.

"No offense, but your feet won't be the only things that kill you if you don't shut up," Zack replied, his voice barely more than a mumble.

"Getting tired of hearing my commentary?"

"I wouldn't be tired of hearing you if you would listen to common sense instead of asking the same questions the whole day." Zack sat beside him and handed Travis a piece of bread that he had purchased from a nearby bakery.

Travis nodded his thanks and grabbed the bread from Zack. "Well, I don't know if this will make you feel any better, but it's only been half a day so 'whole day' isn't really the right context."

Zack playfully punched Travis's shoulder.

"Ouch!" Travis scooted away from Zack to avoid any more blows. "What was that for?"

"Anger management." Zack winked at Travis and he began to fill his face with bread.

"If that really worked, I don't know how much of me would be left." Travis took a bite of bread and continued, "Thistle would have killed me by now by using me as her personal punching bag." Thistle was the nickname that they had chosen for Sarora while in the city. Travis came up with the pet name all by himself, thinking of how sometimes Sarora could be so prickly.

Zack laughed. "That would be her, alright." Zack's expression then became a little serious. "But just remember, everyone does what they do for a reason, whether good or bad."

Though a little confused by the sudden change of the conversation's mood, Travis nodded. Even though his legs still ached, he wanted to get moving so that they could return home to Sarora. So, after stuffing the rest of his bread into his mouth, Travis stood up, wiped the dirt off of his pants, and held out a hand for Zack to take.

"Come on, Emeka. We should be going."

Zack nodded, stuffing the rest of his bread into his mouth before taking Travis's hand. With effort, Travis leaned back and hauled Zack to his feet, surprised not only by how heavy Zack was, but also by the fact that he could pull Zack up.

Wiping his brow, Travis looked around at the city area. In contrast to the place they had arrived, this area of the city was a little more rural—the buildings weren't as tall or large, and instead of being wall-to-wall, many houses were surrounded by picketed fences. Some people even had clotheslines hanging between the corners of their houses, and one house that Travis had spotted had chickens in its front yard. Travis had never seen such a diverse city.

"Devon," Zack began, awakening Travis from his thoughts, "I think that it's time we split up for a while. We need to find this last ingredient." Turning, Zack pointed to the central part of the city. "I'm going to look over in that general area, but I won't go more than a tenth of a mile away from you."

"Where should I look then?" Travis asked, excited for some time alone to explore.

"Walk along the line of homes here," Zack instructed Travis. "Sometimes families will own shops in or by their homes."

Travis nodded. "That sounds fine. What time shall we meet back up?"

Zack sighed as he put his hand over his mouth and looked up to the sky. The sun was at about midpoint, just before noon. If they wanted to be home before dark, they would have to leave in the next couple of hours.

"...How about I'll come find you when I've either given up or when I've found what I'm looking for," Zack finally suggested.

"But what if I find the item?" Travis asked.

"Just... stay put and stay out of trouble. Remember, it's minty-green in color, and it usually comes in a ground up powder."

"Green powder, got it."

Zack shook his head. "Come on, we'd both better get going."

"Alright then, see you later." Travis turned and began to walk down the line of homes. As he walked along the path, Travis looked back and forth from the dirt road to the line of houses. With his hands in his pockets, Travis dragged his feet along the ground. A few yards down, a group of young girls were running under a clothesline, giant grins on their faces as they chased each other in circles. Stopping for a moment, Travis watched them play their version of tag. Chickens squawked and fluttered nervously as the girls darted in between them. As the feathers flew, the girls laughed, not seeming to run out of energy.

Spotting Travis, one girl, a blue-eyed seven-year-old, stopped and stared at Travis. He smiled and waved to her, hoping to make a friendly gesture. Seeing the friendliness in Travis's eyes, the young girl smiled back and waved her small hand at him before turning to play with her friends once more. Travis chuckled and continued on his way, trying to bring his mind back to the item search.

On his way Travis tried to be friendly to each person he passed. Sometimes, when he would smile and nod at another person, they would return the gesture and continue on their way. However, most of the time, people either didn't look at Travis or gave him a dark glare that said something like, "I don't know you, leave me alone."

Finally spotting a shop, Travis veered to his right and walked inside the little place. The shop reminded him of the store that belonged to Elizabeth's family, only this one had a few more cobwebs hanging from the ceiling. At the counter sat a plump woman, her dress straining to stay together. Trying not to be rude, Travis chose not to stare at the woman's poor choice of clothing size and instead looked to her bright cheery face.

"Hello there, young lad," the lady spoke in a kind and welcoming tone, her voice ringing with an Irish-like accent. "What can I help you with today?"

Trying to remember the whole description, Travis spoke, "Well, I am looking for this minty-colored powder. You wouldn't happen to have any of it, would you?"

The woman shook her head. "No, sorry lad. I don't reckon

I've heard of anything like it. You wouldn't happen to know what it's called, would ya now?"

Travis shook his head.

"Well," the woman sighed, "I'm afraid that I can't help you find what you're looking for." The woman looked at Travis with an apologetic expression.

Travis thanked her anyway and turned to leave, but stopped and turned back when the woman called to him.

"Young lad! I just remembered, there is a shop—about seventy yards up the street. There is this man who sells lots of strange things. No one ever goes to his shop because they all say he's a wee bit eccentric. I don't know much about him but it wouldn't hurt to go and see if he has what you're lookin' for."

Travis thanked her again and walked out of the store. With new hope, he strode down the street to the other shop. He wasn't sure what the shop looked like, but he headed in its general direction, just hoping that he would be able to tell which one it was.

And for once, Travis was right. The man's shop stood out like a sore thumb. In contrast to the other buildings, which were made of a tan colored substance, the man's shop was a dull gray color. While some of the other shops had no doors, this doorway was covered by a purple curtain that waved even when the gentlest breeze passed by.

Nervously, Travis stepped forward and pulled the curtain aside. He took a quick peek inside, and to his surprise, he found that the inside of the store was a little more decorative than he had bargained for. The inside of the store had dark gray, almost black walls. Like many other places Travis had seen, candles lit the room with their flickering glow. Though the lights brightened the room a little, the store still had a sinister look. Cobwebs dangled from the ceiling, tall bookcases cast dark, tall shadows across the floors, a few large dark spiders scuttled across the ceiling, and many strange superstitious items sat on shelves attached to the walls.

Travis walked over to the closest shelf with a feeling of unease. He looked in wonder at the strange items that were lined up in no apparent order—an animal skull, a dark purple potion in a vial, some bubbling goop in a test tube, and a jar labeled 'worms'. Long, thin, white worms were stuffed inside the jars, looking like they might soon burst out of their encasement.

A twinkle of light caught Travis's eye and he turned and walked farther down the shelf. He was looking at what appeared to be a gem with a rich, dark purple color. As Travis drew nearer, the gem seemed to beckon him closer. He wasn't sure why, but Travis thought that, for some strange reason, the object was calling to him, almost like when the Crystal of Courage had called him.

The nearer that Travis came to the gem, the more he felt the urge to reach out and grab the object. Timidly, he stretched out his arm and placed his hand on the strange crystal. With a blast of energy, a vision passed through Travis's mind; something that he had not seen in a long while.

Travis ran through the dark woods as fast as he could, although he knew that the creature he chased was very dangerous. Ahead of him ran a shadowy figure. It had a long flowing tail and mane and its hooves beat the ground heavily. Its coat was darker than the night itself.

Travis continued to keep up with the form until it turned on him. He tried to move out of the way and grab his staff, but his feet and arms seemed to be held in place. In a split second, the animal reared, and its hooves beat at Travis's head. Travis felt a short sting of pain before everything went pitch black.

With a gasp, his eyes snapped open. As his pupils adjusted back to the dimness of the room, he tried to slow down his frantic heart. For months, he had escaped having that dream. For months he had pushed that dream back into oblivion and crushed the memory of it until it was only a little speck of his past. After trying to fight the frightening scene that had haunted him since he had received his crystal, Travis had always discovered the clarity of the image increasing each time.

Travis pulled back his arm from the purple-crystal. Eyes wide with fright, Travis backed up a few steps and spun around to leave.

Travis's heart just about stopped when he turned to find a figure blocking his escape. Frozen with fear, Travis didn't know what was going to happen, but he had a foreboding feeling that it wasn't a good ending to a short story.

DIVINATION

"Oh, I'm sorry," the man finally spoke. His voice reminded Travis of a curious little weasel. "Did I startle you? I surely didn't want that now, did I?" The old-looking man smiled at Travis, who was still rooted in place.

Travis tried to gather his bearings as he studied the man. He had thin, white messy hair that seemed to poke out from every spot of his head. His worn eyes shone with loneliness and untamed excitement. Compared to his store and facial expression, the man's clothing looked as if it had come from the nineteen hundreds. Instead of bright colors or a wild pattern which Travis expected to see, the man wore a black tux-like tunic with a white undershirt. Around his neck was a thin, leather necklace.

With a wild grin, the man grabbed Travis's arm. "Come with me, dear boy. I rarely ever have visitors, and I welcome all that come with open arms."

To his own surprise, Travis allowed himself to be led to a small, round table that sat in the middle of the large room. Motioning for Travis to sit, the man let go of Travis's hand and sat in the seat opposite of him.

"Now, dear boy, I wish to give you a little gift, something to just say thanks for being someone who would take the time out of their day to visit me," the man said as Travis sat down, afraid of what was going to happen.

Corners of his mouth tweaking, the man introduced himself, "I, my lad, am the Great Loki, seer of the past, present, and future. In thanks for visiting, I will now read your life story."

Travis felt his palms grow sweaty. This is not what he had in mind for a little gift. A small line repeated through the back of his mind, one he had read in a book long ago... *Do not turn to mediums or necromancers; do not seek them out...*

"Uh, thank you, um, Loki, but, not to be rude, but, I uh... I would prefer not getting any of my stories read," Travis stammered.

"Oh, pish-posh, my lad." Loki waved his hand as if to sweep away any doubt that Travis had. "Seeing is not a burden like many say. It is not a curse filled with dangers. No, none at all. Seeing everything in your life in front of you can help you become stronger. And just by the looks of you, I can tell that you want to become stronger, don't you, lad?"

Travis nodded, but just a little. "Well, yes, I do want to get stronger—"

"Then let me begin reading your life story," Loki cut in.

"But I wish to become stronger on my own." Travis placed one hand on the round table.

A hurt look crossed Loki's face. "Well, alright then, if you must be strong on your own, then so be it."

Travis nodded to Loki. "Thanks for understanding. Now, you wouldn't happen to have any of this green powder looking stuff, would you?" Travis asked the man.

Loki nodded. "Depends on which green powder stuff you mean." He stood and walked over to his counter. In contrast to many other stores, it looked like Loki's counter was part of his store wall.

"Let me see here..." Travis watched as Loki bent down and looked through several small drawers under the counter.

"Grasshopper cinders, grass clips, mint leaves..." Loki rattled off the names of many strange ingredients. "Can you tell me what you'll be making? Maybe that'll help me find the right thing."

"Uh..." Travis searched for the right words. "It's a silver liquid is all that I can remember," Travis lied.

"Then you'll be needing this." Loki stood back up with a small pouch. "This is firefly powder—very rare, as you may know." Loki then handed the powder to Travis. "Will that be all?"

Travis nodded. "Yes, thanks. What do I owe you?"

"Nothing." Loki smiled. "Take that as a gift for coming in."

"But you just told me that this is rare," Travis objected. "I couldn't possibly take this without paying."

"Nonsense, lad." The man waved his hand as if he were excusing the thought. "It's a gift. All gifts are free." His grin looked a little too goofy for Travis's comfort.

Seeing that he wasn't about to win the argument, Travis nodded his thanks. "Well, I better get going then. It was nice meeting you, Loki."

Loki smiled back. "It was nice meeting you too, lad."

Travis nodded and smiled once more before turning to leave. Just as he reached out to pull the curtain to the side so that he may exit, Loki's words stopped him in his tracks.

"The past is unchangeable, and though the present may change future occurrences, it will not change one's destiny."

Travis froze, his hand held in midair. The words that Loki spoke didn't repel Travis, but instead they enticed him to turn around. Looking back out of the corner of his eye, Travis saw the wild-looking man standing by his table, his eyes glowing a ghostly gray.

Travis's tongue felt dry, but still he asked, "What do you mean?"

"Your past, it has been a rough road. You've lost relatives, and friends, and yet you still aim at your goal full force."

Travis completely turned around and narrowed his eyes. "So?"

"Your future has many rough roads ahead, but you may

change your paths and correct them earlier on if you hear what I have to say." Loki's eyes still seemed clouded, as if he had electrically-powered cataracts. "Will you accept the chance to listen to some untold pages of your story?"

Although his conscience—the one that had usually gotten him into trouble—was ordering him to get away, Travis was still transfixed. What could possibly be so bad about knowing something that may help him in the long run?

With his fist clenched and his face straight, Travis finally nodded and stepped towards Loki.

The Great Loki smiled, his yellow teeth sticking out like a sore thumb. "As it is your wish, listen to what your story says...

> *Setting sun and waxing moon,*
> *Knights hiding beneath their armor,*
> *All must fight for their faith,*
> *But must not use the easy road.*
>
> *When your days grow dark,*
> *And your enemies become your allies,*
> *You will learn that betrayal is unavoidable,*
> *When chilling ice cools hearts around you.*
>
> *So be forewarned about things to come,*
> *Darkening skies are not the way to go,*
> *But when the ultimate sacrifice is made,*
> *All promises must be obeyed."*

Travis listened to every word that Loki spoke, desperately trying to drink in the reading's every meaning. *Setting sun? Days grow dark? Ultimate sacrifice?* Travis's mind told him that this prophecy was more than he was looking for. Instead of being filled with words of hope and light, the words that Loki spoke told of dark times. As difficult as times were then, Travis was afraid to know how the days ahead were going to darken.

"Is there something troubling you?" Travis looked at Loki, who had cocked his head like a confused puppy when he spoke. To Travis's surprise, Loki's eyes were no longer clouded, and his wild looking face no longer scared Travis as it had before.

"Uh..." Travis had no idea how to reply, so he merely shook his head. "No, I'm fine. I better get going now, my friend is waiting for me. Thanks again for the, err, life story." Travis turned to leave the room and free himself of the sickening feelings in his stomach.

Loki's voice came one last time across the room, his tongue seeming to do friendly skips as he spoke. "You are most welcome, Travis. Yes, you'd best be going. You wouldn't want to keep Zack waiting!"

Travis's eyes widened in shock, but he forced his feet to keep moving. How had Loki known his name? In fact, how had he even known about Zack? His brain for once was agreeing with his conscience; it was time to scram.

As soon as Travis walked out of the doorway, he ran for it, his heart pumping vigorously. The people that walked around him were a blur, barely visible to Travis. His arms swung back and forth as he continued to run down the street. He didn't know exactly where he was headed, and he didn't care. He just wanted to get away from Loki.

Barely noticing the corner, Travis began to turn to his left...
Bam!

Travis fell in a crumpled heap. Feeling the bruise forming on his head, he lifted his hand to cover the sore spot as if that was going to make it feel better. Opening his eyes, Travis looked for what, or whom, he had collided with. A sickening feeling formed in the pits of Travis's stomach—all around him piles of clothing were scattered. Looking across from him, Travis spotted a middle-aged woman, who, like Travis, had reached for her forehead. She wore a rundown work dress, and her brunette hair was streaked with gray, but her face didn't show many wrinkles.

Travis, feeling guilty about the whole situation, quickly got to his feet and held out his hand to her. "Sorry, Ma'am. I'm so sorry." Travis pulled the woman to her feet as he tried to explain himself. "I didn't mean to—I was running so fast that I just, well, I wasn't watching where I was going."

The woman cut him off with a smile and dusted the dirt off her dress. "Don't worry about it, young man. I'm sure you didn't mean any harm." She waved her hand, excusing his blunder. Quietly, the woman picked up her basket, which lay overturned on the dusty path. While still bent over, she began to pick up some of the garments on the ground.

"Here, let me help you," Travis said as he bent over, took the basket from the woman, and began to fill it with the clothes.

Once he had finished picking everything up, he stood back to his full height, his back aching from the strain. "Here you go," he told the woman as he handed the basket back to her.

"Why, thank you, young man. You are very genuine, you know that?" she complimented him with a warm voice.

Suddenly, another voice boomed from somewhere nearby, "Chloe? Are you okay?"

Travis looked over the woman's shoulder to see a man striding toward them. Compared to his deep voice, the man was actually not very large. He was no taller than the woman, and he was stocky. Like Chloe's hair, his was brown, but he was balding.

"Chloe?" the man spoke again. "Is this young man bothering you? 'Cause if he is..."

Chloe shook her head. "Oh, no, Reginald, not at all. We just bumped into each other and he was helping pick up the clothes that I had dropped."

Gees, what an understatement, Travis couldn't help but think.

Reginald nodded his head once. "Okay. I was just worried 'bout ya, you know, with all of these troublemakers lurking around recently."

Chloe blushed, her fair skin showing pink. "Oh no, I'm fine. But I appreciate that you were looking out for me."

"Well, why shouldn't I?" the man asked. "You're my wife.

What kind of husband would I be if I didn't look out for you?" Chloe just smiled warmly back at him.

Reginald turned back to Travis. "So, who are you, young man? I've not seen many fellows like you walking around with your dark brown hair."

Travis's heart dropped to his feet. *Brown hair? Oh no! The potion! It wore off!*

Suddenly, a hand grabbed Travis's arm and he turned to see a young man hiding under a cloak. *No, not any young man—Zack!*

"Excuse me," Zack spoke, his voice deepened as he tried to disguise it. "My cousin and I have to get going, *now*."

"Oh, well that's too bad," Chloe said, a disappointed expression on her face. "Are you sure that you couldn't stay for a small meal?"

Travis shook his head. "No, sorry. I have to get going. Good day." He nodded to them as Zack forcefully yanked on his arm. With the force that Zack used, Travis was surprised that he didn't topple over.

Once they had rounded the corner, Zack pulled another cloak out from under his own. "Here, put it on. We have to go."

Travis quickly slipped the hood of the cloak over his head and he continued his sprint after Zack. Although he tried to focus on the current events, his mind kept swarming back to when Loki had spoken his name. Had his appearance changed back then? *No.* Travis shook his head. It couldn't have, or else he would have noticed. The only possible time that he could think of was when he had run away from Loki. Maybe he had just been too distracted to notice his change.

As Zack and Travis continued to run to the gate, Travis had a really bad feeling about the speech Zack was going to give him when they were out of the city. And he guessed that it was going to involve not speaking to strangers.

No Right Moves

Drenched in sweat and gasping for breath, Zack slowed down just outside of the city. As he and Travis had run through the town in a mad dash to hide their identities, he had been able to pick up the baskets that he had hidden that morning. No longer afraid of hiding his face, Zack ripped back the hood of his cloak and let the gentle wind cool his overheated face. Next to him, Travis slipped off his hood as well. Out of the corner of his eye Zack watched Travis as he slowed his pace and looked up into the sky. Knowing how tired that he himself was from the quick run, he figured that Travis must be exhausted.

"Okay," Travis was the first to speak through his heaving. "We're away from the city and it looks like nobody recognized us as we ran away. So, are we gonna cool ourselves off and walk the rest of the way home, or are we just taking a break before you make us sprint?" He turned his head to look at Zack, who forced a smile.

"What difference would it make?" Zack asked Travis. "If we used either of your brilliant ideas, we'd be exhausted and/or late."

Zack saw Travis look at him with curiosity. "Do you have other means of transportation then?"

Zack smiled. "Look who's catching on." After setting down the many baskets, Zack took in a deep breath that filled his lungs and let out a long, bird-like whistle.

Looking over to Travis, Zack saw the other boy's large grin appear, then disappear. "Wait, if you're calling Mesha and Shadra, won't it take them a while to get here?"

"It would," Zack began, "if I had not called them before now." Zack pointed out toward the horizon. He noted Travis following his hand and both boys saw two horses running at them full-force. One was Mesha, but the other, instead of Shadra, was Seraphi. Zack still hadn't mentioned Shadra's pregnancy to Travis, and he told himself that he might want to explain in the next couple minutes.

With a quick stop, the two horses stood before the boys, their nostrils flaring in a great effort to fill their blood with oxygen. Quickly, Zack tied the baskets to Mesha, who protested a little as he did a small dance in place. Forcing his muscles to pull, Zack heaved himself onto Mesha's back, careful to not bang his legs against the more delicate packages that were attached to the saddle.

Seeing that Travis was weary about getting onto Seraphi's back, Zack spoke words of encouragement. "Don't worry. Ole' Seraphi's never hurt anyone before."

"It's not that," Travis objected as he pulled himself onto the white horse's back. "It's just that I was expecting Shadra."

"Well, Travis," Zack smiled at his friend, "Shadra can't be your steed for a while."

"Why's that?"

"Shadra is going to have a foal," Zack said simply.

"A foal!?" Travis exclaimed. "When? Soon? Why didn't you tell me before?"

"I just found out myself a couple days ago. You won't be able to ride her until after she's had her foal. Acer horses have very precarious pregnancies—Shadra's last foal didn't make it, so we don't want to take any risks with her this time."

"Do you think she'll be okay?" Travis sounded a little unhappy at first.

Zack chose his words carefully. "There's nothing we can do besides ensure that she's safe and stays hidden. But I'm sure she'll be fine. Now come on, let's go so that I can tell you exactly what you did wrong today when we split up." Zack smiled as he nudged Mesha gently with his legs, and the gelding took off again.

Zack looked behind him and watched as Travis urged Seraphi on. The stallion was old, but far from worn out. With his easy strides, Seraphi caught Travis up with Zack and Mesha. Zack wondered how awesome the sight of the two horses looked—running side-by-side simultaneously, their hooves beating the ground together.

Beside Zack, Travis let out delighted laughter. The younger boy spread his arms out wide as if to catch the air as it zoomed past them. Travis held his position until Seraphi jumped a log that blocked the middle of the path.

"Whoa!" Travis exclaimed as he tried to regain his balance. Zack watched as Travis's hands grasped for the horn of the saddle and he hung on for all he was worth.

Now Zack laughed—seeing Travis, his eyes wide in shock and his nervous breaths were too much of a sight not to laugh at. Zack turned his head to get the full view of Travis's embarrassed scowl. The look in Travis's eyes that were meant to fill Zack with fright only made him crack up. He laughed so hard that a couple of tears escaped and he let go of the horn of the saddle to wipe them away. Zack was too busy laughing to notice the obstacle in Mesha's path. Suddenly, Zack felt the force of a tree branch smack against the side of his head. The impact was so great that it nearly ripped him off Mesha's back.

"Ow!" Zack cried out and reached for the side of his head. It continued to throb with pain as Travis, seeing his friend, burst out into a fit of laughter. Zack playfully swung his arm at Travis. The friendly attack missed by only a couple inches when Travis leaned to his right to avoid the blow. The boys continued to laugh as their mini fights raged between them while they rode on. One second Zack would appear to have the upper hand when he was able to reach out and grab Travis, and then the next second Travis would surprise Zack with a different way of evading him. Once, Travis had Seraphi move a couple inches to his right, and then, as if he had done so many times before, Travis stood on top of Seraphi's back, almost perfectly balanced. Though as talented at standing on a moving horse's back as Travis seemed, he lasted only short while before he smacked his rear-end back onto the saddle after losing a fight with gravity.

After a long while play fighting, Zack slowed Mesha to a walk. Seeing that Zack and Mesha had slowed down, Seraphi immediately followed suit.

"Now," Zack began as he started to regain his breath, "we have some un-fun business to go over." Zack watched Travis's smile fade. "Oh, yes, we must speak about this 'stranger danger' business."

Zack could barely hear Travis's quiet groan, and that told Zack that he had expected this talk. Just as much as Travis didn't want to hear it, Zack did not want to preach it. No matter what the others might think, he really didn't like bringing down the hammer. However, he knew that it had to be done.

"Travis, do you remember some of the things that we spoke of before we entered the city and while inside?" Zack asked Travis.

"Uh, yeah. My name is Devon, yours is Emeka," Travis replied, his eyes no longer looking at Zack.

"Yes, but no." Zack could understand why Travis wanted to avoid the subject. "We talked about how we needed to blend in and keep quiet. You can't go speaking to random people."

"Well, uh, yeah I knew that." The corner of Travis's mouth twitched. "It wasn't that I brought up a conversation, but rather that in the process of running away from a potential threat, I ran the lady—Chloe—over."

"You ran her over?" Zack looked at Travis, his eyes wide.

"Well, heh, funny story really..." Travis was trying to lighten up the moment by not cutting to the chase. "You see, I was running down the street after finding the ingredient that you wanted, and well, I turned without looking and well, you know, pretty much plowed her over."

Zack groaned and closed his eyes. "Must I ask why, one, you were heading the wrong way; two, why you were running; and three, why you weren't watching the wrong path that you were running on?"

"Well, heh, another funny story, you see..."

"Travis, stop beating around the bush. Who or what were you running from?"

"Loki."

Zack had no idea what Travis was speaking of. "What is a loki?"

Travis shook his head. "Not a, the Loki."

"Sorry." Zack pretended to clean out his ear with his finger. "'Loki who' was my real question. Who is Loki and why were you running from him?"

Travis told Zack about how he had been given directions to go to Loki's odd shop and how the man had offered to read his future.

"And you said 'yes', didn't you?" Zack asked, bewildered.

"Well, not at first. Let me finish," Travis replied before continuing his story, describing everything that he saw, heard, and felt.

When Travis finished, Zack could only shake his head. "Great! Not only do we need to stay away from that side of town entirely, but I must change my name and appearance."

"Do you think that Loki possibly knew who I was because I changed back and didn't notice it?" Travis asked him.

Zack shook his head. "From the sound of your story, I think that he really could read your life story, and that by giving him your permission to read a bit to you, he looked the whole novel up and down as well."

"Oh, I would have never thought of that," Travis spoke sarcastically. "Listen, Zack, I know what's at stake—"

"Then why did you let him continue?" Zack asked him, his gaze as hard as diamond. "I know it's tempting to listen to words about the future—every person in this world wants to know what will happen—but didn't you think that, by asking him, you allowed him to shape your future. Not only that, but whomever else was involved in that prophecy no longer can escape that path. Did you think of that?"

Travis kept a constant, calm gaze focused on Zack. "I did not think of that, but I do know that it was risky to listen to him. Put yourself in my shoes, Zack, and tell me what you would have done instead. Would you have turned your back on a poor old man? Should I have left the shop the second I entered? Should I have slapped Loki over the mouth when, potentially, he had no idea of what he was saying or doing? Tell me, Zack, what should I have done?"

Zack looked away from Travis. What would he have done? *Well, I would have left.* He told himself quietly. *Well, no that wouldn't have worked out. Then I would have asked Loki to please keep his readings to himself. No, from what Travis says, Loki was persistent and wouldn't have listened anyways.*

Stumped, Zack looked back to his friend. "I cannot say that what I would have done would be right either, but I know that there must be a correct solution somewhere in this world."

Leaning over from his saddle, Travis placed one hand on Zack's shoulder. "Zack, maybe there aren't any right solutions. What if there are only solutions?" When Zack didn't respond, Travis leaned back into his seat and looked away from his friend. Out of the corner of Zack's eye, he followed Travis's gaze—the boy was looking out at the horizon, his eyes scrunched tightly together. Ahead of them, the grassy plains seemed to stretch on forever, but Zack knew that it would only be a few hours before they were both back home with Sarora.

With a sigh, Zack stared out at the long way ahead of them.

"Maybe you're right, Travis. Maybe there is no correct solution. Just, in the future, make sure you observe all of your possible answers before making a decision."

From the corner of his eye, Zack saw Travis nod. "Don't worry, I will." And the two continued on their long trek home.

SCARS

Heart racing, Sarora awoke. All of her feathers were ruffled and her tail twitched nervously. Gasping for air, she tried to collect herself. When she tried to stand, she felt her legs shake beneath her. Slowly, she unfurled her wings and carefully studied each of them. It had only been a dream, so why had it scared her so much? Shaking her head, Sarora walked out from underneath the shade of a large oak tree. She had been watching for Zack and Travis for hours before she had fallen asleep. Thankfully she had not been attacked while she was out, but she told herself that she could not fall asleep outside of the tent again.

As the gentle breeze blew she felt her fur and feathers begin to lay flat. Her heart steadied back to its usual pace and Sarora walked on. The sun had just risen in the sky and she was really beginning to worry about her friends. She knew Zack had told her that they might have to spend the night in the city, but she had almost convinced herself that they would have been home last night. *Why must my reasoning skills torture me so?*

Picking a fruit from a nearby tree, she held it in one talon while she used her beak to slice it in half. After swallowing both halves, Sarora looked back to the sky. It was still early, so it could still be a few more hours before Travis and Zack would return. Sighing, she wondered why she had allowed both of them to go. Sure, it was nice to have some quiet time alone, but it felt very strange not to at least have Travis asking questions with painfully obvious answers.

"Boys," Sarora grumbled to herself as she walked the outskirts of the trees. "Can't live with them, can't live without them."

Stretching her wings once more, Sarora strolled with them fully extended as she worked her way to the river. Only the birds could commiserate with her—the feeling of the heat that would build up between her wings and her body. Especially on warm days like this, she wished she could dive into the deep waters and cool her body. But she knew if she were to swim, she risked ruining her feathers. Sure, she preened them every once in a while, but it still wasn't fun keeping them clean with the inside of her beak. She wasn't a duck or a swan. She hardly felt like an animal.

Reaching the small river, Sarora followed it into the woods until she came to the small pool. She smiled as she remembered walking upon Travis while he had been bathing. What good was it to have the ears of a hawk when she could never seem to use it?

Folding her wings back at her sides, Sarora approached the cool water's edge and drank. After quenching her thirst, Sarora glared at her reflection in the shallow waters. First, she looked into her golden eyes—why did her pupils always seem so large? Then she looked at her beak, telling herself that she needed to trim it down some before it would begin to grow too long.

Looking back at her eyes, Sarora gazed at the long pink scar that ran from the top of her eye, across its lid, and then down to the center of her cheek. Disgusted at the awful mark, she struck her reflection with her talons, making water fly everywhere. Turning away from the pool with a huff, Sarora tried to tell herself that at least she was lucky not to have lost the eye. But no matter what she said to try to make herself feel better, she knew that the scar would remain there for her lifetime—a constant reminder of the day Master Racht had been killed.

With her head hanging, she tried to calm her thoughts. She tried desperately to think of the good in every situation instead of the bad. But today, her method just wasn't working—no matter what she tried, she hated the mark for all it was worth, even more so than the bitterness she had felt about the scar on her wing. While she could hide the scar on her wing easily, it was hard to hide her large bird-like head from anyone.

Forcing herself to look at her reflection again, Sarora looked into her eyes, searching for what she was really feeling. The eyes that were reflected were pitiful—full of sadness, stress, and exhaustion. Although she had finally gotten a chance to fall asleep, her rest obviously hadn't been enough.

"How different I am from four years ago..." Sarora thought aloud, still gazing at her worn expression. "And yet I'm more worried about a scar on my face. Where has my tenacity gone?"

Snap!

Sarora's head shot up and she looked in the direction from where the noise had come. "Who's there?" she called, but there was no response.

"Answer me," Sarora ordered. "I know you are there and until you give me an answer, my beak and talons are ready for you— razor sharp."

Suddenly, a form leapt out from the bushes, and Sarora quickly sprang into action—her wings spread out and her talons stretched in front of her.

CALL FROM THE ALPHA

The sun had passed its halfway-point in the sky and was now working its way back to the horizon. Travis, although having had fun on the trip, was wishing that he could make the time fly faster. He had already tried for the past two hours to get any additional information out of Zack. However, Zack was being awfully quiet for his normal self. *If it gets any quieter, I think I'll rip my hair out of my head,* Travis thought to himself.

Finally, after what had felt like an eternity to Travis, they spotted the rows of trees far ahead of them. "Zack!" Travis exclaimed in excitement. "I see them, Zack! We're almost there!"

"Goodness, I never thought I'd see you so excited to go back to doing training and chores." Travis shot him a glare while Zack laughed.

"Come on! Bet I can beat you back to camp!" Travis egged his friend on as he gave Seraphi a little kick.

"Bet you can't!" Zack called from behind the speeding Seraphi. However, Travis knew better. Seraphi was the fastest horse, and when he got a head start, the winner was already decided. Manes and tails whipping in the wind, hooves drumming, and spirits flying, the two riders flew across the open plains.

Dust sprayed out behind them and hung in the air as the horses joined in the joyful return home.

Travis let out a loud "Whoop!" as he spotted their home. They had been gone for only a day, but any time spent away from home felt like infinity to him.

"Sarora! We're back!" Zack called from just behind Travis. Although Seraphi was the fastest, Mesha had the most stamina and he was beginning to gain on them.

The second they reached the tent, Travis signaled to Seraphi for an immediate stop. The large white horse quickly leaned back and dug his hooves into the ground. Dust rose as Travis leapt off the stallion's back and onto the ground. As he walked into the humble home, Zack jumped off of Mesha and followed him inside.

"Sarora?" Travis called to his friend, but his voice was wasted when he realized that the gryphon was not at home. The smile that had formed on Travis's face diminished until it was not a smile at all. "Where could she be?" Travis turned to Zack and asked.

"Don't worry," Zack told Travis. "I'm sure she's probably just out scouting or something. She won't be gone for long."

Travis let out a nervous sigh. "I sure hope you're right."

Zack smiled, trying to help his friend cheer up. "Come on," Zack said as he draped his arm over Travis's shoulders. "Let's go outside and wait for her." Travis just nodded and let himself be led outside.

In silence, Zack brought Travis over to the small ledge just outside of the tent. Memories flooded through Travis's head as he remembered the night that Master Racht had given him the book —the very one that was now resting underneath his pillow in his room.

Travis let out another sigh as they both sat down and dangled their legs over the edge. Travis could see Zack staring at him from the corner of his eye, but he didn't look over at his friend. He was intent on watching for any sign of Sarora. During the few quiet minutes they sat, Travis had continually mistaken trees, branches, and bushes for their friend. A half-an-hour went by before Zack finally spoke. "Stop it! Just stop it, okay? You are killing me with that look."

"What look?" Travis mumbled without looking at his friend.

"The one that makes you look like a beaten puppy. Cheer up, would ya? I'm sure Sarora will be back soon." Zack's optimism was really driving Travis insane.

"Unless she got captured," Travis mumbled.

"You know Sarora, she would never allow herself to be captured."

"Or tortured."

"But she would have to be captured for that to happen."

"Or killed."

Zack let out an antagonizing groan. "Ugh... Will you just listen to yourself? You're worrying about nothing. Just shut up and put a smile on your face before I spin that frown back to where I want it."

Travis exhaled through his nose. Why couldn't Zack look at the possibilities? Really, what was the chance that their friend had been captured or even killed?

"I sure hope you're right," Travis sighed before leaning back and closing his eyes.

"Don't worry," Zack reassured Travis as he lay on his back as well. "I'm a know-it-all, remember?" Zack's joke had no effect on Travis—he had not even heard his friend.

Under the cover of his closed eyes, Travis's mind whirled with pictures of Gore and Sievan leaping at Sarora. He imagined his unsuspecting friend was torn to shreds as he stood and watched the horrific scene. No matter how he tried to block the image, whether by picturing his friends and himself smiling together, or by picturing some other wonderful everyday fantasy, the nightmare always returned, each time stronger than the last.

Travis grunted when Zack jabbed him in the ribs with his

elbow. "Travis, wake up and stand," his friend whispered in a quiet voice.

Travis opened one eye. "Not unless Sarora's—"

"Sarora's back."

Without a second's hesitation, Travis was on his feet. Looking over at the woods, he spotted the gryphon running at the two of them.

"Sarora!" Travis shouted in excitement. "Sarora! We're back! We thought that—" Travis was stopped by a hushed look from Zack.

"She's not alone. Hold your tongue."

Travis followed Zack's gaze and spotted a form running just behind Sarora. They were both too far away for Travis to see clearly, but he had a sickening feeling in the pit of his stomach. Surely they hadn't been discovered by Gore?

"It's a wolf," Zack commented, shooing away Travis's worry. With a relieved sigh, Travis felt his heart begin to beat once more.

"Which one?" Travis asked, wondering whom Sarora had met up with.

Zack shook his head. "I don't know. They're still too far away to tell."

Squinting, Travis strained his eyes to find the color of the wolf 's pelt. It wasn't black or white, that much he was sure, but it was still hard to be certain if it was gray or brown.

"Travis! Zack!" Sarora cried joyfully as she continued at a breakneck pace. Within a few seconds, she was upon them. In one motion she leapt, wrapped her bird-like legs around them, and held them close. Travis drank in her familiar scent with a smile. What was I so worried about again? he wondered to himself. Sarora was a strong individual, and there was no reason why she wouldn't be able to hold her own.

After a few seconds of closeness, Sarora pulled away from them, her friendly gaze hardening. "Talk about giving me a heart attack. Not only did you not return last night, but when I saw the two of you lying down there on the ground, I was sure someone had killed the both of you."

Zack burst out into laughter. "You thought someone killed us? You should've heard him!" Zack pointed at Travis with his thumb. "He was convinced that you were never coming back."

Sarora gave Travis a quizzical look.

"I, I was just worried that..." Travis shook his head. "Never mind."

Sarora merely nodded before replying, "Not that I don't enjoy this happy reunion, but there is something that needs to come to your attention." Sarora paused for a moment to look at the wolf behind her. The figure stood a few yards back, obviously trying to give the three friends some privacy. Seeing Sarora look back at him, the brown wolf approached, his head held at mid-level. His golden eyes looked from Sarora, to Zack, and finally they came to rest on Travis. Travis recognized him as the wolf that helped him suit up before the battle. With a smile, Travis returned the gaze. "Welcome, Bratislav, what brings you here today?"

The brown wolf smiled as he replied, "If you don't mind, Apprentice Travis, I believe that it would be best if we spoke inside the comfort of your home. Even the trees of the forest can have ears."

Travis nodded in understanding as he led the group to the tent. Travis, once inside, took his usual place sitting in a chair beside Zack's desk, which had been given to him in Master Racht's will. Zack followed Travis and sat down in the chair behind the desk. Bratislav timidly came in next, followed by the front half of Sarora—there was not enough room for her to fit inside with the others.

"Now," Zack was the first to speak once they were all settled in, "not that I don't appreciate an update from the wolves every once in a while, what exactly are you doing here, Bratislav?"

"Eager as Master Racht," Bratislav commented, but before Zack could respond, he continued. "There is much news that must be shared with the three of you, seeing as we have not made contact with you since the battle. Firstly, we all send our thanks for the help in the battle."

"But we still lost," Sarora mumbled from where she sat.

Bratislav looked at her with sympathetic eyes. "That makes no difference in our thanks. You were still willing to make that sacrifice to help us, and that is what matters."

"Well," Zack put in, "it's not that we all hate this 'bright side' of things, but the sacrifice makes no difference if we lose."

"You have a point," Bratislav agreed. "But even though it was a loss, we say 'thank you' for trying—an 'A' for effort if you will. But I didn't just come here to say 'thanks for helping, sorry we lost'." Clearing his throat, Bratislav continued.

"As you were all there to witness, Oberon, leader of the wolves, died bravely in battle. Now, Second-in-Command Timur has stepped up to the position. The thing is, although the ceremony went well, there are many who still oppose his rule. Some wolves claim that since he has not had any previous experience in leading, that he should not be the leader. Rather, they are following another wolf that is ready to take over his position. We are unaware of the wolf's name at this time, but we have come up with a solution.

"A group of wolves, including myself, are convinced that if you three were to show up and speak in Timur's favor, then he would be able to regain control of the pack.

"Now, you must understand that this is no overnight trip. At the very least, you would have to stay for a week—possibly two if you are needed that long. Whether or not you come is not my decision, but I'm sure Timur would welcome the support. Not only would it be a chance to help cheer him up, but possibly also a chance to clear names." Bratislav's eyes flashed over to Sarora, but only for a second.

Could he be insinuating that it would clear Sarora's name from the time when she had left those wolves to their deaths and ran off with the Crystal of Courage? Maybe the trip would be worthwhile.

Travis woke from his thoughts and looked to Sarora, who in turn, looked to Zack and asked, "What do you think?"

Zack let out a small sigh. "Does it really matter what I think? I can see it in your eyes, Sarora. No matter what I could say to keep you from going, I know that you would just disobey me and go anyway." When Zack's head was turned, Sarora jokingly stuck her tongue out at him, which made it hard for Travis to stifle his laughter. Sighing again, Zack rubbed his temples with his fingers and closed his eyes. "Fine, we will come."

Travis caught a moment's glimpse of the twinkle in Sarora's eyes. "Thank you, Zack."

"Yes, thank you, all of you." Bratislav said gratefully as he rose from where he sat. "I promise you will not be disappointed."

"We'll just see about that," Zack remarked as he looked at Bratislav. "When are we to leave?" he asked the large brown wolf.

"As soon as possible. I have been on the road for half a moon and I wish to return."

"Fine, we leave tomorrow morning," Zack decided.

Tomorrow morning! Travis exclaimed in his mind. *But we only just got back. Do we really have to leave this soon?* Though he wanted to voice his complaints, Travis bit his tongue. This next adventure was not about him—it was about helping Timur and Sarora—and for once, someone else's needs had to come before his own.

"Travis, are you okay?"

Travis stirred from his thoughts to see Sarora looking at him with concern. "Yeah, I'm fine. I just need some rest." Travis tried to convince his friend with a small yawn.

Although he expected Sarora to contradict, she said nothing and just nodded. The concern in Sarora's eyes faded away like mist until there was no trace left.

"If rest is what you need," Travis turned to look at Zack as the boy spoke, "then you stay here and converse with Sarora about what you have learned. I'm sure there are more stories that I can learn about the wolves." He looked to Bratislav. "Care for a stroll?"

The brown wolf nodded. "I'd be obliged."

With a quick smile toward his friends, Zack led the way out of the tent. Travis listened carefully to be sure that the other two were far away before turning to Sarora. "Um... Unless you have an 'interesting' story," Travis added quotations with his fingers, "then I have something that needs to be shared with you."

"Great," Sarora remarked sarcastically as she rolled her eyes. "I have a bad feeling about what you are going to tell me."

STUDYING

"You'd better be kidding me." Sarora glared at Travis after he told her of the encounter with Loki. The tip of her tailed twitched in annoyance.

Travis raised his hands up in surrender. "Sorry, it's the truth. And that's not the last of it either."

"You spoke to him again?!"

"No." Travis gave Sarora a small glare. "Actually, while I was running from Loki—well, it was more like a blind panic—I sort of, well, ran into a lady who lived down the street." He looked at Sarora sheepishly.

"You did what?"

Travis nodded. "I ran into a lady. And by then, the potion had worn off..."

Sarora's eyes reflected her shock as she gazed at him. "You were so lucky that I wasn't there to kill you!"

"Well, I can't exactly choose when I want to change back. But anyways, here is the rest of the story..." And Travis proceeded to tell Sarora of his encounter with Chloe and Reginald.

"Well?" Travis asked when he had finished recounting his tale. Sarora wasn't looking at Travis; with a distant gaze, she stared at the side of the tent.

"Sarora?"

"Hm, oh, what?" she asked after turning her head back to him.

"You okay?"

Sarora looked at him quizzically. "Why wouldn't I be?"

"You just, well, you weren't—" Travis shook his head. "Never mind. Anyways, what do you think of what happened?"

Sarora sighed and looked away from Travis again. "I don't know, Travis. What do you want me to think? I mean, they were only two people and very insignificant to the roles of our lives. Other than they'll know who you are the next time you go to town, I don't think you'll have any trouble with them. Come on, do you think that they would even work for Trazon?" she asked, finally looking back at him.

Travis shook his head. "No, you're probably right. It's just, well, I don't know." Travis looked into Sarora's hawk-like eyes. "I don't really know, Sarora. I don't know anything about Loki, or Stephen, or Ben, or-or even Zack for that matter." Travis let out an aggravated sigh.

"What about Zack?" Sarora asked, her eyes glaring back into his.

"Well, assuming you know his past, I feel kind of, well, left out," Travis replied, trying to keep his out-of-the-blue discussion peaceful. "I don't know where he's from, who his family is, or even how he and you met."

Sarora's eyes flickered in a way that would be the equivalent to a human biting their lip. "Well, it's not really in my place to tell you anything that you don't know about Zack. That is for him to share with you."

"I know that." Travis sat down with his elbows on his knees. "But what do you think is the probability of him actually telling me anything?"

"Telling you anything, I'd say is a fifty-fifty shot. Telling a whole lot of his past, more like a one to ninety-nine. Just like you have the right to not tell us something, Zack also has the right to remain silent," Sarora mused. "Not to get your hopes down. No, I'm not trying to do that at all. You can ask him for all I care, but I don't think you'll get a whole lot of what you're looking for."

"What do you think that I'm looking for?" Travis asked as he folded his hands.

"I don't know," she replied, shrugging her shoulders. "You always surprise me, Travis, so I'm not even going to guess. It would probably just give me a migraine." She lifted her front leg to hold her head as if she could already feel the headache.

"Then I won't tell you," Travis said to lift the worry off of Sarora's shoulders. He thought that perhaps she was being melodramatic— then again, she was probably just kidding around.

"Good. Now, since we have a bit of free time, remember the last time we spoke at our lesson?" Sarora asked him with a grin.

"Uh, I read, then you quizzed me?" Travis couldn't quite remember all of the details.

Sarora nodded. "And then I gave you an assignment." Gesturing to the bookcase with her tail, Sarora smiled. "Have fun!"

"B-but," Travis stammered.

"Oh, don't tell me that you're just too exhausted to read for enjoyment," Sarora said.

"It's an assignment."

"Right, it's *my* enjoyment that it's your assignment." Sarora smirked at him.

"You're awful." Travis smiled back at Sarora as he walked over to the large bookcase. It was as tall as he was and filled with books of all sizes and colors. Travis couldn't quite decide which book to take.

"Hmm... Eeny, meeny, miny, mo..." Travis pointed to a red book with gold detailing on the binding. Carefully, he pulled the thick book off the shelf and opened the front cover as he moved to his seat.

On the title page was large wording that read,
Terrium Gabster's Firmarian Dictionary

"You've got to be kidding me..." Travis groaned as he sat his rear down on his small chair.

"What is it?" Sarora asked him from where she lay relaxing.

Travis breathed out heavily. "The most exciting book, the first one that I took, is a dictionary."

"Bummer." Sarora looked at him with pity for a moment and then beamed brightly, "Have fun!"

"You're not serious, are you?" Travis asked, desperate to get out of reading the worst book in the world.

"Oh, I'm serious all right," Sarora said as she grinned teasingly at Travis. "Really, you must read it. Not always the most exciting book in the world, but it can really help you learn more about this realm."

Groaning, Travis gave up his complaining and opened the book to the first page. Starting with the A's, Travis read until his eyes hurt from the small print. The last word he read zoomed through his head because it was the only one he was able to remember.

-amicable
\AM-ih-kuh-bul\ adjective
: characterized by friendly goodwill: peaceable

"Amicable..." Travis mumbled before closing the book.

"Hm?" Sarora opened one eye as she woke from her slumber. "What were you saying?"

"Amicable—it means to be friendly or peaceful," Travis replied before rubbing his eyes. "Sarora, why must I read this?"

"Because."

"Because why?"

"It makes you smarter and it makes me laugh."

"It makes you laugh to see me being tortured?"

"No, because you are so upset about being 'tortured' is why I laugh."

Travis, try as he might, could barely hold back a smile. Even though he thought it rude of Sarora to pick on him, whatever she said almost always made him smile.

"Okay, here, let me make you a deal," Travis began as he conjured up a devious plan in his mind. "I'll read this whole dictionary, cover to cover, only on one condition."

"It's not like you have a choice," Sarora smirked at him, "but let's hear what you have to say."

"The one condition—you have to read it as well." Travis's smile broadened.

"Ha!" Sarora burst out. "I've already read it cover to cover. Looks like I won't have to read it anytime soon."

"A good book's worth reading twice," Travis still pressed.

"Yes, too bad that isn't a good book. Come on, can't you think of another deal?"

Travis looked away from Sarora and his gaze drifted toward the bookcase. Slowly, Travis stood and walked over to where the thicker books were set up on higher shelves. Some of the large books had titles, and others didn't. Sweeping his gaze over the titled books, Travis's light bulb flicked on in his mind. Putting the dictionary in his left hand, Travis reached up and grabbed a large dark blue book. With a wily smile, Travis turned back to Sarora, the book behind his back.

"Here is the new deal," Travis began. "I'll read the dictionary if you read the book that I have behind my back."

Sarora rolled her eyes. "Most likely I've already read it, but, sure. What harm could it possibly bring me? You have a deal, Travis. Now, what is the book?"

From behind his back he carefully flipped the book so that the front cover looked at Sarora. Travis could barely keep himself from bursting out into hysterical laughter when he saw the expression on Sarora's face. The book that he had pulled off the shelf was A Bogus's Guide to Psychology.

If a pair of eyes could ever speak the foulest language, it would be Sarora's. With one look, she could say all that she needed to without uttering a word. The look, however, which was meant to scare Travis, only made him bust his gut. His laughter rang through the tent and he could barely even keep his voice at a steady pitch. For one of the first times of his life, Travis's voice bounced up and down, high and low. With red cheeks, Travis's laughing ceased and his eyes widened in shock. Now it was Sarora's revenge.

Sarora laughed so hard her words were barely audible. "The best... payback...ever...and it... was caused...by nature!" Sarora fell into a fit of laughter as she rolled about the floor of the tent. Nothing Travis did was able to stop his embarrassment and Sarora's ecstatic laughter.

Slow Trudge

Travis let out a huge, lion-like yawn as he stretched his arms from where he sat on Seraphi's back. The morning sun shone brightly through the trees and the dapples of light that hit him warmed his body. His muscles felt refreshed after a good night's sleep, and his eyes were bright with energy. Though he had felt like walking through the woods, his friends insisted on riding part of the way—what good would he be if they arrived and he was too exhausted?

To Seraphi's left, Mesha walked with an extra skip in his step. Though a gelding, the young horse was still high-strung and eager to keep moving. It's a wonder how Zack handles him so well, Travis thought to himself as he watched the palomino from the corner of his eyes.

In contrast to Mesha's behavior, Seraphi walked with his head out in front of him. The stallion was far from over-excited. Instead, he had a bored expression, as if this was just another job, no different from the many hundred others that he had seen in his lifetime. Every now and then, when Mesha would get too jumpy and too close for Seraphi's comfort, the stallion would nip the other horse, ears pinned back. The rebuke would cause Mesha to settle down, though within a few minutes he would be at it again. This scene had occurred four times in the past hour.

Zack scolded his horse each time he got too rambunctious, but though Mesha would listen, it wasn't for very long. Travis also tried to talk Seraphi into just ignoring the naïve gelding, but the wisdom of the horse's years obviously contradicted Travis's reasoning, and Seraphi would ignore him every time Travis tried to tell him what to do.

To Travis's right, Sarora walked with an impatient look upon her face. She had tried to convince Zack earlier that she and Travis could fly there alone, and that way the journey could be made more quickly. But Zack, being his normal bossy self, had told Sarora that the idea was ridiculous and that it was best if he tagged along. Although he knew that Zack was in charge, Travis still agreed with Sarora. There was no true reason for Zack to tag along, but he could also reason with the older boy's side. When Bratislav had asked for them, he probably wanted all of them. Though Zack's word would probably be strongest among the three of them, Travis really didn't feel up for another journey with the older boy. It wasn't that he didn't like Zack, but they just needed to be apart sometimes.

Travis was woken from his thoughts when Mesha let out another squeal. Once again, the bouncy gelding had driven Seraphi to the breaking point, and so to reprimand the young horse, the stallion had nipped Mesha on the hindquarters. Trying to comfort the old horse, Travis leaned forward in his saddle, patted his neck, and whispered into his ear. With a sigh, Seraphi at least listened to Travis's words this time, and he sidestepped away from Mesha, ignoring the gelding's annoyed snort.

"Mesha, settle down." Zack gently pulled back on the palomino's reigns. Biting at the bit, ears pointed back, Mesha grumpily obeyed.

Ahead of the complaining horses, the boys heard Bratislav chuckle, "Have those two always been that way?"

Zack shook his head. "No. I think the reason is that Mesha is just a little too excited—he doesn't go anywhere. And Seraphi, well, he's a bit jaded. I can't blame him though—he's been doing the same thing for at least a hundred years."

Bratislav dropped back a little so that he could walk alongside the group. The wolf's face held a tiny smirk as he looked from one horse to another. "It's just in their nature, and no matter what you try, they won't ever grow out of it." Suddenly, the wolf stopped, his head erect and ears straight up. Travis pulled Seraphi to a stop and watched Bratislav's nose twitch as he scented the air.

"What is it?" Travis asked, his voice just a little more than a whisper.

"It smells like dog." Bratislav's eyes held a fire that showed not worry, but anger.

"Where? And what does it smell like?" Travis asked, looking about him to try and spot any movement in the woods.

"Here. It's following us, and it smells horrid."

"Definition of horrid?" Travis asked the brown wolf.

"Like garbage, but much worse."

"Pran..." Travis mumbled under his breath. The young dog hated to be alone for more than a couple hours at a time. He must have taken notice of his master's leave and followed Zack.

"Hey, Zack!" Travis called to his friend, who, with Sarora, had just realized that the other two had fallen back.

"Yes?" came the reply from in the front.

"Did you visit Pran before we left?" Travis asked Zack.

Zack nodded. "Yes, I told him that we were leaving and would be back as soon as possible."

"Did you tell him that he could come along?" Travis pondered.

"What?" Zack's face was twisted in confusion. "No, of course not. I told him he would be staying. Why?"

"He's here," Travis replied just as the bushes next to him shook. Out of the bushes a medium-sized dog padded out. His creamy tan fur was dusted with dirt and his dark eyes were shining. As he bounded over to Travis, his tail wagged ecstatically over the top of his back.

"Oh no..." Travis heard Zack moan as he jumped off Mesha's back and walked over to the group. Before he reached them however, Pran spotted Bratislav. With a yip of excitement, Pran playfully bounced over to where the wolf was. Surprisingly, as much of a coward as Pran was, he didn't have the sense to stay away from a wolf that was more than twice his size.

As Pran approached, Bratislav's whole human personality disappeared. With a growl, Bratislav held his massive head high in the air, his teeth glittering a bright white. His tail was also held high as he displayed the dominant position of a wolf. In this position, he told Pran, "I am in no mood for child's play. I'm the boss."

Obediently, Pran pressed his body close to the ground as he wriggled beneath Bratislav, his tongue just reaching up to lick Bratislav's chin. Pran's body language said, "You are boss."

"Pran! Get over here!" Zack called angrily to the young dog. With tail drooping and eyes staring at the ground, Pran slowly walked over to Zack. With a guilty look, he focused his large dark eyes on the tall boy, begging Zack to forgive him.

"Pran, I told you that you couldn't come," Zack scolded the dog.

Travis thought that the older boy was being rather ridiculous. The dog couldn't really understand a word that he was saying. "Zack, what are you going to do with him?" Travis asked.

Zack shook his head and sighed. "I could tell him to go home, but he wouldn't listen to me even then. Or, I could have Sarora fly him home in less than an hour, but that won't stop him from catching back up to us in a little while. Either way, it looks like we'll still be stuck with him."

Happily, as if he understood the whole conversation, Pran's eyes brightened and he began to bounce in a circle around Zack. The dog's joyful whines rose in pitch with each bounce, and the more he whined, the faster his curly tail whipped back and forth.

Zack sighed and put his head in his hands. "Where again did I find a dog like you?"

Sarora chuckled aloud, "That'll teach you for adopting strays. Once they have their puppy love, they won't ever give it up."

Bratislav finally seemed to relax from his dominant state and his human-like qualities began to return. As his fur began to lay flat, his upper lip uncurl, and his head start to lower, Bratislav shook himself.

"He may come," Bratislav told Zack, "but I make no promise of his safety. The wolves may, or may not, try to kill him. Most of us older wolves don't have that much toleration for a young dog like him." The fire that had filled Bratislav's eyes began to slowly fade away.

After taking a quick look around at his surroundings, Bratislav moved back to the front of the group. "Come, let's be off," he said, his deep voice containing an edge of annoyance. "We have to get to our new camp before dusk, or my brother will have my pelt."

Travis nodded in agreement and Zack was quick to climb back onto Mesha's back. With a trot in his step, Pran followed the palomino horse. Sarora shot Travis a glance as they followed behind the others. "I'm willing to bet that Zack will only be able to tolerate the two of them for so long," she whispered as she gave one of her 'gryphon smiles'.

Travis tried hard not to laugh. "I'm not going to bet against you. With two young, hyper animals nipping at his heels, it won't be long before he explodes."

Sarora chuckled in reply as the two followed Zack and Bratislav through the woods.

Soon, Travis drifted back into a sea of boredom. To him, the journey seemed to drag on forever. Bratislav had insisted upon traveling slowly and making Travis and Zack ride so that the group would be at full strength at any given moment. Travis knew that the forest could be dangerous and that they all needed to be ready to defend themselves if the need arose, but he still wished that they could forget about their energy for a moment and run to the new camp. If Bratislav wanted them to get there quickly, why would the wolf insist upon walking the whole journey? Traveling a bit faster than a snail's pace couldn't hurt, could it?

Sighing to himself, Travis watched the rustling leaves of the trees in a feeble attempt to entertain himself. A gentle breeze seemed to whisper softly against the branches of the large oaks as it swept along its way. On the breeze, Travis could faintly detect the smell of flowers, and as they reached a clearing that was covered in bright colors, he smiled at the sight.

Seeing the large patch of flowers, Pran excitedly leapt into the floral forest. Travis and Sarora laughed as they watched the keyed up dog prance through the tall fields, whose flowers were well above Pran's head. With a joyful yip, Pran landed in one patch and then another, sneezing time after time. His ebony nose wrinkled up as the scents of the flowers overwhelmed him.

"Who would have thought..." Bratislav even seemed to be enjoying the sight.

"Thought what?" Zack asked the wolf.

"Who would have thought that a dog that smells like a skunk cabbage would actually enjoy the perfumes of the summer flowers?" Bratislav's face grew a large smile as he amused himself with the sight of the perplexing little dog.

"Travis," Sarora whispered into the boy's ear as they continued. "Travis, are you still awake?"

"Wha—?" Travis replied groggily, lifting his head off his chest. He had been nodding in and out of sleep for the past hour. But who could blame him? They had practically been walking in one boring straight line for the past eight hours, and not only was the ride boring, but it hurt. Only once had Travis and Zack had a chance to get off their horses and stretch before Bratislav would usher them on their way. And although they had traveled over thirty miles that day, they still had another half-a-day's journey to go. If only we could have traveled faster, Travis had complained to himself earlier. *We could be with the wolves right now. But of course Bratislav would insist on doing the impractical. Humph, just my luck.*

"I said," Sarora began again, "are you still awake?"

"I am now," Travis mumbled as he let out a lion-like yawn and stretched his arms high above his head. "How long have I been nodding off?" he asked her in a whisper.

"Only an hour. I'm the only one who noticed," Sarora whispered back to him. Then she looked ahead of them to where Zack sat on Mesha. "But don't worry—you're not the only one having a tough time trying to stay awake." Sarora motioned to both Zack and Pran. Zack was leaning forward in the saddle, obviously trying to take the strain off his back. Pran was a similar story to that of Travis's. The poor dog was dragging his tail in the dirt behind him and his head was hanging low. The energy that he had shown in the beginning of the day was nowhere to be seen.

In contrast to the three, Bratislav and Sarora both still seemed full of life. Travis knew that he shouldn't be surprised with the wolf's amazing stamina, and yet, he was. The whole time Bratislav had kept his head high and his ears erect.

Travis looked to Sarora. Though her eyes seemed to hold some wish to rest, she kept a steady pace. In the dimming light, her golden eyes seemed to glow. When she looked back to Travis, he smiled at her and she returned the look. It was something that they found strangely entertaining as they went along. One would smile to the other, and then the other would smile back. This had occurred more than twice during the long, dreary day.

Travis blinked away the tiredness in his eyes and remarked sarcastically, "If I ever get any sleep on this journey, it'll be too soon."

Sarora caught on and nodded once to him. "You'll rest eventually."

"But, Sarora," Travis began, "can't you see? Maybe if we had traveled faster, we could have gotten there by now."

Sarora sighed and dipped her head. "Yes, I know. But Bratislav must have a good reason for keeping at this slow pace."

"He'd better," Travis mumbled angrily. "If there is no real reason for this torturously slow trek, I'm gonna kill Bratislav."

Sarora glared at Travis, her head still hanging low. "Now, Travis, you and I both know that you wouldn't harm a single hair on that wolf's pelt."

"And what makes you so sure of that?"

Sarora replied, "Because you're too much of a softy." Then she turned and trotted away from Travis to walk next to Zack. Travis glared at Sarora behind her back, a revenge-wanting smile on his face. His expression remained the same all the while Sarora and Zack chatted together. Once, Zack turned his head to look at Travis from the corner of his eye, smiled, and then he turned back to talk with Sarora.

Travis carefully watched the movement of Zack's lips to see if he could identify their conversation. He even urged Seraphi to walk closer behind the other horse. However, try as he might, Travis only picked up invaluable snippets of their conversation.

Leaning back in the saddle, Travis sighed. What was there to do but sit and watch the sun move above the treetops? The birds and other animals of the forest had already begun to bunker down for the night. Yet, as if oblivious to his changing surroundings, Bratislav kept his pace slow and steady.

Finally, Travis's annoyance got to him. Pressing Seraphi on, he trotted up to Bratislav's side and let the white horse walk beside him. Looking down at the brown wolf, Travis asked, "When are we going to settle down for the night?"

"Hm?" Bratislav looked up to Travis. "Oh, yes, you say you want to rest for the night? Well, I was just planning on walking through the night so that we could reach the camp by morning."

"Well, that's all good and well," Travis tried to keep an even tone, "but even if I am able to sleep on the horse, the horses will grow tired. Not just them, though, Sarora will probably need rest soon."

Bratislav glanced behind them at Sarora. "Does she look like she needs rest?" Looking back to the boy, he continued, "And I believe at a steady pace such as this, the horses have hardly even had a workout." Wagging his tail, Bratislav looked for a moment into Travis's eyes. "Are there more reasons for your way of thinking?"

Travis looked away from the wolf. He had told Sarora that he was going to let Bratislav know what he was feeling, and in every detail too. But Sarora, knowing her friend, had told Travis that he wouldn't even try it. A weird feeling gripped Travis's stomach as he realized that she had been right. He really didn't want Bratislav to know how upset he was.

Travis shook his head and looked back at the wolf. "No, just curious"

"Hm, curious huh?" Bratislav chuckled, his rich, deep voice rumbling. "You must have a very curious streak, but I wonder where you get it from? I don't know your origins so that makes it hard to compare you with others."

Travis shook his head and lied as he smiled, "I don't even know any of my origins, other than my mother."

"Well, that's too bad," Bratislav said as he looked away from Travis. "What can one take pride in if he has no family to be proud of?"

I do have a family to be proud of, Travis told himself. *I am proud of my mom, and I am proud of Arlen. He smiled as he thought of the old man. I am also proud of Zack and his courage, and Sarora and her faith. But most of all, I am proud of Master Racht, because of his trust in the promise of happiness in the future.*

LITTERMATES

"What did I tell you? We have arrived!" Bratislav leapt to the front of the group. The brown wolf held his head high as he paraded to the entrance of the wolves' camp. Travis glanced back at his friends. They were both smiling with relief that their travels were over.

The forest opened at a point where a large, bracken wall stood high. At the bracken wall, two large wolves stood guard, and when they saw the group, they welcomed Bratislav with a couple excited yaps.

"Welcome, Bratislav," the large male said in greeting. His fur was a light gray and his ears were black. "We have missed your leadership while you have been gone."

Bratislav nodded to the large wolf. "Hello, Wafai. I would stay and talk longer, but I must visit my brother."

Wafai nodded. "Of course, but there is one problem."

"And what would that be?"

"Timur is out hunting."

Bratislav looked away as he focused on the forest around them, as if searching carefully for his brother. "Oh, I see."

Wafai wagged his tail. "No worry." Looking at his partner, he ordered, "Thuy, go and find Timur please."

The tawny she-wolf nodded, turned, and ran off without a word.

Wafai looked back to Bratislav and the others. "In the meantime, your pass is granted. You can hang around his den, but I would advise not going in. You know how touchy Timur is, especially nowadays..."

Bratislav nodded. "Thank you, Wafai." Glancing at the group, Bratislav said, "You may want to leave your animals out here, including Pran—the horses would have a hard time getting in and Pran, well, you know your pet. As for you, Sarora," he looked to the she-gryphon, "you can probably fly over. But do this only once I have called for you from the other side. We don't want to incite panic."

Sarora nodded to the wolf as the boys got off their horses. "Of course."

"Pran, you follow Mesha and Seraphi," Zack ordered his dog. "It will be your job to keep an eye on them and protect them, okay?" Pran gave a sharp yip of excitement at his special assignment.

Cautiously, Travis followed behind Bratislav, Zack just behind him. Single file, the three of them squeezed through the small opening in the large bracken wall. Once on the other side, Bratislav barked. Within a couple seconds, Sarora glided over the edge of the wall and into the wolf camp. Coming to a gentle land, she smiled at Travis and then looked around as Travis followed her gaze.

Slightly similar to the wolves' old camp, the new camp had many standing tents, though the number of them was less than before. This was because of the small hiding place, and because the number of the pack had greatly decreased from what it had been before. The hundreds were now only few—somewhere between forty and sixty wolves.

Small pits still smoked from when they had been lit. Armory was divided up among the site, to protect it from all being stolen if the camp was found. The remaining swords and other weapons were not near the quantity that they had been before the battle, and those that weren't in need of repair were few.

Travis watched the wolves as they stared back at the group. Some wolves that had heard them enter had left their chores to watch the guests. However, many others gave them a cold shoulder or a wide berth, being careful not to look their way. It seemed that only the younger wolves paid any attention to the newcomers. One even stopped fighting with another pup and he looked with admiring eyes at Bratislav. Bratislav noticed the youngster and smiled at him. The young gray wolf smiled back and then began bragging to his friends about how one day he would be as good of a fighter as Bratislav.

Bratislav led them to a cave that sat at the back of the clearing. With a quick, questioning glance at Sarora, Travis asked Bratislav, "What happened to the tent where the leader stays?"

"Well," Bratislav gave a nervous glance at the den, "Oberon's was...misplaced by a younger recruit. But that's not the only problem—some of the other wolves have refused to build Timur a new tent."

"What?!" Travis exclaimed. "I mean, how hard would it be for them to make a new one for their leader?"

"In your question lies the problem." Bratislav looked to Travis. "The majority of the wolves don't want Timur as their leader, and therefore, they have begun to protest."

"That's not right." Zack looked to Bratislav. "Can't they just accept that they have a new leader rather than moon over the loss of their past one?"

Bratislav sighed and shook his head. "Even though Oberon's relatives followed darkness, many thought of him as a great leader. Not that Timur is any different from Oberon, though. No, Timur's personality reflects much of Oberon's. However, while Oberon would refrain from mentioning some of his other ideas, well, Timur has decided to share them."

"What ideas?" Zack asked the wolf. "How bad could these ideas be that no one else would agree with him?"

"Don't misread me," Bratislav admonished, looking back at Zack. "There are some that greatly agree with Timur's ideas, including myself. But there are two sides to this pack now—those who ride on Timur's boat, and those who would rather swim." Bratislav gave a quick glance around the huddled group before he leaned in and whispered, "He wants to ask for help from the other animals."

"Other animals?" Travis looked at Bratislav. "What other animals?"

"Those animals whose intelligence exceeds the expectation of the humans." Bratislav looked at Travis. "Among these are the foxes, the hawks, the panthers..." Bratislav's voice grew even quieter so that it was barely audible, "and the dragons."

"Dragons!" Travis exclaimed loudly.

"SHHH!" Bratislav glared angrily at Travis. "Don't let the wolves hear you. They don't know about asking the dragons yet, and as well as everything else is going, that's why Timur has only entrusted every detail to myself and on other wolf."

"Well, not to be a downer or anything, but," Zack said to Bratislav quietly, "how does Timur expect to find the flying lizards? They've been in hiding for over a decade."

"Yes," Bratislav nodded in agreement, "but does it ever hurt to hope or dream that they could lend us their strength once more?"

Sarora spoke for the first time since they had entered the camp. "If that hope or dream leads you into the arms of Trazon, then, yes, it hurts very much." Her face, though the joke was meant to lighten up the moment, was serious as she looked at Bratislav, waiting for his response.

"Agreed," the brown wolf looked back at Sarora, "but since we are already on the road to losing this war, why not try? A loss is a loss, and a win is a win, no matter by how much."

"Unless you just scrape by in winning," Travis pointed out. "If nearly all of the population of the world is killed and you have nothing left to cherish, then it really doesn't matter."

"I second that," Zack glanced momentarily at Travis, "but I

see what Timur means, Bratislav. If we are behind in the race, why don't we look for more speed and strength while we work on our endurance? We may be fairly strong already with the unwritten alliance with the wolves but it would most definitely be in our best interest to find more allies to add to our strength."

Bratislav smiled gratefully at Zack before continuing, "Not only would it give us more strength in having more on our side, but Timur hopes that it would boost the morale of all those who are struggling to keep a strong and firm faith. We need hope more than anything else about now." The rest of the group silently agreed as they each dipped their heads.

"Aaawooo!"

The group snapped their heads up to see the wolves racing towards them. Travis smiled as he recognized the sleek timber wolf pelt of Timur as he led a small party of wolves towards them. Slowing down as he approached the new arrivals, Timur barked out a couple of commands to his followers. Obediently, more than half of the group broke away and trotted off to their own living quarters. Two wolves remained at Timur's side—Thuy and a beautiful white she-wolf. The she-wolf's yellow eyes danced with curiosity at the group as she walked harmoniously with Timur.

Each of the group turned to face Timur—Bratislav a little ways ahead of the others. The wolf's head ducked in submission as his brother met him. However, Timur did not acknowledge his brother at first—his attention was focused on three figures—Travis, Zack, and Sarora.

With a smile and a wag of the tail, Timur happily spoke to them. "Welcome. I did not expect to see you all so soon. It is nice to see familiar faces of friends, but if you don't mind me asking, what are you doing here?"

Zack smiled in reply to Timur's welcome. "It is nice to see you too, Timur. But as for your question, what do you mean what are we doing here? Didn't you send for us?"

Timur shook his head. "No, I'm afraid not, but it is good to see you all."

"But," Travis looked at Bratislav, "didn't you say that Timur wanted us?"

"What?" Timur looked at his older brother, confused. "You went without my permission to find them?"

Bratislav ducked even lower and he pushed himself closer to the ground. "Forgive me, brother, but I was only looking out for your best interest. I have noticed how low you have been over these past days, and I wanted to cheer you up..."

"Silence!" Timur boomed so loudly that Travis was surprised that they were even speaking to the same quiet wolf that he had known in the forest. "I know I am your brother, but you must remember that I am now your leader, so you must refer to me as I am in that command! Secondly, I know you always look out for my best interest, but can't you see that you may have hurt me more than helped?" The brown-gray wolf shook his head in anger. "Now many others may disobey me or otherwise not follow in the paws that I lead because you have so conveniently done this work."

"I am sorry, Timur." Travis had never seen Bratislav so low to any other wolf. "I thought that maybe they could also promote you to full leadership."

"Promote me!" Timur barked again. With an apologetic look to his guests, Timur said, "No offense to any of you, but many here don't respect the three of you, or even like a hair on your heads for that matter. So the only thing that you have done for me, Bratislav," Timur looked down at his brother, "is get the wolves that are for me to take a new vote on whether they like me or not."

Bratislav did not reply—he only hung his large brown head in shame.

Standing, watching the whole scene, Travis felt awkward and out of place. *How could we have known that we would be a burden to him?* Travis wondered to himself. He hadn't ever imagined that this trip would lead to this kind of problem.

Sighing, Timur backed away from his submissive brother and walked over to the others. "My apologies to all of you." He dipped his head in respect to them. "I am grateful that you came to help, but unfortunately, there is little that you can do to help me. But as long as you are here, you may stay a couple nights if you need to rest."

Zack assumed his natural role as group leader. "Thank you. We will stay, but outside of your camp to help prevent any further troubles."

Timur dipped his head again. "Of course, but don't any of you think for once that you are not my guests. I welcome you with open, er, paws. Feel free to talk with me as long as you are here. Any questions that you may have, come and find me." With a quick glance at the she-wolves next to him, Timur added, "I have a small business to attend to first, but Thuy and Eira will give you a heads up on all that is to be." Timur then nodded farewell to each of them and left with Bratislav slinking slowly behind him.

Thuy, a bit smaller but more muscular than the white wolf, Eira, looked over to her companion. "I'm sorry, Mistress, but may I please be excused? I promised Wafai that I would be back on watch with him soon..."

The white she-wolf nodded understandingly. "It's alright—I give you my leave, you may go. I'll show the others around the camp."

The tawny wolf nodded a brief 'thank-you' before turning and jogging back out of the camp entrance. Turning back to her guests, Eira gave one wag of her tail and smiled. "Welcome to each of you. I have heard much about you from Timur."

Zack stepped forward before Travis had a chance to say anything to the she-wolf. "Hello, Eira, it is nice to meet you as well."

"Aren't you the same she-wolf that told us to come to battle back when we were in the woods?" Travis asked, recognizing the white messenger wolf.

Eira grinned and nodded. "Yes, I was."

"Eira?" Zack asked quickly, obviously trying to look like he was the leader again. "Would it be rude if I asked you your position in this pack?"

Eira shook her head. "No, not at all. But Timur has told me of how cunning and clever each of you are. So, you tell me, where am I in this pack chain?"

After a second's silence, it was Sarora who spoke. "You are the Alpha female, second in command only to Timur." Her voice seemed to convey a smile as she answered the she-wolf.

Eira nodded. "Very good, how did you know?"

"Thuy called you 'Mistress'," Sarora explained, "and there's only one other wolf that I know of who's been called that—Quail, Oberon's mate." Her tone saddened as she finished speaking. Travis tried to make a mental note to ask Sarora what had happened to Quail, as he had never heard of her before.

"Well done," Eira said with a smile. "And I don't mean that in a mentor to student format. Even for you, I am surprised that anyone would know this much about us wolves. Many of our ways are hard to see, for though we are bonded to the ways of our ancestors, with each new generation comes improvement and fallbacks."

Zack nodded. "As is the same with humans." He was having a difficult time trying to hide his need to be in control of everything that is said and done—Travis could see it in his face and hear it in the tone of his voice. "As different as we are, everything in nature faces the same hurdles in one way or another. But anyway, you were going to show us around?"

"Yes, of course," Eira replied, her voice barely holding surprise. Turning away from them, she flicked her tail. "Please, follow me."

Eira led the small group around the camp. To Travis, every scene they passed by was almost identical. Wherever they went, wolves would nod in respect to Eira and ask her of her day. Then, Eira would reply and turn and introduce them to her visitors. The occasional good-sided wolf would nod and give a brief smile, but most just glared at them. Eira tried to assure the three that it was that particular wolf's way of saying, "Hello." However, Travis believed less of it the more he saw it happen.

Once they had finished, Eira led them back out of camp—much to Travis's relief—and then brought them to a clearing nearby. Seeing that their owners had returned, Mesha, Seraphi, and Pran welcomed the group back, although Pran seemed more excited to see the she-wolf than anyone else. With his tail doing flips over his backend, Pran wriggled with excitement as he worked his way closer to her.

Though he should have seen it coming, Travis was surprised how dominant Eira could be. As soon as Pran had bounded over to her, Eira's lip curled back in a deep growl. Her head held high, Travis could see the vibrations in the she-wolf's throat as she told Pran to respect her. Although Eira was strong and independent, her body told another story—she had a delicate figure, though not small, and her paw steps seemed to be so light that the ground might not even notice her walking at all.

Pran, tired of being bossed around, turned and trotted away from Eira and back into the woods. Zack called for the young dog, but Pran did not return at the sound of his master's call. Barely able to suppress an eye-roll, Zack apologized to Eira for his dog's behavior, wished her a good day, and then walked off looking for Pran.

Eira then turned to Travis and Sarora. "As you probably have already figured out, this is where you may stay. It's just far enough outside of camp to give you some privacy and to keep the pack relaxed."

"Thank you, Eira." Sarora's eyes showed her gratitude.

"You are welcome," Eira chuckled as she turned to trot away. Looking back over her shoulder, Eira called, "Be sure to call for us if you need anything."

"The same to you," Sarora replied to the she-wolf before turning to Travis. "Now, what do we do?"

Travis studied the ground for a moment before looking back to Sarora. "I don't know, but I'm sure you're going to tell me."

Sarora chuckled as her tail swept over the top of Travis's head, ruffling his hair. "You've got me all figured out. So, since you are so smart, go and find us some firewood for a nice brunch. We need all the strength that we can get."

"You eat wood now, do ya?" Travis joked. He had to duck quickly to avoid Sarora's bird-like front leg as it swept at him. "Kidding, just kidding," Travis laughed as Sarora's smiling eyes glared at him. Turning around he walked back off into the woods.

Heart-Hardened

Travis sat the wood in the center of the circle that he had drawn in the ground. Wiping his brow, he was glad that he was finally beginning to cool down. He had spent that afternoon chopping wood—with a sword. Not only had the sword been previously dulled, but now it had shattered at the end from hitting the tree just the right way. Why hadn't Travis asked for Sarora or Zack's help? The answer was stubborn pride. For once, he had wanted to do something on his own without the help of his friends. Unfortunately, he had forgotten that he didn't have the common tools used to chop down trees, and in his bull-headedness, Travis had spent the past hour sitting around after a long bout of chopping with a dull sword.

"You're not tired at all, are you?" Sarora asked sarcastically as she walked up from behind him. With a dull thud, Sarora dropped a small furry object by Travis's side. Grimacing, Travis turned and looked down to see a small gray rabbit lying at his feet.

"Hey, Travis," Sarora awoke Travis from his quiet state, "if you don't mind, I think both you and Zack would prefer to eat sometime today. So stop staring down at the dead rabbit, make a tepee out of the logs, and get us a fire going please."

"Um, oh yeah..." Travis looked back to Sarora, his stomach

still churning. Turning away from Sarora, Travis stacked the logs in a tepee-like structure. Then he sat down and remained quiet.

"Excuse me." Sarora walked forward and nudged Travis with her beak. "When would you like to light this thing?"

"Oh, right," Travis replied. He had decided to see how long he could get out of trying to use his powers. Ever since the battle, he had not been able to call upon them. He shuddered a little as he thought of the gruesome fight, and then how he had not been capable of using fire.

Nervously, Travis held out his hand, cleared his mind, and focused his power on the logs. His eyes remained shut as the seconds ticked by. The forest was quiet and still, and as Sarora watched in silence, to her surprise, no fire appeared. A gentle wind encouraged her to speak to Travis.

"Travis, is there a problem?" she asked, her head dipping down to Travis's level.

Travis shook his head, eyes still closed. "No, gimme one more second..." Another few seconds ticked by before Sarora pushed herself to speak again.

"Travis, what's wrong?" Sarora asked. When Travis still did not reply, Sarora looked at him, worry in her eyes. "Travis, you know you can tell me anything."

Sighing, Travis grudgingly began to speak. "You wanna know the truth? Well..."

"I'm finally back!" Zack's voice sounded through the forest. In his mind, Travis let out a sigh of relief. He didn't want his friends to worry about him or think of him as weak. Together, Travis and Sarora both looked up to spot Zack walking back towards them. He had been gone all afternoon, and they had not seen him since before Eira had left. In his arms, Zack held the elusive Pran, who hung his head, panting heavily.

"You two wouldn't believe how far I had to chase this guy," Zack smiled as he stood by his friends. "He had me going for over a mile before I was able to catch up with him. I had to leap over streams, jump over logs, and crawl through bushes to follow him.

Finally, he got trapped between a large boulder and me, so I was able to nab him before he could get away."

"Huh," Sarora mused as she looked at Pran carefully, "I wonder what has gotten into him?"

Zack shook his head. "I don't know, but I'll have to keep a close eye on him so he doesn't—" Zack was cut short as he struggled to keep a firm hold on the squirming Pran. Before he could regain his grasp, Pran pushed off Zack's chest and leaped onto the ground. With a delighted yip, Pran turned around and ran back into the woods, the same way that he had gone before.

"You've got to be kidding me!" Zack's eyes bulged out of his head with exasperation. With a loud groan, Zack ran after his dog. "Pran! Get back here!"

"Zack!" Sarora called after the boy. "What about lunch?"

"You guys eat!" came the voice. "I'll pick something up later!" Zack's voice echoed through the trees.

Wanting to avoid another confrontation with Sarora, Travis looked up at Sarora. "Should I go help him?"

Sarora shook her head. "No, he's got to learn how to bond with Pran on his own. Honestly, though, I would think that Zack would have more control of his own pet." Shaking her head and chuckling softly, Sarora walked a little ways off and lay down near a tree.

With another sigh of relief, Travis was sure that Sarora wasn't going to press him about using his magic. Thinking quickly, Travis grabbed a couple of rocks that sat around the teepee of logs. With a small prayer, Travis struck the rocks together. For once his luck was with him. With a sizzling spark, the rocks brought ignition to a leaf that sat near the logs. Hastily, Travis grabbed the leaf and threw it onto the logs. With a strengthening light, the fire slowly began to brighten.

Smiling to himself, Travis stood, wiped his hands off and walked over to Sarora. With a sigh, Travis sat by the gryphon. Together, the two relaxed in silence, watching the fire begin to grow.

Remembering what he had reminded himself earlier, Travis asked, "Who was Quail?"

"Hm?" Sarora took her gaze off the flames. "Oh, Quail. She was the previous alpha female of the wolf pack."

Travis glared at the gryphon with a smile on his face. "I gathered as much. Did you know anything else about her?"

"Well," Sarora looked away from Travis and back to the fire, "she was Oberon's mate."

"I'm not stupid. What are you hiding?" Travis asked, still looking at Sarora.

The gryphon was silent before replying, "You know how Oberon was a mountain wolf, right?"

"Yes."

"And you know how his breed is, mostly filled with darkness and hatred, not following the paths of light."

"Yes, Sarora, get on with it," Travis urged.

"Quail was a gray wolf, Travis." Sarora's voice was barely more than a whisper.

"And?" Travis pressed. "What has that to do with Oberon?"

"Many didn't trust Oberon, and so they were too busy to see the danger right in front of them—"

"What happened?"

Sarora looked to Travis, her eyes filled with sadness. "It was Quail, Travis. It was her that first put fear into the minds of the wolves. She betrayed them all."

Travis fell silent, and the forest was entirely still for the third time that day.

"But why? What happened?" Travis asked, afraid of the answer.

Sarora sighed as she laid her head on her front legs. "I can only remember parts of the tale, so don't quote me on it.

"It happened five winters ago. Zack and I had just begun our training with Master Racht when this all occurred. The night was dark, and the winter harsh. A blizzard was moving in from the north, and at an alarming rate too. The council of wolves—a group of seven wolves, generally elders, headed by the alpha—was meeting to discuss the next battle plan.

"Oberon had been a leader for three years at that point and was still trying to gain the trust of his comrades. Wanting to show his loyalty and strength, he insisted that the group fall back, to prevent another fight before they were ready.

"The council, genuinely surprised by the cocky young leader's decision, was all for giving the idea a shot. When the meeting was adjourned, Quail went up to her mate and asked him why he had decided so. 'Well, to protect the lives of those I love, of course,' Oberon had replied, hoping to sweet talk the she-wolf.

"But Quail, not wanting to hear the sound of retreat, brought up the debate with her mate. She argued that if they gave up their position now, they would be unable to get back into the fight later. But Oberon would not hear of it, so he told Quail to leave his sight.

"Enraged by the lack of faith that Oberon had in her, Quail went on her way. And supposedly not wanting her mate to take the blame for the loss in battle, she went among the captains of the wolves, and she told them that they were to hold their post. The wolves, not even knowing about Oberon's decision, went along with the Alpha female's orders.

"At midnight the next night, Oberon let out a howl to call the troops back, but because of Quail's orders, the troops did the opposite, and as one they pressed forward." Sarora sighed and became silent once more.

"Wait," Travis broke the lapse of calm, "I don't see how this works. How had Quail betrayed them? I mean, she was only looking out for Oberon, doing what she thought was best."

"That was the first thought that came to mind when they all found out what she had done," Sarora agreed, shifting her weight to her other side. "At midnight, the number of rebel wolves of the light was greater than ten thousand. By the time Oberon had received word of Quail's doing, there were only four thousand left.

"This was not just because Quail had told the wolves a different command, this was not only done for the love of Oberon. No, Quail had betrayed them all, for she had fallen in love with the commander of the dark wolves, Radbound.

"As she mockingly bowed to Oberon, Quail confessed with a smile that she had, indeed, betrayed them. With evil in her stare, Quail whispered into Oberon's ear, and the large wolf's muscular form seemed to crumple under reality. The second-in-command at that time—Timur's father—called to the guards, who immediately took Quail out of Oberon's sight and executed her for her infidelity." Sarora sighed again as she looked to Travis. "Broken-hearted, Oberon decreed a new law. That was the last time an Alpha female ruled, until now."

Travis looked away from Sarora's gaze. Never once had he felt the sting of betrayal, and for Oberon to have felt it from the one he loved most... Travis would have thought that it had destroyed every bit of love in him. But somehow, the strong wolf must have found a way to move on and become the greatest leader the wolves had ever known. Travis's heart began to pick up pace as he remembered the prophecy.

"When your days grow dark, and your enemies become your allies, you will learn that betrayal is unavoidable, when chilling ice cools hearts around you," Travis quoted the verse under his breath.

"What was that?" Sarora asked. Travis had never told Zack or Sarora the exact words of the prophecy. More or less, he had lied that he couldn't remember much about the prophecy.

"Nothing, just nothing..." Travis replied to Sarora, but his mind was still inundated with the foreboding prophecy. Who were the enemies becoming his allies? Who was the chilling ice that was cooling the hearts around him? Most importantly, who was going to play the part of betrayer?

QUARREL

Timur walked into the group's camp, his eyes full of weariness. He had been hunting for two days straight before returning to the main camp. Now not only did he have to work hard to show energy and effort, but he also had to be alert at all times. This became more and more difficult with each passing day as he was faced with more and more stress as he fought for control of the pack. He had yet to see a day where no one objected to his orders.

Travis looked up from where he sat by the dying light of the fire. He had only just noticed the presence of the wolf, as did his friends. Sarora lifted her head to see who had come. Seeing that it was none other than Timur, she quickly leapt to her feet, scrambling as she balanced herself.

"Greetings, Timur," Sarora said as she dipped her head in welcome. On the other side of the camp, Zack turned around from where he was tying Pran up to a tree. His electric blue eyes shone with genuine surprise, as he had not expected the alpha to visit them that day.

Seeing that he was the only one left sitting, Travis quickly spun on his seat and stood without using his hands. With a smile, he spoke to Timur as a friend and as a leader, "Hello, Alpha Timur."

"Greetings, Sarora," Timur returned, nodding to Sarora. Then looking at Travis, he smiled back at him and acknowledged their friendship. "Hello, Travis." Spotting Zack at the back of the group, Timur said, "Zachary," addressing him in a very formal manner. Travis remembered that the two had not been thoroughly introduced, and that he and Sarora had been the only ones to visit the wolf pack nearly five months ago.

Forcing back a yawn, Timur spoke as the group came closer and stood by the wolf. "Please, sit. I wish that I could have arranged seating for you, but at the current time, I wish to keep our meetings private."

Zack nodded to Timur as he sat down. "Don't worry about it, we understand." He shot a glance at both of his friends, who nodded in agreement.

"I thank you all for being so grateful for the little that I can do for you." Timur gave a faint smile. "But I do hope for better times in the future in which these kinds of actions will not be necessary."

"As we all do," Zack said, which made Travis's blood warm to an uncomfortable temperature. He wasn't entirely sure of his feelings, but Travis began to learn of a new trigger—Zack's all-too-willingness to speak for him.

Travis again spoke to Timur as a friend. "Are you sure that there is nothing that we can do to help?" Out of the corner of his eyes Travis thought that he saw Zack shoot an irritated glare at him, but no matter what the boy may do, Travis wasn't going to let it faze him.

Timur sighed and gazed at the woodland floor. "I wish, but I fear that there is nothing that you can do to help me. The only thing still keeping me in leadership is that there are more for me than against me, but that number varies each day. Only time will tell if I will lead as long as Oberon was able to." Timur looked up at Travis, struggling to hide the nervous emotion in his eyes.

Travis pained for the wolf, but he had no idea how to show him any comfort. He thought of reaching out and patting Timur on the shoulder, but he only figured that this would offend Timur, so he kept his hands to himself.

"If there is one thing we can do," Sarora spoke and all eyes turned on her, "we can help you recruit those that you need. Bratislav told us of your plan to gain the help of the other animals, and I would gladly take responsibility of the project if need be."

"Well," Timur's eyes shone with surprise and gratitude, "I had never expected this, I assure you. If the time comes, then, yes, I will gladly give you this responsibility."

"You mean 'when' the time comes," Travis corrected. "You have to believe in hope for it to exist, Timur. If there is hope, there is always a chance."

"You know what, Travis?" Timur smiled with a new determination as he looked at the dark-haired boy. "You're right. I should learn to be less pessimistic and have faith that one day things may be different." Breaking out into laughter that no one had ever seen on the wolf before, Timur proclaimed, "You know you are a fool when it takes a boy to knock common sense into you."

Along with him, Zack and Sarora also laughed. Travis couldn't help but chuckle to himself as he replied, "Not as embarrassing as when you think you're smart and you're really not." The laughter suddenly subdued and all eyes went to Travis.

"Don't you guys get it?" Travis grinned. "I'm bagging on myself."

"Travis," Sarora started off kindly, "you don't even have to try to bag yourself, it happens naturally on its own." The group laughed again and Travis gave Sarora a friendly glare.

Zack tossed and turned on the ground, unaware that the danger at hand was merely a nightmare. His body was sweating from head to toe, and his hair was damp. As he rolled from side to side, he tried to push back the awful pictures and escape the dark voices in his head...

"Run, run!" a woman's voice screamed in his mind.

"But I can't leave without you!" The figure next to her had desperation written in his eyes.

The two were standing in a dark room, and soldiers were banging at the door. The man and the woman were frantically searching their minds for an escape.

"Yes! You will, and you must!" The woman grabbed a hold of her husband and pushed him towards the window. "Take our child with you!"

"But what about—"

"There is no chance for us two." The woman's eyes were welling up with tears. "The lord can see into our minds—there is no escaping his powers."

"No! No, it can't be true!" The man shook his head, trying desperately to remove the dark truth.

"It is true!" The woman put her hands on her husband's shoulders. "But you and the youngest are free of this man's curse. Quickly! You both must flee. Go far away from this place! Leave this land behind! It is the only way to save our second-born child! Now go!"

Realizing that this was the only way to save the baby boy, the man nodded bitterly, kissed his wife for the last time, and cradled the sleepy child in his arms as he leapt from the window.

As he ran into the inky darkness, the quiet, dangerous night was filled with a blood-curdling scream. Tears ran down the man's cheeks as he forced back the thought of the woman now lying dead on the bedroom floor. Through his sadness he kept running, afraid for his future—his child's future. What would happen to the child if he were unable to care for it?

Zack's mind whirled with agony and confusion. He had had bits of this dream before and thought of it only as a silly dream that his fears aroused to scare him. But now, the image began to alarm him—what if this was real? What if this was a picture of things to come?

"Zack!" Sarora screeched into her friend's ear, frantically trying to wake him. "Zack, wake up!"

Finally, Zack's eyes snapped open and he sat up. His heart thudded and adrenaline pumped through his veins. His blue eyes were wild with fear, and he gasped for breath as Sarora looked worriedly at him.

"Zack, what's the matter?" the gryphon asked, her eyes full of anxiety. In the moonlight, her brown feathers were hinted with silver and her gold eyes shone like sterling.

Feeling the nervous numbness begin to leave his lips, Zack shook his head and looked away from Sarora. "Nothing, it was only a nightmare." He began to settle back down along with his heart rate. "Go back to bed, there's nothing to worry about."

Sarora sighed, her own pounding heart slowing back down. "You gave me a real fright," she told Zack. "I'm surprised that you didn't wake Travis, what with your voice and all."

"My voice?" Zack looked at Sarora quizzically. "What do you mean? What was I saying?"

Sarora shook her head. "I have no idea. It was like some strange foreign language. It sounded nothing like Firsoman and you repeated the same thing many times. Do you have any idea what you were saying?"

Zack shook his head. "Sorry, I have no clue."

"Maybe if you told me what happened in your dream," Sarora thought out loud, "then maybe we can put the puzzle pieces together."

Zack shook his head again. "Sorry, but I can't remember anything," he lied. He didn't want to alarm Sarora, especially not at this late hour in which sleep was critical.

"Hm..." Sarora looked down at her front feet. "Well, you think it over, and if you remember anything, be sure to let me know. If there is anyone who can solve this, it would be myself or one of the wolves."

"Don't worry about it." Zack dismissed Sarora's thought with a wave of his hand. "I'm sure it was only a dream."

"A dream in which you knew another language?" Sarora challenged him.

"It was probably just gibberish." The corner of Zack's mouth curved.

"Right..." Sarora narrowed her eyes at him. "The second that gibberish makes you scream and sweat like a banshee, let me know, because then we'll know that something really is wrong with you."

Zack watched Sarora cautiously because her back hairs began to stand on end and her feathers were ruffled. She obviously knew that he was hiding something, but she hoped that he would tell her openly rather than have to drag it out of him. However, Zack wasn't going to do what Sarora wanted—he was thinking for himself at the moment. Both stared into each other's eyes, holding onto every bit of their bullheadedness. Sarora's hackles began to rise higher with each passing moment, and Zack saw how hard she was fighting back the will to retaliate. Seeing her under so much strain and pressure pushed Zack to his limits, and some of his strength broke.

"Fine," Zack snapped. "I admit it—I know more than I am giving away, but I'm not ready to tell you. Are you happy now?"

Zack flinched when he saw the expression of hurt on Sarora's face. Her voice was full of painful emotions. "I had never suspected you of hiding anything from me, Zack. But now that I know how you really feel, maybe it is best if you don't tell me anything at all, because I don't want to help someone who won't help himself." Without another word, Sarora turned and leapt into the air, spreading her massive wings and soaring off into the starlit night.

"Sarora, wait!" Zack called out to her, but Sarora was already too far away to hear him even if she had wanted to. Fists clenching in anger, Zack looked for a punching bag that he could take out his aggression on. Finding only a branch by the fire pit, Zack picked it up, held it out in front of him, and snapped it in two with one quick jab of his knee. The branch let out a sound that sounded like a quick lightning crack, loud enough that Zack was surprised to see that Travis was still asleep. Biting his lip in anger, Zack knelt on the ground, his fists clenched once more. He and Sarora never quarreled—ever. And never in their lives had they fought like this, but Zack knew that if this confrontation would break their friendship, it would be too soon.

Looking up to the crystal-clear night, Zack's eyes reflected the pins of light that were scattered across the sky. Seeing a star streak across the sky seemed to lift Zack's spirit. If something like that could shine so brightly on its own, well, maybe he could too.

Picking his heart up off the ground, Zack whispered a wish that no one would have expected him to utter. "Whoever is up there, if you can hear me, make me strong on my own; and when my friends need help, bring me to help them, but to also make the right decisions in doing so. If one must go, let it be none from the prophecy."

JURISDICTION

"Hey, you." A wolf approached Zack as he entered the camp. "Yeah, you," he said gruffly. "Where's the big feathered one? The giant hybrid?"

It was the next morning, and the summer sun shone brightly through the trees. Beneath Zack's feet, the ground was dusty and trodden. Though the day looked good from a passerby's view, Zack and Travis were playing a desperate hide-and-seek game with Sarora. Since the gryphon had left late that night, they had not seen their friend at all.

Trying to remain as kind as possible, Zack smiled at the wolf, not giving direct eye contact. "I was going to ask you the same, kind wolf. Why? Is someone looking for us?"

"Looking for you!" The wolf's accent sounded strange to Zack. "Oye, that's a good one. Why would anyone want to look for the lot of you outcasts?"

"Well, if you have no need of me," Zack forced back an inappropriate retort, "I'll be on my way. Would you be so kind as to tell me where Bratislav is?"

"Tell you where the captain is?" The wolf burst into laughter again. "You better stop pulling my tail. I only wanted to know why none of us have seen neither beak nor tail of that scrawny thing you call a gryphon. We want to be sure when to clean up camp, 'cause she likes to make quite an entrance."

"And what would you mean by that?" Zack asked, walking closer to the bulky old wolf. His fur was a dark gray and his eyes a livid green.

The wolf seemed less confident as Zack drew closer. "Well, she flew by last night and caused quite a racket, she did. Scared one of the pups so bad he nearly wet his den."

"Scared him how?" Zack asked again, coming even closer to the wolf. The boy's fears were growing for the sake of his friend.

"Well, to start," the wolf began confidently, but his voice was not as strong as before, "you must have been deaf 'cause when she flew o'er us, her awful screech shook us all. Then, she landed in camp with a loud THUD an' stomped her talons and paws good and hard on the ground. We got super scared when the she-gryph' ran 'round camp and grabbed all of our weapons."

"What?!" Zack exclaimed, finding it hard to believe a word of what the wolf was saying. "I don't believe you. Steal all of your weapons? Not even Sarora has the strength to do all that."

The dark wolf chuckled, walked past Zack, and pointed with his paw at the ground. "If that's not her tracks, whose are they? It sure ain't any of ours."

His heart thudding slowly with dread, Zack walked over to where the wolf stood. Bending his knees, he carefully began to examine the tracks. But no matter how he looked at them, he brought himself to a fact that he would have never thought to be true—inevitably, the tracks mirrored those of Sarora's.

The wolf began again, "If I was you, I wouldn't be sticking 'round camp any longer."

Zack looked at the dark-colored wolf. "Really? Why's that?" He was becoming more distant with each second that led him to believe that his friend had caused this problem.

"Well why do 'ya think?" The wolf rolled his eyes at Zack. "Timur has been searchin' for the lot of you this very morning, he has. He told any wolf to bring you to him for a prosecution.

'Course, no one from the council is likely to side wit' you after what happened."

"The wolves are looking for us?"

"In't that what I jus' said?" The wolf shook his head. "You better be goin' else the troops find you and your friends."

Suddenly, Zack heard a howl sound—the pure melody sung sweetly in his ears. However, this song was not meant to bring Zack peace. Zack turned just in time to see a familiar face speaking to him.

"Um, Zack, we have a problem." Travis's eyes darted nervously as he watched the group of wolves that had captured him back in the forest. Zack could only watch as the wolves pushed Travis on, forcing him along with constant growling and nips at his heels.

"So," the lead wolf barked to Zack, "you dare come back to the crime scene yourself." Glaring at the tall boy through narrowed eyes, the wolf cried out in a howl, "But justice shall be served!"

Around him, the other wolves echoed, "Justice will be served!" As if being moved by one mind, the wolves opened a space in their ranks and forced Zack in. Though the boy was nervous about the wolves' treatment, he was confident in Timur to back them up.

Travis and Zack exchanged several nervous glances as the search pack led them closer to Timur's den. They dared not speak in fear that the wolves may hear them. The sunny day had suddenly brought a foreboding omen—one that was hard to escape.

The band of wolves stopped at the entrance to Timur's cave den. With a grunt and then a howl, the lead wolf called, "Alpha! We have found the traitors!"

Well, Zack thought to himself optimistically, *at least he is for Timur.*

Zack strained his eyes to focus on the opening to the cave. His heart hammering, Zack watched as Timur stepped out, his fur glistening in the morning sun, with Eira at his side. To Zack, her snow-white fur shone like a beacon of light in the dim forest.

Both boys and the wolves watched as the pair approached, their eyes not showing any obvious emotions.

"Timur, what's going on—"

Timur's glare was enough to shut Travis up. With a short bark, Timur greeted the captain and then said, "Thank you for bringing them to me. Lead them into my den and the council and I will decide what to do with them." The wolf nodded to his leader and obediently led the boys in with the help of his companions.

As Zack's eyes adjusted to the lack of light, he saw nothing spectacular about the alpha's den. It merely seemed to be a stone-hard cave and nothing more, though there was a pile of moss that lay at the back. Zack supposed that this was Timur's bed.

Once the prisoners were led inside, the patrol of wolves departed, only to be replaced by another group of regal-looking elders. There were six of them, and none looked thrilled at the guests with whom they were going to have to deal with. Each of them had spent time in the army, and having been lucky to survive many battles, they were serving as the decision-makers of the pack. Zack was not surprised to see that there was only one female in the group, for males were mainly dominant in the wolves' pecking order. Not to say that females couldn't hold authority—many of the past leaders of the pack had been females, and many of them well before Oberon.

The group of wolves eyed the two boys suspiciously as they sat in an oval formation inside the den. Travis and Zack sat near the back of the den, their backs facing the cold den wall. Still they did not speak to each other, but they really had no need to, for they both could look into each other's eyes and see their own worry reflected in them.

Timur sat at the front of the ovular formation, his expression still emotionless, as if it pained him to have any feelings for the supposed criminals. His head high, the alpha began to speak.

"Great Wolf Council," his voice echoed slightly against the rocky walls, "you all have been told of the crime that took place last night, and many of you have already come to a decision. But," Timur looked at each wolf in turn, "I ask you that you do not cast your votes before we can review all details of the crime."

"Alpha Timur," a cream-colored male began. His face showed his age, though his muscles were still finely toned and his eyes were bright. "I wish to relay some of the evidence from the crime scene."

Timur nodded his head once to the wolf. "Very well, Havilah, you may begin."

Clearing his throat, the wolf stood and began his speech. "Last night, at quarter after moon high, we all experienced the awful sounds that came from the center of our camp. By the time we had all conquered our own fear and looked to the place of the noise, the creature took to the skies and we noticed our supply of weapons was gone. Looking to the ground, we spotted large tracks of both a bird and a large cat-like animal. Immediately, we assumed that our guest, Sarora, was the culprit of this crime.

"Our fears and suspicions only grew as we scented and spotted blood on the ground around the tracks. It was not just the blood of our own, but it was also the blood of the supposed culprit. Although, strangely enough, no wolf has been reported missing, hurt, or has admitted to fighting with the creature in question.

"Therefore, I believe that there is lacking evidence to prove that the crime was committed by our guest," Havilah finished, dipping his head to Timur.

"Lack of evidence!" a wolf in the council howled out in objection. He was a large silver male with daring yellow eyes. "Brethren, could you not see the missing items? Could you not smell the scent of the foul creature?"

Timur spoke out, his voice strong. "Peace, Achan, yes, there is reason to still believe that Sarora is the perpetrator, but is there still doubt among the council aside from Havilah's?"

The lone she-wolf stepped forward. Though still beautiful in her old age, one eye was clouded. She had not been able to see clearly out of the misty orb for many years, and with each passing day she began to doubt that the eye would see anything at all in a short while. Her fur was a light roan color, and down her back ran black hairs mixed with white.

"I share the same doubts as Havilah, Alpha Timur." The she-wolf's voice cracked a little as she explained gently, "I believe that since the perpetrator of the crime was not seen, we still may lack the evidence to bring out a punishment sentence of any kind. There is also the questioning of why our guards were not on top of this, because certainly it is their job to sound the alarm at any threat."

"Well-reasoned, Tirzah," Timur commended, nodding to the she-wolf. Looking to the rest of the group, he asked them, "Are there any more who wish to speak before the vote?"

"I would, Alpha Timur." An elderly gray wolf stepped forward. His muzzle was covered with white hairs, and his once-bright eyes had seemed to sullen over time. "Though I have been in favor of the help that the Acers have brought to Firmara, I must admit where my opinion stands. Unfortunately for the she-gryphon, I believe that she is the one to blame for this crime. It only seems reasonable that she was the one to steal the weapons, seeing as both bird and cat tracks were found in the sand."

"I agree with Eran," another wolf spoke up. "The evidence is just too much. Is it not obvious that the she-gryphon committed the crime?"

The whole council was silent and Zack and Travis exchanged nervous glances. What would happen to them if Sarora was found guilty?

Finally, Timur raised his head and addressed them, "If that is all there is to say, let us take a vote. Those who say guilty, step forward." Zack watched nervously as half the council stepped forward—Eran, Achan, and the last wolf to speak—although Havilah, Tirzah, and the wolf that did not speak stayed back.

"Then we are divided," Timur sighed as the wolves returned to their places.

"You know what must happen, then," Havilah said to his leader. "Alpha Timur, what is your vote?" The room fell to a still hush as all eyes turned on the young leader. Timur's eyes fell on each of the council members before gazing back at Zack and Travis. Between Travis and Timur, there seemed to be an unspoken conversation in which Zack could only guess what their eyes were telling each other. Sighing once more, Timur looked at the council and took a step back.

"For the time being, I declare Sarora not guilty. The vote is four to three, not guilty. For now, we shall look for the gryphon, and when we find her and question her, we will be able to come to a full conclusion. Council dismissed." Timur ended with his head held high as if he was daring the council to oppose his authority. But none of them said anything. The three for "guilty" shot him angry glances before they padded out while the rest of the council nodded to him in respect before going on their ways.

Zack felt his whole body sigh with relief. They had dodged a bullet... for now. But when they found Sarora, he knew that they would be in much more trouble than they were bargaining for if the wolves found her guilty.

Timur watched the group of wolves leave as he stood at the entrance to the den. The wolf's demeanor quickly changed from that of a strong leader to a lone wolf. Seeing his stress, Eira padded over to him and licked him on the cheek, comforting him with her touch. The tip of Timur's tail twitched in an effort to wag, but it was as if he couldn't summon enough energy for happiness. Nodding once to the white wolf, Timur turned to face Zack and Travis. Behind him, Eira's golden eyes were filled with worry, but she remained silent.

"Thank you, Timur," Travis said ardently, trying to express his gratitude toward the alpha. "Without you, I don't think that the council—"

"Your thanks is unneeded, thank you, Travis," Timur cut in,

his voice emotionless toward the boy. Taken aback, Travis let the grateful look on his face drain away. To some extent, Zack thought that Travis should have kept his mouth shut and let Timur speak first—however, he was also ticked off that the alpha wouldn't show any sympathy for the ones who were blameless. Zack felt his pit for the wolf slowly begin to disappear.

The room was filled with an uneasy silence as the air grew stale. There was an edge to everyone's consciousness and Zack found it hard to bottle up his feelings. Biting his lip, the boy waited for Timur to speak.

"I'm sorry for this unhappy meeting," Timur's voice showed little more emotion than it had before, "but it was necessary for the council to talk of this trouble, although I wish that the council wasn't split in half."

"Well," Travis again tried to remove the uneasiness from the air, "at least we can be thankful that Sarora isn't going to be prosecuted."

A small growl came from the back of Timur's throat. "You have no idea what I have just done, do you?" The wolf's voice was filled with irritation. "You have yet to feel what it is like to have this terrible weight on your shoulders! You..."

"Timur," Eira soothed, stepping forward and licking Timur's cheek again, her voice gentler than the calmest wind. After whispering a few words to her mate, she turned her bright eyes on the two boys. "I think what Timur is trying to say is that by making the decision he just did, not only did he save you for the time being, but he may have just crucified his leadership."

"What do you mean?" Zack asked, although he already knew the answer.

"I mean that because he defended Sarora, if she is later found guilty," the she-wolf's eyes glowed with foreshadowed thought, "the wolves may no longer see my mate as the leader that they want."

THE GLITTERY-FURRED
JAGUAR

Travis's heart hung like a hound dog's ears as he sat in the small camp. The night sky was clear, just like it had been two nights ago when Sarora had disappeared. The stars glowed brightly, as if unaware of what Travis's heart felt.

For the past two days, he and Zack had searched nearly every inch of the forest, that is, the inches of forest inside the wolf pack's territory. Because the verdict of the case wasn't final, the two friends were ordered to stay inside the pack's boundaries. If they left, they faced the verdict of "guilty." And "guilty" was not something that the wolves' smiled upon, for anyone who was claimed a traitor—wolf or not—was to be executed on the spot. *Just like Quail,* Travis thought darkly to himself as he sat staring at the starlit sky.

Zack was fidgeting next to a tree, deep in an uneasy sleep. Twice, Travis had woken him to help calm his friend's nerves. But both times, Zack had ignored what his obvious feelings were and told Travis to worry about himself. It seemed that as each day passed, Zack tried to become even more independent of his friends.

Closing his eyes and sighing, Travis whispered to himself, "If only we could find Sarora, then maybe things would start to brighten up..."

A soft wind blew Travis's hair and it seemed to calm his worries. Opening his eyes, Travis looked for the invisible winds that had brought him comfort. The wind came a second time and rustled a pile of leaves next to him. He gazed on as the light leaves floated gracefully into the air. Smiling at a blissful little leaf, Travis watched as it floated into the woods.

A seemingly normal night was about to change.

Travis watched and his nerves grew as the leaf returned to him and hung in the air. Though the winds were still there, it was certainly most unnatural and unnerving that the inanimate object would come back to him.

With a quick glance at Zack, Travis stood. Part of him wished to wake his friend, but what good would it do if Zack was awake? Figuring that it was best not to wake the older boy, Travis returned his attention to the leaf that still hung in midair.

A new curiosity drove Travis on and he reached out his hand and put it underneath the leaf. To his surprise, the leaf floated higher above his hand, avoiding his contact. The leaf hovered over Travis's right hand until he reached for it with his left. As if it saw Travis's oncoming hand, the leaf floated away and upward. When Travis brought his arms back down to his sides, the leaf returned and hung a few inches in front of his face.

Taking a step toward the leaf, Travis watched as it glided a few feet farther away from him. His curiosity grew as Travis took another step forward and the leaf again did the same.

An unusual thought crossed Travis's mind and he shared it with the leaf. "Do you want me to follow you?"

The leaf fell a little before being picked up by the wind. Travis thought that in a weird way, the leaf seemed to be nodding to him. Taking a deep breath and shaking his head, Travis made up his mind. "Fine. Lead the way," he whispered.

Travis followed the little leaf through the obstacle course of the woods. Ducking under the tree branches, he discovered that the bushes liked to cut at his legs with their thorns. Travis found it hard to watch the leaf as it seemingly camouflaged itself among the trees. Tripping over unearthed tree roots as he hurried along, Travis fought to keep the leaf in sight.

After a tedious few minutes, the leaf led Travis into a clearing where the bright moon shone on the both of them. Off to the side of the clearing sat a crystal clear pond, which gleefully reflected the moon's cold light. When the leaf hung motionlessly in the air once more, Travis bent over his knees and gasped for breath. He wasn't sure what was tiring him more—the fact that it was late at night, or the realization that he had just followed a leaf for almost a mile in the woods.

As he panted, Travis lifted his head to see that the little leaf had disappeared. His head filling with disbelief, Travis spun around himself, desperately looking for any sign of the tiny leaf. "You have got to be kidding me," Travis groaned as he began to wonder why he had followed the leaf with such hope in the first place. "Good job, Travis," the boy shook his head at himself, "not only did you just win the stupidity award for thinking that a leaf was trying to communicate with you, but now you are lost in an unfamiliar place. How could things get any worse?"

Travis's breath caught in his throat when the wind blew again and he noticed movement at the other side of the clearing. A figure was slipping between the trees with fluid, graceful movements. In the moonlight, two eerie, golden eyes glared back at Travis through the dark forest. With a silent gulp, Travis took a few steps back, not sure whether to be afraid or intrigued by whatever was watching him.

Suddenly the figure leapt from the shadowy veil. Its body was a golden color, overlaid by many dark spots. Its round ears perked forward as it landed in the clearing. Travis watched as it completed its form by carefully balancing itself using its wide-based tail. Its large claws went in and out of its wide paws, and Travis watched nervously as the large animal yawned, its powerful jaws displaying some of the largest canines that Travis had ever seen. Although the creature's shoulders didn't reach Travis's waist in height, he was still deathly afraid of the damage that the animal could cause.

The jaguar's unusual golden eyes blinked back at him as it seemingly stared into Travis's soul. His heart, that had stopped only moments before, was now leaping inside his throat. Never once in his training had he been taught how to fight a jaguar.

"This world never ceases to surprise me," Travis mumbled as he mulled his future actions over in his head. He could stand there and become cat food, or he could run and see how far his attempt would take him. *Die now, or die later... not very optimistic choices.*

Taking slow steps backward, Travis kept his focus on the large cat standing in front of him. It watched him with its bright eyes while the tip of its tail twitched, as if its prey amused it. After a few steps, Travis took a quick glance behind himself. He was now on the edge of the clearing, only a couple feet from the dark forest. His heart flying, Travis spun on his heels and turned away from the jaguar that watched him closely. However, before Travis was able to reach the woods, a figure leapt in front of him and blocked his path, its coat sparkling as it appeared in front of him. In some amazing way, the jaguar had been able to pass Travis without him noticing and was now blocking what had seemed to be his only chance at survival. Travis skidded to a quick stop. His heart seemed to have left his throat. He felt lightheaded and dizzy as he watched the jaguar's claws slice in and out of its massive paws. Though stocky, this cat was not to be underestimated. Not wanting to see his end come, Travis shielded his face with his arms and tightly shut his eyes. There he stood, motionless.

A second passed by...

More seconds...

Wondering why his death had not yet come, Travis lowered his arms in time to see the large cat pawing the ground as it gave a couple loud 'cher-uffs'. Using large sweeping motions, the jaguar used its paws to make patterns in the dirt in front of it.

Wait, not patterns, Travis thought, *a word.*

Travis watched in disbelief as the spotted cat stepped back and waited for a response as Travis read the message aloud:

"Peace."

Travis cautiously looked back up at the large cat, who was staring back at him. Though he found it hard to believe, Travis thought that the eyes, which had once frightened him, now shone with cordial friendship. Travis watched as the cat stepped back once more and wrote in the dirt a second time. When he had finished, Travis read:

"You called?"

Travis looked at the jaguar's glowing eyes as he replied, "Not specifically."

"But I am here."

Travis felt awkward speaking to the large carnivore. He chose his words carefully. "Then, do you have an answer for me? Do you know where my friend is?"

The jaguar's throat rumbled once and he dipped his head. Travis's heart started to fumble again when he thought that the cat was going to leap at him. However, the jaguar gracefully strutted over to the single pond that sat to the side of the clearing. Anxiously, Travis followed behind the cat.

At the pool, the jaguar gestured for him to sit down with a flick of his tail, kind of like what Sarora would do. Travis sat close to the edge of the pool and looked up at the jaguar, who stood next to him. Blinking his eyes once, the jaguar wrote in the dirt,

"Look into the waters."

With hesitation, Travis turned his head and gazed into the still water. As he watched, the jaguar reached out with one of its large front paws and placed it on top of the glassy surface, breaking the water with glitters of gold. All the forest seemed to still as small gold ripples formed around the jaguar's paw.

Breathing in, the jaguar pulled back its paw. Travis watched in amazement as he began to see light coming from the inside of the pond. Leaning in closer, Travis watched anxiously as a picture began to form...

The first things that Travis could make out were the trees looming over the picture. They were large oaks and birches, though they were not as massive as the ones in the area where Travis now sat. Not fifty yards from the line of trees, water lapped at the surface of a sandy shore. The foamy waves beat in a rhythmic pattern. Travis felt as if he could hear the calming sound of the ocean's shore, but this time he was sure that the sounds were in his head. Between the woods and the lapping waves sat three tents and a wagon. Travis squinted to make out a large form that was sleeping beside the wagon.

"Sarora," Travis breathed, happy to see his friend still alive. He watched as a couple of human forms walked past the sleeping gryphon. He could see that they were deep in conversation, but obviously, he could neither hear them nor could he read their lips. As the men turned to leave, Travis saw Sarora stir and was greatly unnerved when he spotted a large line that seemed to tie Sarora to the wagon.

"No," Travis breathed again, this time not with relief. "This can't be. Sarora would never let Trazon's men take her alive." Even as he spoke, the image began to fade away. With longing, Travis reached his hand out to feel the image in front of him but was taken aback when he touched the water's surface. The water broken, the image quickly disappeared through the fading golden ripples.

Eyes wide in shock, Travis turned to his right, looking for the jaguar. He was disappointed when he saw that the cat had left, though not without a farewell. In the dirt next to him, Travis read, "Seek and you will find."

Travis stood and looked all around him for any sign of the large cat. Carefully, he studied the ground for the large cat's tracks and was baffled when he could not find them anywhere. Though he wished to stay and look for the jaguar, Travis turned and ran, eager to tell Zack what had happened.

Wounds Of The Past

"Are you sure?" Zack's mouth was dry after hanging agape for so long. Travis had just recounted the tale of the meeting with the jaguar and the boys were debating the next steps to their plan.

"I'm positive," Travis replied, excitement in his voice. "There's no doubt that it was her."

Zack looked away from Travis. The morning sun crept through the tree line. Travis sat on the ground, his legs sprawled out. He had been gone for nearly three hours by the time Zack woke. Though mad at Travis for leaving camp, Zack was now trying to work through a bunch of confused emotions in his head. The fight with Sarora still left an awful bile in his stomach, but he was closer to her than to anyone else. He knew that he must find his friend, not just for his own need, but also for the fate of others around him.

"Recount again exactly what the vision looked like," Zack said, letting out a sigh as he stared into space.

Once more, Travis described the vision in the pool. This time, Zack listened to every detail, for each piece of information could lead them in one direction or another. When Travis had finished, only one area of Firmara stuck in Zack's mind.

WOUNDS OF THE PAST

"Capricious," Zack breathed, imagining the place in his mind.

"Capri-what?" Travis asked.

"The Capricious Ocean," Zack explained. "It's to our south. Sarora's probably on a beach in the bay of the Capricious Ocean." Travis still looked confused, so Zack bent over and drew a map of Firmara in the dirt.

"See this place here?" Zack pointed to a spot on the map. "That's where we are. We are to the north-east of the portal and to the north of the Capricious Ocean." Zack moved his finger across the map and pointed to the south where the ocean was. "Sarora is probably somewhere not too far from where we're at, because it doesn't seem likely that she would have gone as far south as Pelagius, which is the largest city on Firmara's west coast. So she's probably a three day journey or less from here."

"Unless they take her north to Trazon." Travis mumbled pessimistically.

"Well, then it'll mean that she is closer," Zack retorted, trying to bring both optimism and common sense into the picture. "Come on, Travis. What do you think the probability of Sarora getting caught by Trazon's men is?"

Travis's next comment held a sugar coated darkness. "Pretty high."

"But..." Zack stopped and then thought for a moment. "Well, I guess you're right, for once. But that doesn't mean that it's Trazon's men who have her. Maybe they are just innocent civilians who thought that a gryphon would make a good pet."

"Zack," Travis let out the faintest smile, "you and I both know Sarora, and so in what world would someone want her for a pet?"

"Huh, good point," Zack admitted with a sigh. He snapped his fingers after a moment of thinking. "What if it isn't people?"

Travis rolled his eyes at Zack. "Now, come on, and I thought I was the bonehead. If not humans, what other creatures with two arms, two legs, hair on their heads, and front-facing eyes are there that speak?"

"Well, none, but," Zack continued, "something could have taken on the shape of a human."

"Such as?" Travis asked as he stood up and absentmindedly plucked bark off the nearest tree.

"Such as, well," Zack had wanted to keep the name of this creature away from Travis for as long as possible, but he thought it best to tell him now, "a lucifera."

"A what?"

"A lucifera," Zack breathed. "When in human form, they look just like any other person, but they are creatures with dark magic."

Travis stopped peeling bark off the tree. "Dark magic?" he asked, looking over to Zack.

Zack nodded. "Yes, but they're so ancient that they might as well be mythical beings." Clearing his throat and hoping that he had dodged a bullet, Zack changed the conversation back to Sarora. "Well, standing around gossiping is not helping Sarora at all. Let's get the wolves' permission and be on our way."

"What about Pran?" Travis thrust his thumb in the direction of the young dog, who was tied to a tree and sleeping happily.

Zack thought for a second before replying, "Well, most likely he'll follow us, but it wouldn't hurt to tell him to go home. Whether he'll listen or not is out of my hands." Travis nodded in agreement and the boys walked out of their clearing to the pack's camp.

They were lucky enough not to encounter any of the wolves before they reached the bracken entrance, but, as usual, two large, stone-faced guards were posted. Cautiously, Travis and Zack approached the wolves.

Nodding once to Travis, Zack looked to the wolves and stated, "We wish to seek permission to leave."

While one wolf held a constant, hard gaze, his friend's eyes flickered with curiosity. "Whom are you seeking this permission from?" the latter wolf asked. He was a young male.

"From whoever is in charge of letting us go on our way," Zack replied, trying to keep his tone even. Though he was nervous of the wolves' response, he knew that he must keep his composure.

The young male wolf glanced at his partner, who shook his head. Turning back to look at Zack, the young wolf spoke. "I'm sorry, but you are not permitted to come in. There is, uh, trouble being discussed right now. Is there any other way that we may be of help?"

Zack bit back a nasty reply. "We must speak to someone about us leaving." Taking a quick glance at Travis, Zack continued, "We think we know where Sarora is."

The younger wolf's eyes widened in wonder but the veteran guard was the one who spoke. "We can't answer for that. For all we know and are concerned, you are lying."

"But..."

"But nothing!" the wolf's voice boomed. It was so commanding that even his comrade took a step back. "Until the true leader of this pack is brought into position, you have no one's permission to enter our camp or to speak with the Council!"

Travis took a step forward. "Now, come on, listen to what we're trying to tell you..."

"Stand back, you two-legged freak!" the old wolf cried out with a snarl forming in his throat, "or I will be forced to kill you, prophecy or not!"

"Yutzu!" a loud bark sounded from nearby. The whole group looked to see Eira approaching, her beautiful white head held high and her yellow eyes reflecting the sun's light. "Why are you harassing our guests?"

"But Mistress Eira," Yutzu tried to explain himself, "they have no regard for our law! They were just about to enter without permission!"

"Oh, and so you were afraid that you wouldn't be able to stop them," Eira growled and looked into the eyes of the guard. "Yutzu, go and find another wolf—preferably one with an open mind who can listen to two sides of reasoning. You are relieved of your duty for today." Eira turned away from the wolf who stood there gaping at her orders.

"But Mistress...!"

"Those are my orders! Now go, before I call the guards on you!" Eira's voice sounded as demanding as ever.

With a dirty look at Travis and Zack, Yutzu bowed his head. "Your will is done, Eira." Zack noticed how he left out the title of respect for the white-wolf.

Once Yutzu was gone, Eira looked to Zack, then to Travis and sighed. "What am I to do with the two of you?"

"Would you like me to explain?" Zack asked civilly.

Eira shook her head. "No need, I heard the whole thing. I would have thought that a guard like Yutzu would have heard or even have smelled me, for his attitude toward the two of you is certainly different when I'm around." Sighing once more, the she-wolf looked up at both of the boys. "You are sure you know where your friend is?"

"As sure as we'll ever be," Travis put in before Zack could say anything. Zack felt like slapping his hand over his friend's mouth but refrained from doing so. He didn't want to make it look like they knew exactly where they were going. Especially not to Eira, who could be in serious trouble if she let them go and they never found their friend.

Blinking once, Eira spoke with the voice of a friend and a leader. "Then go. I give you my permission. Grab your horses and be swift. You must return within a week or we will all be forced to claim you as fugitives and you will be wanted, higher than the most murderous wolf of our kind."

"What if we find her and are unable to return?" Travis asked the white wolf.

"Then send a message—whenever you find her, say aloud 'the wolf's talons'." Eira looked at both boys. "We have a fortune teller in our pack who will be able to hear your words from miles away. But you asked for my permission to leave, and I gave it to you, so be off!"

Travis nodded and jogged away. Zack was just about to follow when Eira stopped him. "Zack."

Zack turned back to look at the she-wolf. "Yes, Alpha Eira?"

"Be on your guard and open to new ideas."

"What are you telling me this for?" Zack asked, eager to leave but trying not to be impolite.

After glancing back at the young wolf, Eira looked Zack straight in the eyes. "To tell you the truth, I wasn't just out wandering. I was looking for you. That was a message from our fortune teller. She said that I must relay the message to you."

"Are her words to be reflected on?" Zack asked, afraid of what the fortune teller may have meant.

Eira nodded. "Oh, yes, very much so. Her words are not to be sent away without thought. Be careful with what you do, Zack, for one of your future choices will be life changing, and not just for your life."

Zack nodded once, wished Eira good fortune, and left in a hurry.

Eira sighed as she watched Zack disappear from her sight, though she could still hear and picture him in her mind running through the woods for many minutes. Behind her, the young wolf walked closer. Though he had seemed to be deep in thought, he had heard every word of the conversation. Though he was young, he had a special connection with Eira, one that not even her mate, Timur, shared with her.

"Eira," the young wolf stood by her side, "why didn't you tell him about..."

Eira shook her head, silencing the wolf. "To them, their destiny will forever lie in the unknown. There will come a time when we can share some of the Sights, but it is not now. Now brother," Eira turned to the gray wolf, "why don't we go find something to hunt? It would do our Alpha a world of good. His stress is still eating away at him day and night."

Her brother nodded in reply. "Sometimes I wish your Sight or my Sense would be able to help him..."

"I wish I could help all of them..." The she-wolf stared off into the distance. "I would give all of my powers if I thought it would protect any one of them from danger..."

"Same here, same here..." The littermates stood together as silence enveloped them.

"Zack! Slow Mesha down! Seraphi can't keep up in woods like these!" Travis called from farther behind his friend.

Zack slowed his excited gelding down a little. "Sorry, Mesha can sense my nervousness." He watched as Travis slowly caught up to him.

"As does Seraphi, but you can see that he's too worn to do much galloping," Travis sighed when the boys and their horses were moving side-by-side. The boys had left the territory of the wolves no more than five minutes ago and they were now maintaining a steady speed heading south. Their plan was to reach the bay by tomorrow evening at the latest. From there, they would search the shore for the tents, the wagon, and the gryphon.

"I know, but we have to keep going." Zack spoke again. "Although we've left the wolf pack's territory and have been granted permission to leave by Eira, I don't think even that will be enough to convince the wolves to let us go."

Travis nodded once. "I agree, but can you take it easy? We don't want to lose the wisest one of us."

Zack smiled, thinking that Travis was jokingly worried for him. "Oh, don't worry, I'll be fine."

Travis let out an exaggerated sigh. "I wasn't talking about you —Seraphi's probably smarter than the two of us combined."

For a moment, Zack felt his face grow warm with embarrassment. But it was only for a moment, and then Zack was back to his usual sophisticated-leader status. "Well, um, yes, I guess he is."

Zack heard Travis chuckle next to him, "Don't worry, Zack, you're still pretty smart..."

"Well, thanks," Zack replied and smiled at his friend.

"...compared to me," Travis smiled back, finishing his statement. While Zack sat glaring at Travis, the boy urged Seraphi on and took the lead.

With a sigh, Zack took off his shirt. His skin seemed to soak in the air as the heat around it disappeared. Clucking to Mesha, he made the younger horse walk beside Seraphi. Taking his shirt, Zack wiped his forehead.

"What a warm day," Zack commented as the sweat drops that had formed on him seemed to slowly disappear.

Travis nodded and looked over at Zack. Suddenly, a look of great surprise crossed his face.

"What is it?" Zack asked, his concern growing.

Travis pointed to Zack's shoulder. "When did you get that?"

Zack looked down at his right shoulder. "Oh, that. I've had it for a while now," Zack said vaguely as memories rushed through him, but he kept them all to himself.

"That's a nasty-looking scar," Travis commented.

Zack nodded and studied the pink-red scar on his shoulder. It was a lot smaller than it had been a year ago. It was about half of a thumb's length wide, and it still was indented about half a centimeter.

"What happened to you?" Travis asked, looking from Zack to the scar and back to Zack again.

Zack shook his head as if Travis's question was of little importance. "Just a battle. I guess we all bit off more than we could chew."

"But that's not a sword cut, is it?" Travis asked, sounding as if he already knew the answer.

Zack shook his head again. "Nope—spear."

"A spear?" Travis exclaimed. "How in the world were you able to keep your arm?"

Zack shrugged his shoulders. "Just got lucky I guess. I was fighting, preparing to knock my next opponent to the ground, and then the spear was thrown at me. It came, went through my shoulder, and pinned me against a wall." It wasn't the whole story, but that was all of the details that he was going to share.

"Ouch," Travis said, wincing at the thought of a spear breaking his skin.

"Yeah, big time ouch." Zack could recall the burning pain that seemed to set his skin afire. Then he shook his head to push away the memory. "That's part of why I'm able to battle with both hands. After this shoulder got speared, I had to learn to use my left for fighting. Even now my right shoulder will ache and I'll have to switch things up. So even though it hurt, that part of the battle worked out for the better in the end."

Travis gave Zack an odd look. "I guess so, but you couldn't pay me to do what you've gone through just so I can use my left arm. My right works just fine."

Zack laughed. "Good."

The boys kept their horses moving through the night. Only once did they stop by a small stream to get a drink of water and rest. Mesha and Seraphi severely disagreed on the decision to skip lunch and dinner, and their anger grew with every hour they were ridden.

In the moonlight, Zack found it hard not to reflect on his argument with Sarora and his dream. His heart full of guilt, Zack hung his head and relied on Mesha to follow Seraphi. Letting go of the reins, Zack wiped away the grime that had been collecting at the corners of his eyes. Exhaling heavily, Zack fought back a tired yawn. He had to stay awake for a while longer. Eventually, the boys would begin to take watch, and Zack wanted to be the first to lead.

"Travis?" The wait had finally gotten to Zack. "When would you like a rest?"

The reply came a couple of seconds later, "I'll watch right now, if you'd like me to."

No, I would not like you to. Zack bit back the reply and instead told Travis, "Well, I was thinking that I would like to take the first watch."

Zack thought that he heard Travis sigh, but he wasn't sure. "Whatever you want, Zack."

Zack was almost taken aback by Travis's reply. Hardly ever would he receive an answer that made him question his actions. Now Zack really didn't know what to do—follow his own bull-headed brain, or give Travis a chance to take the wheel for once.

Sighing quietly to himself, Zack listened to his heart and conceded, "If you really want the first shift, I wouldn't mind getting some rest."

Travis turned back to look at Zack, his eyes showing just a shadow of his surprise. With a smile of understanding, Travis nodded. "Sure thing, Zack. Go ahead and get some rest." Then he turned back to look at the forest that went on forever ahead of him. With one last prayer that Travis would keep his direction and not get them completely lost, Zack leaned forward in the saddle and fell into a deep sleep.

CAPRICIOUS BAY

The morning of the third day, Travis walked beside Seraphi, tired of sitting on the old stallion. Zack, wanting to move quicker, decided it best to send Mesha home to keep an eye on Pran. Not only would it keep the mischievous dog away, but it would also save Seraphi the pain of being annoyed for the rest of their journey. Now both of the boys would either walk with the horse or take turns riding him. Surprisingly, the journey's length seemed to shorten because of this.

As the sun shone on, the woods began to part, and for the first time, Travis saw the Capricious Ocean. A beautiful blue-green, the salty waters splashed upon the white, sandy shore. His spirits beginning to lift, Travis urged Zack and Seraphi on, and soon they were running down the shore.

Travis was so enthused by his surroundings that he wanted to throw up his hands and have fun on the beach. But for once, his conscience kept him on the sane track and he kept focused on the mission. Sarora was the most important thing on his mind right now and he would rest no more until he found her.

Suddenly, Zack stopped. Turning, Travis looked back at his friend. Seraphi stopped as well and perceived the lapse in running as time to eat.

"Travis," Zack whispered, looking at the ground. "I think we're getting close."

Travis looked behind himself in the direction they had been going and asked, "Are you sure?"

Zack nodded and knelt. "Yes, look at these tracks." Travis walked from where he had been standing and knelt down next to Zack.

In the sand were fresh boot tracks.

"But that doesn't necessarily mean that they belong to the people that are keeping Sarora captive," Travis had to put in.

Zack nodded. "You may be right, but I have to believe that these are soldier boots, and if they're soldier boot prints, then we could very well be looking at Sarora's captors."

Travis felt his heart miss a beat. Sure, he had thought about trying to escape alive with Sarora, but never once had his mind thought it through. Would there be fighting? Death? Worse? He didn't know what would be worse than death, and he didn't want to find out.

Standing up, Zack wiped the sand from his pants. "We need a plan..."

"Yes, so you got one?" Travis asked, unaware of how to handle the situation.

Zack shook his head. "You know me—if I had one, then I would have boasted about it ten seconds ago." Sighing, he turned to Travis. "Looks like this one's up to you. What do you want to do?"

"Me?!" Travis tried to keep his voice down, fearing that whoever was out there would hear them. "Do you have a death wish? If yes, then I've got plenty of plans! All kidding aside," Travis looked into Zack's eyes, "wouldn't it be best if you set something up?"

Zack stared back at Travis. "I know your heart, Travis. You're a novice, but determined, and you have a ton of natural ability despite your naivety. And I know you want to play a bigger role in our group. So, prove me wrong and let's save Sarora."

Travis couldn't meet Zack's eyes. What if what he had in mind led them to their deaths? What if it ultimately killed one of his friends and not him? He would never be able to live with the guilt.

Inside his mind, Travis shook his head. *No, it's all or nothing, and I want all.* Looking back to Zack, Travis felt his heart begin to swell with confidence. "I think that I might have something that may work..."

Later, Travis hid in the bushes, his ears listening for all they were worth. With every little twirling of a leaf or cracking of a twig, Travis felt his muscles tense. He had been sitting in that uncomfortable bush for half an hour and his calves cramped under his weight. Nevertheless, he held his position and waited for Zack's cue.

Zack watched the camp below his tree with caution. Travis had sent him ahead to scout for the camp, but this wasn't his only job. As he waited for the soldiers to relax their senses, Zack's blue eyes flashed as he studied each of them.

There were only three men sitting around the campfire, smiling as they took turns joking around and stirring a cooking pot. *Just a couple more minutes and then they'll know fear,* Zack thought with a sly grin. Taking his eyes off the soldiers, Zack looked at the wagon. Though he couldn't fully see her, Zack thought that he could make out Sarora's shadow and her bird-like front feet from under the wagon.

Sarora, if that really is you, why aren't you trying to escape? I mean, come on, these guys are a bunch of pushovers. Zack's attention was quickly moved from Sarora to the tent closest to the campfire. As he watched, the tent's green entry opened up, and out came a man that could hardly be compared to the others.

"Hey, Trayka!" One of the men looked up from where he sat

stirring the pot and added, "You finally got out of bed, sleepy-head?"

A nagging sensation suddenly floated around on the surface of Zack's memories, making him feel as if he had forgotten or missed something important. Brushing the feeling aside, Zack concentrated on the person who had emerged from the tent. The man, *More like a boy,* Zack thought, moved next to a man opposite the one who had spoken. With a smile, he sat and replied, "If you can recall, first of all, the rest of you went to bed at sunset while I stayed out with our friend." Trayka gestured toward the side of the wagon with his thumb. "Secondly, you know that I wasn't sleeping. I was checking our map. If we stay here too long, we'll all be in big trouble."

Ha! Zack thought. *So they are working for Trazon.* He watched Trayka closely as anger began to boil in his stomach. With a smile, Trayka slapped his comrade's back, who had just relayed a joke to him. "Spoken like a true veteran," Trayka laughed, letting go a large grin.

Veteran? Zack wondered and then shook his head. *No matter —once for the darkness, always for the darkness.*

"So, Trayka," the last man spoke, "when do we head out with the she-gryph?"

Trayka's smile disappeared. "We will not refer to our guest as a she-gryph, Mortimous. Though not human, Sarora is probably smarter than all of us put together. So do not devalue her."

Mortimous hung his head. "My apologies, Trayka."

"It is alright, my friend, do not worry," Trayka forgave the soldier. "At one time, I, myself, did not fully respect Sarora. But now that I have learned more about her character, I trust her as any other comrade."

Okay, Zack thought to himself as he shifted in the tree. *I've heard enough of this garbage.* Taking in a deep breath, Zack pointed a finger to the sky and let loose a crashing bolt of lightning.

The woods rang with the sound of thunder as the lightning

exploded. Trayka and his men leapt to their feet, eyes darting around with fear. Trayka, though, seemed the calmest out of the group.

While his men shouted in fear, Trayka looked to the sky, searching for storm clouds. Zack thought he saw Sarora move as she woke from a slumber.

"Wait," Trayka spoke, trying to calm the soldiers, "do any of you know where the lightning came from?" The men were too busy running around and grabbing their things to reply.

"Thomas!" Trayka called to one man. "Do you know anything about this lightning?"

Thomas stopped in his tracks and shook his head. "No, Trayka I only know of a legend that haunts this place."

"What legend?" Trayka asked.

Mortimous also stopped in his tracks. "The legend of the Great Water Dragon."

"Now, come on, Mortimous." Trayka obviously thought that the man was joking. "No dragon can cast lightning. It's only a story meant to scare children."

Zack saw his opportunity and he set out another bolt, this time out across the camp to make it hard to tell if it had come from the woods or from the salty waters.

The men cried out in surprise and fell to the ground as the lightning struck. The third soldier was the first to his feet. He cried out, "Quick! To the woods! The beast can't get us there!"

The three soldiers quickly dashed into the woods. Zack watched with a smile as they ran below the tree that he was in. Trayka was the last to go. Calling out to his men, he pleaded for them to come back, "Halt! Wait! Stop! There's no way..." his voice disappeared as he continued into the distance.

Seeing that the soldiers had all left, Zack leapt down from his hiding place. After recovering from the impact on his legs, he ran over to the wagon, his heart pounding excitedly in his chest. As Zack rounded the wagon's side, a large figure leapt on top of him and pinned him to the ground. "Sarora!" Zack called out in surprise as his friend held him to the ground, her talons digging into the earth around his shoulders.

"Zack! What are you doing here?" Sarora asked, her eyes showing great surprise as she let him off the ground.

Zack wiped the sand and dirt off of his arms and legs. "What do you think I'm doing? We're rescuing you!"

"*We're* rescuing?" Sarora asked. "Where's Travis?"

"He's coming," Zack reassured her.

"Why did you leave him behind?" Sarora cried out. "You know how he is! So reckless and brain dead—"

"Sarora, it's okay, this was his plan..."

"Yeah, that makes me feel a whole lot better!" Sarora retorted.

Zack sighed. "Never, mind that. Here," he said, moving to Sarora's side, "let me untie you."

"Untie me?" Sarora asked. She lifted a wing and showed him the rags that covered it. "You want to undo my bandages?"

Zack stepped back. "What...?" He was cut short as a figure leapt at him. Zack grunted in surprise as he rolled around on the ground, trying to stay on top of his attacker.

"Trayka! Zack! Stop!" Sarora screeched, but it appeared that neither of them could—or wanted to—hear her. Before she could stop them, they were fighting to get to their feet while throwing wild punches at each other.

Zack was just shorter than his attacker. Trayka was about a head taller than Zack, but generally they had the same lanky build with strong arms and an even stronger heart for fighting. When Sarora flew away over their heads, Zack became momentarily distracted. With a smirk, Trayka pushed Zack backward into the trees before grabbing his sword from his belt. His heart racing to calm down and his eyes barely showing a flash of fear, Zack instinctively held his hand above his head and did something that he had never done before. Feeling power surge through his body, he searched for a feeling that lay behind him. Once he found what his mind was searching for, with a new ease, he reached out with the energy... and was surprised to see vines shoot out from the trees.

Seeing the fear in Trayka's eyes boosted Zack's confidence. Using his newfound powers, Zack stood and moved his body as he remembered Master Racht had done. Putting one foot back, Zack pointed both hands forward and the vines shot toward Trayka.

Though he cut the first vine with his sword, the next vine wrapped itself around Trayka's right arm. As the man gasped with shock at the vine's strength, the second vine came and wrapped itself around his other wrist. Immediately, Trayka dropped his sword and it hit the ground with a clank. With a grin of revenge, Zack used his earth powers to lift Trayka off the ground.

"This is for keeping my friend captive!" he shouted as Trayka was dangling twenty feet in the air.

"Zack, stop!"

Zack turned around to see Travis and Sarora racing toward him. Travis ran in a dramatic fashion, his right hand held out.

"Zack," Travis huffed as he stopped by his friend. "Stop, let Trayka down!"

"Why should I?" Zack asked, though he lowered Trayka a little.

"Because he wasn't holding me captive," Sarora explained, her eyes pleading for him to believe her.

"I thought you were attempting to take her captive!" Trayka's voice called from where he still hung fifteen feet off the ground.

Travis nodded once to Zack, reminding the older boy that he had put him in charge. Inwardly groaning at his own stupidity, both for letting Travis take charge and then for not listening to Sarora in the first place, Zack lowered Trayka to the ground, pulled the vines back, and set them in their original places in the trees.

With a small grin, Trayka picked his sword off the ground and wiped sand from his pants. "I must say, I felt that we were evenly matched until you pulled the Acer magic."

Zack rolled his eyes. "You know, if these two hadn't shown up just in time, I would have killed you with a flick of my wrist.

Trayka's smile faltered a little. "Yes, but you didn't, did you?" Trayka came forward and held out his hand for Zack to shake.

Zack felt like Trayka's personality and character had done a complete one-eighty. Though as stubborn as he was, Zack wasn't stupid. He knew that deep, deep down—somewhere—he'd rather have Trayka as an ally over an enemy.

Grudgingly, Zack shook Trayka's hand and the two stared into each other's eyes: electric blue against electric blue. They stood there for a couple of seconds until Trayka's smile disappeared, a look of shock replacing the friendliness in his eyes. Letting go of Zack's hand, Trayka took a small step back.

"It can't be..." His eyes widened in shock like a deep, swelling sea.

"Trayka, what's the matter?" Sarora asked, both her and Travis wondering what had been spoken through the eyes of the two similar characters.

"Zachraus?" Trayka wondered. "Is it really you?"

Zack felt uncomfortable under everyone's gaze. "Excuse me?" Zack asked, trying to remove the awkward feeling. "I'm Zachary, but my friends call me Zack."

An enormous grin formed on Trayka's mouth, one that made Zack nervous. "Zachraus, it is you! Even after all these years, I could never forget your face." Trayka wrapped his arms around Zack. "It is you! I can't believe it! I've found my brother!"

OH, BROTHERS

"Zachraus! Hey, Zachraus, wait up!" Trayka called after his long-lost brother. After hearing the news and realizing the possibility Trayka could be telling the truth, Zack had turned his back on his own blood and walked away from the situation. The hot afternoon sun filtered through the leaves of the trees and heated the top of Zack's head. Working his way mindlessly among the trees, he followed an invisible path away from the beach. Zack had left, hoping to get some time alone. But again, he was wrong and his so-called 'brother' had followed him.

"Zachraus!" Trayka called again. "Zachraus, wait up a second!" the older boy called to Zack as he caught up with him.

Zack glared at Trayka. "My name is Zack."

Trayka leapt in front of Zack, and the magic wielder was surprised by how similar Trayka's body movements were to his.

"Zachraus, please, just hear me out," Trayka panted as he stepped in front of Zack.

"Not if you keep calling me that." Zack looked through Trayka as if he were invisible and shouldered past the young soldier.

Zack felt a firm hand grip his shoulder and he spun his head to look at Trayka as the dark-haired boy spoke. "Fine, Zack, please, just give me a chance to explain."

Zack turned around with a sigh. "Fine, explain to me why in the world, if you're my brother, that I've never met you before? Where have you been all my life?"

Trayka swept his tongue over his cracked lips. "You've seen me before, but not for quite some time." Trayka turned and sat down on a nearby log. Zack, to his own surprise, followed him and sat down next to his brother.

"You were only a year old and quite a trouble maker..." Trayka began.

"Me? Now that makes all this even harder to believe." Zack never could remember a time where he caused much trouble.

Trayka smiled. "Yes, you were. I was six when you were born. You were a very small child, but your eyes held the fire of survival. It was that will to survive, I guess, that led you to cause so much trouble.

"Once, our mother told the both of us to stay inside the bedroom. But, when I had my back turned, you crawled to the door and somehow managed to escape. Mother nearly gave me a good lashing for letting you out of my sight."

"Mother?" Zack couldn't help but say the word. He had always wondered what his real mother had been like. "Tell me about her."

Trayka grinned at Zack when he noticed that his brother was no longer fighting him. "She was the best mother in the world. I remember sitting on her lap and she would tell me stories while she brushed my hair out of my face." Trayka involuntarily reached up and pushed his dark bangs behind his ear. "And when you were born, we'd sit on her lap together, and she would smile as she sang to us. Occasionally I would join in. You were barely old enough to say anything, so if your dribbling sounded anywhere close to the melody, you would do it as loud as possible."

Zack smiled. He wished with all his heart that he could remember those days.

"And our father was one of the bravest men alive," Trayka continued, his proud smile flashing white. "Though he wasn't home too often, when he was, he would scoop us both up in his arms, and he would call me King Trayka and you Prince Zacky and he would tell us of how one day we would change Firmara..." Trayka's smile faded.

"Trayka?" Zack asked, afraid of what was the matter.

Trayka couldn't look at Zack. "Though you may have been here for the good of Firmara, I most certainly have not."

Zack wanted to reach out and comfort his older brother, but he had no idea how. Nervously, Zack reached out his hand and placed it on his brother's shoulder.

"You know," Zack tried to find the words written in his heart, "I used to always think that once someone had ink poured on their heart, that there was no way to make it pure again. But you could prove me wrong."

Trayka looked into Zack's eyes, blue meeting blue once more. "I promise, Zack, that I'll do my best to prove you wrong. I'll spend every second of my life working to fight Lord Trazon, and never again will he have hold of my heart."

Zack dipped his head with a smile. "And I'll promise not to be so judgmental of someone. I'll always look for the good in everyone's heart." When there was a small lapse of silence, Zack asked the question that he dreaded to hear the answer of. "Trayka, where are our parents?"

Trayka's smile disappeared and his eyes became clouded with sadness. "Mother made her way to the great beyond thirteen years ago."

Zack's heart nearly was torn apart. He had always carried the slightest hope that his mom was still alive.

"What of our father?" Zack dared to ask.

"The night our mother—" he shook his head. "The night mother died, he left with you, and he... I haven't seen him since." Trayka said in a clipped voice

Zack couldn't help but let his hope stir inside him. "So there is a chance that he is alive?"

Trayka nodded ever so slightly. "Don't hold out hope for meeting him. He probably found you a place to live and then left you with your adopted parents. By the way, why aren't you with them?"

Zack looked at his hands. "Well, it's a long and complicated story..."

"We have time, and I'm all ears." Trayka patted Zack on the back. Zack smiled and then he began to tell the story of his past to his brother. For once, he wasn't going to hide anything.

SUSPICIONS

Sarora and Travis sat together around the campfire. Trayka's men had still not returned, and after the shocking truth that Trayka had shared, they were both too stunned to speak. Every few seconds, Travis would glance at Sarora, hoping to catch her eye and spark up a conversation. But for the first few minutes, Sarora merely sat and stared off into the ocean. The breeze that swept over the ocean ruffled her feathers every few seconds, and then she would sigh ever so slightly.

A thought jumped to the front of his mind. "Oh, the wolf's talons." Travis remembered aloud.

Sarora looked at him. "What was that?"

"It's nothing, never mind," Travis replied, shaking his head. Sarora gave a small nod and gazed back off into the distance.

Finally, unnerved that Sarora would take so long to speak, Travis moved next to her and sat beside the she-gryphon. Gazing in the direction she was looking, Travis asked, "So, what's going through your head?"

"Zack has bloodlines that are still alive," Sarora answered simply.

"And why is that such a surprise to you?"

Sarora glanced at Travis and then returned to gazing at the

ocean. "It's just that I've never known him like this... I always considered him as my family and no one else's, but now, to know that part of his family is still alive..."

Travis caught on to what was bothering Sarora. "So you think that after all this time, Zack will just up and leave us for Trayka?"

Sarora hung her head. "It's always a possibility, especially since..." Sarora stopped again without finishing.

"Since what?" Travis pressed.

"Since we fought the night I left."

Travis had no idea that this had occurred. "What happened? You two are closer than anyone else I've ever met."

Sarora looked at her front feet. "Well, it all started when he had this dream."

"Dream?" Travis sat up straight. "What was in this dream?"

Sarora shook her head. "I don't know—he wouldn't tell me."

There was silence before Travis asked, "So, you left because Zack wouldn't share his dream with you?"

"Well, no, that wasn't the whole problem..."

"So, then, what were you mad about?"

Sarora looked at Travis. "I told him that I was there for him, and he refused my offer."

"Meaning?" Travis asked, not seeing the big deal.

"Travis, I don't expect you to understand—"

"Try me," Travis interrupted and folded his arms across his chest.

Sarora lifted her right front foot and studied it as she spoke. "Well, it's just," Sarora sighed, "we've always been honest and up-front with one another, and whenever we needed help, we would lean on the other's shoulder. And now, Zack has this dream that scares him so much, and he won't talk to me about it."

Travis looked at his own hands, struggling to find a way to let Sarora lean on him. "Well, what exactly did you say to him when this, um, confrontation happened?" Travis asked, looking back to Sarora.

"Well, to put it simply, I told him that he was an idiot."

Though Sarora put forth the effort to joke, the jest merely died like a whisper against the wind.

"And if I tell you that you're an idiot, and then ask if you need my help, would you accept it?"

"Well, maybe—"

"Sarora?" Travis cocked an eyebrow.

Sarora hung her head once more and gave a small chuckle. "No, probably not—especially if it came from you." Sarora smiled.

Travis smiled back. "Now that sounds more like the Sarora I know."

Sarora flicked both of her feathery ears back.

Travis heard a twig snap, and both he and Sarora turned to see Zack, Trayka, and Trayka's men walking toward them. With a smile, Travis waved to them and was surprised to see one of Trayka's men wave awkwardly back, along with Zack.

When the group reached Travis and Sarora, Travis asked, "So, no hard feelings?"

One of the men, old and gruff-looking, smiled back at him. "Are you kidding me? You gave us the scare of our lives!" Travis felt guilt begin to eat at his stomach. Then, the man's smile broadened. "Don't ya see, lad? We're thankful!"

"Thankful?" Travis questioned the word, confused on what this man's definition of it was.

"Yes! Thankful!" another man, looking almost identical to the first, spoke up. "If it weren't for you guys bringing us to our senses, why, Trazon's men could have stormed in here at any time and taken us."

"I just wish that Trazon would give up on catching you, already," the last of Trayka's men spoke up. "It would be nice to relax a bit."

Sarora turned to the man who had just spoken. "Well, Thomas," the man jumped, apparently shocked that Sarora knew his name, "considering that Lord Trazon probably isn't too fond of deserters, I'd say that it'll be quite a while longer before Trayka is out of the woods."

"So wait," one of Trayka's men began, his expression one of confusion, "you're under Trazon's command? You're one of his *soldiers?*"

Trayka shook his head. "Not since he tried to have me killed."

Trayka's three friends turned and looked at him in shock.

"You forgot to tell us that precious bit of information," one of the men grumbled gruffly. "We knew that you were in trouble, and that Trazon's men were after you, but we assumed you were on the run because of some petty crime. We never thought that the Dark Lord himself sought your blood."

Trayka apologetically nodded to them. "I promise to explain, but we must get going." He looked at Travis and Zack. "Your 'surprise attack' made us realize how vulnerable we really are."

Zack and Sarora nodded in agreement before gathering with Travis in a small group.

"I'm going to head south just a little ways," Zack told them, speaking first. "I'd like to make sure that no one from a small village nearby heard us and is coming for a visit."

"Won't that take too much time?" Travis asked.

Zack shook his head. "Not if I'm just scouting a mile ahead and not sightseeing."

"Good idea," Sarora agreed. "Travis and I'll check up north by Dragon River. There may also be a chance of finding some 'friends' while we keep an eye out for enemies."

A thought crossed Travis's mind. If Dragon River was the name of the body of water, then did that mean—"Are dragons in these waters?" Travis voiced his conclusion.

Sarora shrugged. "Possibly, but even if they are, they're masters at hiding. Even you should know that bit of information."

Travis nodded—water dragons. That's what he had based his plan on. There was a legend of an electricity-controlling water dragon that lived in this area. They were very good at hiding in the rivers and oceans. So good, that Travis wondered if he would ever see one. He was woken from his thoughts when he noticed that he was the only person still standing in that spot.

"Hey! Empty-Head!" Travis turned to see Sarora calling to him. "Are you coming or what?"

Travis followed Sarora across the beach, watching out for the occasional stone or long tree root that he might trip over. He wanted to spark up another conversation with Sarora, but she didn't seem as eager to do so. Anytime Travis would ask her a question, Sarora would do one of two things: give her answer in short, or give no direct answer at all.

"You know, the wolves aren't exactly happy with you right now," Travis put in. When she looked at him quizzically, he responded, "More than the usual."

Sarora shook her head in slight confusion. "What did I do? I've been gone!"

"Well, you see, they're blaming you..."

"For what?!"

That's when Travis finally got the chance to explain everything that had happened after she had left.

Sarora looked like she was on the verge of losing it. "But... that wasn't me! I left—end of story! I got mad, flew away—a bit too far I must admit—but I found Trayka, and his men accidentally ambushed me because they thought I was Sievan..."

"It's okay!" Travis cut her off, stopping her from going any further. "I know you didn't do it. It'll be the wolves that will need a thorough convincing. But for now, at least we know that you're innocent, and from there we can figure out who really broke into the camp."

"It must be Sievan," Sarora muttered as she gazed at the sky, her eyes narrowed.

Travis nodded in agreement. "Maybe, but why and how could his scent not have told the wolves a different story?"

"True... unless...."

"Unless what?" Travis asked.

Sarora looked at him. "Unless some of the wolves 'ignored' him."

The thought struck a chord with Travis. "If that's true, then Timur's situation is much worse than we thought."

"Even our own allies can't be trusted..." Sarora sighed.

"So, what do you think of Trayka?" Travis found himself asking yet another question as they continued on. The wolf topic was on hold until they could sit down with Zack and really dig for details.

Sarora shrugged her shoulders. "He's okay."

"Okay as in..."

"He's not entirely full of himself and hasn't tried to kill us yet."

Travis sighed. "Is that all?"

Sarora turned her head to glance at him. "He does remind me a lot of Zack."

They're brothers, duh! Travis bit back in retort. When Sarora looked away, Travis shook his head. *Maybe I should just start the conversation myself. Get some info out of her thick skull.*

"You know," Travis began, "I kind of like Trayka. Sure, he's been on the wrong side for pretty much his whole life, but I guess we can't blame him, huh?"

Travis thought that Sarora's eyes held a flicker of nerves. "Why would you not blame him?" she asked.

"Well, we shouldn't judge and all that, you know," Travis continued in his casual conversation, wanting to somehow connect it to Sarora's past. He had tried several times to talk to the she-gryphon about what her history contained. Now was the time. He wanted to know everything that he could.

"Meaning?" Sarora asked.

"Well, maybe he was forced into following Trazon. Maybe that's what happened. Maybe Trazon threatened to hurt Zack and the rest of Trayka's family if he didn't join him." Travis was making shots in the dark, not intending to hit the exact target.

Sarora stopped in her tracks and waited until Travis was next to her before she spoke. "Why do you think that?"

Travis shrugged his shoulders, playing nonchalance. Truth be told, he wanted to know everything he could. However, he was able to pull off a casual talk, which seemed to be catching Sarora off guard.

"I don't know, maybe it happened long ago, before you even met him perhaps."

Sarora glared at Travis, though she did so lightly. "I know everything about Zack's past, but it's his business to tell you that, not mine."

"Oh, I know." Travis waved his hand and walked ahead as if he really didn't care.

Confused, Sarora jogged to catch up with Travis. "Do you not care all of a sudden?" she asked him.

"Care about what?" Travis asked, faking his dumb expression.

"Oh, never mind," Sarora huffed, looking away and trying to think of what Travis was trying to pull off now.

"Anyway," Travis continued on, seeing that he was almost at Sarora's breaking point, "as far as I'm concerned, Zack can share when he's ready. It's probably not that exciting anyways, kinda like my past."

Sarora's head turned to look Travis squarely in the eyes. "Now, you listen here," Sarora ordered, her voice angered and her eyes flaming. "As far as I'm concerned, you've led a much easier life than Zack ever has! At least you knew one of your parents for a bit of your life! Zack can't even recall a bit of his past before we met!"

"What?!" Travis forgot about hiding how badly he wanted to know. "What happened? Did he hit his head or something?"

Sarora seemed to choke on her words. "No, that's not what I meant—I mean," Sarora stumbled, "we've known each other a really long time—"

"Sarora, what are you hiding?" Travis asked, looking his friend up and down suspiciously.

"Nothing," Sarora replied, shaking her head. "Why would I be hiding something? Besides, as I said before, it's Zack's business to tell you about his past."

"Dang it, Sarora!" Travis cursed at her. "You're hiding something from me, and I know it!"

"But they're Zack's—"

"No! You have a secret bigger than the both of us, and I'm the only one who doesn't know what it is!" Travis shouted at her, his whole mind working its way around the thought.

Sarora stopped, her voice seemed choked up in her throat.

"So then you do have a secret!" Travis exclaimed, shocked to find out how deep the secret actually was. "Why can't you share it with me?"

Sarora looked away for a moment before admitting, "Yes, I have a secret, and yes, I've kept it this whole time I've known you." Turning her head back to him, Sarora scowled. "But I've done it for your safety. And just like Zack has the right to privacy, so do I."

Travis wasn't sure what he had planned to say next, but unkind words found their way out of his mouth. "Safety for me? When has hiding secrets from me ever kept me safe? I think that whether you tell me or not, the subject will still come back to bite you in the butt."

"Travis, you have to understand—" Sarora tried to explain herself.

"Sarora, the only thing I can't understand is: why are you keeping this secret from me? Zack obviously knows, and I'm willing to bet that even Stephen knows as well—and Stephen's not even your friend! So why does he get to know and I don't?"

"Well, first of all, I don't care nearly as much about what happens to Stephen as much as I care about what might happen to you." Sarora glared at Travis. "I may have known Stephen longer, but you're a better friend than he'll ever be. I've lost so many friends and family already, and if I ever lost you..." Sarora's voice got choked up again.

Travis lowered his gaze. "But what if there's a chance that nothing will happen to me if you tell me?"

Sarora shook her head. "I know you, Travis. If I told you, your focus would shift, and we can't afford to be distracted from our destiny of defeating Trazon. Honestly, I wouldn't keep anything from you if it wasn't this important."

"That's what happened last time, when you lied about being my spirit animal. And look at what it did to us then?" Looking into Sarora's eyes, he said, "It almost destroyed our friendship."

Sarora looked away and said quietly, "Better our friendship than both of our lives."

Travis burned with anger. "How could you say that! I'd rather die than not be friends with you or Zack!"

Sarora looked back up. "Travis, I didn't mean it like that—"

Travis waved his hand at her as if dismissing her comment. "Never mind, Sarora. Let's finish up this scouting mission. We've wasted time over a lost cause."

"But Travis..."

Travis walked on and didn't look at Sarora. He was determined to stay mad at her until she told him the secret. Her secret. And until that happened, Travis felt he could nearly forget about their friendship altogether.

THE FIERY BLADE

Sarora and Travis walked side-by-side along the ocean shore until they came to Dragon River. The day—though it was almost August's end—was quite hot, and Travis felt beads of sweat begin to gather on his body. He had found it hard to keep up with Sarora's pace, but he trudged on and was able to walk alongside her.

Sarora must have noticed how hot and tired Travis was. Once they reached the river, she turned to him. "The river is not too deep if you want to take a quick dip, though it looks like you already took one."

Travis leaned forward to get a better look at the river. Seeing the rushing water churn and froth until it reached the ocean made Travis's head spin. With shaky knees, Travis took a step back and shook his head.

"No thanks, you can go without me."

Sarora shook her head. "I don't swim; it ruins feathers." Though she said no, Travis thought that Sarora's eyes longed to show her overheated body to the cool waters. Shaking her head once more, she told him, "I'm going to take a quick flight around. That'll cool me off." Looking to Travis, she added, "Please stay here and don't get into any trouble."

"Me, trouble? After you up and disappeared for days? Really, Sarora?"

"Track records speak for themselves," Sarora rolled her eyes and unfolded her wings. A single rag dropped from her right wing. Sarora had told Travis that Trayka had accidentally cut it when he mistook her for Sievan, but the cut hadn't been that deep or long, so it had healed quickly.

"I won't go far. I'll be back soon." Sarora avoided Travis's gaze, crouched, and then expertly leapt into the air. For a couple heartbeats she seemed to run on the air, but soon her wings lifted her and Travis watched as she became smaller and smaller until her shape was unrecognizable.

Travis stood in place, wondering what to do next. "Let me see," Travis mumbled to himself. "What can I do that won't cause any trouble?"

Nothing, Travis's mind disputed, which made him smile. There had to be something that he could do.

Behind him, Travis heard hoofbeats approaching. He turned to see Seraphi walking toward him. The stallion had been waiting by the river for Travis and Zack to return.

Stopping in front of Travis, the white horse snorted in the boy's face.

"Well, hello there." Travis patted Seraphi on the neck. "Sorry it took us a while. You didn't happen to know that Zack had a brother, did you?" Seraphi didn't seem to listen, but Travis continued on anyway. "I thought not. So, Seraphi, what can I do that won't get me into any trouble?"

Seraphi pawed the ground with his front hoof, just missing Travis's foot. Travis took a step back when Seraphi nodded his head up and down vigorously.

"Well, why don't you show me if you're so sure," Travis told the horse.

With a nicker, Seraphi nosed Travis's back. The boy sighed. "Fine, I'll get on. But we can't go too far, okay?"

Seraphi became all the more excited when Travis got on his back. Before Travis could give the signal to go, Seraphi took off.

Travis found himself scrabbling for the reins as Seraphi cantered toward the woods near the river. Several times, Travis had to duck to avoid low-hanging branches.

"Whoa! Seraphi, take it easy!" Travis pulled back slightly on the reins, but the horse's speed did not change. Praying that Sarora wouldn't kill him, Travis hung on to Seraphi as the stallion carried him deeper into the forest.

Heart pounding in his chest, Travis watched as the trees and shrubs seemed to zip by and become a blur. Underneath him, he could feel Seraphi's strong muscles as he pushed himself harder and harder. Sweat began to break the white horse's skin and white foam appeared at the corners of his mouth.

Fearing for his horse, Travis yelled, "Woah, Seraphi! Halt!"

The next thing Travis knew was that he was flying over Seraphi's head. With an aching thud, Travis hit the ground, lucky to have not hit a large stone in front of him. Not only did it hurt to fall off a horse, but it hurt even worse to fall off one that had been cantering at top speed.

Wincing, Travis reached up and felt the back of his head. "I didn't mean that quickly," Travis complained to Seraphi, who stared back at him indifferently.

Forcing his knees to straighten, Travis stood up and scowled at the white stallion. "Next time you want to play obstacle course, let me know ahead of time." Looking at the surrounding trees, Travis sighed. "I sure hope you know how to get us back."

With an angry nicker, Seraphi stepped forward and nudged Travis's head with such force it nearly knocked him to the ground.

"Seraphi! What's your deal—"

Travis stopped. Something shiny had caught his attention. Turning, Travis spotted one of the most bizarre sights that he thought he'd ever see.

"It's—it's just like out of a legend..." Travis breathed to

himself as he stared at the sword, whose blade was implanted in the large boulder.

Stepping forward, Travis could see in great detail how strong and beautiful the sword was. In the forest light, the sword's golden hilt seemed to glow. The ends of the hilt were decorated with three carvings—each was a bird with a long, flowing, feathered tail. In the center of the hilt, between the three birds, sat a red ruby. When it reflected the sun's light, the ruby glared with an orange-red vibe that reminded Travis of his crystal. A thought struck his mind—had this been the sword that Master Racht had written to him about in his will? It had to be! Why else would Seraphi act so recklessly?

"Well, if it's mine, I ought to take it." Travis climbed up on top of the boulder. Travis grasped the hilt of the sword in both hands. He was surprised by how comfortable the grip felt. Taking in a deep breath, Travis pulled as hard as he could, but the sword did not budge.

Retightening his grip, Travis pulled a second time. As he continued his stubborn pull, Travis felt his muscles begin to shake. Seeing that he was getting nowhere, Travis stopped pulling and released his grip from the sword.

Catching his breath, Travis looked to Seraphi, who stared back at him as if he were crazy.

"Well, what do you want me to do?" Travis puffed at the horse.

Seraphi walked up to the boulder, stretched out his neck, and rubbed his muzzle over the top, clearing its surface.

When the dirt and leaves were removed, Travis could make out writing on the rock right next to the sword. Kneeling, he rubbed his right hand over the surface to see if he could clean it more.

Travis's hope grew as he uncovered an 'E', but it was quickly dashed as he noticed that the 'E' was part of a word in a different language.

"Firsoma," Travis breathed, very aware that he knew little to nothing of the language.

"Well, what next?" Travis questioned Seraphi, who gave him a look that read, 'I wouldn't know, I can't read it!'

Closing his eyes, Travis sighed. He could go and look for Sarora for help, but a foolish pride was residing in his heart. For once, Travis wanted to do something good without help.

Opening his eyes, Travis focused on the first word. "Ma," Travis spoke to himself. "Well, for sure it doesn't mean mother, but then what?" Shaking his head, Travis read the next word.

"Chronos." Travis's eyes lit up. "Wait a second! Doesn't Chronos have something to do with time?" Nodding to himself, Travis spoke to himself out loud, "Ma time? My time?" Travis shook his head again and moved to the next two words.

"Ti eb. Well, I've got no clue what that means!" Travis yelled, though not loud enough for his friends to hear him.

What am I supposed to do? I can't read Firsoman!

A gust of wind suddenly blew through the trees, and the sun's light grew brighter. And though these were natural occurrences, Travis watched as a miracle occurred right before his eyes. Slowly, the words on the stone rearranged themselves. In awe, Travis read aloud, "At times, it is better to have gentle hands than an iron fist." Though surprised by what had occurred, Travis came up with a new idea. As if he were holding a precious gem, he grasped the sword's hilt. With great gentleness, Travis slowly pulled up on the sword and to his surprise, the sword slid out of the boulder.

With a smile of triumph, Travis examined the blade of the sword. "Undamaged," Travis said to himself and smiled with relief, glad to see the sword free of any and all blemishes. After jumping down off the boulder, Travis looked at Seraphi and nodded. "Thanks, friend." For once, the stallion returned a welcoming nod and then signaled for Travis to climb aboard him once more.

. . .

Travis sat on a ridge overlooking the ocean. Across his lap lay his sword, bringing a new hope to his world. The sun, which had heralded a long day, was working its way back to the horizon. Sarora had still not returned, but Travis was not worried. If she needed time alone, then he'd let her have it.

His feet dangled off the edge of the ridge several feet above the rolling waves that crashed against the stony shore. Travis forced himself to look at his new enemy—deep waters. Though he watched the waters in the horizon, he could scarcely bring himself to look down. Anytime he would try, his eyes would command his mind to let them stay shut. After a couple of tries, Travis had given up hope of overcoming his fear. Instead, he ran his hand across the sword's hilt and the flat of the blade. The cool metals felt refreshing on his warm skin. The red gem glinted warmly as it reflected the sunbeams. Standing, Travis held the sword in his right hand. Picturing Master Racht with his own sword, Travis formed a crude replica of his stance. When held by one hand, the sword began to grow heavy, though it was not much heavier than the sword he had used at the battle.

Closing his eyes, Travis held the sword out ahead of him. Carefully, he pictured his fire form that he had used with his staff in his head. After calculating his movements, Travis opened his eyes and swung the sword to his right. Taking his weapon in both hands, Travis spun on his feet and cut at an invisible enemy with precision. With a flick of his wrist, he knocked a soldier's sword out of his hand and then dispatched him with a quick slash downwards. Turning to his right, Travis jabbed, ducked, rolled to his left, jumped to his feet, and slashed at the imaginary soldier. His grin enlarging, Travis flipped the sword in his hand and thrust it toward the ocean. Spinning three-sixty, Travis swung his sword around, then, with great strength, he thrust his sword three times, each time bringing down his foot to stomp on the ground. Smiling, Travis thought of how he had just defeated the ocean. That is, until...

Travis felt the ground crumble beneath him. Before he could

do anything, he was falling, sword still in hand. His heart flew to his throat as he realized that there was no stopping his fall and there was no way to slow down. His body hit the water.

For a couple seconds he sank because of his speed. But as he held on to his sword, he began to sink deeper and deeper. Holding his sword in his right hand, Travis kicked his legs as hard as he could and used his left arm to help propel himself upward. But his fear and the weight of the sword were too great, and Travis found himself struggling to find oxygen to fuel him. The deeper he fell, the harder the cold water compressed him. He struggled even harder now to pull himself up. The voice at the back of his mind told him to drop the sword and escape with his life, but Travis could not bring himself to do so. Even though he had only held the sword for an hour, he felt that it was already a part of him. Now the determination to live was the only thing keeping his aching body moving. His lungs screamed for air, but Travis could not supply them. If he would breathe in, he would surely drown. However, as the light began to fade from Travis's vision, he was ready to accept his fate—he wasn't going to make it.

As Travis's lungs ran out of air, a sort of calm began to surround his body. Though he would be dead, at least he wouldn't have to suffer any more—no more bad memories, no more arguments... *No more hidden secrets,* Travis thought. As his body began to shut down and his eyes began to close, Travis was vaguely aware of a large moving figure swimming toward him.

A Living Legend

"Travis! Oh, Travis! Please wake up!" A voice called urgently through the dark. Numbly, Travis stirred a little. His body seemed to suddenly realize that it couldn't get any air to his lungs. With great effort, Travis coughed up seawater by the mouthful. As the water dribbled down the sides of his mouth, Travis slowly opened his eyes. He was on the beach. The sandy shore felt rough against his arms and legs. The sun hit every part of his body except his head. *I'm alive!*

Looking up, Travis saw Sarora, her frightened expression still planted on her face. Her legs and wings were dripping with water and her beak gleamed with dampness.

"Are you okay?" she asked nervously, searching Travis with fearful eyes.

Travis tried to nod but found that he could not. "I thought that you couldn't swim," he mumbled.

"I said I didn't, I never said that I couldn't."

"You're soaking wet. Did you save me?" Travis asked, confused.

Sarora shook her head. "No, I didn't."

Travis sat up. "But then who—" He stopped abruptly when he noticed that they were not alone.

An elongated form stood with its head resting on its long neck. Thin white fur covered every inch of its body besides its underbelly, which was protected by tightly-placed, tan-colored scales. Along its spine, thin green spikes flexible like fins pointed backwards as they continued down from the base of its neck to its tail. Its legs, in comparison to its body, were short but slim like its body. Its sleek, graceful head reminded Travis more of a dog than what the creature really was. Compared to similar species, it had two ears that were easily visible. The left ear had a hole in it, most likely from a past fight. Its two tan-colored horns elegantly pointed back. At the sides of its muzzle, just behind its nose, two long whiskers seemed to hold themselves up and float in the air.

"Y-you're a water dragon," Travis breathed, his eyes wide in shock.

With a twinkle in its blue-green eyes, the water dragon smiled. "Yes, I am. My name is Kaelin. I take it you're Travis?"

Travis could barely nod, still exhausted from his struggle and in awe of the presence of such a beautiful, powerful creature.

Kaelin laughed, a sound like twinkling chimes. "Ah, speechless in my presence after all! You do not need to be afraid, Magic Wielder. I saved you after all, so why would I want to harm you now?"

Sarora jabbed Travis from behind with her talons. "Say thanks..." she whispered so quietly that Travis could barely hear her.

"Oh, um, thank you, Kaelin," Travis replied after he had gotten to his feet and given an awkward bow.

"You are most welcome, Travis. It is an honor to have saved one from the prophecy."

When Kaelin looked away momentarily as he bowed in return, Travis shot a glance at Sarora and mouthed, "Prophecy?"

"I'll explain later."

Nodding, Travis looked back at Kaelin. The water dragon got back up from his bow with a smile. "Now, let me get a good look at the two of you. Who might I be fighting alongside before too long?"

Without looking to Sarora for her consent, Travis walked slowly up to the white dragon. Though he was longer than he was tall, Kaelin's shoulder was just below Travis's head. His neck made his head rise so high that Travis couldn't have reached it if he stood on his toes. Up close, the hole in Kaelin's ear was a little larger than he had first thought. It was about two inches in diameter, however the hole was clean and healed, suggesting that it had been damaged long ago.

"Kaelin?" Sarora began quietly from behind Travis. The water dragon moved his gaze from Travis to the she-gryphon. "I don't suppose you have time to, um, talk?"

"Well," Kaelin chuckled once more, "I've had time to stay this long, have I not? Yes, I can stay for a while longer if it is necessary. I just need to be sure that no one is trailing me." Lowering his body, Kaelin slowly lay down on the ground.

Travis, seeing that they were going nowhere in a hurry, sat down as well. Suddenly, a fragment of his memory returned to him.

"My sword!" Travis stood back up in a hurry and looked around frantically.

"Your sword?" Sarora asked confusedly, but Travis didn't really hear her.

"Kaelin, you didn't happen to grab my sword while you were saving me, did you?" Travis asked, despair flickering in his eyes.

Kaelin looked away from Travis and reached under his body. "Well, look here, I was wondering what was poking me." From underneath him, the water dragon pulled out the shining sword.

Travis sighed with relief and then took the sword from Kaelin. "Thank you so much, Kaelin," Travis exclaimed and bowed to the dragon once more.

"You are welcome," Kaelin replied, smiling in return. "I figured if you were willing to drown with it in hand, then it must be special."

"Is that why you couldn't swim?" Sarora questioned Travis, her voice irritated. "Less than a week ago you were carelessly using a sword to chop wood, and now you're willing to die for one?"

The corner of Travis's mouth formed a smile. "This one is different." He held the sword out for Sarora to examine. With wondering eyes, Sarora looked the sword up and down.

Sarora looked up at Travis, her eyes questioning. "How did you get a hold of this?"

Travis just remembered how mad he had been at Sarora before this had occurred. Turning sideways, he removed as much of the sword as he could from her view. "Not like it's any of your business, but Seraphi rode me to it."

Sarora seemed taken aback by Travis's cold shoulder, and for a moment, Travis felt the sting of hurt when he saw Sarora flinch at his voice. But his heart forced him to remain stubborn and he blocked the hurt and guilt from entering his heart.

Though Sarora was obviously hurt, she had an odd way of lashing back—in a formal manner. "Well then, good for you. I'm happy you found a lost sword."

Now Travis was stunned. He had expected for Sarora to retort in an obvious way, but she had managed to take him by surprise by hitting him with kindness. That was her whole idea—when someone fires hatred at you, shoot friendship back and you'll succeed in annoying the heck out of them.

Ignoring Travis's stunned expression, Sarora looked back to Kaelin. "The thing that I wanted to talk to you about involves the wolves."

Interest seemed to spark in the water dragon's eyes. "The wolves? Last I heard of them, they wanted to kill their new leader."

Sarora nodded once. "Yes, the pack, well, many of them, still aren't too pleased with Alpha Timur. It's because of him that I want to talk to you."

Kaelin studied one of his talons on his front leg. "I'm not an assassin."

"No, that's not it at all," Sarora quickly clarified. "Timur is our friend—we'd do anything to help him. That's why I volunteered to find the dragons and talk to them about his plan..." Sarora then began to explain Timur's idea to Kaelin.

When Sarora was finished speaking, Kaelin looked at her with seriousness in his eyes. "I agree with the alpha's thinking, and I'd be glad to serve Firmara. Hiding these many years has been quite boring. But I can't promise what my brothers will think. A couple may follow, but as far as water dragons go, we're built for doing nearly anything but fighting."

"What of the other dragons?" Travis asked. "Will they fight too?"

Kaelin looked over to Travis, who was sitting on the ground Indian style. "Fire dragons, it depends. They're up for fighting for what's right, but I haven't heard from them since our last great battle with Trazon. Most left Firmara a century ago and haven't returned. Those that remained on the mainland up until the battle fifteen years ago retreated to their island as well. As for ice dragons, I highly doubt he'll help."

"Why is that?" Travis asked.

Sarora was the first to answer. "Pardon my unintentional pun, but they lived in isolation. In fact, only two are likely left. One lives freely, and one—if you want to call him 'alive'—is Trazon's spirit animal."

Travis felt dumb in Sarora's presence. Sometimes he hated the fact that she knew so much more than him. *Of course, that's how everything goes nowadays. Everyone knows everything except for poor, stupid Travis,* Travis thought angrily to himself.

A call from somewhere down the beach made the group turn. As they watched, Zack, Trayka, and the other three men appeared. First, they waved hello, then, seeing the large water dragon in front of them, the three men turned tail and hid among the forest and bushes, whispering to each other to be quiet so that the monster wouldn't "hear" them.

"Well, what an honor," Zack said as he bowed before the water dragon. "And what would your name be, mighty dragon?"

Kaelin chuckled. "Are you trying to flatter me? I'm not a god, I should hope you would know. Respect is always good, but you don't need to exalt me. There are others who deserve that kind of praise." Smiling, Kaelin continued, "But as for your question, my name is Kaelin. And you would be...?"

"Zachary," he answered, emphasized his full name. Travis thought he saw an annoyed look on Trayka, who was standing by his brother. Though he looked nervous around the dragon, he had a much calmer demeanor around Kaelin compared to his men.

"Hm, another of the prophecy then," Kaelin commented before turning away from Zack to look at his brother. "And you are..."

"Trayka," Trayka responded, his blue eyes dancing timidly. He shuffled his weight from one foot to the other, obviously uncomfortable being in the dragon's attention.

Kaelin leaned in, and his nostrils flared as he took in Trayka's scent. "You remind me of someone..."

Trayka stiffened, quickly looking away. "I, uh, get that a lot. I must just have one of those faces."

"Hm." Kaelin obviously didn't believe him—his cat-like eyes were slits as they bore into Trayka.

"Well, um," Trayka took another step back before looking at Travis and Sarora, "we better get going if we want to remain undetected."

Sarora slowly nodded. "We should, but I was really hoping to speak with Kaelin more about the dragons and the wolves meeting."

"I'm eager to find a better place to hide. Is there a way we could contact you later, Kaelin?"

"You're leaving so soon?" Kaelin asked. "Where might you be headed?"

"Home. Not mine, but theirs," Trayka replied, gesturing toward Sarora, Travis, and Zack.

"It's a ways into the Anima Forest," Zack explained further.

"And you're taking them with you?" Kaelin looked away from the group to the three soldiers who were peeking out from behind the bushes. When they saw the dragon look their way, they quickly dove back into the scrubs.

Trayka nodded and sighed. "Yes. To be truthful, I wish that they would return to their own homes and stay away from any danger that follows me. But they insist on coming with me, especially now that they know I'm one of Lord Trazon's most wanted."

"Ah, so you are a soldier?" Kaelin asked.

"Was," Zack corrected as he placed a hand on his brother's shoulder for moral support.

Kaelin dipped his head. "I see. Will it not take your group an awfully long time to travel through the woods to your camp?"

"Probably," Zack said.

There was silence for a moment while Kaelin seemed deep in thought. Then he lifted his head and asked, "Would it help if I gave you a lift?"

Travis was both surprised and excited about the offer. "That would be…"

"I don't know," Zack cut him off with a glare. "We wouldn't want to cause you any trouble."

"Trouble?" Kaelin let out a hearty laugh. "I have faced greater troubles in my life than being a ferry for a group of younglings. I can get you home in a day's journey."

"You can go that fast?" Sarora asked.

Kaelin nodded. "In fact, it is a little slower than what I could usually go, but if I carry two or three people it will slow me."

Another thought occurred to Travis. "Wait a second, you fly?" Travis asked.

"I am a dragon—of course I fly." Kaelin looked at Travis as if it had been quite obvious that he could do so.

"But, how could you? You don't have any wings."

Kaelin gave a wolfish grin. "I don't need them."

"But then how do you..."

"Magic, Travis, magic." Kaelin replied. "Like how some beings can use magic to cast lightning." He side-eyed Zack, who smiled sheepishly. "Do you accept?" Kaelin asked the leader of the group.

"Well," Zack looked around at his exhausted company, who all seemed to plead to have him answer yes. With a sigh, he said to Kaelin. "That would be excellent. Thank you."

"You are welcome. Who would like to ride with me?" He looked over to Travis with a twinkle in his eyes. "Would you like to?" he asked him.

"Um, well I don't know." Travis looked at his friends. *I usually ride on Sarora.* Then, he remembered that they weren't getting along. "Um, sure. I'd love to join you."

"If you don't mind," Trayka took his first step during this meeting toward the dragon, "I'd like to ride as well."

Kaelin nodded. "Of course."

"Then I'll go with Sarora," Zack decided as he looked at his friend with regret in his eyes. "We have some catching up to do." Sarora gave a 'gryphon smile' back at him.

"What about those three?" Kaelin glanced at the men, who were trying to sneak their way out of the bushes.

"I guess they could follow behind on their horses," Trayka decided. "They would probably be uncomfortable coming anywhere near you anyway, no offense."

Kaelin nodded, amusement glittering in his eyes as he watched the terrified threesome. "None taken. Now, climb aboard," he said cheerfully, turning back to Trayka And Travis. "If we start now, we can hopefully reach your home by tomorrow morning."

"Just a moment, please," Trayka said. He dashed off, spoke to the three soldiers, and then returned to the group. "All set. They'll follow, but they are doing so grudgingly. They think I'm putting myself in too much danger," Trayka chuckled.

Travis approached Kaelin and contemplated how he should get onto the dragon without looking like an idiot.

"Put your right foot on my front elbow and grab my horn with your right hand," Kaelin explained. "Then, lift your left leg over top of me and sit tight," he added with a mischievous twinkle in his eyes.

Travis carefully sat on top of the water dragon's back. A moment later he felt Trayka sit behind him. It felt weird. Travis had expected to feel cold, hard scales underneath him. Instead, as he sat just in front of the dragon's shoulders, he felt warm, soft, white fur beneath him.

"Ready?" Zack asked from where he already sat upon Sarora's back.

"I just need to…" Travis remembered and reached down to the ground for his sword. Sitting back up, Travis looked for a place to put his sword.

"Here," Trayka offered, "I have an extra sheath."

He handed a leather sword sheath to Travis, who took it with a grateful, "Thanks."

Quickly, Travis put the sword in the sheath and hooked it to his belt. "Ready," he finally said, wondering whether to grip Kaelin's fur or one of his spikes.

"Let us be off!" Kaelin let out an excited roar as he gracefully loped into the sky.

AERO-AQUATIC DYNAMICS

Travis gasped as Kaelin flew through the sky like a wavering arrow. His long whiskers flew backwards as his body danced through the clouds with elegance.

Behind Travis, Trayka held onto the younger boy with one arm and onto a leathery, green spike with his other. Seeing the scared expression on Trayka's face from the corner of his eye, Travis tried to muster any confidence inside of him. At least Travis had previous experience flying with Sarora. He didn't want the young man to be as frightened as he was. It was odd putting on a brave front for someone who was older than him.

Suddenly, Kaelin's whole body dropped a few feet and Travis thought that his heart had just about stopped. "Hang on and be careful," Kaelin said to him. "There are lots of air pockets in this spot."

"Great, just what I need, more unneeded excitement," Travis mumbled so that neither Trayka nor the water dragon could hear him. Looking to his right, Travis spotted glimpses of Zack and Sarora diving in and out of clouds. With Zack riding her, Sarora seemed to do more tricks in the air, none that she had ever done with Travis. Once, she flipped over backwards and dove for a few feet before propelling them back up. Another time, she did a kind of corkscrew move that dispatched a cloud and left Zack damp.

"Do you like tricks?" Kaelin asked, following Travis's gaze.

Startled, Travis replied, "Depends on what you mean by 'tricks'."

Kaelin's lip drew back to reveal his pearly white teeth in a smile. "Oh, I have some good ones. Like this for example..."

Tilting his head downward, Kaelin shot to the ground like a speedy arrow, his long tail being the only thing that kept them from falling too fast. His eyes wide in terror, Travis heard both Trayka and himself shout with surprise. The air rushed past them and pushed on them with great force. Below them, Travis wished he wasn't seeing what he saw—the river.

"Dragon-Wing River, here we come!" Kaelin called back to them without turning his head. Only then, did Travis realize what they were going to do. Before he could protest, Kaelin broke the surface of the widest part of the river.

Travis's mind forced him to hold his breath as soon as the first drop of water hit his skin. Behind him, he barely felt Trayka tighten his grip around Travis. Forcing his eyes closed, Travis felt them submerge into the deep water.

One second went by, then two, three, and four...

Finally, the suspense got to him, and nervously, Travis opened one eye and then the other. Surrounding them were the waters of the Dragon-Wing River. Above them, the sun's light fought to penetrate into the darkness of the depths. Something shiny flickered not far from Travis's side, and he turned to see a school of fish swimming past them.

Travis smiled, forgetting that he couldn't breathe. Immediately, water found its way through the gaps between his teeth. Travis quickly forced the smile away and the water flow stopped.

"Don't forget to hold your breath." Kaelin's voice was a little distorted by the water, but clear enough to tell what he was saying.

The water dragon's body moved fluidly through the water

like, well, a fish. Travis watched in awe at all the world found in the water. The experience made him a little less frightened of his foe, but he knew that this fear would never be cured completely.

Travis felt something squeeze his stomach, and he turned his head to see Trayka pointing to the surface. His face was blue, and it looked like he couldn't afford to stay under any longer. Travis nodded and tapped Kaelin's side once. The white-furred dragon nodded back to him and then shot up towards the surface of the water.

Just as they had entered the water, they exited it—Kaelin's body shot like an arrow straight into the sky. Travis and Trayka both gasped for breath and panted heavily as water dripped off their soaking wet heads and clothes.

The sun was tremendously bright compared to the underwater world. At the same time, it also brought the warmth that the deep waters seemed to forbid. As Kaelin continued to soar speedily through the air, Travis felt his skin begin to dry quickly.

Behind him, he heard Trayka laugh aloud. "That was awesome!"

Travis nodded back in agreement while Kaelin spoke. "Glad you thought so. See why riding a water dragon is so much more fun than riding anything else? We can swim as well as fly, so nearly every terrain can be covered."

"Hey, you guys look a little wet!"

Travis and Trayka looked up to see Zack teasing them from on top of Sarora. His own hair was mildly damp along with his clothes.

Kaelin flew up higher so that his riders could speak with them.

"Take a look at yourself," Trayka chuckled. "Who dunked you in a lake?"

"Hey, I didn't actually visit a large body of water!"

"But I bet you're jealous that you didn't see the river," Trayka countered. "It was amazing—there were fish and boulders covered in lichen..."

"Gee, I've never seen those before," Zack snickered at his older brother.

Trayka gave Zack a friendly glare, the one that Travis had seen Zack use so many times. "I bet you haven't seen them underwater while on a water dragon."

Zack smiled and shook his head. "No, I have not. Have to add that to my list of things to do before I die."

"Well, what if your death came right now?" Sarora flipped over backwards and fell upside-down for a split second. Though it had been short, it had been enough to make Zack shout out in surprise.

Kaelin chuckled at the scene. "Maybe I ought to be spending more time with young ones rather than by myself. It seems a lot more..."

"Fun?" Travis offered.

"Interesting," Kaelin finished with a smile.

The night passed quickly as they flew through the starry skies without a hitch. Travis woke as the dawn's first light began to appear beyond the horizon.

"Sleep well?" Kaelin's voice startled Travis a little.

"Mm-hmm." Travis rubbed his eyes and then let out a huge yawn.

Trayka stirred behind him. Travis felt him release his grip from around Travis's waist and quickly Travis reached with one hand to hold Trayka's arm in place before he fell off the dragon.

Trayka almost immediately realized his mistake. "Whoops. Thanks. That could've been bad."

"Very bad." Travis smirked at him before turning back to Kaelin. "So, when do you suppose we'll get there?"

"A few more minutes," Travis heard Zack's voice come from somewhere to their right. "We're over the Anima Forest and we're almost to the Vitaker Plains."

Travis nodded. Vitaker Plains was the formal name for the

large open area that surrounded the area outside Olegraro. But since there weren't any other plains anywhere near where they lived, he usually just referred to them as 'the plains'.

"Look! There it is!" Sarora cried out in excitement, very much like she had done when she and Travis had arrived at the camp together for the first time.

With anticipation, Travis looked over Kaelin's shoulder. In the shadowy distance, he could just make out the silhouette of their tent.

"There! Down there!" Travis pointed with glee.

"Where?" Trayka questioned. "I don't see what you're pointing at."

"That tan-colored tent!" Travis pointed again, trying to show Trayka. "It's so large, you can't miss it!"

As they got closer and the tent became unmistakable in Travis's sight, Trayka asked again, "Where? I don't see it."

"Oh yeah..." Travis had finally figured out what was wrong. "You can't see the tent because you're not an Acer or an apprentice."

"That's why Lord Trazon's so ticked!" Trayka exclaimed. "He always used to get so mad because we would seem to get so close on your trail, and then, we could never find your hiding place. Now it makes sense! Why wouldn't he ever think that you guys would make something like that?"

"Probably because his head is too fat for its own good," Kaelin replied, surprising Travis.

"Fat, yes," Trayka agreed, "but never underestimate him. He has plans—so many great and evil plans. Anything else that previous Acers have come up with pale in comparison to what he's got in mind!"

Travis looked at Trayka with a worried expression. "Like what?"

"Oh, well," Trayka looked away from Travis, "you see, well, I can't really tell you..."

"Why? Can't you remember them?"

"No, I remember them as if he had told them to me yesterday. But, well, I'm not allowed to."

Travis looked at Trayka quizzically. "He wouldn't be able to find out, would he?"

Trayka wouldn't look at him. "There is a good possibility that, through me, he could be learning things about you now."

"What?!" Travis almost fell off of Kaelin. "What do you mean by that?"

"Hey, is everything okay over there?" Zack called from where he sat on Sarora, who had glided a little ahead of Kaelin to lead the way.

"Yes, of course!" Trayka replied.

"What was Travis yelling about then?"

Trayka gave Travis a pleading look, asking him not to tell Zack what he had just said.

"Uh," Travis thought quickly for a believable response, "Trayka was just being sarcastic with me and I didn't get it, as usual."

Zack seemed to believe him. "Huh, guess he's part of the family already." Then, Zack turned and continued to wait for Sarora to drop down to their camp.

Turning back to Trayka, Travis whispered, "What do you mean?"

Trayka shot a nervous glance at Zack as if to be sure that his younger brother wasn't looking at them. Deciding that his brother had his mind on other things, Trayka turned back to Travis and whispered, "Have you ever met Lord Trazon?"

Travis shook his head. Trayka continued, "Then you have no idea how powerful he really is."

"Can he read minds or something?" Travis guessed. "Is that why you're so afraid of him?"

"Afraid?" Trayka looked surprised. "I'm not afraid of him."

"Oh, no, you're right," Travis began with sarcasm. "You two are like best buds, and the big yellow sun smiles at you when you think of him. Come on, Trayka, I can see it in your eyes. Whenever you hear 'Lord' or 'Trazon', your eyes darken and you flinch ever so slightly. Like you just did," Travis exclaimed as he spotted the same signs again.

"No, I didn't," Trayka debated.

"Yes, you did."

"No I—"

"Trazon," Travis cut him off, and Trayka jumped.

"Don't do that!" Trayka grasped Travis's upper arm with his right hand and squeezed.

"Told you." Travis had proven his point more easily than what he thought that it was going to take.

"Okay, fine. I'm terrified of him... immensely." Trayka finally admitted. "But can you blame me? I've been tortured by him before. I've seen him torture others with his powers. How do you expect me to feel about him? A lesson to learn for the future, Travis, is to never spend too long of a time in his presence."

"Why?"

"Because, the longer the time that you spend with him," Trayka glanced at Zack nervously once more and then whispered quietly to Travis, "the easier it is for him to overtake you and enter your mind."

Travis didn't know how to reply. Overtake someone and enter his or her mind? He had never heard of such a thing! Sure, he had heard Trazon was powerful, but he had not thought that someone could ever be powerful enough to enter someone's mind.

"Don't ever expect him to go down easily, because his powers are strong—stronger than those of any other Acer that has ever lived." Trayka's blue eyes seemed to flash with intensity. He meant every word that he said.

"I suggest that you hang on," Kaelin told them. "We're going down."

Once on the ground, Travis eagerly jumped off the water dragon. His bottom hurt horribly and he ached from sitting in the same position for hours. The sun's light turned the long grasses of the plains a golden-yellow that seemed to smile at the world around it.

Zack stepped next to Travis and breathed deeply. "Ah, what a beautiful day. It's so nice to be home—for good." He smiled at Travis.

Travis nodded. "It feels like it's been months since we've been home for more than a night."

"But in reality, it's only been a little longer than two weeks," Zack breathed.

Travis could hardly believe it—the most eventful times of the past couple months had happened in two weeks. Seeing the wolves, meeting Trayka, going to town...

Travis smiled as he remembered Elizabeth. He wanted to ask Zack what time they would be leaving to visit the town again, but he knew that that wouldn't be for quite a while. They had just gotten home, and he was sure that his friends wanted to stay for a long time.

Trayka looked around at what, to him, must have been the vast, empty plains. "Hm, nice place. Wish I could actually see the place where my brother grew up," Trayka teased Zack and ruffled his brother's blond hair.

"Me too, but you'd have to go back about six years ago, keep the rest of the crystals from being destroyed, and then find one that accepts you," Zack teased back. Grabbing his brother's arm, he led Trayka toward the tent. "But, I'm sure that you'll still be able to see the inside."

JADED

One week had passed since the group had returned home with Trayka. August had finally met its end, and the days quickly grew shorter in the long preparation for winter. Together, the group of four had lived happily as a family. Not to mention, they had been able to continue training, and everyday, Zack had to admit that Travis grew more skilled in battle. With the help of his sword, Kader, he had several times come close to beating Zack during practice.

Travis had found the sword's name in his book from Master Racht. Supposedly, one of the Acers of the past had wielded Kader many times in battle. Zack would see Travis polish the sword every day, as if it was a precious gem that must be treasured for all eternity.

Pran seemed to be the one who was the most excited about the group's return. His curled tail swept over his back like a fly zipping in the air. Zack had been the first to fall victim to Pran's puppy tackle, followed by Travis, and then Trayka, to whom Pran took a quick liking.

Kaelin, the kind water dragon that had helped them on their way, had opted to leave not long after they had arrived. He said that if he was to call his dragons together to discuss the wolves seeking their help, he must act quickly. So with short goodbyes, he launched himself into the sky and disappeared into the clouds.

Trayka's three men—Mortimous, Thomas, and Straton—had sent word ahead by a pigeon that they were going to take a side route. Supposedly, Trazon's army had caught bits of their trail and were following close behind. In order to keep Trayka safe, they were now heading south towards Pelagius, a large city on the shore of the Capricious Ocean. From there, they would hide and send an occasional letter to Trayka, letting him know every movement of Trazon's men. Though Trayka was obviously happy to be free of his men, he didn't do well with staying put.

"For the past three months I have traveled, only stopping once or twice for a few days," he had explained to his new friends. "My whole body itches to keep moving. It's so weird not to be on the run constantly."

Trayka had talked to Zack later on and decided that he would be leaving soon. He would probably head east towards Myrddin, a seaport on the opposite side of Firmara, and hope to find an apprenticeship in which he could get a new identity.

Trayka had spoken with Zack when they were alone together. "I-I hope you understand."

"Of course I understand." Zack had tried to cover up his disappointment. He didn't want his brother to know how badly he would miss his company. He had spent his whole life wondering where he came from, and as soon as he found his kin, they were to be parted.

"It's just, well, I can't risk him finding you guys when he's looking for me." Trayka meant Lord Trazon. Zack's older brother was always paranoid about him finding them, and part of Zack thought Trayka was right to be so on edge.

"Just be sure to keep yourself safe, Trayka," Zack had said and smiled back at his brother. "Don't go sticking your neck out for all of us all the time."

Later that evening, Trayka announced that he was ready to leave.

"I really wish I could stay, but I have to go. My being here only puts the rest of you in greater danger of being found." Trayka tried to explain himself once more, but everyone already understood. Trayka was a loner—a fugitive—and that's the way it would be until Trazon was vanquished.

Sarora walked over to Trayka and placed a talon on his shoulder. "Be careful. And make sure you know who or what you're striking before you bring out your sword," she added with a twinkle in her eyes.

"And friends before enemies, please," Travis reminded Trayka as well. "Friends shape you—enemies break you."

Huh, been reading from Master Racht's book again, I suppose, Zack commented to himself.

Trayka smiled at all of them. "Thank you, all of you. I promise I'll never forget you." Turning to Zack, the two brothers embraced in a large hug. Trayka whispered into Zack's ear, "If you ever need me, send for me, and I'll come running, full speed."

"Thanks, Trayka." Zack didn't know what else to say. However strong of a friendship that he shared with Travis or Sarora, he knew that he would never be closer to anyone than his own blood.

Zack tossed his sword over Travis's head as he avoided another blow from the younger boy. Twisting, he moved away from the silver blade of Kader and caught his own sword by the hilt. Flipping it in his hands, he went for the fatal blow that would kill any opponent. But Travis was ready. With a newfound agility, Travis turned and blocked Zack's attack. The two swords flashed like bolts of lightning as they collided full force. The shock from the collision vibrated up Zack's arms, but he fought back the urge to drop his weapon. With a grunt, he dropped the attack, stepped back, and readied himself for Travis to strike. Travis waited a moment before attacking with part of his fire form. Zack saw the whole move coming. He readied himself and at the last second, he slipped out of Travis's way and held the sword to his friend's neck.

"You're dead." Zack grinned as he remembered speaking the same words to Travis almost a month ago.

"Not if you'd had a change of heart..." Travis replied with a smile as Zack lowered his sword. Then, before Zack realized what he was doing, Travis fell to the ground, wrapped his legs around Zack's ankles, and twisted. With a thud, Zack hit the ground, stomach first. The air rushed out of his lungs and Zack struggled to get it back.

"Or a distraction came your way," Travis finished his statement.

Zack couldn't help but laugh—he'd been tricked, by Travis nonetheless. As the two of them lay on the ground, laughing their guts out, Sarora appeared over the horizon. She usually came to check on the boys a little after this time. But today she was early, cantering toward them at top speed.

"Zack!" she called to get his attention.

Zack stopped laughing and sat up. Seeing Sarora heading toward them, he stood up and ruffled his hair free of dirt. "Sarora, what's the matter?" he asked as the gryphon came to a sliding stop beside them.

"I've gotten news from Trayka's friends. They say that some of Trazon's men have stopped following them and are now headed this way!" Sarora panted, anxiously looking to Zack for advice.

"Well, I think we'll be just fine if we keep a low profile..."

"A low profile!" Sarora exclaimed and she unfurled her wings. "Sure, we could do that, but what if one of them just happened to stumble upon our camp? Imagine a soldier just searching the plains and he ran into our 'invisible' tent? What then?"

"Well, we're not going to fight them, if that's what you want," Zack said, crossing his arms.

"But, why can't we?" Travis wondered aloud. Looking at Sarora, he asked, "How many did they say were coming?"

Sarora shook her head. "They weren't sure, but they figure more than ten, less than twenty-three."

"Twenty-three? How did they get that number?" Zack mused.

Once more, Sarora shook her head. "I don't know—from what I've witnessed, they are all very 'unique' individuals."

"Well, let's round that number down to twenty-one. That's seven for every one of us," Travis figured, trying to sound smart. "We fought odds a lot worse than that at the battle."

"Yes, but we still lost the battle," Zack reminded him. "We can't just go picking fights with Lord Trazon's men. They're practically trained assassins!"

"Zack, all soldiers are trained assassins, but—"

"But nothing," Zack cut him off, knowing that this was a time to put his foot down. "We're not going to fight them and risk dying."

"But what if we just gave it a shot?" Travis suggested. "We can do it, I've seen us! When we work together, we're nearly unstoppable!"

"Yes, but that alone won't be enough to keep us alive." Zack scowled at him. "Let's look at it this way—if we stay in hiding and keep ourselves alive, the prophecy can still live on for another year."

"What prophecy?!" Travis cried out as if this confrontation was the final straw. "I don't know what's going on, and the best excuse that you two can come up with is that it's for my own 'safety'. What good is that safety if I die because I don't know enough?" Travis's brown eyes held a fire of determination that Zack had never seen in them before.

"But, what if—" Zack tried to ask, but Travis cut him off.

"Zack, I have to be honest with you," Travis's tone was beginning to push Zack off the edge, "ever since Master Racht died, you seem to have tried to become his replica—you act like you know it all, you boss us around, and you never miss a chance to claim your authority over us! But no matter how hard you seem to try, you always miss the point."

Now for once, Zack was confused. "What have I missed?"

"There was only one Master Racht, and there shall never be another to walk precisely in his footsteps!" And with that, Travis got up from where he had been sitting and walked away, ignoring Sarora's call to come back.

Zack watched Travis in wonder as the brown-haired boy's figure disappeared into the horizon. Dumbfounded by the whole outburst, Zack pressed the palms of his hands against his forehead. He could feel the 'nervous sweat' that had fallen from his brow. In exasperation, Zack sat down heavily on a rock that was a ways away from the tent. With his head in his hands, Zack groaned, "Where could we have possibly gone wrong?" Looking up to the sky, he cried, "I'm just doing the best that I can!"

THE SIGN OF THE SHADOWS

Travis began his long trek home after the sun had set. His heart still burned passionately from the words that he'd spoken, and the corners of his eyes held back tears. He had wanted to give up and sob, but his faith forced him to keep his chin up and continue to walk on. Travis could feel strong emotions that he had never felt before, welling up inside of him like a strong tide. It would disappear, then slowly grow, then disappear, then grow stronger than the first time, and it would keep welling until he thought that his heart would burst. He was so entranced by his feelings that Travis had not noticed how far he had walked off into the horizon, and he now continued his four mile hike back home. He didn't know what Zack and Sarora would say to him when he returned. However, he figured that it would go something like, "Wow, I'm impressed," or "I never thought that you..." and then also conclude with, "What were you thinking, walking off like that?" and "Empty-Head, I would have thought that even you would have known not to stay out after dark."

It was so dark now that even the moon was afraid to come out from its hiding place behind the clouds. For the first time, Travis shivered in Firmara's cold night, and he began to look for something that might help him find his way back.

Crack!

Travis thought that he had heard something move. Nervously, he spun around and did his best to see with his eyes in the dark. His heart rate began to slow back down after he convinced himself that it was all in his head. So, he continued to look around for something that would light his path.

Spotting a large stick, and without putting much thought into what he was doing, Travis grabbed a hold of it and held the tip of it in his right hand. "Ignite," he told it, and, to his surprise, the tip of the stick lit on fire. Instantly, the spirit that had made his pride soar disappeared and the flames transfixed Travis as his mind flashed back,

After several seconds, Travis reopened his eyes. "Zack, I can't find it!" he called to his friend, who was having a difficult time aiming the bolts of lightning at Sievan.

"Then dig deeper!" Zack instructed him, still trying to concentrate.

"I... I just can't!" Travis exclaimed, after trying again for another couple seconds.

"Dig... even... deeper!" Zack managed to grunt. A second later, Master Racht's vines withered and the older man fell backward, exhausted.

...As he watched Sievan leap at him, out of the corner of his eyes he saw Zack and Sarora's terrified expressions. "Travis! No!" he thought he heard Sarora's voice, though in slow motion, everything was dreamlike and quiet.

However, just before the talons of death reached Travis, Master Racht leapt between the two of them. Travis's heart plummeted as he watched Sievan's talons rip through Master Racht's armor...

Travis was losing control of his emotions. He felt the sadness in his heart begin to overpower him and take control. He tried to fight it back. Travis dropped the stick that he had lit, which was extinguished as soon as it hit the ground, and held his head between his hands as pain seared through his mind. He could feel his shoulders jerk as he tried to force back his sobs. Travis clenched his fists, hoping that this pressure would help hold back his emotions. Finally, Travis could take it no more. He lifted his head to the sky and let out an angry cry. He became someone— something—else. In his rage, Travis didn't realize that he had brought forth fire, and his fists were now covered in dark crimson flames. Ready to rid himself of the awful guilt, Travis began lashing out in a fighting form that he had never done before.

In anger, Travis punched with his right hand, then with his left. Fire flew from his fists in balls of fury. Some of the smaller flames dwindled as soon as they hit the ground, but unfortunately, and unknown to Travis, the majority of the flames lit a wildfire as soon as they touched the ground.

In his state, Travis didn't realize what he was doing. He spun around and punched twice more. Then, Travis turned to his left and kicked out with both legs, landing perfectly on the ground as the flames that had come from his feet shot away from him. Travis let out another cry as he continued his reckless actions. Something inside him felt almost as if he was an entirely different person— strong, confident, and in-control. His brows scrunched closer together as his vision blurred and his eyes began to glow, an evil grin replacing his look of despair. Then a single, crooked thought crossed his mind, but the thought was not his own. *Now this is power! Let them come find me.*

Zack walked alongside Sarora in the dark. The night's lights hid behind the clouds, so they were forced to look around with only Sarora's keen eyesight. "Where could he be?" Zack asked for about the eleventh time. For the past hour, Zack and Sarora had searched for Travis. When the younger boy had not returned from his walk, Sarora had insisted that they find him so that Zack could apologize

"But I haven't done anything wrong!" Zack had complained to her.

"That doesn't matter at this point now, does it?" Sarora had replied. "He's obviously upset with us, so whether or not we're in the right, we should still talk to him."

Zack couldn't help but sigh and shake his head at the memory. Why did things like this always have to happen to him?

Zack nearly jumped out of his skin when Sarora stumbled beside him. "Sorry," she apologized. "Didn't see that rock." Zack bit back a rhetorical reply. It would do him no good to be joking around right now.

Suddenly, a small flicker of light caught Zack's eye. Zack turned his head to look ahead of them. He thought that he must have been seeing things until the flame appeared again, only bigger this time.

Zack and Sarora turned to each other. "Travis," they said in unison.

"Quick," Sarora ordered Zack, "hop onto my back. Travis needs our help!"

Without replying, Zack leapt onto the gryphon's back and grabbed a hold of her feathers. Even before Zack was ready to go, Sarora had begun her sprint and lifted them high into the air.

"What do you think is going on?" Zack asked her. Once again, he spotted another flame. This time it had been fired into the sky.

"Whatever it is," Sarora began, "it's definitely not good. I think that this is the first time Travis has used his powers since before the battle." She bent her head as she strained her eyes against the light to see what exactly Travis could be fighting. "What has provoked his fire to come back?"

Zack could not answer her question—he had been just about to ask the same thing.

Sarora rapidly beat her wings as they continued to approach

the great light. As they neared, Zack noticed that the fire wasn't just placed out randomly. No, from the sky, it took a shape. And, to Zack's fear, he knew what the shape was.

"Sarora? Do you see what that is?" he exclaimed as fear overtook him.

Sarora nodded, the same grim expression on her face. "Yes— the Sign of the Shadows. I prayed I'd seen the last of that sign three years ago." Those words sent shivers of fear down Zack's spine as he shook away the memories. The Sign of the Shadows was an emblem of evil. It was a thirteen-sided ring, and inside of it was the Eye of Malevolence, a catlike dragon's eye. But the sight of the dark sign was not what scared Zack the most. In order for the Sign of Shadows to appear, it had to be conjured by dark magic, which only came from those whose hearts had been tortured and tainted dark with pain. And this time, instead of an evil sorcerer inside of the eye, there stood Travis.

As they neared the enraged boy, Zack could see the glow of the fires reflecting in his eyes. *No, they're not reflecting the fires; his eyes are glowing red!* Zack realized, recognizing another evil sign on his friend.

"Sarora!" Zack shouted to the gryphon over the roar of the fire below. "Fly me over top of the eye and I'll jump off your back. While I hold Travis down, find a way to put the fire out before it has any more time to spread and attract more attention!" Sarora nodded in agreement and did not argue with Zack. In the face of danger is when they seemed more like siblings than ever before— an older brother and younger sister.

Nervously, Zack released his grasp on Sarora and he began to balance himself carefully on her back. When they neared the drop-off, Zack stood, ready to hurl himself down at Travis. Just before he leapt, time slowed. He could see the evil grin on Travis's face as he continued to release the fire from his palms. His eyes continued to glow a sinister red, and his dark brown hair whipped back and forth in the winds that his fire created. This was definitely not the kind boy that Zack had met several months ago.

No, something was wrong with Travis, and Zack knew it. Travis was not making the decision to conjure this evil mark. Something was controlling him from the inside, and Zack knew that in order for things to stop, he must break that evil link between the evil-doer and Travis.

With a resounding cry, Zack leapt off Sarora and flew through the air towards Travis. Zack landed on top of his friend before Travis was able to defend himself. With tremendous force, Zack pinned him to the ground as he had done before.

Now that Travis saw what was going on, the angry flames that gathered in his eyes looked directly at Zack, and they seemed to burn a hole in Zack's heart. With great effort, Zack pushed aside his feelings and he straddled Travis, making sure that he held his friend's arms down so that his powers could not hit him.

"Travis!" Zack tried to snap the evil conscience out of his friend. "This has to stop! Someone is going to get hurt!"

Travis struggled under Zack's weight as he tried to break free. "You shall not tell me what to do, Iceblood," Travis snickered and his eyes glowed with an evil red. His voice was deep, and it sounded like more than one person was speaking through him.

Now Zack knew for certain that someone must be controlling Travis. The younger boy had never been told the many foul names that were used to describe people like Zack in Firmara.

Trying to ignore Travis's cruelness, Zack continued to pin down the younger boy as he looked to the sky for Sarora. Luckily, the gryphon was just swooping by and was close enough to talk to.

"Zack!" she called to him above the roar of the fire. "I don't know how to put the fire out!"

"I do," Zack shouted back. "Use your keen eye-sight, Sarora. There must be an enchanter around here that is causing this evil magic! Be quick and find him!"

Sarora's eyes widened as she understood, and she nodded and quickly took off. Zack's heart thudded nervously as he looked around for any sign of another figure. Suddenly, a bright flash flew toward Zack, and he yelped and jumped up off of Travis as the flames scorched his cheek. Zack frantically reached his hand up to feel his face. Luckily, the flames didn't seem to have done any fatal damage to him.

While Zack was distracted, Travis stood back up and laughed menacingly. "Why is it that those who claim to bring the better fire always get burned worse?" he cackled. Zack was mortified by the look of evil joy that flashed across Travis's face. How was he going to rescue this boy's heart if he had no idea how to stop the evil pains inside of him?

"Travis, stop." Zack tried desperately to get through to his friend. "This is not what you want. You have a good heart—stop blaming yourself for Master Racht's death. We both know it's all my fault."

Travis scowled at him. "You cannot get him back from my control, Iceblood. Can you not see the power that I have been given by taking him?" Travis stretched his arms high and wide as he looked around at the flames that he had created. "I have the most powerful element ever known, and combined with my sorcery, I am the strongest being in Firmara aside from the Great Lord himself. Tell me, Iceblood, why should I not deserve to have the perfect life if I am, indeed, perfect?"

Zack's mind raced to find a way to stop Travis. The fact that his friend was calling him 'Iceblood' made him all the more sick to his stomach. He feared anyone but Sarora knowing the truth behind that name—he hated that it was the only information his father had left him with when he left Zack behind.

"So, Iceblood, what's your plan?" Travis's snickering awoke Zack from his thoughts. Looking back to Travis, he saw only the red in his eyes. Obviously, Travis was someone else, which meant that he probably wouldn't remember any of the practice battle tricks that Zack used to pull on him. Zack reached to his side and pulled his sword out of its sheath. In the firelight, the silver blade flickered orange.

Seeing the weapon, Travis cackled, "You bring a sword to kill a

Magic Wielder and a sorcerer? How pitiful. Don't you see that I can melt it as easily as I can melt wax or even bend it with my mind?"

"Of course," Zack replied, trying to keep calm. With one last doubting thought about his plan, Zack tossed the sword to the ground and saw it skid across the dirt.

The Oversight

Even the evil Travis seemed genuinely surprised. He froze, eyeing Zack suspiciously. "You're surrendering? Just like that?"

"I'm not going to fight you, Travis," Zack told him, keeping his head up and his eyes level with Travis's.

"But—but why not?"

"Because you're one of my best friends, and no matter what you do, I will never look to bring harm to you."

Travis was in awe of his actions. For a moment, Zack thought he saw his old friend's good nature flicker across his face. But the evil inside Travis quickly returned with a smirk. "Then your death will come much quicker." And Travis lunged at Zack after pulling his sword, Kader, out of its sheath.

Time slowed once more for Zack, and just at the right time. He saw Travis's blow coming, and he jumped out of Travis's way at the last second. Avoiding Kader's blade, Zack watched as Travis kept moving. Before Travis could turn and attack again, Zack used the side of his arm and hit Travis on his left shoulder with all might as a spark of electric current transferred between their bodies.

Time began to speed back up when Travis's face became filled with shock before he collapsed. Kader fell from his hands and clattered on the ground, just in front of Travis's falling body. After Travis fell, Zack was quick to kneel beside his friend. With worry, Zack put his ear to Travis's back, and with relief, he heard the soft beating of his friend's heart.

"He's alive," Zack sighed with relief. Still kneeling on the ground, Zack flipped Travis over so that he could see his face. For now, at least, Zack could avoid explaining everything that he and Sarora had been hiding from him, because Travis was knocked out.

Around them, the flames that formed the Sign of the Shadows were growing dimmer and dimmer until finally, all that was left of them was smoldering piles of ashes. The evil inside Travis must have left when Travis's body had fallen to physical and magical contact. Maybe there was a way to fight magic with magic...

"Zack!"

Zack looked up to see Sarora flying in towards them in the moonlight, which had just worked its way from behind the clouds. Her face was filled with anguish as she landed next to Zack and saw Travis on the ground.

"Oh, Zack, you didn't..."

"No, he's not dead—yet," Zack assured the gryphon. "I just hit one of his pressure points. He should be waking up soon."

"But the flames are gone. Does that mean—"

Zack nodded, seemingly reading her mind. "I think so. The second Travis blacked out, the flames died, and our evil friend left him. I think that whoever was possessing him lost control when he passed out."

There was a small lapse in silence before Sarora turned her head to look at Zack. "Zack, I think maybe we should tell him."

Zack nodded at once. "Yes, we should. But how do we explain it in a way in which he won't black out again in complete shock and awe or call us liars? He might think we're just messing with him."

"I know," Sarora sighed. "But at least we'll be telling him the truth. Whether he believes us or not, it'll be his choice." Then, Sarora positioned herself down on the ground and folded her wings at her side. "Put him on my back—it'll make it easier to get him home if I carry him."

Sliding his arms underneath Travis, Zack found his balance and lifted the boy off the ground. Stumbling, Zack hefted Travis onto Sarora's back and hung him over her sides like a lifeless sack.

Slowly, Sarora stood up to make sure that Travis would not fall off. "I think I'll walk for a while," she told Zack.

"Fine by me, but is it such a good idea to head for home if he might come back to his previous state?" Zack asked her.

"I'm sure he'll be fine as long as his emotions don't go haywire again."

"But what about you? Can you handle it?" Zack asked, afraid for his friend.

Sarora looked into Zack's eyes, emotion brimming inside of them. "You know what I've been through, Zack. I think telling the truth will be a lot easier than hiding our biggest secrets from him. We just have to trust him to do what's right afterwards."

Zack followed Sarora back to the tent, making sure that Travis wasn't about to fall off her.

"Sarora," Zack finally spoke once they were almost home, "I've been thinking about what may have allowed Travis to be possessed."

"Yeah? Well, we know for sure that he hasn't been around Lord Trazon, so that option's out of the question."

"But what else can cause him to act like that?" Zack asked her. "What else had Master Racht said that made possessing another being possible?"

Sarora thought for a moment and then stopped. Looking at Zack, she asked, "When you and Travis were in town, what did you do?"

"Well, we went around looking for supplies..."

"Let me rephrase that question. What did Travis tell you about doing when he was alone?"

Zack thought carefully. "He went and got starstruck on the first day..."

"Starstruck?" Sarora looked at Zack quizzically. "Who was he mooning over?"

Zack shook his head. "I don't know—I didn't see her. But I doubt that Trazon has any female assassins working for him, so whoever the girl was, she's out of the question."

"What about the next day?" Sarora asked.

"Well, we met Stephen and his new friend."

"Stephen's a jerk, but he doesn't have the kind of brilliance needed to do this. Next."

"Travis met Loki."

"Loki... he's the one that gave Travis a prophecy?"

"Against his will," Zack reminded her.

Sarora sighed in frustration. "But that's not enough to cause what just happened. Do you remember Travis saying anything about something else happening before then?"

"I..." Zack stopped as he fit the pieces of the puzzle together. "I've got it."

"What is it?"

Zack began to explain, "Loki lives in this shop, full of sorcery items. Travis did mention looking at one of the shelves and finding a purple stone."

"But he didn't touch it, did he?" Sarora asked nervously.

Zack nodded, not liking what he was saying. "He did. He said he laid his hand on it and kind of blacked out for a moment before he woke to find Loki standing beside him."

Sarora's eyes widened in shock. "Zack, what if that was..."

"It must have been," Zack affirmed her fear. "Somehow, Loki got a hold of the stone and Travis just 'happened' to find it. They've had an idea of where we've been going all along, Sarora."

"But, how?"

"Well, Loki is a psychic, so he must have been keeping an eye on us for Trazon. That's how I see it," Zack figured.

"But then, if Travis touched it..."

Zack nodded. "Travis touched Trazon's Acer Bane. Which can only mean that they know where we've been going. Trazon is most likely aware of the fact that we've been going to Olegraro for supplies, and his men are probably heading there, looking for us right now.

Relief seemed to flood over the plains as the sun's rays grew in the east. The warmth of the light brought hope to Zack while his heart dreaded the moment in which Travis would finally learn the truth. Right now, Travis was sleeping soundly inside the tent. Sarora was out looking for their next meal and keeping watch for someone who might have caused Travis's strange behavior. Zack kept watch for any signs that would cause him worry—like the possessor or Trazon's men. Those two things could cause big trouble. Closing his eyes, Zack listened to the whispering breeze. Serenity filled the growing void of uncertainty, and Zack welcomed its company.

"Zack?" a groan sounded from behind him.

Zack turned his head to look at Travis, who still had a sleepy expression on his face. His brown hair was all messy, and his clothes were stained everywhere, seeing as it was really his only pair of clothes.

"Travis, you're awake!" Zack smiled and stood up quickly to give Travis a large hug. "We were so worried about you."

"Zack," Travis broke away from the hug, regret flashing in his eyes, "I'm so sorry."

"For what? None of us died. Sarora and I were more worried for you than we were for ourselves."

Travis's eyes flickered with sorrow. "I-I hurt you, and I-I couldn't stop myself. It was like I was watching a whole other world while something controlled my body. I tried to hold myself back, and I fought whatever was controlling me, but I couldn't help myself."

"Hurt me?" Zack asked him. "Do I look mortally wounded to you?"

Travis looked at Zack's cheek where the one fireball had hit him. "You're burned."

Zack had only checked his face once. His cheek had swollen a little and turned a pinkish-brown where it had been hit by the fire, but other than that, he was perfectly fine.

"It's not a big deal. It'll heal quick enough," he tried to assure Travis.

Travis shook his head. "No, it won't. I did something bad. Worse than anything else I can think of!"

"Don't worry, we'll work through it," Zack tried to comfort him.

Travis shook his head again, more urgently this time. "No, you don't understand! While my mind was under someone else's control, a voice spoke to me. I was too scared to know any better! I couldn't even control my actions or my thoughts! The words just slipped!"

Zack became really worried. "Travis, what happened?"

"Why, he gave your coordinatesss to me, of courssse."

Travis and Zack spun in horror as they came face to face with one of their worst enemies.

"Well, hello there," the creature cackled at them, his crow-like wings shining with a dark purple in the sunlight. A gray beak with jagged edges seemed to smile back at the boys menacingly. In place of the snake's tail that Sarora had removed from him, the creature's tail was now made of a crystal-looking compound, which gleamed an evil ice-blue in the sun's light. "Long time, no sssee," Sievan cackled as his red eyes danced in the sunlight.

KIDNAP

Travis couldn't take his eyes off of Sievan. His heart thudded in his chest as with each passing second, the realization that their enemies had finally found them sunk in even deeper. It was bad enough that Sievan had found them, but he had found them with *his* help. Travis felt awful.

Seeing the fear of his opponents must have boosted Sievan's morale. With a devilish smile, he strutted forward, his wings held high against his sides. "You know, we had alwaysss wondered why we could never find you thrrree. But to find that you had been hiding in plain sssight for all these yearsss?" Sievan shook his head. "No matter. Lord Trazon will be pleasssed to know that I have found you."

Zack ever so slightly elbowed Travis and whispered, "Grab your sword slowly..."

"Now," Sievan continued as he approached the boys, "I'm sure neither of you will caussse me too much trouble. Right?"

Travis felt his sheath for his sword, but to his dismay, it wasn't there. *Zack must've taken it in the tent after I blacked-out.* He tried his best to hide the fear that was growing in the pit of his stomach. Travis quickly jabbed Zack back and pointed at his empty sheath without taking his eyes off of Sievan. Out of the corner of his eye,

Travis saw Zack sneak a quick glance at the sheath, and he then shot Travis an "oops" in the same motion.

Sievan glared at the boys. "What are you whissspering about?"

"Oh, we weren't whispering," Zack replied calmly. "I was just telling Travis that of all the camps I've seen, most of them have *tents.*"

Travis caught on quickly. *Kader must be in the tent. But where?*

"Right." Travis spoke cautiously as Sievan eyed them suspiciously. "Some of the tents are very large. They are almost like mansions!"

"But the best part of the big tents are the *study* rooms," Zack added. "Lots of the study rooms also have large *desks* where the leader of the camp sits."

"Would you two imbecilesss ssstop blabbering about nothing?" Sievan hissed, his ice-tail lashing back and forth. "Either come with me peacefully, or I will be forced to kill you," he ended with an all-too-eager expression.

"You know, death is kinda harsh," Zack commented, stepping away from Travis and towards Sievan's left. "What if you get to take us, and then can I join you?"

"J-j-join usss?" Sievan stammered, surprised by Zack's response. "But why—"

"Well, Lord Trazon is very powerful, and I'm very tired of disagreeing and fighting all the time," Zack continued dramatically. He stepped further away from Travis, keeping Sievan's full attention. "I mean, I wouldn't want to be on the losing side, so why not join you...?" While Zack continued to drag on his explanation, Travis quietly slipped into the tent.

He headed straight to the desk where, just as Zack had hinted, sat Kader, ready for a good fight.

Silently, Travis slipped the sword off the table and walked out the opening of the tent.

"...and in that way, Trazon would finally be able to rule," Travis heard Zack finish his explanation.

"Well, I've never thought of it like that," Sievan pondered, still unaware of what Travis was up to.

"Yes, it is a new thought," Zack continued on. "In that way, the Dark Lord could keep himself safe from any *attacks*."

While Sievan was nodding in agreement, Travis got the picture. Quickly, he crept up behind Sievan and swung his sword at the dargryph's wing. The next thing Travis knew, Sievan's ice-tail had wrapped around his wrist. With a yelp of pain, he struggled to hang onto Kader as the cold tail seemed to freeze against his skin. Zack was a little slow on his attack. He had grabbed for his sword, but by the time he swung it, Sievan was ready for him. Tossing Travis to the side, Sievan's tail whipped ahead of him and he slapped Zack's sword out of his hand.

"What? Did you think that the two of you could actually take me on?" Sievan sneered. "Do you not rrremember that during the lassst battle, even while the odds were five to one in your favor, I ssstill killed two of you and won! And now that I have been graced with this new tail by the Great Lord himself, I am unstoppable!"

Travis wouldn't hear of defeat. This time it was Sievan's turn to lose. Taking his sword, Travis charged again. When Sievan's tail came in for another attack, he quickly dodged it and slid underneath Sievan. He had just reached up to rake the dargryph's underside with his sword when Sievan's tail came underneath him, and with extreme flexibility, it grabbed a hold of Travis's right hand and dragged him the rest of the way under.

Seeing the danger Travis was in, Zack came to his friend's aid and chopped off the greater length of Sievan's tail. Like ice, the tail cracked under the sword's blade and split evenly. While Sievan was momentarily distracted, Zack grabbed Travis's wrist and pulled him onto his feet.

"Thanks," Travis told Zack as he ripped off the end of Sievan's icy tail, which was still wrapped around his wrist.

Zack nodded quickly. "No problem, but he's not dead yet."

"I mossst certainly am not," Sievan cackled, and when Travis looked at Sievan, he saw no pain in the dargryph's eyes. As Sievan continued to laugh, the part of the tail that Zack had just removed slowly grew back.

"You can regenerate!" Travis exclaimed.

"Prrretty awesssome, huh?" Sievan's eyes glared evilly at the boys. "Now, wherrre wasss I? Oh, yesss. If you two are going to make this difficult, I really only need one of you." With his panther-like grace, Sievan leapt at Zack.

"You're not taking either of us!" Travis cried out, and in a split second, he found himself in front of Zack, between his friend and the beast. His sword held out in front of him, Travis was ready for a good fight.

Sievan momentarily stopped his attack. With an evil grin, he struck at Travis with his beak so that the boy had to duck to avoid getting his eye pecked out. The second Travis went down, Sievan swiped at him with one of his large front talons. The next thing Travis knew, he was flying through the air until he hit the ground with a 'thud'. His head ached horribly, and he was vaguely aware of a cut that went through his shirt to his arm. As he watched in a daze, Sievan went for Zack. Zack raised his sword to defend himself, but alone he was no match for the mighty dargryph. After batting Zack's sword from his hands once again with his tail, Sievan knocked the boy to the ground with a swipe of his massive talons. Before Travis could get up to help his friend, Sievan stretched out his tail and wrapped it all the way around Zack—from his feet all the way up to his mouth—plastering his arms to his sides.

"Got you now. The Dark Lord needs to have one Iceblood for safekeeping." Sievan cackled evilly as he launched himself into the air, Zack in tow.

"Zack! No!" Travis finally felt his legs and, grabbing his sword, he followed Sievan's form as fast as he could.

His legs flying, Travis ran across the plains, keeping Sievan and Zack just ahead of him. Putting Kader in his left hand, Travis mustered every bit of courage that he could find, and he shot a spitting ball of fire out of his right hand.

The fire hit its mark, but it only caused Sievan to momentarily falter in his flight. Looking down at Travis, Sievan taunted him, "Nice trrry, boy. But you'll never bring me down, and you'll never catch me now!"

Determination welled up inside of Travis. He felt his legs pick up more speed and his heart pumped oxygen quicker than it ever had before as his adrenaline took full effect.

"Zack! Hang in there!" he called up to his friend. "I'll get you!" But the dargryph had carried his friend away in a blink.

Something sent Travis sprawling down across the ground. The impact hurt just nearly as badly as the strike from Sievan had.

Forcing back his pain, Travis looked up to see what had collided with him.

"Sarora!" Travis felt relief flood through him. Quickly, Travis got back on his feet once more. "Come on, we have to hurry! Sievan has Zack! Give me a ride!" Without waiting for a response, Travis moved to Sarora's side to hop aboard, but Sarora knocked him down once more. Her eyes flickered with so much emotion that Travis was not able to decipher what exactly was going through her head.

"Sarora, what are you doing?" Travis cried out as he sat up. It was really hard to ignore the pain he was feeling now. "We have to get Zack back! Sievan has him!" Travis turned and looked at the sky. I know which way they went. We have to follow them!" Travis went to stand up, but Sarora pinned Travis to the ground.

Travis could hardly believe what his friend was doing. "Sarora? Why are you holding us back? Zack is in danger!"

"I know that!" Sarora cried angrily back at him.

"But then, why don't you..." Travis cut himself off as he remembered the prophecy. "No, it can't be!"

"What now?" Sarora asked him.

"You-you're the betrayer!" Travis cried out.

Sarora looked at Travis with bewilderment. "What do you mean?"

"The prophecy! The one that Loki told me! He spoke of an

enemy that would become my ally. It's you! You betrayed Zack and me!"

"Have you lost your mind?" Sarora asked in shock.

"I was about to ask you the same thing," Travis retorted.

Sarora sighed. "No, Travis, I would never betray you or Zack. Ever. I'm only stopping you from making a big mistake."

Travis glared into Sarora's eyes. "What mistake?! Zack is in trouble, and he needs our help! So why won't you help him?"

Sarora leaned her head in closer to Travis's. "Think, Empty-Head! Did you see how fast he left? We have no hope of keeping up with him after he ingested Speed Spruce. And what did Sievan say? He said he only needed one of us! Doesn't that just scream 'it's a trap!'?"

Travis stopped his rampage. He hated to admit it, but Sarora was most likely correct.

"Just think, if we found their trail and followed now, Sievan would lead us right to an ambush, where they would obliterate all three of us! But, not before torturing us for information about the wolves and other magic animals."

"Wait a second." A thought caught Travis's mind. "How did you hear our conversation? You weren't even there!"

"I have the ears of a hawk, if that helps any," Sarora explained. "I was headed home from hunting when I heard Sievan gloating to the two of you. I stopped to listen—which was my mistake. I should have continued on to help you guys. But what's done is done. The matter can't be helped much now." Sarora stepped off of Travis and offered her wing to help him up.

"But what about Zack?" Travis asked as he retrieved Kader from the ground. "We can't just leave him in the hands of the enemy."

Sarora looked away from Travis, sadness welling in her eyes. "I don't think that there's much that we can do for him now. We'll have to contact the wolves, but I doubt they'll want to rescue Zack. After all, we still haven't returned for my trial."

"But then, what do we do?" Travis asked, anguish filling his heart.

"We do all we can do," Sarora said. "We send a letter to Trayka and hope that he can help. But for now, we should go into the woods, lay low, and wait to move until we have a plan. There's no telling if Trazon's men will be headed to the tent."

Travis didn't want to give in, but there was nothing that he could think of that would help Zack.

"Fine, just let me grab Master Racht's book from the tent," Travis told her.

"Already done," Sarora stopped Travis. Unfurling her right wing, she revealed his leather-bound book. Normally, Travis would have been upset by the fact that Sarora would take his book out of his room without permission, but his emotions were too dull to attack her again.

"Thanks," he mumbled to her as Sarora led him across the plains and into the shade of the Anima Forest.

FRIENDS IN ALL
PLACES

S omething wet pressed against Zack's head. His whole body ached, especially his right shoulder and his head. The last thing he remembered was flying with Sievan full speed through the mountains. When passing through the gaps between them, Sievan had carelessly let Zack hit the rocks and cliffs that were in his way. After about the third hit, Zack had blacked out, and now he had the worst headache that he could imagine. Again, something wet pressed against his forehead and Zack began to open his eyes. The room he was in was dark and had a wooden door, which had one window fitted with bars. On the opposite wall there was another window, this one also with bars and high up. He was lying on a cold, hard, concrete floor. Above him, the ceiling was made of stone, just like the four walls of the cell. At least the floor had straw scattered across it to use for bedding.

Seeing his surroundings, Zack tried to sit up, but pain shot up from his ribcage. Something gentle touched his shoulder and spoke softly, "Be still, all is well."

"Sarora?" Zack asked as he tried to settle himself back down, still in a daze. He looked to his left and saw a figure kneeling next to him. He could barely make out her form in the dim, cold cell.

The figure shook her head. "No, I'm afraid I'm not the gryphon."

"Where am I?" Zack asked, trying to bite back the pain coming from his head.

The girl placed the wet towel on Zack's head again and told him softly, "You are in a cell in Sir Donigan's castle, which is located in the middle of the Sendoa Mountains."

"Donigan?" Zack wasn't as surprised as he sounded. "Well, that's...great." He said as he lowered himself back onto the floor slowly.

"Master Sievan brought you here," the girl explained further. "He ordered you to these quarters until your friends made their way here."

"Travis and Sarora?" Zack asked nervously. "They didn't follow me, did they?"

The girl looked at Zack with sympathy. "I don't know. I haven't heard anything from the guards about them coming, so I would assume that if they are coming, they won't get here for quite a while."

Zack let out a sigh of relief. "Good. Sarora must have grabbed Travis before he could follow me any farther. I'm sure they'll be fine without me for now."

"You-you do know that they are holding you hostage, right?" the girl asked Zack.

Zack tried to nod, but his head hurt too badly to do so. "I don't care how long I must stay here as long as my friends are safe." The girl nodded once and moved her hands to Zack's arm. In silence, she wrapped cloth around a cut on his arm. When she tied in the ends tight and pulled, Zack grunted.

"Sorry," the girl apologized and then continued checking him over. "So, you can use magic then?" The girl's shyness seemed to slip away and was replaced with curiosity.

"Yes," Zack replied shortly, not quite sure what to think of the girl yet. She sounded as if she weren't all that much older than

Zack, so he concluded that she was probably just a young servant of the castle.

"That's pretty useful, I guess."

"Unless it puts a target on your back and gets you killed," Zack grunted as he forced a smile, trying to be polite to the person who was helping him.

The girl smiled back. "I guess that would be pretty bad. I prefer to not mess with anything having to do with magic."

Zack searched the darkness for the girl's expression. "Then why are you helping me?"

The girl turned her head away. "I was cleaning when I saw the soldiers drag you in and toss you on the floor. I just couldn't leave you lying there."

"Well then, thanks." Zack didn't know what else to say.

The girl smiled back once more. "You're welcome. At least you gave me someone I can talk to. There are only a couple other maids here, and Donigan likes to keep them busy cleaning his quarters."

"Sounds like Donigan, all right," Zack thought darkly.

"You've met him? And lived?"

Zack managed a nod this time. "He's got a ruthless hand in battle, but a gut of mush."

The girl chuckled softly, "You describe him perfectly. All his strength is in his arms and voice, though you would think that he could eat steal without dying."

Far away, there was a creaking of a door. The girl immediately stood up and grabbed the cloth that she had been using for bandages.

"I'm sorry, but I must go," she told Zack. "If they catch me speaking with you, they'll have our heads."

Zack understood. He wouldn't want the girl to get into trouble on his behalf. She seemed pretty nice for having to deal with a life like hers.

The girl went to open the door, and she turned once more to smile at Zack. He could now tell that she had long, wavy hair and that she wore a worn maid's dress. The light coming through the door's window reflected her round, warm brown eyes.

"I'll come back the next chance I get," she whispered to Zack as she began to slip out the door.

"Wait!" Zack whispered as loudly as he could. The girl stopped and looked at him. "What's your name?" he asked her.

"Jezebel," the girl whispered and then walked out of the cell, silently closing the door behind her.

DREAMS OF A
GRYPHON

The sky was still alight, but the sun finally sank deep enough to where the forest's shadows overcame it. Bits of orange and red peeked through breaks in the trees and peered at Sarora as she lay next to the river. Her head hung while she watched Travis sitting across from her, leaning against a large oak tree as the sun set. His eyes were drooping as well while he read from Master Racht's book.

Yesterday Zack had been taken from them. The sorrow of the day seemed to drag the hours on. The trickling of the river was soothing to Sarora, but she wanted to talk with Travis. Though she had been hard on him about letting Zack go, she knew that the blow had hurt her worse. They were more than friends—she considered Zack a brother.

Travis sat in silence, one finger held up, lit at the tip like a little torch.

"Travis?" Sarora finally spoke up, tired of the silence.

"Yeah?" came a quiet reply. Travis still had his face in the book.

"I was wondering... what does Master Racht say about me in your book?"

Travis flipped through the pages quickly, as if he remembered where he had last read of her in it. Finally, he stopped and read aloud:

"As you continue on your journey, plenty of mysteries will be revealed, not to mention the chance to find secrets in them."

When Travis stopped, Sarora asked, "That's it?"

Travis shook his head. "He also said you're stubborn, but that there's a possibility that Zack is worse."

Sarora sighed. "Travis, I know that you have a lot of reasons for being mad at me, and I understand that. But, I just want to be friends again. Please?"

Near the tree, Sarora heard Travis sigh. "I really want to trust you, Sarora. But don't you see how hard it is to do that when you don't trust me enough to share secrets?"

Sarora tried to find Travis's eyes in the dark, but she found this hard even for her hawk-like eyesight. "Travis, I swear, Zack and I were going to tell you everything once you had woken up, but now that he isn't here..." she trailed off before continuing, "Zack's a big part of what I want to tell you, and if he's not here, I-I just—"

"It's fine, Sarora."

"It is?" Sarora was puzzled.

"Yeah." Travis extinguished his finger with his thumb and swiped his hand over the book, which was quick to lock itself back up. "I'm just going to get some rest. Maybe sleep will give one of us an idea of how to get Zack back."

Although she knew that Travis couldn't see her, Sarora nodded in agreement, laid her head down, and then closed her eyes, falling into a dream-filled sleep.

Sarora sat in a large cavern that brought memories of both joy and pain. Magic crystals rested in recesses, their powers casting a rainbow glow all around her. The clicks of her talons echoed in the chamber as she surveyed the crystals with intrigue. She quickly recognized Master Racht's crystal. Its deep green gave the impression of being earthy while still bearing the precious resemblance of an emerald.

With a smile, she walked over to the Crystal of Knowledge and touched it gently with her beak. It gleamed in the dim light with a modest brilliance. She had visited this place many times in her dreams, and each time it had been the same—today was no exception.

Suddenly, the serenity of the cave was disrupted with screeching, and Sarora watched in horror as Trazon's soldiers marched in and began to destroy every point of light they saw. Each time a crystal shattered, she heard the spirit animal within it cry out in agony. Sarora tried to stop the men, but they just passed right through her as if she were a ghost.

Master Racht's crystal remained untouched, as if the soldiers hadn't seen it. Sarora covered the crystal with her body, trying to ensure that it remained hidden. The screams of anguish grew louder, so she covered her ears with her talons, knowing that there was no way she could help them. But though she blocked the sound from her ears, she could still hear the screams vibrating in her head.

"Stop it!" Sarora screeched. "Please, someone, make it stop!"

This was usually the part of the dream in which she would awaken, but this time, something interrupted the soldiers' rampage.

A brilliant light radiated from Master Racht's crystal. Sarora could barely keep her eyes open as it illuminated every remaining crystal in the room. In a chorus, the crystals seemed to speak using their light, and Sarora understood every word.

Those of great prophecy go fraught,
One with gift of fire burning,
Your enemy of fate will be naught,
But your friends with woe be mourning.

The soldiers disintegrated in the light, and the screaming stopped abruptly. At the end of the cavern rested four last crystals— three of which she recognized.

Sarora's whole being shook with fright and awe at the brilliance. Though the screams and the strangely worded prophecy had stopped, she remained bowed on the floor covering her ears.

Then, from the center of the cave, a familiar form appeared. A hand rested on her shoulder as he spoke, "Do not fear. It is just me, and all other things seen are of the past."

Sarora uncovered her ears as she looked upon the figure. He wore a kind smile and his eyes were warm. His white-silver hair shone brightly against his dark green tunic, which had a pleasant gold pattern running across its seams. Like his crystal, he also appeared to glow.

"Master Racht!" Sarora cried out with joy. Quickly, she stood up to greet him. "But I thought you were dead!"

Master Racht smiled at his long ago apprentice. "Ah, my dear, you have thought correctly. Though at the moment you wish to deny it, I have left and shall never return to live with you."

Sarora's heart sank. Though she realized that there was no way possible for her mentor to be alive, she had still hoped that by some miracle she would find him again.

"But then," Sarora tried not to sound disappointed, "why are you here?"

Master Racht's smile disappeared. "Though I am gone from your life, I have been sent to pass along knowledge. I have been granted the opportunity to share your own pasts with you and Zack."

"So you gave Zack his dream too?" Sarora asked. "Why would a message from you scare him?"

"Just like you, I showed him pictures that were connected with his past. He didn't know it at the time, but he was seeing his past life, before he met you." Master Racht explained.

Sarora reminded herself to ask Zack, if and when he returned to them, about his dream.

Master Racht seemed to have read her thoughts. "You wish for your friend's return?"

Sarora nodded. "Yes, but I don't see how we can rescue him. If he's with Trazon, it's a trap for certain. And if he's with Donigan and Sievan...well, that's probably a trap as well..."

"Sarora?"

"Yes?"

"You and Zack are very close, are you not?" Master Racht asked.

Sarora was puzzled. Why would her master ask such a thing? "Closer than ever, but—"

"And you'd do anything for him, am I correct?"

"Of course! But I don't see how—"

Master Racht cut her off again. "And what would Zack do if he were in your position and you in his?"

Sarora's answer came a couple seconds later. "He would rally Travis, come up with a plan, and recklessly come to rescue me."

Master Racht's eyes held a twinkle. "Is being reckless always a bad thing? At first, sure, it will have its snags, but inaction more often leads to failure than haste. Look at how your own recklessness has served you—if not for it, would Travis be in your midst?"

Sarora wasn't sure how to answer. Looking away from her master, she found her heart being torn in two for the safety of both of her friends.

"What does your heart say, my dear?" Master Racht asked her. "You know what you must do."

Sarora looked up to respond, but her master had already begun to dissolve from her sight. As he faded away, Sarora heard him softly say, "You will make the right choice, of this I am sure." And then he was gone.

Steeling her resolve, Sarora woke. The starry night was almost over, so she sprang to her feet. "We will go. But this time, I will not be so negligent."

Sarora spotted Travis's form sleeping soundly next to the tree. Quietly, she skirted around him and stole away back to the camp. The dovish morning sky cast an eerie light on the still campsite. Landing next to the tent, Sarora shot one quick look around her, just waiting for some large monster to jump out and attack. But when nothing happened, she quietly slipped inside.

Walking next to the desk, Sarora pried open a drawer with a talon. Carefully, she shuffled through its contents until she found a box. Inside the box she found the Crystal of Courage in its bag. Delicately, Sarora picked it up with her beak and set it on the table.

Something clanged underneath the crystal. With curiosity, Sarora sat down the box and lifted the sack up with her talon. On the table sat a yellow-gold crystal on a thin chain. It was a necklace that would belong to an Acer. *Isn't this Zack's?* Sarora wondered. *Why isn't he wearing his crystal? Doesn't he know that even though he never finished his ceremony that he still has earned the right to wear this?* Along with the red crystal, Sarora grabbed Zack's Crystal of Justice and put it in the sack. Then, she walked into her room for one last item.

The room, once filled and lined with books and scrolls and musings of her own, was now empty to make way for her nest-like bed. She reached under her bed, gingerly sliding the item out from underneath. Warily she held it in her foot before daring to look at it. Sarora felt a twinge of pain in her heart when she beheld it and it failed to gleam at her. She couldn't even remember the last time she had looked at it—it had to have been years. She had forced herself to put the past behind her, and she intended to still move only forward. But perhaps this small token could serve as a reminder of who she was and the aid she could lend her friends.

Sarora took all three items and left the tent.

The stars were just beginning to fade. A beautiful pink dawn dotted with clouds welcomed the new day. With hope and worry dwelling in her heart, Sarora looked to the northern star in the sky

—the Acer Star. After a prayer for guidance, Sarora searched for her heart in that star as she wondered aloud, "Is this really my destiny?"

To The Rescue

When Travis woke with a start, it took him a moment to realize that Sarora was missing. The morning sun leaked a gentle light through the treetops. Though dark clouds covered the northern skies, it looked as if this day was going to be a normal one—that is, until he remembered that Zack had been kidnapped.

Forcing his legs to stand, Travis grabbed Master Racht's book from the ground, which he had sort of used as a pillow. Wiping any dirt from its cover, Travis studied the design of the golden seal. Three animals chased each other around the circle, and with wonder, he realized for the first time that Zack's qilin and that a gryphon—which could be related to Sarora—were two of the three animals. The last animal was a fearsome looking creature—a dragon. It was nothing like Kaelin, who was lithe in build and cautious in nature. No, when this piece of gold was brought to life, it seemed to glare at Travis with the fire of a beast. Once, it had even hissed at him when he had tried to pick it up.

Well, at least it doesn't spit fire. Travis tried to lighten his mood with humor, but his efforts were futile.

Just as Travis was about to put the book down on the ground, there was a flapping of wings, and he turned to see Sarora landing next to him. In her right talons she carried a small bundle.

Hastily she told him, "Grab the horses. We're leaving."

"Leaving? You mean we're going after Zack?" Travis felt hope stir within him.

"You're going to get the horses and lead them behind me. I'm going to fly ahead, sneak into Donigan's castle, and find Zack before I'm detected," Sarora explained her plan in short.

"Wait a second!" Travis looked at Sarora in disbelief. "Are you trying to tell me that I'm going to horse-sit while you go and rescue our friend? No way, Sarora. Not this time. I want in."

Sarora sighed as she handed him the sack. "I was afraid that you were going to say that. Here, take it. Inside are the Crystals of Courage and Justice."

Travis opened the bag and carefully pulled out a yellow crystal on a silver chain. "This is Zack's crystal? A necklace?"

Sarora nodded. "Once you have found your spirit animal and used your powers, then your crystal grows smaller and is fitted on a chain. That way, not only can you use even greater powers than before, but it's also easier to carry around."

"Sounds like I should have been trying to call my spirit animal months ago." Shaking his head, Travis dismissed the thought. "Anyway, you giving me a ride?"

"No, I'm gonna make you run," Sarora snapped gently at him. "What do you think? Just let the horses know where we are headed and then we'll be off. And don't lose that sack. We'll need it when we find Zack—I'm sure he'll need the boost to his strength."

"Speaking of strength, shouldn't we wait for the wolves?" Travis asked. "Or Trayka? He'll surely want to help." They had sent for the pack's help through a message yesterday morning. They had also sent word to Zack's brother, but they doubted that the message would reach him for some time.

Sarora shook her head. "There is no time to wait for help, and if we want to bring the element of surprise into a trap, we better keep a low profile."

Sword in his sheath, crystal in his pocket, and the bitter wind clawing at his face, Travis sat on Sarora's back, hanging on to her feathers and fur. Below them, storm clouds boomed and thundered. Each time one struck, the shock waves would shake the air as they vibrated against everything in their way. The atmosphere was alert with the uneasiness of the situation—so was Sarora. Storms frightened her, especially when she was in flight. Travis couldn't blame her, though. If they weren't on their way to rescue their friend, they wouldn't take the chance of being electrocuted. Ever since her flight from Firmara, she never felt quite comfortable in the air when it was dark. She had told Travis that it felt like Sievan would appear at any moment and attack her directly.

But both of them knew that, for now, they must both set their fears aside and look ahead at the task before them. Zack needed their help, and if they were going to avoid falling into the trap that had been set, then they were going to have to execute a perfect plan. What the plan was—they were yet to find out. Silence would have been useful to help them think, but the storm didn't seem to want them to get organized.

"Sarora!" Travis leaned forward and shouted to his friend. "Can you go any faster?"

Sarora's reply was muffled slightly by the wind, but it still carried back to Travis. "I took what I could from the Speed Spruce but it's worn off. If I fly higher to go faster now, you may pass out from lack of oxygen!"

"Please, Sarora," Travis asked her desperately. "Just a few yards higher? I'm sure that wouldn't hurt, would it?"

"Fine," Sarora sighed. "But if you fall off, I'm not turning to pick you back up." Flapping her wings, Sarora used the lift around them to bring them up higher in the air. As they went higher, the wind that had blown Travis's hair seemed to die down, and Sarora was able to move forward at a quicker pace.

Another hour passed before either of them spoke. Sarora was the first to break the silence. "I'm going down below the clouds. I think we've passed the heart of the storm, and I want to make sure of where we are."

Travis nodded. "I'm ready—go for it."

Pulling her wings in, Sarora dove almost straight down. As they plunged through the clouds, puffy wisps of gray and white circled around them. Travis wanted to let out a shout, but he clenched his jaw shut. If they were anywhere close to Donigan and Sievan, proclaiming their arrival would be the worst thing they could do when they wanted to stay undetected. Finally, they broke through the bottom layer of clouds. Sarora was quick to tilt back up and snap her wings open. Thousands of feet below them, the Anima Forest had broken apart into separate clumps of trees. As they continued to fly on, the clumps grew smaller and smaller until only a few lonesome trees dotted the grassy ground.

Travis felt Sarora's muscles shift underneath him. "Look ahead closely."

Squinting, Travis searched for what Sarora was looking at. Finally, he spotted the outline of several dark, tall silhouettes looming not ten miles ahead of them.

"The Sendoa Mountains," Sarora told Travis, her voice just loud enough to be heard.

"That's where they're keeping Zack?" Travis asked.

Sarora nodded towards a specific peak. "Between that mountain and another is a high valley. In the heart of it rests a stone castle with high walls. Soldiers guard the place day and night, so it'll be very difficult to try and sneak in."

"Quite a vivid description," Travis commented sourly.

Sarora sighed. "Fine. Here comes the first secret—I have been there before. Zack, Master Racht, and I have fought Donigan there once before and barely won. Unfortunately, we didn't kill him, but at least he didn't come looking for us for a while."

Travis felt something in his heart flutter. He couldn't exactly place the emotion—it was like something unexpected had finally happened, and his mind was trying to digest the surprise as it reminded him that this was a breakthrough that he had hoped for all along.

"We were stupid, Travis," Sarora continued before Travis could ask more. "We were young, and cocky, and when Master Racht was taken hostage by Donigan and his soldiers, Zack and I raced to his rescue, against Master Racht's wishes. We may have made the right decision in the end, but we paid a lot for the results we wanted. Both Zack and I were injured, he more than I."

"That scar on the outer side of his shoulder," Travis thought aloud. "Is that the injury that he received?"

Sarora confirmed his question with a nod. "Yes, and it took him three months before his muscle tissue began to work okay together, and then another couple months before he could use that arm again properly. His arm never has fully healed, but he copes with the pain—though he won't admit that the spot hurts him."

Travis was quiet at first. Although he could not see her face, he was able to tell by the tone of her voice that Sarora hadn't felt very open to sharing the secret with Travis. Yet, she had done so. Guilt began to grow inside of him. What if Sarora had only shared those secrets because he had pestered her so much about it? He really didn't want it to seem that way, but there was a possibility that this was so.

Travis finally found his voice. "Um, Sarora?"

"No, Travis, we are not there yet," came an exasperated reply.

"No, that's not what I was going to ask—well, I was going to, but not after you said what I was going to say. Sarora, I'm sorry."

"Sorry for what?"

"For being a jerk of a friend and moreover, an idiot. I'm sorry if I forced you to share something that you weren't comfortable with sharing—you don't have to tell me anything else."

There was a lapse of silence, and then, "Travis, I don't blame you. I forgive you, if that is something that you must hear, but as much as it might pain me to reopen an old wound, it brings relief to my heart to let you know everything about Zack and I..."

Before Sarora could continue on, Travis interrupted her. "If it's not immediately important to this mission, we can share more after the battle. We are almost at the mountain's base—we should probably start going through some plans before we reach the castle."

"You're right," Sarora agreed, though her voice held disappointment. "Well, what if we came in through the east side of the mountains? Since the sun is working its way west, then the shadows from the mountains will be cast east, which will hide us from the soldiers' sight."

Travis nodded. "Sounds good enough, but how do we enter the castle if it's heavily guarded?"

Sarora seemed to take this into deep consideration before she replied, "We'll go in through the escape in the back."

"But won't Donigan expect that? Going through the front would be dumb, so he'll figure that we'll come through the back," Travis brought up.

Sarora shook her head. "Donigan thinks too many steps ahead. He'll assume we will come from the front because no one would ever try to sneak in through the main door. So, he'll think that it is the most obvious place we'll enter from, because we'll think that he'll have left it nearly unguarded. It's complicated, the way he thinks, but I am positive that the back is the best entrance."

"I hope you're right, Sarora," Travis said, quieting his voice as Sarora turned them east and headed for the shadows of the mountains.

BREAK-IN

Upon finding cover in the mountains, Sarora flew Travis down over their steep sides. Without words, they contemplated where to land. Deciding that it was best to land on a ledge and slip through a window, Sarora glided over and landed so quietly that Travis didn't even hear the clicks of her talons on the slate.

Silently, Travis slid off Sarora's back and set his feet on the cold stone castle floor. In every way, Donigan's castle reminded Travis of when Sleeping Beauty's kingdom had fallen under its curse—it had all the makings to be warm and welcoming, and yet, the dark stones whispered of shadowy days and evil paths.

The castle had four towers, one at each corner of its square-like layout. Sarora had told Travis that they were probably used as dungeons. Though they were almost certain that Zack was in one of them, they were also convinced that he was heavily guarded, so it would be suicidal to go directly to his tower. Instead, they were going to take their chances at scaling the tower from the heart of Donigan and Sievan's home.

If Zack could see us now, he would assume that this was my plan and not Sarora's, Travis thought to himself. *It's so simple and full of foolishness that we might as well just turn ourselves in.*

Nodding to Travis, Sarora pointed at the barred window. Travis nodded back to her in understanding. Holding out his hands, Travis grasped the center bars. Concentrating, he was able to make the bars flex without melting them too much. Pushing as hard as he could, Travis spread all of the bars out as far as he could so that the both of them could slip through the opening. Standing back, Travis turned to Sarora and smiled as he whispered, "Bet even you can't do that."

Holding a talon to her beak, Sarora told Travis to remain silent. With the nimbleness of a cat, she crept up to the window and slipped through it. With one last look over his shoulder, Travis followed closely behind her.

Except for the glowing, candle-sized torches on the walls, the halls of the castle were utterly dark. The air held a chill that sent shivers down Travis's spine. From somewhere down the hall, Travis could hear a steady dripping of water.

Looking back at Travis, Sarora mouthed, "Grab a hold of my tail." Travis did so.

Using her wings, Sarora extinguished every other torch as they walked, making sure that she did so silently.

Quietly, the two of them crept through the long halls filled with darkness. For a long while, they heard and saw nothing of anyone else. *Strange,* Travis thought to himself. *Maybe we've been giving Donigan more credit than he's due...*

Suddenly, a door opened and then slammed shut not thirty yards ahead of them. In the dim light, Travis saw Sarora's eyes flash with fear—they were caught in the open.

Straining his eyes to see in the dark, Travis spotted a storage room door to their right. After tugging on Sarora's tail, Travis moved to the half-open door. While he struggled to pull it open enough for Sarora to squeeze through, the footsteps grew louder from down the hall. Finally, Travis was able to pry it open and slip inside the cramped storage closet. Sarora followed closely behind, but it was a very tight fit. Travis had his back pressed against the cold, stone walls. Under Sarora's weight, his arm dug into old wooden shelves. She leaned back on her two hind, lion-like legs, and her back was just touched the walls. Her wings were pinned at her sides, and her head was bent inward to prevent it from bumping the ceiling.

Outside the door, the footsteps stopped abruptly. The deep voice of a soldier grumbled something about how boring the watch duty was. Then, just when Travis thought that he was going to make a noise and topple over, the footsteps started up again, and the man began to walk away.

Travis breathed a sigh of relief as soon as he was sure that the man was gone.

"Quiet," Sarora whispered. She still hadn't moved from her spot. "He may still be out there."

Travis tried to remain silent, but one thought after another suddenly swarmed in his head like angry bees. If they were really in great danger, he needed to share with Sarora the prophecy he had received from Loki. Surely it was better to know it than be left in the dark...figuratively.

Since Travis's face was practically in Sarora's ear, he whispered very softly, "Sarora, there's something that I've neglected to share with you."

Sarora was quiet, but Travis didn't take offense. He figured that she was trying to do the right thing and remain silent, but as far as Travis was concerned, this wasn't his silent time.

"You-you haven't been the only one keeping secrets," Travis managed to say. He thought that he saw Sarora's eyes flash with curiosity and warning, but he continued.

"I haven't spoken the truth. That is, I do remember Loki's prophecy. All of it—word for word." And then and there, Travis told Sarora the whole prophecy.

Travis was surprised by how well Sarora took the news. He had expected her to at least smack him over the head, and yet, she listened to him in silence.

Only after he was finished did Sarora reply, "Thank you for telling me, Travis. I know how hard it is to admit something that you've done, trust me." Looking away from Travis, Sarora leaned forward and slowly opened the door of the closet. Nervously, she worked her way out of the storage room and back into the hall. Turning her head, Sarora whispered over her shoulder, "Come on, the coast is clear."

Feeling the elbowroom increase around him, Travis walked forward and peeked out the doorway. Though it was dark, he could tell that they were the only ones in the long hall. This time, Travis led the way and Sarora followed behind. For the rest of the walk down the hall, no one appeared ahead of or behind them. *Strange,* Travis found himself thinking again. *Why, if this was a trap, wouldn't Donigan have more soldiers guarding the inside of his castle?* As they reached a corner of the castle and the hallway ended, Travis peeked around the bend to make sure that no one else was coming their way. Behind him, Sarora shuffled her feet with unease. Finally, her nerves must have gotten to her, so she spoke.

"Travis, there is something else that I must tell you before we go to fight Donigan," she finally whispered to him.

Travis was trying to focus on their surroundings. As far as he was concerned, the time for talking had been back when they were stuck in the nearly soundproof closet.

"Sh, I think I heard someone," Travis tried to quiet his friend as he strained to listen once more.

"But Travis," Sarora didn't seem to want to give up, "I have to tell you the truth. It's—"

Travis held his hand up for silence. Ahead of him, he saw a guard appear around the corner. Quickly, Travis pressed his back against the wall and fell into the cover of the shadows. Sarora did the same.

The soldier, obviously oblivious to all that was going on, walked past them. As he walked through a door further down the hall, he shouted, "Oye! Glendor, you got the keys?" The reply was muffled, but Travis could still hear the first soldier say in response, "Well, then, you better grab her. We got another hour 'till the captain wants to be at full force..." The voice slowly disappeared as the soldier walked further away.

With a sigh of relief, Travis peeked around the corner once more. Seeing no one else, Travis whispered, "Let's go," and then continued to lead the way.

Coming to the door where the soldier had come from, Travis carefully swung it open to find that it led to a tall staircase.

"Found our way up," Travis told Sarora, his confidence growing with his nervous excitement. Without looking behind to see if his friend was going to follow, Travis began sprinting up the stairs as stealthily as he could. His legs hefted him up the stone stairs and his feet padded quietly. Behind him, he could hear Sarora's talons scraping the ground as her cat feet stepped softly at the same time.

The staircase was narrow, but still fairly easy to walk up. Except for the windows that let in glimpses of the moon, the tower was dark. Inside of himself, Travis's heart seemed to be flying at a hundred miles an hour. Would Zack be at the top of this tower?

Once they reached the top of the stairs, Travis quietly tried to get a hold of his breath. Huffing and puffing, he bent over and looked at his surroundings. Like the floor below, there was another hall, only, this one led to an open bridge that was connected to another tower. Between Travis and the open bridge were four cells, each with barred windows and locked doors.

Travis stood tall once more and was about to continue on when Sarora grabbed his shoulder.

"Look," Sarora whispered and motioned with her beak toward one of the dungeons. Looking very carefully, Travis was able to spot a shadowy figure moving in the entrance of one of the farther cells. Travis nodded to let Sarora know that he had spotted the figure, and then he carefully crept forward, reaching for his sword, which was in the sheath attached to his belt.

As Travis got closer, he noticed how small and slim the figure was. It was a girl, probably around his age, possibly a bit older.

Her brown hair fell down her back, tangled and unkempt. She was wearing a sandy-brown, tattered dress, which fell to her ankles. In one hand, she held the keys to the dungeon. Her other hand was pushed up against the door, helping her to keep balance while she peered into the empty cell.

As carefully as possible, Travis slowly slid his sword back into its sheath. Keeping his shadow away from the girl's sight, Travis came up behind her and slowly moved his hands forward. Once he was right behind her, Travis shot his hands forward and put them over the girl's mouth.

Immediately, the girl began to fight back, kicking and trying to turn to look at her captor. Under his hands, Travis felt the girl try to scream, but he managed to muffle the sound. Behind him, Travis knew that Sarora was approaching, but he didn't turn to look—he was too focused on keeping a hold on the girl. After a couple more seconds of fighting, the girl seemed to give up, but her nervous breathing increased. Travis, though he knew she was with the enemy, realized that the girl was just as frightened for her life as he was for his own. No matter where they had come from, they both had faced dangers in their pasts. Travis thought quickly on how to help reassure the girl and calm her down.

"Hold still," Travis whispered into her ear. The girl didn't seem to want to take his orders, but she stiffened.

"Now, if you promise to shut up and not make a sound, I'll let you go, okay? Then we can have a little talk. Maybe we can help each other. Nod if you understand."

The girl nodded, but not too enthusiastically—she obviously didn't trust him. *And rightfully so...* Travis smiled inside his head.

"Okay, I'll let go on three," Travis told her as calmly as he possibly could. "One, two, three..." Travis withdrew his hands, no longer holding the girl back. Instantly, the girl fell forward, having still been fighting against Travis's hold. After falling to her knees, the girl was quick to turn and glare at Travis. Her eyes burned with fire that seemed to pierce Travis straight through his heart. But upon seeing that the person that had restrained her was merely a boy, not much younger than her, her eyes softened, though only a little.

"Now," Travis searched for words while trying to keep a quiet tone to his voice, "if you could just hand me the keys and tell me where my friend is, then I'll be out of your hair." Slowly, Travis reached for the keys that the girl held in her right hand.

The fire seemed to reignite in her eyes as the girl stood up. "So you are the friend that Zack was praying wouldn't be stupid enough to come and save him!"

"Sh!" Travis tried to quiet the girl. "If they hear you, they'll come and find us. Now, calmly and quietly explain to me how and why you know about us."

The girl stood tall, but not confidently. Travis now noticed that her feet were bare and her skin was white, as if she hadn't seen the sun's light for quite some time.

She nodded slowly and then spoke. "My name is Jezebel—I'm a servant here. I was doing my chores when they brought your friend Zack in. He was hurt, and he needed help, so I came in and healed him as best as I could. Just a few hours ago, I visited him for quite some time, and he made me promise to tell you—if you showed up—that you are brain dead and need to get away before Lord Donigan finds you."

"*Lord* Donigan?" Sarora stepped into the girl's view from the shadows. "Now when did he start calling himself that?"

Jezebel's eyes grew round in fear as she spotted the gryphon. Her mouth opened wide to scream, but before she could, Travis put his hand over it.

"It's okay," Travis tried to reassure her. "She's a friend. And her screech is definitely worse than her bite." Travis removed his hand from the girl's mouth. She obviously still didn't trust Sarora, but at least she was willing—and able—to keep her mouth shut.

"Now," Travis began again, "would you be so kind as to tell us where Zack is?"

Jezebel shot a nervous glance at Sarora. "He didn't want me to tell you."

Travis tried not to sigh in exasperation. "Yes, I know what he told you not to do. But, could you tell us where he is so we can save his life?"

"Oh, I'm pretty sure that they won't kill him until you two show up," Jezebel said, trying to sound confident.

Travis felt his fists begin to clench. "Yes, but let's not find out if that's true or not. So, would you please tell us where he is?"

Jezebel shook her head. "No, I promised not to tell."

Travis thought that his eyes were going to roll into the back of his head. Thankfully, Sarora spoke up before he could say anything that he would regret.

"Um, Jezebel, you must know Zack really well by now, seeing as you know enough about us. But, did Zack specifically make you promise to not *tell* us where he would be?"

Jezebel nodded.

Travis looked at Sarora, whose eyes lit up with an idea.

Sarora quickly continued, "Then, if you can't tell us, I'm sure you could *show* us, right?"

"But I..." Jezebel stopped herself, and it appeared that she was trying to think back. A small smile formed on her lips. "I never did promise him that I wouldn't show you guys where he was."

The Shadow's Face

Jezebel led the way at a hushed sprint. She was obviously accustomed to sneaking around the castle—every move she made was very fluid and calculated. All three of them were able to bypass several soldiers who had fallen asleep while on sentry duty. Travis eventually realized that Jezebel was leading them into the heart of the castle. *If she leads us into a trap, I'm gonna kill her, and then grab Zack and run for it,* Travis told himself as he thought about the dangers that awaited them.

A silent nervousness settled over the three of them as they ran to aid their friend. Every once in a while Jezebel would mutter something under her breath. Sarora had tried to relay the messages to Travis, but most of the time Jezebel's phrasing was hard to understand. She spoke quickly and softly, but Travis just wished that she would just be quiet and focus on getting them to Zack.

Finally, they reached a new hall near the center of the castle. Slowly, the group came to a stop. Controlling her breathing, Jezebel whispered, "He-he should be down the hall here. To-to the right, there should be a large wooden door. It leads to Lord Donigan's throne room—the place where he plays king. I believe that he's been getting impatient about you two not showing up, so he's interrogating Zack, trying to find your whereabouts."

"What's your guess on the number of soldiers and guards in that room?" Sarora asked, shifting her weight from one foot to the other. Her gold eyes glinted with ire.

"Little to none." Jezebel sounded confident for once. "Lord Donigan's fairly confident in his own abilities—but I'm sure you won't give him a chance to correct his mistake," she ended with a scheming smile.

Travis nodded, trying to look hopeful. Turning to Sarora, he asked, "You got a plan?"

"You-you mean you haven't thought this through?" Jezebel stammered, her eyes widening in shock.

Travis shook his head. "We kind of just hoped that Zack would be in one of the towers. In that case, we would have just grabbed him and run for it. But now that he's with Donigan, we have to fight and try not to get ourselves killed."

Sarora caught Travis's attention once more. "I have an idea, but it's risky."

"It's better than nothing," Travis said.

"What if we make a distraction so that Zack could slip away?" Sarora suggested.

Travis nodded, but Jezebel shook her head. "Most likely, he's tied up. Lord Donigan's cocky, but he's not an idiot."

"Then what do you suggest we do?" Travis asked Jezebel.

Jezebel thought for a moment, and then she replied, "What if you two distracted Lord Donigan while I untie Zack? He usually doesn't notice me as much as the other maids. I can go in after you two barge through the door, and while he's momentarily preoccupied, I'll help Zack."

"No, you'll get hurt," Travis disagreed, shaking his head.

"I don't care!" Jezebel's hands flew to her mouth as she tried to stifle her shout. "You don't know how awful it's been to be kept in this godforsaken castle! I don't care what happens next—

as long as I can foil Lord Donigan's plans, then I'd be fine going out raising Enfirma!"

"Enfirma?" Travis asked Sarora.

Sarora nodded. "Haven't heard that word in a while. It's Firsoman for the cursed land of the afterlife."

Turning back to Jezebel, Travis began reluctantly, "If you really are certain about this—"

"I am," Jezebel cut him short.

Travis shot a quick glance at Sarora, who nodded. Looking into Jezebel's eyes, Travis whispered, "Fine. But if any of us tells you to run for it, you go, no questions asked, and no arguments. Deal?"

Jezebel nodded, her eyes gleaming with determination. "Deal. Now let's go."

Sarora led them to the doorway, which was about nine feet high and seven feet wide. The side-by-side doors were made of thick wood, and their hinges were made of a black metal.

"It's probably locked from the inside," Jezebel whispered from behind Sarora and Travis.

"Then we'll have to break through," Sarora said simply, stating the obvious. "Got any brilliant ideas, Travis?"

Travis shook his head. "My fire can burn, but I don't think it can explode."

"Why don't you give it a shot?" Jezebel asked.

"And why don't you handle a grenade without knowing exactly how to use it?" Travis retorted. "I only got the ability to use fire back a couple days ago—before that, I had forgotten how to use it. So trying to create an exploding ball of fire isn't exactly on my to-do list."

"But for once we need your recklessness."

Travis couldn't believe that Sarora was agreeing with Jezebel. When he looked at her, Sarora's eyes were just as convincing as her voice.

"Travis, I know it sounds like some stupid thing that you would have done a couple months ago, but trust me, you have to try. We need to do more than surprise Donigan—we need to blow away his confidence—literally."

Travis still couldn't believe what he was hearing. Sarora wanted him to do something reckless? *What world have I just entered?*

Shaking his head, Travis looked for an answer. "If I die, you'll be the one with the blood on your hands."

Sarora looked doubtful about her idea for a moment, but she quickly steeled herself. "I know you can do it. But the second you doubt yourself will be the same second that I'll feel guilty— because then you will be dead."

With a sigh, Travis shook his head once more. "Fine, I'll try. But you two need to stand back." Both Sarora and Jezebel stepped back until they were pressed against the other side of the wide hall.

Looking away from them, Travis faced the large doors. Closing his eyes and taking a deep breath, Travis focused on calling forth his powers. Digging deep within himself, Travis found that his hands and arms began to heat up.

Breathing in deeply again, Travis opened his eyes slowly. Taking both his hands, he pressed them against the pressure that was forming between them as if he were holding a ball. Focusing again, Travis concentrated on forcing the heat from his hands into the space between them. Forcing out another breath, Travis brought out the fire that burned from inside of him. Between his hands, a whirling ball of fire formed. Pulling for all his strength, Travis fit the ball of raging fire into his right hand. With all his might he threw the ball at the door as hard as he could...

And the door blew into shambles with a resounding boom.

Travis and Sarora rushed into the room.

Zack knelt on the floor, his head high and his hands bound behind his back. Around him, moonlight filtered in through hard-to-see windows from high above. A yellow-white light also came from the torches that were residing on all four walls. Though the moonlight was cold, the room itself held an even colder tension.

His energy seemed sapped from him—but that's how Donigan always won his battles. Though he wasn't an Acer, the powers that he controlled could be far greater than that of even the most elite of Magic Wielders. He was a sorcerer—his powers had been granted by the darkness, and Donigan knew how to use them well. With his magic, he could drain others of theirs.

Donigan sat on a bronze throne, his arrogant manor sprawling all about him. He wore a dark purple tunic, matched with a hooded cape. His peppered hair was short, and his dark eyes were like cold fire. But though he looked like royalty from Enfirma, he was a very unkempt man. His skin was a bit dirty, and he reeked like nothing Zack had ever smelled before—a combination between sweat and an expensive fragrance.

With a stony glare, Donigan tried to remove any hope from Zack's heart. He had ordered his guards to bring Zack into his throne room so that he may interrogate him.

"You don't speak much, do you?" Donigan's voice was rough as he looked at Zack with a twisted smile.

Zack tried to avoid looking into Donigan's blazing dark brown eyes. He didn't want to speak about anything to him—he was afraid that he might let information slip.

Donigan let out a throaty laugh. "You know what's really funny about this whole plan? It's exactly the same as the last one I pulled, and it still works like a charm!"

Zack couldn't help but glare directly at Donigan. "Sarora won't fall for it."

Donigan looked at him with that same crooked smile. "But for once, you will be wrong. Just as the two of you came running to your master's aid, Sarora and Travis will come running to save you. Then there will be a confrontation, just like before. But unlike last time, I'll use my powers the right way, to make sure that the three of you die, souls and all," Donigan boasted, his eyes flickered with scorn.

Zack continued his hard gaze. "When pigs fly, then will they come." He paused for a moment before continuing, "Oh, wait a minute, incorrect phrase, you fly on Sievan—never mind."

Fire shot from Donigan's eyes, but he didn't reply to Zack's comment. Instead, he stood and began to pace.

"It shouldn't be long now." Donigan strode around the room. "Any second now, either my guards will bring them in, subdued," Donigan said confidently as he pointed to the large double doors to Zack's left. He laughed, "I'm even so sure of it that I told the guards to keep watch by the towers. They'll wait there for your friends and bring them to me so that I may vanquish you three with only Sievan at my side."

Zack felt static buzz between his hands—this sometimes happened when he was angered enough to fight. But, he knew better than to use his powers. Donigan might still underestimate him and not know about them yet—and he was waiting to surprise the dense superior into submission.

"Yes, any second now they will fall into my trap," Donigan muttered to himself, continuing to raise his confidence.

"Your trap?" Zack scoffed. "Wasn't Trazon the one who came up with this idea three years ago?"

Donigan stopped walking. "Well, he brought the idea into thought, but I could have said 'no' if I had wanted to. I can do whatever I want, and his 'Highness' will just have to learn to deal with it."

"Yes, like the 'great' lord himself will ever let you have free will." Zack tried hard not to roll his eyes—he needed to keep focused on Donigan and not get too riled up.

Donigan's eyes bulged. "Look, the second that your friends stow away into my castle undetected and are able to get into this room by blowing that door off its hinges, then I'll obey every order Trazon gives me!"

Suddenly, there was a loud, resounding boom. The whole

room shook with the force as the large door was blown into a million pieces. Donigan lost his footing as the wooden shards and bits of the hinges flew all around them.

After the explosion had done its worst, Zack looked up from where he had ducked his head in close to his chest. When he saw who was standing before him, Zack's stomach flopped over.

As the dust and debris cleared from the air, Travis spotted Zack on the ground. When Zack lifted his head, Travis could see that his friend's face showed his fatigue. His electric blue eyes glowed faintly with exhaustion and fright—the latter part from seeing his friends, who were supposed to be safe at home.

"Sarora! Travis! What in Enfirma are you doing here!?!" Zack's voice was filled with fear and desperation. His blonde hair was covered with dirt and grime, and his face was covered in soot. Around him, bits and pieces of the door were scattered about the floor. But that's not all that Travis and Sarora spotted.

A sluggish form managed to pull itself to its feet. It was a man, possibly in his forties. His hair was short, but Travis could still see the brown-gray color of it. But as his face lifted, Travis's breath hitched.

The man looked up, his brown eyes like a dangerous fire. First, he looked at Sarora. "Well, well, well, what did I tell you, Zack? Your friends are faithful until the end—I knew that they'd show." The man smiled at Sarora. "Nice to see that your wings aren't clipped, Sarora." With fear, Travis finally recognized the man—part of his past that he never wanted to relive.

"Donigan." Sarora glared at the man with unconcealed hatred. "Long time, happily no see."

"Stepdad?" Travis could have fainted.

THE SECRETS ARE EXPOSED

"Your stepfather?" Sarora said, bewildered. Her wings were held out at her sides, and her golden eyes seemed to go wild. "You-you never said that Donigan was your stepfather!"

Travis glared at Sarora. "And you never said my stepdad was Donigan!" he replied rhetorically. "Last time I saw him was almost a year ago! How was I supposed to know that he was Donigan? He didn't exactly come out and say, 'Hey, Travis, by the way, I'm actually an evil minion of Lord Trazon's from another dimension'!"

"Now, now," Donigan stepped forward, the corners of his mouth creeping into a grin, "I wouldn't want the two of you fighting amongst yourselves now, would I?" Donigan strode forward. Soon, he was only feet from Travis, but as scared as he was, Travis wouldn't let his stepfather get the better of him—it was time for a change. Sarora sidestepped so that Donigan could not touch her.

Travis watched as Donigan slowly extended his hand toward Travis. "My, how you've grown." Travis kept his gaze steady and tried not to flinch as his stepfather got closer. "You know, it seems only yesterday that I met your mother—that was, of course, before she met your father."

"My father?" Travis took a step back to stay out of Donigan's reach. "What do you know of my father?"

Donigan smiled, almost too kindly. "He was a very smart man, Travis. Your mother fell for him hard, but that must have not been enough, seeing as he left the two of you."

Travis shook his head. "No. I could never believe a word that came out of your mouth. My dad was a great man, I just know it!"

"Believe me, Travis." Donigan gave him a sympathetic look. "I would never lie to you about your family, and for once, I will tell you the truth—your father abandoned you and your mother before you were even born."

"If that is true, then why'd he do it?" Travis didn't want to believe the words of a follower of the Dark Lord. "What reason would my father have for leaving me behind?"

"Don't listen to him, Travis!" Zack called. He was still bent over on the ground, his hands behind his back. But as Travis glimpsed at him, he noticed a small figure behind his friend. With a small feeling of triumph, he knew that Zack would soon be free and they could all run away.

Donigan ignored Zack and he continued to press Travis. "Why would I lie to you about this, Travis? Am I not practically your family? Did I not feed and clothe you? Did I not give you shelter?"

"Well, you let me stay in the house, that much I can say." Travis scowled at Donigan. Why did it seem he was dragging a simple conversation on forever?

"I can't say exactly why your father left," Donigan sighed. "He was always focused on the fast lane in life. Perhaps he just thought that you and your mother slowed him down."

From behind Donigan, Zack arose. His hands were at his sides and they were beginning to glow yellow. He gave Travis a signal to keep Donigan busy. For once, Travis knew better than to nod—

doing so would kind of make the surprise attack—well—less of a surprise.

"Travis, you're practically my own son," Donigan continued. "I wouldn't ever do anything to hurt you. By locking you up, I simply wanted to keep you safe from the world around you."

Travis stared Donigan down and replied sarcastically, "And by not feeding me, you prepared me for the next Great Depression?"

Donigan appeared genuinely hurt. "I'm sorry, Travis. I really am. I-I guess I was just so sad after the loss of your mother..." It looked as if Donigan was about to tear up. "But I'll make it up to you, Travis. If you join us, I'll treat you like a king. I'll regard you more highly than Trazon or any other of the past lords! Never again will you have to work, or fight, or struggle for survival. You'll be treated like royalty!"

"Travis!" Sarora finally spoke up. "You're not going to believe him, are you? He starved you! Cursed at you! And millions of innocent lives have been destroyed because of *him*!"

Travis looked at Donigan more closely. He realized what was going on—Donigan was placing a mask over his real self. There was no way that Travis would ever be treated like royalty around darkness. But since he was still waiting for Zack to make his move, Travis thought he'd go along with Donigan's trick.

He let his defense appear to crack. "Re-really? I've always wondered what it would be like to be a ruler." Travis acted as if he were truly taking this thought into deep consideration.

"Travis, what are you—?" Sarora tried to ask, but Travis cut her off.

"So, this is a real offer?" Travis asked Donigan.

Donigan nodded fervently. "Oh yes! Of course, my son! This is the offer of a lifetime! You'd be at the same level of power as Trazon, and with your help, we can overthrow him!"

Travis put his hand on his chin and faked a contemplative look. "Well, I don't know. What could you possibly offer me that I don't already have? I have friends who are my family. And though we sometimes *fight*, we always pull things together, like *now* for instance."

Zack took his cue. Stealthily, he shot towards Donigan, small spurts of static shooting out from his hands at his foe. For a moment, Travis's hope arose, and he was nearly sure that Donigan was going down on the first hit. But at the last moment, Donigan twisted around and grabbed his sword from its sheath all in one motion Zack had to dive to his left to avoid being sliced in half.

"Now, you weren't trying to hurt me, were you?" Donigan smiled devilishly at Zack, who was quickly picking himself up off the ground. "If you try to hurt me, I'll be forced to bring your death sooner." He pointed his long sword at Zack, readying himself for the kill.

Donigan's sword was long and thick with a dark gray blade. Its hilt was black, and in the center of it sat a deep purple gem, like the crystal that Travis had touched while in Loki's store.

Donigan noticed Travis regarding his weapon. "You like the sword? I've named it Vehndetia. Its stone you especially seem to like is called Acer's Bane—one of your few weaknesses. Get killed by this sword and I get your powers and your spirit animal."

Suddenly, a screech resounded from the halls. Everyone turned to look. Massive black wings beat the air as Sievan flew over everyone's heads. In his front talons, he carried a petrified figure. As Sievan carried her across the room, the girl beat at him with her fists as she screamed, "L-let me down or I'll—!" Her words choked in her throat.

With an evil grin, Sievan dropped Jezebel. With a scream of terror, Jezebel fell and rolled across the floor.

"Jezebel!" Zack rushed to the girl's aid. Once he reached her, he helped her up. "Are you okay?"

Jezebel nodded shakily. "I'll be alright, but that jerk just dropped me from more than twenty feet!"

Sievan landed behind Donigan, who was still not that far from Travis. "Ssstop whining, you brrrat. It wasss only fifteen feet, and you lived—be thankful for that."

Jezebel looked like she wanted to strangle Sievan, but her anger was being controlled by her fear. Though as brave as she seemed, Travis could sense that she was just as afraid of Sievan as she was Donigan.

"Now, what do we have here?" Donigan smiled evilly at Jezebel, who tried to avoid his gaze.

"She wasss the one who let your prrrisssoner go, Donigan," Sievan explained to his companion. "While you were dissstracted by the child and the oversssized kitten with wingsss, she sssnuck in and untied him."

"Hm, well, you know the punishment for betrayal, my dear," Donigan remarked with a callous grin, looking steadily at Jezebel.

"It isn't betrayal if I wasn't for the darkness in the first place," Jezebel managed to spit back as she stumbled, tripping over herself.

Smiling over his shoulder at Sievan, Sarora, and Travis, Donigan then walked imposingly over toward Jezebel and Zack. Putting Vehndetia out in front of him, Donigan smiled. "Make your prayers to the stars, my dear."

Travis shot a quick glance at Sarora, who caught his gaze and nodded. Then together, both of them sprang into action.

With a battle cry, Sarora leapt on top of Sievan, who let out a surprised screech. In a fury of talons and beating wings, the two of them rolled across the floor.

Travis ran toward Donigan and grabbed Kader from his sheath. With his right hand, Travis drove his sword toward the small of Donigan's back. But his stepfather knew the blow was coming. Like he had done before, Donigan spun around and held his sword up in defense.

With a clanging of metal, Kader and Vehndetia met, creating bright sparks that shot in all directions. Travis was surprised by how strong Donigan was. He had to push with all of his might just to hold Donigan back.

Then, a thought crossed Travis's mind. While his hands were busy fighting sword on sword, Travis lifted a foot and kicked, sending a ball of fire at Donigan. The fire hit, but not very hard. Not to mention, Travis's shoe was burnt black by the fire. But even if the fire didn't wound Donigan, it momentarily distracted him. When Donigan backed away from the surprise attack, Travis leapt back as well, trying to give his arms a break while he thought of what to do next.

Then Travis was reminded of how thankful he was for his friends. After telling Jezebel to run for her life, Zack leapt to Travis's aid. Though he didn't have a sword, Zack's idea was something that he would be proud of for a long time.

Using his powers, he created an electric staff that zapped small bolts of lightning as he wielded it. When he attacked Donigan with it, Zack's lightning staff met with Donigan's sword, and the two made a sort of clanging noise that ended with a zapping sound. The bad thing about the staff though, was that Zack had to use both hands in order to keep it in a solid state.

While Zack fought Donigan, Travis took a second to glance at Sarora, who was still fighting the dargryph. Both were now back on their feet. Sievan's ice-tail lashed like an angry cat's. He looked like he had taken damage, but not enough to stop him from fighting. The old wound on his wing was slightly reopened, and the tip of his beak had been fractured. Over his left eye, it looked like Sarora had gotten payback for her own scar. Sievan's eye—though it was hard to tell because it was red—was bleeding. His black eyelid was half-closed over the wound, but Sievan wasn't one for showing weakness, so he struggled to keep it open.

Sarora wasn't doing too well, either. There were several minor cuts and scrapes on her front and back legs, and one of her feathered ears was torn at the end. Her tail was also bleeding, but at least she still had it. Without a tail, Sarora would struggle to fly, and Travis had no idea how to regenerate a tail for her that was made of fire.

Though he wanted to help her, Travis decided he would only get in her way, so he turned back to Donigan. Zack was struggling to hold his own. Coming up from behind Donigan, Travis carefully, but still with strength, swung his sword at Donigan's back.

Travis should have seen Donigan's next move coming. After Travis swung Kader, Donigan sidestepped to his left, completely dodging Travis's attack.

The sudden loss of an opponent caused Zack to stumble forward. With surprise, both of the boy's weapons met. Travis felt his arms shake as the electric staff vibrated against his metal blade.

As soon as he could, Zack leapt back. Travis's arms now felt like jello, and it was not a good feeling. He found it hard to hold Kader in one hand, so now he was forced to use both.

Donigan smiled at the two boys. "That staff you got there is kinda shocking, huh?" Turning away from them, Donigan spotted Jezebel breaking for the doorway. She was almost home free, but then, with amazing speed, Donigan beat her to the exit.

Travis couldn't see Jezebel's expression, but he certainly heard her yelp in surprise.

"Now, where are you going, my dear?" Donigan snickered. "Aren't you going to help your new friends fight?" Donigan held his sword out toward Jezebel's neck.

In fear, Jezebel spun on her heels and ran for the other wall, which, Travis noticed, had had a hole blasted through it. Why she hadn't tried to use that escape route before, Travis had no idea.

Donigan leisurely paced after her, as if he knew that she wouldn't be able to escape him. With another devilish grin, Donigan pressed the gem of his sword. Travis watched in horrified awe as Donigan's sword glowed purple and then magically transformed into a javelin.

Zack must have known what was coming. With a shout, he tried to warn Jezebel as he sprinted in her direction. The girl looked over her shoulder, and when she spotted the long spear aimed at her, she screamed and ran even faster.

"Take this, slave!" Donigan cried out as he flung the javelin at Jezebel.

"Jezebel! Get out of the way!" Zack cried as he ran toward her.

At the last second, Zack pushed Jezebel to safety. But to Travis's horror, the javelin still hit a mark—Zack.

"No!" Travis cried out, as did Jezebel, who was on the ground. Travis watched in terror as the javelin went through Zack's arm and pinned him to the wall.

Sarora looked up from where she was facing Sievan. When she saw Zack, she let out a screech. "No! This can't happen again! We nearly lost him last time!"

As Travis looked carefully, his heart twisting in fright, he saw Zack stir. Thankfully, the spear hadn't penetrated any of his vital areas, but the real shock was that it had speared his arm, right where his scar was.

Zack let out a cry of pain. His arm was bleeding heavily and his blue eyes were screwed shut. His teeth gnashed as he tried to fight back the searing pain.

Donigan's smile was sickening. "Now look how history repeats itself! I wonder what else this glorious day has in store for us?"

Travis thought as fast as he could. He realized something— Donigan no longer had a weapon! As fast as he could, Travis charged Donigan, Kader aimed at his foe's heart. Upon reaching his stepfather, Travis let out a battle cry and once more swung the sword at him. He had almost hit him too, but thanks to his impeccable speed, Donigan just managed to duck and roll out of the way.

"Nice try, kid," Donigan sneered. "You know, I knew your father quite well, and if there is anything I can say about the two of you, it's this: neither of you thought about the consequences of your actions. Both of you were so blind as to underestimate my true powers..." Donigan then did something strange. He brought his hands together. As his hands met, his eyes began to glow an eerie purple. Looking directly at Travis, Donigan began to chant in some other language. Around him, purple fire began to grow, slowly at first, but as he continued, the fire intensified more quickly.

"Travis!" Sarora leapt at her friend and pushed him out of the way just in time. The purple fire shot forward in a fury of darkness. Unfortunately, the fire still grazed Sarora's wings and burnt the tips of her feathers.

"Are you okay?" Sarora asked Travis as she helped him to his feet.

Travis got up and nodded. "Yeah. How the heck did he do that?"

Sarora glanced at Donigan, whose fire had begun to die down. "He can look at your own powers and duplicate them with the power of darkness. Even when he's weaponless, it doesn't mean that he's defenseless."

Looking toward the wall, Travis saw Jezebel desperately trying to help Zack—tears streamed down her face.

"Zack, oh Zack, how can I help you? What am I supposed to do?" Jezebel's voice shook as she tried to free him.

Zack shook his head, his face twisted in anguish. "You can't help me. It takes a lot of skill to remove the spear from my arm. And you, well, you don't have that particular skill. If you're not careful, you can damage my arm permanently."

Jezebel began to sob, "But-but then what am I supposed to do?"

Travis wanted to help his friend so badly, but he couldn't do that while he was fighting Sievan and Donigan. He stood there, petrified, and his only power left was to pray—pray that there was an answer and that they would all make it out alive. And sometimes, all you have to do is give a small prayer and believe something good will come from it.

That's when a heroic bark called from the doorway. All eyes turned just in time to see the small and tame house dog leap onto Sievan's back and clamp onto him with razor-sharp teeth.

Sievan's head shot up in shock, but although the wound he was receiving was very painful, he laughed when he saw that he was being attacked by a little dog.

"Pran!" Travis cried in alarm. *I can't believe it! He followed us!*

Growling, Pran dug his teeth deeper into Sievan's neck. But instead of crying in pain, Sievan seemed to smirk with near satisfaction.

"I knew it all along!" the dargryph proclaimed. "I knew you were the betrayer, Praesul!" Turning, he grabbed the dog by his scruff and tossed Pran off of him. But before he hit the ground, Pran spun in the air and landed gracefully on his feet.

"Pr-pran?" Zack stuttered. "Betrayer? But—"

That's when another miracle happened.

Pran grew larger and his face contorted. His fur darkened a little, but it also grew thicker. His paws grew very large compared to their original dainty size. Pran's tail extended outward and lost its natural curl, and the area around his lips blackened. His eyes glowed with a new intelligence, and when the transformation was complete, he smiled a large smile that showed his pure white teeth.

Pran, in a dark way, looked happy to see Sievan and Donigan. Then, Travis almost passed out when Pran spoke in a deep, commanding voice, "Good to see you again, Masters."

Sarora couldn't believe it either. Pran, a small wimpy, whiny, spoiled, stinky little brat of a cute dog, was really a mountain wolf, which were known for their magic. In this case, his shape-shifting abilities.

Donigan glared at the wolf through narrowed eyes. "Praesul! What are you thinking? By attacking Sievan, you show opposition!"

Praesul lifted his large head even higher. "I'm not just showing it, Donigan, I'm proclaiming it! No longer will I spy on them for you! No longer will I serve you when you condemn innocent lives to death!" He let out a roar of a growl as he continued, "No longer will blood cover my paw steps where I have trod, unless it is your blood!"

Donigan seethed inside. The second-in-command of his wolf squadron had betrayed them. Travis wondered how many more of Trazon's wolves were now against the darkness.

"I sent you to them because I knew that you could find them!

I trusted you! I knew you were very capable of being a spy, but I didn't know that you were doing a double job!" Donigan yelled.

"It was my mistake to take the mission," Praesul replied. "A year ago, when you sent me to find them, I was as lost in Enfirma as you are still! But after I got to know them through my house pet life, I discovered that we were the ones who were in the wrong. We fight for glory and fame! We fight for gold! But what do they fight for?" Pran looked at his friend, his amber eyes glowing in admiration. "They fight for their lives! They fight for their loved ones! They fight to be free, and they fight for peace!" His bark was like a whip against a hardened rock. "There will never be peace as long as Trazon lives!"

Donigan looked scared. "Praesul, how could you do this to me?"

"Turn back your tide, Donigan," Praesul commanded. "Turn away from your evil ways! You had the law written in your heart! So why don't you follow it?"

Donigan considered what was being said, and for a moment, Travis thought that Praesul may have quelled the man's evil ways. But then Donigan shook his head, his anger rising like the sun. "No, turncoat! It is you who is wrong! Trazon will bring us peace! He will give me back what is rightfully MINE!"

"You can't bring back the dead!"

Donigan glared at him as he whispered, "Try me."

Praesul snarled ferociously, "You child of Enfirma! You king of hatred and vengeance! I no longer call you my brother in arms! We shall never again fight side-by-side in this war!" Then, he took up a long howl, "Long live the king! Long live King Devon!"

Before Donigan could do anything, Praesul produced a glowing light that shone the brightest yellow-orange. The light then flew at him and Sievan, and both evildoers fell to their knees.

"What just happened?" Travis had to ask.

Amber eyes turned to him as Praesul explained tiredly, "I have broken the barrier that has protected them from death by their enemies—the gift that Trazon bestows on all of his most trusted. Now they are vulnerable to death by any means."

"But power like that—" Sarora spoke up, but Praesul cut her off.

"Gives you enough of an upper hand to take back control of the battle."

Donigan struggled back to his feet. "But it weakens you and destroys your protection from my magic as well!" That's when he returned the volley, his light a dark purple. Before Praesul could muster the strength to dodge, the orb went through his heart and he screamed in pain.

"King Devon is dead!" Donigan shouted and repeated his magic.

"Long live the King!" Praesul cried weakly. "Long live the Loyal King! Long live King Devon!" His paws glittered as they began to disappear.

"Pran!" Zack reached out to his dog, but his arm remained pinned to the wall.

Praesul let his gaze drift towards the teen. "Zack, you are my true companion, and I've done everything in my power to protect you in this life." His paws continued to fade as the glitter reached his tail and his shoulders. "If I could live again, I would start anew, fighting alongside you. We would've been the best of friends..."

Zack let tears fall as he grimaced from both the spear in his arm and the thorn in his heart. "Pran, or Praesul, whoever you are, you are one of my closest friends. I may not have heard you speak before today, but I shared everything that was on my mind with you. Before this week, you could have betrayed us all, but you kept us hidden. I trust you, Praesul, and despite the fact that you're really a wolf, you're the best dog that I've ever had!"

Praesul smiled a tired smile. "I am Pran, and I am proud that you can call me your friend and loyal dog." His legs were gone and his head was beginning to fade. He could barely be seen now. "I will still be with you—I will be your shield, Zack. As long as you remember what I have done in my loyalty to you, know that your back is protected from danger.

"In return, please carry this message to my true pack, to my father's home! There is poison in the pack... led by the one with the steel tooth and thirst for vengeance. They must find out before it's too late!" Pran grimaced as another wave of pain went through him. "For the sake of Firmara, long live the king!" he howled, and was gone.

Travis signaled to Sarora, and even though they were in the depths of pain, he knew they must take advantage of the situation. Quickly, she dove back into another round of attacks with Sievan and Donigan as he ran toward Jezebel and Zack. Zack was hardly conscious—Jezebel's words struggled to keep him awake through the pain and sorrow. Travis turned to Jezebel and whispered, "I have something for you to do—it's really important."

Jezebel wiped her tears off her cheeks with her dirty sleeve. "What is it?"

"I need you to get through that hole in the wall. Once you get just outside of the castle, I need you to whistle three times like a bird. Three horses will come to meet you. I need you to keep the horses in check and wait for us to meet you. As soon as we get a moment to escape, we'll come and meet you, and we'll all make a run for it," Travis explained as quickly and as quietly as he could.

Jezebel nodded, fighting back her sadness with great success. "Okay, I'll do it. Just promise me that you'll bring Zack. I've been healing him for two days, and I don't intend to lose him now."

Travis nodded. "Of course, Sarora and I will do our best. And now that Pran is with him, he will be safe, I am sure. Go. Sarora and I will try to wrap things up here."

With one last nod, Jezebel stood, and looked at Zack. "Don't leave us yet. I want to see you when you're not in chains." And then, she leapt up and disappeared out the hole.

Just then, Sarora jumped back out of the fray. Turning to her, Travis looked for an answer in the gryphon's eyes. Donigan and

Sievan were regrouping in the center of the room—a similar evil gleam in both of their eyes.

Sarora glided as best as she could toward Travis, but he could tell that it pained her to fly. Landing next to Travis, Sarora asked him, "What's the plan?"

Travis shook his head. "I was hoping someone with your intelligence would have that all figured out."

Sarora looked at Travis while using her peripherals to keep an eye on Sievan and Donigan. "Look, I'm not perfect, and, as much as I hate to admit it, I'm not always right,"

"Then what do we do?" Travis asked her.

Sarora shook her head. "I have no plans, and the will to fight is dying inside of me, Travis. We must finish this up before we all die."

Travis looked around himself desperately. "Where is a prophecy of hope when you need one? Has Pran died for us in vain?"

Sarora shook her head. "I don't..." she trailed off as words rushed into her head.

"Darkening skies are not the way to go," she gasped, reciting part of Travis's prophecy from Loki. "Travis, that just happened twice!"

"I don't see what..." Travis began, but Sarora explained quickly.

"You decided not to follow in Donigan's footsteps, and Pran stood up for what he believed was right! Oh, what's the next line again?" Sarora muttered as she racked her brain.

Donigan and Sievan were watching them speak together. Donigan finally called over to them, "So, when are you two cowards going to be ready to fight again?" But his challenge was weak. He was still recuperating from Praesul's attack.

Sarora's mind worked faster than it ever had before. *'Those of great prophecy go fraught...'* Well, *that's all three of us. 'One with gift of fire burning...' Doesn't that mean Travis? 'Your enemy of fate will be naught...' Either Sievan or Donigan is going down. 'But your friends with woe be mourning...' There will be a death.'* Sarora glanced at Zack, but then shook her head. *No, Zack will live. Pran is already dead, but...* Sarora shot a glance at Travis. He had the element of fire, but what would happen to the world if he died? Then, a memory from three years before appeared in Sarora's mind.

She stood in front of Master Racht, her head hanging low. "I just wish that I could be myself once more. I hate who I am!"

Master Racht sighed, "I know, my dear. But there is a brighter future in store for you—I have a good feeling about it." Reaching forward, Master Racht placed his hand on her shoulder and whispered, "Sometimes helping others must come before helping yourself. Though it is a hard decision to make, you may be rewarded. Maybe not in the way you want during this life. But the fruits of your sacrifice will be greater than any gift."

Sarora's mind snapped back to the present. A thought occurred to her.

One with gift of fire burning... She couldn't believe what she had figured out. She had found all the pieces to the puzzles of the prophecies! And yet, though they would be fulfilled, it was the most difficult thing that she would ever do.

Sarora, you're crazier than Travis, she told herself as she faced Sievan and spoke. "Travis, you know that I've been keeping a secret from you. Well, Sievan also knows just as well about this secret, don't you?"

Sievan glared at her. "Of courssse, why do you think I'm ssssstanding here today? I couldn't brrreathe if that had neverrr happened."

"What-what do you mean?" Travis looked at Sarora, confused. "Why wouldn't Sievan be alive?"

"You insssolent boy!" Sievan snarled at Travis. "Don't you

know that the only way for a dargryph to be created is when a spirit animal is ripped from an Acer's soul?"

"What?" Travis sounded scared. "But, Sarora, who died then to give Sievan life?"

Sarora looked at him from the corner of her eyes. "You know, Travis. Think. It doesn't take much to figure the answer out." Sarora then closed her eyes and focused the energy of her body towards the object around her neck, hidden under her feathers. She felt it lift from her chest and she heard Travis gasp.

Opening her eyes, Sarora watched as a clear crystal necklace, like the one that Zack had, floated in front of her face. The chain was tied around her neck—her secret was now revealed before her friend's eyes.

Travis could barely speak. "You-you're not a gryphon! You-you were human!"

Sarora sighed sadly. "Keyword, was. Last time we fought Donigan, he tried to strip me from my spirit animal using his sword, but his attempt was futile. He stole most of my powers and I was transformed into a gryphon. I've been a gryphon for three years, Travis. I was only eleven—as stupid and naïve as could be. And now I am a prime example of my mistakes."

"But—why didn't you tell me before?"

Sarora shook her head. "You might not have believed me. And if you had, you would have insisted we find a way to change me back. But I couldn't be that selfless—there are greater evils to overcome." Sarora let her crystal drop back and rest against her chest. Then, she turned her head to look at Travis. "I'm sorry I never told you before, but I want to make things right, Travis. I'll need your help to do so."

Surprisingly, Travis nodded. "What do you want me to do, Sarora? I promise to help you."

When the ultimate sacrifice is made, all promises must be obeyed. Sarora recognized the last pieces of the puzzle as they fell into place.

Turning away from Travis, Sarora stared Sievan down.

"Travis, grab your crystal and then hold out your hand." She paused for a moment while Travis did so.

"Now what?" Travis asked.

"Now dig deep within you. Find your true fire." She paused once more while Travis did as she instructed.

"I think I feel it."

"Good. You remember Zack's ceremony?"

Travis nodded from behind Sarora. "Yes."

"Travis, you gave me your word, and to fulfill your prophecy and my own, you must keep your promise. Travis, as stupid as this is going to sound, you'd better do it." Sarora took a shaky breath and then spoke words that she could never have imagined saying. "Call upon your true spirit animal, Travis, and then aim it full force at me."

The Ultimate
Sacrifice

"What?!" Travis cried out, her words crashing into him in unrelenting waves. "Sarora, you could die!"

"I know," Sarora sighed, fighting to keep her resolve. "But this is all fate, Travis. I received a prophecy, which is the reason why we came running for Zack. I know you think that killing me would be wrong, but just trust me, Travis. Sievan and I are bound by the fact that he carries the dark form of my soul, and I carry what is left of mine in the body of my spirit animal. Kill me, and we both die. Now Travis, honor your promise."

Visions of Master Racht flooded Travis's mind. His master had begged Travis to kill him, but Travis had refused, and Zack received their master's power. Now Sarora was asking the same difficult question, and he found it even harder to bring himself to do it.

"Please, Travis," Sarora begged him. "I know what I'm doing."

Tears pooled in his eyes—he knew what he had to do. "Fine, Sarora. I'll do it for you, but don't think it doesn't shatter my heart to do it."

Sarora's eyes welled with regret. "You're my best friend. If it didn't bring you pain, you would be more evil than Trazon," Sarora said grimly. "On the count of three, okay Travis?" She stepped between Travis and Sievan.

Behind them, Zack stirred. "Sarora?" He asked, his voice hoarse.

"Fine. One," Travis replied to Sarora, closing his eyes and digging deep.

"Sarora, what are you—?" Zack's voice was laced with terror.

"Two," Sarora added, cutting Zack off and unfolding her wings.

"Sarora, NO!"

"Three!" they shouted together, and Travis cried with all his might as he held the Crystal of Courage out ahead of him.

"I call upon the power of fire to bring forth the dragon!"

With a great burst of energy, a figure erupted from Travis's hand and passed through his crystal. Red fire mixed with red wisps of smoke and shot upward, first, creating thick legs, then, a strong chest and neck, and lastly, tapering off to the tail and the square head of a giant fire dragon. The dragon sped forward and engulfed Sarora with flames. As the dragon hit her, she flew with it at full speed.

"No!" Donigan cried out and he called forth his magic. "You can't do this!" Dark flames flashed from Donigan's hands and engulfed Sarora as well, and together, Sarora and Travis's spirit dragon flew into Sievan.

Sievan cried out in pure agony. His black feathers exploded as the fires hit him. His ice tail immediately shattered into hundreds of pieces and then evaporated. Then, in a great eruption, Sievan cried out his last, and the dargryph was gone forever.

Sarora, still on fire, couldn't hold back a cry of pain either. She screeched in anguish as the flames began to eat her body. Suddenly, a large chunk of the ceiling fell and landed between Sarora and Travis, so that Travis could no longer see his friend.

"NO!" Donigan cried out in horror. "This cannot be happening!" And then another rock fell, and it looked to have crushed Donigan.

"Sarora!" Travis cried out to his friend, but she did not reply. With a pang of overwhelming regret in his heart, Travis forced back his tears. He needed to get Zack out of there as fast as he could. He suddenly noticed a weight had lifted from his hand. In his crystal's place, Travis held a gem on a silver chain. It looked like Zack and Sarora's crystals, only instead of being clear or yellow, it was a deep, ruby red. Quickly, Travis slipped the necklace on over his head.

Running over to his friend, Travis had to dodge several falling objects—the castle was crumbling around them. Zack's eyes were full of tears. In pain, he cried out, "Travis, how could you? She's gone! I swear I would never lose her again, and now she's gone forever!"

Travis felt for his friend, but he knew that he had to help. "Zack, I need you to focus on me, okay? We have to get out of here." Then, as carefully as he could, Travis broke the javelin that had Zack pinned to the wall. There was still a large hunk of it embedded in his arm, but Travis knew that it must stay there for now to prevent extra bleeding. Grabbing his friend by the hand, Travis looked towards the hole Jezebel had escaped out of, but to his dismay, he saw that falling debris had blocked it. They would have to find another way out. Making a quick decision, Travis helped pull Zack along, and they headed for the doorway where they had entered.

Travis had to constantly pull Zack. His friend was delirious with pain and grief; so much so, that he stumbled easily, and he wouldn't watch where he was going. Around them, the castle was collapsing in flames. Large chunks of the ceiling were on fire, and they fell unexpectedly as the two boys ran. Several times, they had almost been crushed, but thank goodness, luck had been on their side. Travis only had a couple burns and scrapes, and Zack was covered in soot.

Travis led him through the castle until they reached the large entry doors. Using his magic, Travis blasted the iron bar that held the door closed. The explosion blasted the doors with enough force to partially destroy their hinges and make them hang half-open. Not wasting any time, Travis ran through, still dragging Zack with him. Once they had exited the castle, Travis spotted Jezebel, who was holding three very frightened horses—Seraphi, Mesha, and Abendega. The whites of their eyes flashed as they bucked and reared and tried to run from the burning, crumbling castle.

"Travis!" Jezebel called. "What did you do?"

"There's no time," Travis told her as he helped Zack onto Mesha's back and tied him to the saddle with a rope. "We need to get far away from here."

"But where's Sarora?" Jezebel asked, the tone of fear rising in her voice.

Travis felt like he would throw up. "She's not coming."

"But—"

"She's gone." After that, Jezebel didn't say anything else.

Travis leapt onto Abendega's back after helping Jezebel onto Seraphi. "Seraphi, Mesha, follow Abendega and me," Travis told the horses, who nodded, eager to get away as fast as possible. With one last look at the burning castle, Travis inhaled, his breath hitching, and then commanded Abendega, "Get us away from here. Take us somewhere safe and unknown to Trazon." Abendega bobbed his head once and then took off at a full gallop. The other two horses followed closely behind.

They rode through the sunrise, past noon, and then they finally came to a stop late that evening. They had made it to a large mountain, which held a cave that would hide them from any potential pursuers.

Jezebel helped lay Zack down on the ground, and then she immediately began to treat him. Zack had blacked out not long after the ride began, so it was a good thing that Travis had tied him to his saddle.

"Will he be all right?" Travis asked Jezebel as she continued to assess Zack's condition.

Jezebel shook her head worriedly. "I'm not sure. He may make it, but it'll be a long road to recovery. He's lost a lot of blood. And his friend."

Travis nodded, physically and emotionally drained. "Anything that I can do to help, let me know."

"Find some food and fresh water. But don't take too long," she added quickly. "If he's going to survive this emotional trauma of losing Sarora, he'll need someone like you to keep his will to survive alive. And Travis, you will need to fight to do the same." After a slight pause. "I-I've heard that when you die, there is no more pain or sadness; only eternal joy and peace."

Strangely, the words comforted Travis, but only a little. Now that they were safe, his arms began to shake and he felt sick to his stomach. He silently excused himself from Jezebel's presence.

Outside, Travis reached for his neck and found his crystal still hanging there. Curiously, he lifted it to his eyes. As he looked into the deep red crystal, Travis found that he wasn't sure what he was feeling—it was sadness, but tears never formed. It was guilt, but he didn't question the choice he made—at least, he didn't right now. Sarora had asked for his help, and for the first time in a long time, he had kept his promise.

They had lost two friends that day. Sarora, and Pran, the brave infiltrator from the other side, who had died courageously defending what he knew was right. Travis found himself wondering if he could ever do what they had done... to sacrifice your own life for those of your friends... there was no greater love or honor. But the thought scared Travis. Yes, death scared him... but the deaths of those whom he knew scared him even more. And now only he and Zack remained of their found family.

In a trance, Travis looked to the sky. The sun was setting, and the stars were coming out. The northern star, also called the Acer

Star, was the first that Travis saw. Today, he swore that it was the brightest that he had ever seen it. He knew that part of Sarora must be up there now, living in happiness.

As he watched the star, the wind blew against him and brought a strange calmness to the night. And in the wind, he could swear he heard an old friend saying to him:

"Be strong. I'm not going anywhere, Empty-Head. You're my dearest friend..."

His eyes stung, but Travis didn't cry. He couldn't cry—it just wouldn't happen. Instead, he smiled at the brightening stars in the indigo sky and imagined Sarora flying through it on her strength-renewed wings, with her 'gryphon smile' beaming down on him.

Her friends would make it—they would miss her deeply and their grief would never end, but she would never truly leave them. She would watch them and laugh at Travis and his moments, and she would lightheartedly chastise Zack when his head swelled too large. Travis smiled again.

Sarora hadn't left them—she only had become part of their hearts.

And now it was up to them to finish her fight.

THE ADVENTURE CONTINUES IN

SPIRIT HEARTS

THE LAST
CRYSTAL

PRONUNCIATION GUIDE

Hello, and welcome to Firmara. No, don't worry, you have not left your own dimension. I was really welcoming you to learn how to pronounce the names of people, places and things. Some of these names are very hard to read using only sight as a guide. Here are the names that are easily mispronounced.

Abendega – ah-BEN-di-ga
Achan – AY-ken
Afon – AI-phon
Aitasen – ATE-uh-sin
Areem – ah-REEM
Blagasian – Blah-GAY-zee-on
Bratislav – BRAT-iz-slav
Capricious – Cah-PRIH-tious
Derya – DAIR-ya
Devon – DEH-vin
Donigan – DON-i-gan
Eira – EE-ar-ah
Emeka – eh-meh-KAH
Eran – EH-ran
Ferocia – fair-OH-sha

Firmara – fur-MAR-a
Havilah – ha-VEE-la
Jezebel – jez-i-BELL
Kader – KAY-der
Kaelin – KAY-lin
Lacerpenna Animi – lah-sir-PEN-na an-ih-mi
Lucidis – LU-sid-uhs
Mesha – MEE-sha
Mira – MEER-ah
Myrddin – MEER-din
Oberon – OH-ber-on
Orzeł – OR-jou
Pelagius – pel-ah-GEE-us
Praesul – PRAY-sool
Qilin – CHI-lin
Racht – Ract
Radbound – RAHT-bowt
Sarora – sa-ROAR-a
Sendoa – zen-do-a
Seraphi – SAIR-i-fy
Shadra – SHA-dra
Sievan – See-VAN
Silva – SILL-va
Tantillus – TANT-ill-us
Thuy – Ta-hoy
Timur – Tee-MOOR
Tirza – TEER-za
Trayka – TRAY-kah
Trazon – Tray-ZON
Versutia – ver-sue-SHA
Vehndetia – vehn-DEH-she-ah
Wafai – wah-FI
Xue – Zoo
Yutzu – UTE-zoo
Zelophehad – Zeh-lo-PHEE-had

CHARACTER GUIDE

Here is a page of physical descriptions for the main characters of *The Last Secrets*.

Travis – Fourteen-year-old boy with brown hair, and brown eyes. Holds the Crystal of Courage (Fire)

Sarora – Gryphon that is half-lioness and half-hawk with dark, golden-brown feathers and a lighter brown fur pelt. She has a scar over her right eye.

Zack – Fifteen-year-old boy with blond hair and dark blue eyes. Holds the Crystal of Justice (Electricity)

Sievan – A dargryph that has the body of a black leopard, a tail made of magic ice, and the talons, wings, and head of a crow. His beak has several jutting spikes that are set around the sides of the opening.

Donigan – Sturdy man with short hair and stony brown eyes. He uses evil sorcery from an ancient dark crystal to copy a magic wielder's powers. Donigan is a follower of Lord Trazon and second-in-command of his dark forces.

Lord Trazon – Dark, malicious man. Titan ruler of Firmara.

Elizabeth – Fourteen-year-old girl with blonde hair and gray eyes. She lives with her mother and father above her family's store in Olegraro.

Stephen – Tenacious sixteen-year-old boy with dirty blonde hair and brown eyes. He spends most of his time in Olegraro, committing theft as a bad habit.

Timur – Timber wolf with gray-brown fur and yellow eyes. Leader of the wolf pack. His older half-brother is Bratislav.

Bratislav – Large, muscular brown wolf with golden-amber eyes. His younger half-brother is Timur.

Eira – Beautiful white she-wolf with yellow eyes. She is Timur's mate and the alpha female. Eira holds a very special connection with her brother, Argent.

Argent – Handsome grey wolf with black ears. Holds a special connection with his sister, Eira.

Kaelin – Old and wise water dragon with an elongated body covered in white fur, a scaly tan underbelly, and green spikes.

Trayka – Young man with near shoulder-length dark brown, almost black hair and bright blue eyes. A refugee of Lord Trazon's army.

About the Author

McKenzie began writing and published her first book, *The Last Acer*, at fifteen. Through high school and college she has continued to write and develop the *Spirit Hearts* series. She now resides with her husband and children in Grand Rapids, Michigan.

facebook.com/spiritheartsseries

instagram.com/spiritheartsseries